# CHASING
# PRINCE
# CHARMING

Cover Design by Melissa Williams Design

Carriage created by Melissa Williams Design, using images from: Vladimir Zadvinskii on AdobeStock and Pagina on AdobeStock

Published by Garden Ninja Books

ExtraSeriesBooks.com

First Edition: August 2021

0 9 8 7 6 5 4 3 2 1

# CHASING PRINCE CHARMING

THE EXTRA SERIES *Book 13*

## MEGAN WALKER & JANCI PATTERSON

*For Toni Grey,*
*the best not-evil Evil Stepmother ever*

# ONE

## Becca

The day I'm to film my preliminary interviews as a contestant on *Chasing Prince Charming*, I stand in front of my ten-year-old daughter who is critically eyeing my floral tank top and knee-length denim skirt. This outfit seemed fine when I bought it for this purpose, but now I think I look less like a potential princess and more like a mom who shops at discount stores.

Which is exactly what I am, though I'd prefer it be less obvious to the camera.

"That's definitely the one," my daughter Thea signs to me.

I arch an eyebrow. "Really?" I sign back. "Or are you just saying that so I won't try on my entire closet again?" She's been a trooper dealing with my last-minute wardrobe regrets. The only thing I haven't tried on is a yellow t-shirt that I once wore as part of a Minions costume.

"You look really pretty in that," Thea says, dodging the question.

I glance back at my outfit in the mirror. On the show I'll be wearing ball gowns—got to look the part to keep Prince Charming from running—but the orientation package specified to dress normally in these introductory interviews. Like I would look in my regular life, they said, though there was no way I was going to wear my actual normal clothes, which is more often than not a pair of stained jeans with an old t-shirt and a messy bun.

Today I'm wearing makeup, which seems to make my blue eyes brighter, and I went to the salon for the first time in forever and got a blow-out, which has partially survived all the clothing changes.

"Pretty enough for TV?" I sign to Thea. Apparently I'm still nervous enough that I need the fashion approval of a tween who only recently stopped wearing the same rainbow unicorn sweatshirt nearly every day.

She looks me up and down, twirling a lock of her curly hair—a gorgeous orange-red color she got from her father. Then she shrugs and walks off.

Sigh. I tug at the tank top, wondering if it's showing too little cleavage. Or too much.

Either way, I doubt I have time to change again, as the producers should be here any—

The doorbell rings, and my heart lurches like a bad car battery.

They're here. The people who are going to film me for the first of many, many hours are here.

What have I done?

"Mom!" my other daughter Rosie shrieks from the bedroom across the hall. "Mom! The TV people! I see their truck outside!"

She comes hurtling out of her room just as I leave mine. She dodges around me, a blond five-year-old whirlwind wearing the most sparkly pink princess dress she owns, along with a pair of equally sparkly fairy wings. She gets to the front door before me and jumps up and down with her hands behind her back, her wings askew. "Come here! They're going to bring the cameras in!"

I'm incredibly nervous about said cameras, but the sight of her beaming face—so happy about her mom being on a show with the words "Prince Charming" in the title—does calm me somewhat. I smile at her. "Okay, okay," I say, and reach for the doorknob—

With a squeal, Rosie throws two fistfuls of glitter right in my face.

"Aaaghhhaaahh," I say, coughing and spitting and blinking glitter.

"Look, Mom, you're a *princess!*" Rosie shouts, and she flings open the door.

I'm caught still coughing out puffs of glitter while a small TV crew stare at me wide-eyed on my porch. The one in front, a tall Black guy wearing dark jeans and a blue t-shirt with the outline of a mountain range on it, recovers quickly.

"Hey," he says, a smile broadening on his face. A face which, I notice now that I don't feel like I'm looking through a disco ball, is incredibly handsome. "I'm Nathaniel Coleman, one of the producers, but you can call me Nate." He introduces me to two cameramen—a short guy with a light brown soul patch and a beefy guy with a bored expression—and Kristin, the interpreter, a middle-aged woman with a short blond bob and wire-frame glasses.

"Hi," I say with a forced breeziness, pretending that I don't look like I just came from a New Year's Eve party at a strip club. "I'm Becca."

Rosie tugs on my hand, bouncing up and down again. "My mom is a princess!"

"Yes, she is." Nate tries to smother that grin. Which, with a smile like that, is something he should never do. Not even to spare an embarrassed woman covered in glitter. "It looks like you are, too."

"I'm not really a princess," Rosie says. "I have to marry a prince for that."

The feminist in me (who maybe shouldn't be going on a show about women competing for Prince Charming) feels the need to clarify. "You don't need a prince. You can be a princess all on your own."

Rosie gives me a skeptical look, but I probably shouldn't go into the details of royal birthright while a television crew is still standing on my porch.

"Sorry!" I say. "Come on in." I step back so they and their camera equipment can fit into the hallway. "You've met Rosie here, and my daughter Thea is—" I turn around and startle, because Thea is suddenly standing about two inches behind me. "Apparently practicing her teleportation skills." I sign this as I say it.

Thea's eyes grow huge when she sees my sparkle-covered face. "What happened to you?"

"One guess," I sign back.

She looks at her sister and snickers. I introduce Thea to the crew while the cameramen try to get their equipment past Rosie, who is dancing around them, possibly thinking they're filming right now.

I gently tug her down the very crowded hallway to break up the traffic jam. We're already off to a stellar start.

"Does this work?" I ask, gesturing to the living room. "It's not big, but . . ."

But I did manage to clean up the twenty-some semi-naked Barbies and also vacuumed up the crumbs from Thea's toasted bagel this morning, since she—way more than her five-year-old sister—can never seem to eat anything without making it look like a bomb went off.

"This'll be fantastic," Nate says. "Let us set up and we can get started."

Kristin signs this for Thea, and Nate and the cameramen check out the lighting in my living room and get things set up— including mic packs for me and my daughters. Kristin pulls over a chair from the kitchen table for herself, and Thea and Rosie settle in the loveseat together; no way are they missing this. Thea signs at Rosie to scoot over, and Rosie signs back that she can't or she'll smoosh her wings. Thea acts exasperated, but she's the one who adjusts Rosie's wings so they can sit even closer.

My heart swells, as it always does when I see them like that. Then I turn to the decorative mirror on one of the walls and check out the glitter damage.

Good god, you can barely see that there's a person under there. I hurriedly grab some wet wipes from a stash in the drawer of the end table and use about a dozen to wipe my face as clean as possible. Meanwhile, I find myself checking out Nate in the mirror.

He's got curly black hair pulled into a short ponytail, and these perfectly sculpted arms. His blue, fitted shirt looks great against his deep copper-brown skin, and—

What the hell am I doing? Ogling a producer of the dating show I'm about to go on, that's what. A dating show in which I will be dating another guy.

I tug my attention away. My face is now mostly visible, though I still have a clump of glitter in my right eyelashes, not to mention in my hair and all over my clothes. So much for my careful outfit selection.

"I don't think I can get this all out," I say, turning back to the crew. Kristin is already signing this for Thea even though I wasn't talking to her, which I appreciate. I try to sign whenever Thea's in the room, even when she doesn't seem to be paying attention. It's not fair for her to miss out on conversation just because she's deaf. "I don't know if even a shower will do it, but I could try."

"Nah," Nate says. "Leave it. The viewers will get lots of chances to see you without glitter."

"I guess if you want to see who I really am, this is it. A mom covered in sparkly craft material. Might as well lean into it."

"Perfect," he says with that grin, and my pulse picks up.

The cameras are set up now, along with some extra lights, and I perch nervously on the edge of the couch. Nate sits in the armchair, positioned out of sight of the cameras, which are on the kids and me.

"Okay," he says. "Why don't you tell us about yourself, Becca."

My mouth goes dry. I've already had to do several casting interviews, but I never thought I would get picked for the show.

"I, um. I'm Becca, like I said. Becca Hale." I clear my throat.

"I'm a single mom, with two incredible girls. Thea is ten and Rosie is five. I'm currently working on a business degree—my in-laws are awesome and really supportive and watch the girls while I'm at school." Now to the part I know they really want to hear. The reasons I got picked for this show, I'm sure. "My girls and I—and my in-laws, too—all know sign language, because my daughter Thea was born deaf. The girls' father—my husband, Rob—passed away three years ago, he was active duty military and—"

I've told this story about a hundred times in my life, but I cut off because I notice my knee is jiggling.

Nate's smile is sympathetic. "Hey, it's okay. I know how nerve-wracking it can be in front of the camera, but it'll get easier as we go. Just remember, we're not out to get you. We just want to learn more about you."

I let out a breath. "Okay, yeah."

"Also, it would be great if you could restate the question with your answer—like 'I decided to apply for the show because . . .' Not to spoil the next question for you." He winks, a gesture I didn't think could be done in a non-creepy way until this very moment.

"So, Becca," he says. "Why did you decide to apply for the show?"

That answer is more complicated than could fit in a sound bite. But I can try.

"My friend Cece signed me up for this, actually. She thinks I've been in a love life slump for a while now, which is probably true." I've been in a love life slump for a lot longer than she or anyone else realizes, but I'm not about to say that. Or mention that I'm not sure I'll ever be ready to get back out there, even with Prince Charming. "I was pretty sure I didn't want to date in front of millions of people—I mean, dates are awkward enough, right? But then I thought it could be an adventure of sorts, and maybe I could use more of that in my life. Not that parenting isn't its own adventure." I cringe because I'm both rambling and sounding ridiculous, even though it's all true. I don't know what to say beyond that, and Nate is looking at me expectantly, so I stutter something nonsensical about proving that I can be brave, which is also true but sounds even worse. Finally I just ask, "Is that enough of an answer?"

"Yeah, for sure. Just so you know, I'm not going to cut you off or interrupt you, because it's bad for the audio. So just answer however you want, and when you're done you can stop talking."

"Instead of babbling like an idiot?"

Nate laughs, a warm sound that's just as amazing as his smile. "Don't worry, they'll edit it out. Unless it's funny," he adds with a one-shoulder shrug.

"Awesome," I say dryly. I am starting to feel better. Nate seems to have a calming effect on me, despite his hotness.

There's a sound of knuckles rapping on the end table—one of Thea's ways to indicate she wants attention. We both look at her.

"She *needs* to date," Thea signs with a pointed look. The interpreter speaks the words faithfully, including the emphasis, though that was pretty clear from her expression.

Nate laughs again. "Do you mind if I ask the girls questions?"

"Go right ahead. You'll probably get better answers from them."

"So, Thea," he starts, but Rosie cuts him off, bouncing in her seat and whapping Thea in the face with a wing.

"Ask me a question!" she says.

I'm impressed she managed to sit quiet and calm for this long, but I still shake my head. "Wait your turn, Rosie, okay?"

She pouts, but only for a couple seconds. Rosie tends toward one of two moods—hyper-happy and meltdown miserable. There is very little in between. I'm hoping we stick with the first, at least for the duration of this interview.

"Thea," Nate continues as Kristin signs. "Why do you think your mom needs to date?"

"Because she should get to be happy," she says.

I put on a mock-wounded expression. "I *am* happy!" I'm happier now, just me and my girls, than I was at any point in my marriage.

Thea rolls her eyes. "Yeah, but you're *Mom* happy. You should get to smile and laugh, not just with us. And not at jokes you told yourself."

I groan. "Yep. Better answers, for sure."

Nate grins. "Kids are great for that. So what kind of man should your mom be dating?"

Thea straightens. Clearly she has answers for this interview locked and loaded. "He should be funny and nice and should treat her like she deserves to be treated. Like a princess." She has a sarcastic expression on that last part—a sarcasm directed at the show theme, not me. I'm guessing the editors will love her saying it, though. I've seen this show before, and apparently there can never be too many references to the fairy tale theme.

I'm prepared to die before I let them maneuver me into saying that tired line about having kissed a lot of frogs.

But this next part melts me: "He should be someone who supports her dreams."

Wouldn't that be nice. I reach over to squeeze her knee, but she pretends she doesn't see. There's only so much mushiness she's willing to publicly accept.

Something flickers in Nate's dark eyes, and I can tell we'll be returning to that. But he wisely decides to give the now-squirming Rosie a turn. "So what kind of man do you think your mom should date, Rosie?"

"He has to be a prince," she says. "Is he a real prince? Is that a lie?"

Nate wobbles his head. "Well, it's like your mom telling you that you're a princess."

"But that's a lie!"

"Hey," I say with another mock-wounded look. Lie or not, she sure doesn't mind when I say it.

"Okay," Nate says. "But sometimes people have prince or princess-like qualities. It's more about the kind of person they are."

He's good at this. Talking to them at their level, but not being condescending. I wonder if he has kids. He doesn't have

12

a wedding ring. Not that I'm checking.

Rosie considers his answer. "Does he have prince clothes?"

"Yes," Nate says.

She seems mollified.

Nate looks back at me, amused, but then he frowns. "I had another question I was going to ask you." He searches my face, like he might find it there.

My cheeks heat up under that gaze. "I figured you did."

His eyes glint; he knows I remember. "I might have to review the footage. Unless you want to remind me."

"It may have been something about my future dreams."

He grins. "Ah, yes. Tell me about your dreams, Becca."

My dreams. This is an easy one—now, at least. "I'd love to open a restaurant one day. I've always loved to cook, and the thought of doing it professionally, having my own place . . . It would be incredible."

"Nice. What type of restaurant would it be?"

"So what I'd love is," I start, then see him give a pointed eyebrow-raise. I rephrase. "The type of restaurant I'd love to open," I begin again, and he gives me a thumbs up, "is one where I'd serve comfort food, but with a new twist. Add unique spices and flavors to something like homemade mac and cheese, you know? Something complimentary, of course, that makes it feel like your favorite childhood dish made even better. And I know this sounds cliché, but I'd love the restaurant itself to feel cozy. Like you're in your family's living room, just casually eating together. Comfy chairs, maybe even couches, but with surfaces to eat on and—" I cut myself off, not because I'm nervously babbling, but because I'm getting so happily caught up in the vision, I think I could go on for another hour. "That kind of thing."

Nate's watching me intently. I feel my palms sweat. Maybe I did go on too long, but he asked, after all.

He blinks and clears his throat. "That sounds amazing." He leans forward with his elbows on his knees, steepling his fingers under his chin. "What would it mean for you to have someone to share it with?" He's got a kind of smug look where he's aware that I know he's leading me to all the cheesy romance stuff they want, and I give him a similar look right back—I'm not just going to give it up to him.

Um.

"I do have someone to share it with," I say. "I've got my girls."

Another rapping sound. "Mom, that is not what he meant!" Thea signs, and Kristin translates.

"Thank you, Thea," Nate says. He bites his lower lip around a teasing smile as he turns back to me. "Go on, Becca."

Rosie has given up paying attention. She's climbed off the chair and is twirling around in the space between the living room and the kitchen. Thea, on the other hand, is watching closely. She's not going to let me get away with talking around things.

"Fine," I say. "It would mean a lot to have someone to share this with." I perhaps overemphasize the restating of the question, and am happy to see that Nate seems more amused than irritated. "It would be nice to have someone alongside me for all of it," I continue, feeling it more deeply than I'd like to admit. "I don't need someone who loves to cook—I like doing my own thing. But to have someone to support me, to want this for me as badly as I do, just because he loves me . . ."

I find myself blinking rapidly, looking away, my chest hollow.

I do want that. And if going on a dating show isn't the way to find it, maybe it could at least help me *believe* in it again.

I'm not sure that it's a good idea to let myself want that, even if Cece and my in-laws and my daughters disagree. Then again, all of them believe I've had a relationship like that before.

Nate pauses, studying me. Then he sits back, his expression unreadable.

"So, tell me about your late husband," he says.

"Sure." This should be the easy part. I'm used to being very careful about how I tell this story.

It does seem different now, though, with the camera on me and Nate taking everything in. My heartbeat feels unsteady.

"My husband Rob was in the army." He enlisted a couple years out of high school. We were married when we were twenty and had Thea soon after. He passed away on active duty overseas. His convoy was attacked." I let out a breath. I may be used to telling this story, but I still have a hard time letting myself picture it. "He was a great dad. He loved the girls so much. They miss him. We all do."

I stop, not willing to say more. No one wants to hear that the military hero and great dad wasn't an equally great husband. And I can't bring myself to tarnish him in the eyes of his parents and daughters.

Nate nods, looking sympathetic. "How do you feel about falling in love again?"

I glance over to Thea, who gives me an expectant look. Maybe I should give the canned answer: I'm excited. I can't wait to start the journey. I know my prince is out there.

I look back at Nate. "Scared," I say. "I said I wanted to get better at putting myself out there, and I do. But . . . it's scary. Risking the loss again."

My hands are gripping my knees too tightly, and I wonder how well he can read what I actually mean. That what scares me is the thought of losing myself all over again, when I feel like I've just barely started to figure out who I am.

But no. There's a reason this story works; everyone believes it, because they want to.

"Maybe everyone's scared, though," I say, "for different reasons. Do all the girls say that?"

He shrugs. "I don't know. I'm new."

"Really? I wouldn't have guessed. You're good at this." I've been able to forget for stretches of time that there are cameras filming my every move. Talking to Nate is like talking to a friend. A really hot friend.

I wonder if I would be comfortable on a date, if it was with him?

"Thanks," he says, and his smile does nothing to discourage this train of thought. "I'm not new as a producer, just on this show. I don't know if you've ever seen the YouTube show, *Jason Climbs Sh!t*, but—" He blinks over at Thea and Rosie. Thea raises her eyebrow—Kristin did translate it, though spelling the last word out with the exclamation point—and Rosie's mouth forms a little "o." Though, really, it's not like they've never heard that word from me before.

"Sorry," he says, cringing. "Is there a swear jar I can put money in?"

Now Rosie gapes even wider. "A what? You put money in a jar?"

"Yeah," he says. "Or I should definitely start now." He shoots me a side-eye and looks relieved when he sees I'm barely holding in a laugh. He looks back at Rosie. "If you get a jar, I'll put some money in it, because I said a bad word."

Rosie dances in place and looks around desperately.

"There's the glitter jar," Thea signs at Rosie. "It's probably empty now."

"Oh my god," I say, as Rosie dashes back to her bedroom. "I actually managed to forget that I'm covered in glitter."

Nate's grin turns devilish. "Yep."

"I really should have cleaned it all off," I say with a sigh, resisting a look to see how much is clumped in my cleavage.

"Could you, though?" Nate asks. "It's *glitter*."

Dustin, one of the cameramen, makes a snorting laugh from behind the camera—their existence was something I'd also managed to forget.

"Good point," I say.

Rosie runs back in the room with the glitter jar. Which is empty, if you don't count the glitter stuck to the sides. She waggles it in front of Nate, and he takes out his wallet.

"Whoa," she says, her jaw dropping again as he puts a dollar in the jar. She doesn't totally understand the varying values of money, but she definitely knows that the bills are better than the coins. "Say another bad word!" She shakes the jar again.

"This is why we don't have a swear jar," I say. "I know my kids too well."

Nate chuckles and sets his wallet out on the table. "You just leave that jar there, kid, and we'll see."

Rosie giggles and starts playing with some Barbies that were apparently hidden under the loveseat. She even manages to get Thea to hold one. For all that Thea acts like she's drowning in ennui (at ten!) she still loves dolls—most of these are hers.

I don't imagine she's going to stop paying attention to us, though.

"So," I say to Nate. "You've worked on Jason's show. That's awesome!"

"You've seen it." He looks impressed, even though it's pretty well-known.

"A couple episodes. I was a huge fan of his *Starving with the Stars* season. Jason's show is great. I was legitimately shocked that he survived every time."

"You're not the only one," he says with a laugh. "Jason's a great climber and really responsible. Not that you'd know it from the show. I was the one always egging him on."

"I remember you!" I say, with possibly too much Rosie-like bouncing enthusiasm, especially given that my boobs are covered in glitter. "That's awesome. But you're new to *Prince Charming*, then."

"Yep. You're my first interview. I guess I got lucky."

My face goes warm. Along with the rest of me—some parts more than others.

He blinks and wets his lips. "I didn't have to fly anywhere," he clarifies quickly. "You're, like, an hour away from where we're going to film."

Oh. Right. That makes sense. He was definitely not flirting with the contestant he's interviewing—on camera—for a dating show that he works for.

I am saved from having to come up with a response by another rap on the coffee table from Thea.

"What are you going to say to Prince Charming when you first meet him?" she asks. Then she picks up a Barbie and Ken (both dressed, thankfully) and has them move back and forth a bit like they're talking to each other. Or dancing weirdly.

"I have no idea," I say. "They said I should come up with some unique thing to do when I first meet him, but . . ." I scrunch up my nose. Having seen this show before, I know how ridiculous it can get. Once, a girl dressed in this big Fruit-of-the-Loom apple costume and asked the prince to "take a bite."

I realize we are all appearing very desperate just by being on this show, and I'm not eager to make it worse.

"You don't have any ideas?" Nate asks.

"Oh, I have ideas. Just none that leave my dignity intact."

"Right." He considers for a moment. "You could sign with him. That's memorable. And not in an 'I'm trying to be a sexy enchanted apple' kind of way."

Dustin laughs again from behind the camera, and I do too. That was pretty infamous.

Thea sets the Barbies down. "You should make him your mashed potatoes. Then he would propose right there."

"Is that so?" Nate raises an eyebrow. He gives me a sly look. "Obviously I need to try these mashed potatoes."

"Only if you're going to propose," she warns solemnly.

"Does everyone propose to your mom after eating the mashed potatoes?" he asks Thea.

She beams at him. "The smart ones do."

"You are crazy," I say to her, and lean over to ruffle her curls. She still lets me do that, at least.

"Is it time to eat?" Rosie pipes up eagerly.

"I can get you a snack soon," I say, then look over at Nate. "Or is now a good time for a break?"

"Now's fine," he assures me. "Actually," he says to Rosie, "do you like to help your mom cook?"

She jumps up and down. One of her wings has somehow broken off during all of this. "Yes! I do! Thea says it's boring."

Rosie doesn't always sign when she talks, but Kristin translates for her, too, and Thea nods.

Nate twists his lips. "It would be great to get some footage of you all cooking together. Any chance you'd be up for that? Boring or not?"

Thea twists her lips right back. "Do I need to pretend to like it?"

"Cooking with me isn't that bad!" I say. Cooking sounds *fantastic*. That's something I can do much better than talking about my non-existent love life or family tragedies. "Come on." I tug her to her feet. "I might have the ingredients for those mashed potatoes."

This brings a grin to her face, and we all head into the kitchen. Dustin and Ken—the other cameraman—get the cameras set up and I dig out all the ingredients. Thea peels potatoes with me, and Rosie puts potato peels over her eyes and pretends to be a monster. We boil and mash and add cream and butter and spices. I'm in my element. Though he mostly stays back and out of the shot, Nate laughs with us and agrees to peel a couple potatoes. He even flicks a peel at Thea when she isn't looking. It sticks in her hair, causing Rosie to giggle.

The cameras might as well not be there; my nerves are long gone. And not for the first time, I think that if I could cook instead of date, putting myself out there would be a whole lot easier.

# TWO

## Nate

I was a little worried about how the first day of shooting for my new job would go. I'm used to filming idiots climbing improbable objects, but I've never gone into someone's house and set up a camera and pried into their personal life.

But I knew what I was signing up for when I left my longterm job as the head producer on *Jason Climbs Sh!t* and took this position as a junior producer on *Chasing Prince Charming*. Despite the difference in my relative power, it's actually a big step up for me. Jason's show is huge on YouTube, but *Charming* has some of the highest ratings on network TV. I never in a million years thought I'd get this job when I applied for it.

And yet, here I am. Becca's kids help mash potatoes, and I mimic (and exaggerate) Thea's wearied expression a bit to get her to smile. I meant it when I said she didn't have to pretend to enjoy cooking, but the editors are probably going to use ten seconds of the cooking footage at a maximum, so a couple of smiles are all they'll need to make it look like she enjoys time with her mom. Afterward, Rosie proudly presents us with bowls of mashed potatoes, and wow, they really are the best I've ever had.

"You have to open that restaurant," I tell Becca as we settle in to do one more round of interviews. "The world needs your mashed potatoes."

"That's what everyone tells me," she says, sitting down on her couch again. She's set the girls up with tablets in the other room so they won't disturb us—we want to get some footage of her without them, mostly focused on her love life. Kristin goes to wait outside in case we need her again, but she won't need to interpret when we don't have Thea in the room.

Becca's face and hair are less glittery now—I think she snuck off to shake more of it loose in the bathroom while she was getting the girls settled—but there are still flecks catching the light.

Which is not surprising. It took me exactly one "Craft Time with Uncle Nate" session with my niece to learn the terrible truth about glitter: that shit does not come off.

"Okay," I say. "I've got a few more questions for you. What do you hope to get out of being on the show?"

"What do I hope to get out of the show?" She looks like she's proud she remembered to state the question, though we probably won't use this one, since it's a bit self-referential. "Oh, you know. I'm here to make friends," she says wryly, a glint in her eyes. "I just want to be the first girl ever to say that on this show."

I laugh. "You probably will be. Is it true?"

Becca shrugs. "Sort of. I'd like to get to know the other girls and hear their stories. I think being on the show could be an adventure, but it would be nice to find love." She smiles tentatively, like she's afraid to hope for it.

Damn, this woman has a beautiful smile. Everything about her is beautiful, actually, which will probably be true of all the contestants. I expected to be surrounded by hot women on this job, which is definitely different from my last one, where I was mostly surrounded by sweaty dudes in helmets and harnesses. What I didn't expect was how weird it would feel to have personal conversations with beautiful women and know I have no chance in hell with them. Becca is incredible—if I met her under normal circumstances, I'd have asked her out in a heartbeat.

But she's looking for Prince Charming. She's not going to date me, and if she did, I could lose my job.

I just need to get used to this. It'll probably get easier the more interviews I do.

When Becca runs out of things to say, I ask a few more questions. The questions are canned and cheesy as hell. Her answers are only slightly less so, but she manages to deliver them charmingly. *I'm* eating it up, which means the audience definitely will.

"You're good at this," I tell her as we're winding the interview down. Tape is still rolling, but we won't use anything I say to her and probably not her responses, either, unless she gives me something really good.

"So are you," Becca says. "I really never would have known it was your first time."

I want to make a crack about how it's not my first time for *some* things, but I bite my lip. This isn't *Jason Climbs Sh!t*. I can't turn everything into a sexual innuendo and expect to get a laugh. I don't want to make Becca uncomfortable, and I definitely don't want her to feel harassed.

"That's good to know," I say. "I may have been producing for a long time, but YouTube is a whole different ball game."

"No doubt. Are you from LA?"

"Yeah, my family all lives in Pasadena."

"That must be nice, having them so close."

"It is," I say, then shrug. "I mean, we don't get together very often, since we're all pretty busy. But my parents make sure we get together for holidays and stuff."

"How big is your family?" she asks.

"Not very. I have a younger sister and an older brother—he's married and has a nine-year-old girl. She's pretty damn cute."

"Aww, I bet." Becca's blue eyes crinkle at the sides with her wide, gorgeous smile. "So did you always want to work in TV?"

I laugh. "No way." It occurs to me that Becca is starting to interview *me*, but part of my job is to befriend her. If she comes to trust me, she'll give me the good stuff later. It all feels a bit manipulative and underhanded, probably because it is.

But I like Becca, so it's easy to pretend I'm talking to her because I want to and not because it's my job. "I got started on YouTube because I knew Jason from a climbing gym. We started climbing together outside the gym, and I had a cell phone camera, and Jason had a habit of doing stupid crap and being like, 'Hey! Take a video of this!' The rest is history, I guess. We never intended to make money at it, but then we *did*. I was working at Target at the time, and I sure as hell quit that job in a hurry."

"You must be really outdoorsy," Becca says. "I tried to take the girls camping once. It rained, and we gave up in the middle of the night because everyone was crying, including me."

I smile. "I camp with thirty-year-old men and even they get a little dramatic when they're sleeping in the dirt."

She grins. "Are there tears?"

"Not a lot. More whining and sniping at each other. I've never been camping with an actual child, but I've been on a lot of backpacking trips with full grown men who turned out to be big babies."

Becca laughs, and god, it's a beautiful sound.

One I absolutely cannot get attached to. This is probably my cue to wrap things up. I look over at Dustin, my camera guy. He's been doing this show a lot longer than me, so I'm hoping he'll tell me if I've missed something.

"I think that's all we have for you today," I say, and Dustin nods. I turn back to Becca. "Was there anything else you wanted me to ask for the camera?"

"Not for the camera, no." She suddenly looks nervous again. I didn't realize how much she'd relaxed until she wasn't anymore. "Am I allowed to talk to you off the record?"

There's no rule that says every word we say has to be filmed. If we give the head producer what he wants, he'll be happy with that. "Give us a minute?" I ask Dustin and Ken.

They nod and schlep their equipment out to the car.

When I turn back to Becca, she's rubbing her face, like she

suspects there's still glitter there. Which there is.

"What's up?" I ask.

"I just wanted to get your perspective about Thea."

This is about the last thing in the world I expected her to ask. I don't know what perspective I could possibly have about her daughter.

"I mean," Becca continues, "I know that part of the reason I got picked for the show is because of her. It's a story that they can use for sympathy. I'm the poor single mother raising a daughter with a disability."

I think she probably got picked for the show because she's articulate and funny and drop-dead gorgeous, but I know what she means. "They're definitely going to use that as part of your story. It makes you sympathetic, helps the audience pick you out of the crowd."

"Right. And I know I can't control the way they portray me. But I'm worried about them exploiting Thea. Having a deaf daughter is part of my story, but I don't want them to make it look like it's so terrible that I have to deal with this *trial*, when really, Thea is amazing, and I love our deaf community. I wouldn't trade it for anything."

I hadn't thought about it that way, but it makes sense. "Yeah, I could see it coming off like that. They're going to focus on the tragedy in your past, but it would suck if it looked like your daughter was part of what made it tragic. Besides, you have *two* awesome daughters."

"Exactly. But I know I don't have control over what story they decide to tell, and I know you don't either."

She's right about that. My job is to do the interviews, develop relationships, and get the footage they need. We're going to take hundreds of hours of footage for every one-hour segment of show. I won't even know what story they ultimately decided to tell until it airs.

"You do have a small amount of control," I say. "You can control what you say to the cameras. So if you talk about your 'daughters,' they can't cut that to focus on Thea alone. But that will be difficult, because we're going to get a lot of footage of you, and they'll pick just a couple of sound bites for the show."

Becca nods. "That's helpful, though. I can try to remember to do that."

"They're going to focus on your personal loss and on the sign language, because awful as this sounds, it's a tag that will help the audience remember you. There are going to be, like, twenty blond girls on this thing, and they need to set you apart. If you're around long enough to get a more complex story, they could go with the pity thing. Personally it's not the story I would tell about you."

"What story would you tell?"

I lean forward, putting my elbows on my knees. "I'd go with, here's this amazing mother and incredible person who has everything except a man." I smile at her. "You can't get away from that last bit. That's everyone's story on this show."

She lights up, like it's unexpected that people could see her this way. That surprises me, because it's so obvious.

"So, on night one," she says, "if I lead with 'I have a deaf daughter,' I'm encouraging them to treat that as my main characteristic, right? And then it's like *I'm* exploiting Thea to be interesting on a dating show, which is the last thing I want to do. But if I keep it back, will it look like I'm ashamed of her?"

I think about that. I'm clearly right—she is a fantastic mother. If she wasn't, she wouldn't be asking these questions. I like to think I'm a pretty good judge of when people are being fake, and while Becca obviously wants to look good on camera, I don't think she's faking anything. She's the same person now with the cameras out of the room as she was before they left.

That's a complicated question, though, and I'm not sure how to answer. I'm used to controlling the narrative—we had an editor for Jason's show, but we had full control over what footage we used and what story we told.

"I think," I say, "that if it were me cutting this together . . ."

I pause. "Which I want to stress that it's not. I won't have any control over the final product."

"I get that. I just want your opinion."

It's wild that she thinks my opinion means anything, but I guess I'm the one who showed up as an official representative of the show. "I could more easily construct a narrative out of the shame thing if you held it back. In some ways, it might be nice for your relationship with Prince Charming if you shared that information up front. Not a lot of women ask anything from the guy on night one, but you're asking him to accept this part of your life that would require something from him if he ended up with you, since he'd have to learn to communicate with your daughter to be part of your life. That looks like you're proud of her, not ashamed. But I'd be careful how you phrase it."

"Right," she says. "I have *two* daughters, one of whom is deaf."

"Exactly. There's no way for them to cut that to focus only on Thea."

"I like that. I need someone who is going to step up for my kids, and if that's not Prince Charming, it's better if he sends me home right away."

I smile. I like Becca more the more I talk to her. She's self-assured and confident, even when her nerves show. She's not desperate to stay on the show if this guy isn't what she needs.

It makes my heart ache a little that she isn't available. I wonder if I'm going to feel this way about every interview. If all the women they've cast are as awesome as Becca, Prince Charming is a lucky guy.

"This is awful," she says, "but it's pretty easy to tell when I meet someone if I don't want them in my life. Thea's deafness turns into kind of a litmus test. I hate that it has to be that way, but it's nice to weed out the assholes."

I get that. Being Black, I see an ugly side of people that white folks tend to miss. I'm not about to bring that up, though. I'm at *work* and I don't want to make waves on day one.

Really, though, I don't want this litmus test to play out right here in her living room. I'm afraid of what I'll find.

Becca gives me a weary look, like she's tired just thinking about all the choices she's going to have to make, all the worries she has about protecting her daughters. "I'm really not going to have much control over how they present me."

"Not a lot," I admit. "They can manipulate your words, but they can't pull things out of thin air. Plus, they can get a lot more out of you when you're drinking. So it depends on how well you can hold your liquor and how much you let the producers feed you drinks."

I'm talking as if I'm not the one who's going to be doing these things, even though that is literally my job description. Becca doesn't seem to notice.

"I'm not a bitchy drunk," she says. "Alcohol makes me sleepy."

"Ha. So they won't want to give you drinks, then. You should be fine. You're very natural in front of the camera."

"I think *you're* the one who's good at this."

That makes me smile. "Well, hopefully I'll get to interview you more."

"Can you? I mean, do you get to choose who you interview?"

"Yes and no," I say. "They'll want you to be interviewed by a producer you trust. So if you prefer to be interviewed by me, that'll be possible more often than not."

"I'd like that," she says.

"Me too," I tell her. Definitely more than I should.

"I want to ask you for a favor, but if you have to say no, I understand."

"Okay."

"You're going to see a lot more than I will behind the scenes," she says. "If you see that the narrative is leaning toward exploiting Thea, will you let me know? I know you won't necessarily know it's happening, but if you catch things going in that direction—"

"I will absolutely give you a heads up." I might not be able to control it, but I should be able to alert Becca without anyone being the wiser. "I would have done that anyway."

"That's so nice of you. It's good to feel like someone will have my back."

I like that she feels this way. "If you're uncomfortable with anything, let me know. I'll do what I can. And if you open up to me in interviews, they're going to want me to keep interviewing you. So you have some control over that, if that's what you want."

She smiles. "It is. Thank you."

"Of course."

I want to put off leaving, to extend the conversation as long as I can. But the cameramen are waiting for me, and I'm only here to do a job. "I should be going. But I'll see you in a couple of weeks at the castle."

"At the castle!" She rolls her eyes up to the ceiling. "Oh my god, this is really happening."

"It is," I tell her with a chuckle, and then I say goodbye and walk out to the car to meet Dustin and Ken. Ken lives nearby, so he took his own car, but I drove out from the studio with Dustin. When I come out, Ken's already gone, and Dustin is sitting in the driver's seat with the key in the ignition and the radio cranked all the way up. I wave goodbye to Kristin, who is waiting in her own car, and then climb in.

Dustin immediately turns the radio down. "Well done, man."

"You think so?"

"Oh, yeah. You had her eating out of the palm of your hand."

That should be good to hear, but I'm not sure it's a compliment that I'm good at manipulating women.

"You guys were in there for a while," Dustin says, starting the car. "What'd you talk about?"

"Just some worries she had."

He nods like that's not out of the ordinary, which is good. I don't want to get a reputation for being too close to the contestants. I imagine a lot of new producers screw this up by getting confused about what's real and what's for show. "That's great.

She trusts you already."

"That's what I was supposed to do, right?" I say. "They wanted me to gain her trust. Is it okay that I let her go off camera like that?"

"Yeah, sure," he says. "Producers do that all the time. It's a good way to get them to feel like they can tell you everything, and then when the cameras are on, you know exactly what buttons to push."

Shit, is that what I was doing in there? That sounds like an awful thing to do to Becca, who I think actually trusts me.

"That's how you get them to be vulnerable on camera," I say.

"Oh, yeah. They start to feel like you're on their side after a while. It's like Stockholm syndrome."

"*Stockholm syndrome*? Like we've *kidnapped* them?"

"Pretty much. I mean, they're stuck in the castle, cut off from the outside world, and they desperately want a friend they can trust, so they'll believe anything you tell them. Why do you think the girls always say they didn't expect to feel the way they do? It's crazy, but it works."

I stare at the dash. Is *that* what I've signed myself up for? When I took this job, I envisioned all these women being as whiny and bitchy as they appear on the show. They signed up for this knowing what was going to happen to them.

But did they really? Are they aware of how much they're going to be manipulated?

Am I really ready to do that to someone as awesome as Becca?

"She seemed like a cool girl, yeah?" I say. I want to hear that I'm not alone in thinking this. That it's normal to feel a little off-kilter after interviewing a gorgeous, incredible woman who is also untouchable.

"Oh, yeah, she's got that hot mom thing going on."

"Hot mom?" That's not exactly what I was thinking. I would go with plain hot and awesome. "Are you calling her a MILF?"

"Yeah, totally," he says. "You don't agree?"

I mean. "She's hot, man. I'll give you that."

"I don't think she'll last long, though," Dustin goes on. "She's got a good sympathy story, so I'd give her a couple weeks. But if she doesn't get in on the drama, she'll probably be gone after that."

"Unless Prince Charming is into her."

"I guess. Though, you know what you should do with her? Figure out who in the group is threatened enough by her that they'll say something bad about her kids. Then Mama Bear will come out."

"So nothing is sacred, then."

"Hell, no."

Ugh. I wonder if I'm going to get used to this. I wonder if it'll be a good thing if I do.

"Do you like your job?" I ask.

"Yeah," he says. "You get to stare at hot girls all the time. It's awesome."

I raise an eyebrow. Dustin is in his forties, if not his early fifties. He's twice the age of some of these girls. "But you can't date them."

He laughs. "Not until the show's over. Then they all hang out at these alumni events, and they hook up with producers all the time. Tech guys, too." He winks.

I sink in my seat. No, I don't think getting comfortable with *that* would be a good thing. Not that I'm not grateful for the chance to ask Becca out. She seems legitimately cool, and Dustin is probably right. The odds aren't great she'll make it to the end of the show.

Then again, I have three more interviews this week. Becca's just the first, and I'm new at this.

Probably it's normal to feel this way. I'll probably fall a little in love with all of them.

# THREE

## Becca

When I arrive at "the castle" for the first night of filming, my phone is immediately confiscated. I have three suitcases filled with ball gowns, cocktail dresses, and loungewear. I was allowed a picture of my kids and a makeup case full of toiletries.

That's it. No contact with the outside world. No electronics, no entertainment. Not even a book.

Just me and a house full of women who will also be dating Prince Charming, each hoping he'll plant a tiara on their heads so they can stick around one more week.

I'm terrified, and I have no idea what I was thinking.

The staff takes my suitcases, which I'm told I can have back when the night is over. The castle is an enormous manor house in Sunset Beach, rented by the show for the first weeks of filming. It's set back from the road and has a gorgeous cobblestone drive-way running up to a stone facade with honest-to-god turrets. I'm not even at the driveway yet, though. My dark blue ball gown and I are loaded into a horse-drawn carriage and parked near the back of a long line of carriages that runs down the drive and out to the road. They shut down the whole street so they could load thirty princesses into individual carriages and leave us to wait.

And wait. And wait.

I lean back and sigh. I'm already wearing a mic pack, so if I started talking, someone might hear me. If I got out of the carriage, one of the production staff would no doubt swoop over to find out what I need and then stuff me back inside. It's a good thing they aren't trying to put more than one of us in a carriage, because the ruffles of my poofy skirt flow out to cover nearly the entire floor.

But I still wouldn't mind having someone to talk to.

I'm desperately wishing that someone was Nate.

Over the last two weeks, I've been getting more and more anxious to begin this whole process, and of course I'm looking forward to meeting Prince Charming. I don't know anything about the guy, though, so most of my daydreaming has centered around what I'm going to say to Nate when I see him again. He was so kind and understanding about my worries, and seems like such a laid-back, sweet guy. And, yeah, he's smoking hot and has featured in more than one of my fantasies.

But he's a producer and was only talking to me for his job. He said he would try to be the one who interviews me, but he probably said that to everyone he interviewed. Maybe he even met someone he likes better and has forgotten about me.

I sigh again, craning my neck, trying to get a look at the girl in the carriage in front of me. The carriages are mostly enclosed, with small windows, so I can't see inside it. Through the rear window of my own carriage I can get a better look at the carriage behind me, but all I can see there is a large brown horse wearing side-blinders on its eyes. There are a couple of production members off to the side, probably keeping an eye on the horses and the contestants to make sure neither runs off.

"Hey," a voice says, and I spin back around in my seat.

There's Nate, leaning in the now-open carriage door.

"Hey!" I say. I sound surprised, and Nate smiles at me.

That smile. It's even more arresting than I remembered.

"Sorry to startle you," he says. "How are you doing?"

"I'm okay." But my voice sounds shaky. I think I'm even more nervous than I thought I was. Or maybe I'm just nervous to see Nate again.

Nate's eyes travel down my dress in an appreciative way. "You look amazing. I love the gown."

I play with the ends of my hair, which I'm wearing half-down so it brushes my arms. I had it done earlier today, and this is the last time I'm going to have a hairdresser to make me look good on camera. After this, I'm on my own, unless I make it into the top six or so, when they'll be down to few enough girls to offer us help.

"Thank you," I say.

"You seem nervous. Mind if I join you?"

He gestures toward the inside of the carriage, and I rush to gather my skirts.

"Of course," I say. "Did you get stuck babysitting me?"

"Are you kidding? I requested to be here."

My heart skips several beats. Which is silly. He told me he'd try to interview me—not that there are any cameras right now, but my mic pack is on, and I imagine if he's here talking to me, they're recording audio they can layer over other shots later.

But it's still so good to see a friendly face. Especially one as handsome as his.

Nate sits on the bench across from me, and his feet are only mostly buried in my skirts when I release them. He's wearing a pair of dark jeans and a forest-green polo shirt. Damn, this is also a good color on him. "So, are you ready for this?" he asks. "You could be meeting your future husband tonight."

I very much doubt it, but I wouldn't be here if I didn't think it was at least a possibility, right?

"It's a little nerve-racking." This is an understatement.

"What are you nervous about?" he asks.

"The whole experience, I guess. How I'll be perceived, and whether I'll do anything stupid on camera. And that I'll be sent home tonight and miss out on the adventure. But I'm also nervous that it'll go *well* and I'll fall in love and get my heart broken. Or I *won't* get my heart broken, but I'll have to open up to someone, and that alone is terrifying."

I close my eyes. I'm babbling again. I seem to do that around Nate, when I'm supposed to be concentrating on being charming and eloquent and generally not looking like an idiot. Nate said they can only use what I give them.

I'm afraid I've already given them more than enough to make a fool out of me.

"That's a lot of things to be afraid of," he says. "I think you hit every possible outcome."

"I think I did!" Except maybe that I'm way too into a producer and will hit on him instead of Prince Charming. I did manage not to say that out loud.

"Have you dated much since you lost your husband?" he asks.

"Not a lot," I admit. "I've been on dates." If you want to call them that, I guess.

"But no relationships."

"Definitely not."

"Why do you think that is?"

I mumble something about not having been ready, and he smiles sympathetically. I realize I haven't been restating his questions, and now I'm not sure if I'm supposed to, since we're not in an official interview with a camera. I'm about to ask, but he speaks first.

"It seems like you're more afraid of having a relationship than losing one," he says. "Am I getting that right?"

I stare at him. He *is* right, but I can't tell him why. There are a hundred reasons not to talk about my marriage on national TV, but my girls and my in-laws are the four most important. "Maybe a little," I say, and he narrows his eyes slightly, like he can tell I'm hedging.

Nate doesn't miss a thing, unfortunately. I hope I'm not being this transparent about my attraction to him. Either way, this could be a problem.

"What makes you so afraid of having a relationship?" he asks softly.

"There's more than one kind of loss," I say carefully. "There are things that are worse than rejection." I expect Nate to pry further, but he just leans back in his seat.

"So, as a single mom, where do you usually meet men?" he asks. "I'm guessing it's not on dating shows."

"I've done some online dating. Have you ever tried it?" I want to ask if he has a girlfriend. I can't believe I didn't think of this over the last few weeks. He's still not wearing a wedding ring, and he didn't mention a wife when talking about his family, but he might have a fiancée or a live-in girlfriend or a serious, long-distance situation. He probably does—a guy as gorgeous and awesome as him is not going to stay on the market for long.

"Yeah, some," he says. "I mostly meet people at parties, though. My friends do a lot of socializing and I tag along. That's where I've met most of the girls I've dated."

There's my chance. "Are you seeing anyone now?"

Nate shakes his head, and I try not to appear visibly relieved.

It shouldn't matter if he's dating anyone. I'm here to date *Prince Charming*, not a producer. Besides, just because Nate's single doesn't mean he's into me.

"I can see why you'd rather meet people in person than online," I say. "Though I imagine you get far fewer dick pics than I do."

Nate laughs. "No, never gotten a dick pic. Nor have I sent one."

I have a brief moment of imagining what one would look like if he did, though I manage to keep from glancing down at his jeans.

*Come on, Becca. Get yourself under control.*

"Really, though, would you admit it if you had?" I ask.

"Probably not, but I wouldn't have volunteered it either."

I smile. "What would you have have said then?"

"I'd probably be an apologist. I mean, have you ever considered that you should be *grateful* for the dick pics?"

I laugh, and it comes out a little high-pitched. The carriage is starting to feel really warm, even with the open windows.

"Tell me the truth," he says. "Have you ever dated a guy based on a dick pic?"

"No. I have never gone out with a guy who sent me a dick pic. Except this guy I went out with once who sent me one *after* the date, but I didn't go out with him *again*."

"Ah. So you're saying pictures of genitalia aren't the chick bait these guys are hoping for."

Nate is grinning as he says this, and I'm grinning like crazy back and wondering why I'm not uncomfortable with the conversation. I don't usually talk about penises with guys I barely know. Or, for that matter, with anyone.

But instead of making me uncomfortable, it's just making me want to tear off all of Nate's clothes, which is probably not the effect he is going for.

"Look at that," he says. "You're not nervous anymore."

He's right. I'm not. I'm sexually frustrated and ready to jump into his lap, but for the moment, not nervous.

"I guess I have the antics of the dudes on Tinder to thank for that." Though, really, it's talking with Nate.

"Wait, wait," he says. "You meet people on *Tinder*? No wonder you're getting all the dick pics. What are you doing on Tinder?"

Oh, shit. I did not mean to admit that. I guess I'm committed now, because there's really only one reason anyone's on Tinder. "Um, looking for hookups?"

Nate's eyes widen, and I swear his face is flushed. But maybe that's because it's hot in here. It is warm, right? It's not just me?

"*Really*," he says. "For some reason, I had this vision of you as this conservative, good-girl mom type."

"I am," I say. "But I'm a good-girl mom who hasn't had a husband in three years and who still has a sex drive. And, you know, a fear of relationships. So . . ."

"So how does this work? Do your kids stay with your in-laws?

36

Do you bring guys home, or do you go somewhere else?"

I can't imagine that he's asking this for the show, which, for all its skeeziness, keeps the sex stuff deniable enough to avoid Mature ratings—so I'm not particularly worried that my voice will be talking about dick pics in every promo.

But I don't want to assume Nate is asking because he's interested in me. He's probably just trying to distract me, keep me from getting nervous again.

And I *am* distracted.

The carriage starts to move, but we roll up one carriage-length and then stop. "It begins," Nate says.

I don't want to think about that. Just minutes ago I was eager to meet Prince Charming and get it over with, and now I never want to get out of this carriage.

"I do leave my kids with my in-laws," I say. "But no, I don't bring guys home. I don't want these randos to know where I live." I hesitate. "Are you telling me you've never used Tinder for hookups? Or is it more okay for you because you don't have kids?"

"I have been on Tinder," Nate says carefully. "And no, I wasn't judging you, just surprised. But I don't use Tinder a lot. I'm not into one-night stands."

"Really?"

Now Nate looks uncomfortable, and I wonder if I've overstepped, though this is much more tame than the stuff he was asking me.

"I've actually never had sex on the first date," Nate says, wincing like this is a bad thing.

Yeah, okay. So he definitely doesn't want me to pounce on him—even if we weren't on a reality show, and I wasn't about to start dating someone else, and he wouldn't lose his job over it. "Huh," is all I manage to say over the ridiculous wash of disappointment.

"Now who's judging who?" He sounds like he's joking, but given his reticence, I'm not sure that he is.

"I'm not judging!" I say. "Just surprised. That's a little old-fashioned."

Nate laughs. "Yeah, well, in Ye Olden Days, I don't think they were like, 'Yes, let's have sex on the *second* date.'" He winces again. "I don't always bring a girl home then, either."

"Why?" I can't help but ask.

He shrugs, almost seeming ashamed. "I'm not comfortable with it, I guess. It feels . . . too personal. I want to get to know a girl first."

That's sweet, actually. And not at all what I'm used to. Probably because I've been "dating" on Tinder. "I think that's the way I would be, too, if I weren't scared of getting into a relationship. I like the idea of getting to know someone first, having it mean something, but I haven't been in a place for that."

"How often do you date?" Nate asks.

"There have been a total of five guys in three years. Counting that guy with the dick pic, who I didn't sleep with. I got a vibe from him on that date that led me to bail. The pic just confirmed it."

Nate's tone softens. "How long did it take you to be ready to date after your husband died?"

"A year," I admit.

"And how long ago was your last date?"

This stuff, he's probably asking for the show, so I remember to restate. "My last date was five months ago."

Nate smiles. "Okay, yeah. So you've got to be sexually frustrated. You know you're not going to be able to hook up with Prince Charming the first time you meet him, right? Not unless you want to do that in front of the cameras and quite possibly other contestants."

I groan, and it comes out a little too orgasmic. "I *know*. But trust me. I've had sex four times in three years. I know how to control myself." And I make liberal use of my vibrator, which I unfortunately did not pack for this adventure. I'll have roommates the whole time anyway, but given how tense I feel even now, I'm clearly going to take care of myself in the shower.

Nate looks like he wants to say something, but thinks better of it. I want to ask what he was thinking, but there's this thread of tension between us. Not an awkwardness, but this electric current, like the moment right before a first kiss. He looks into my eyes, and my sexual frustration is stronger than it's been in a long while, maybe ever. I know he's just trying to get me to loosen up so I'll do better when they get me on camera—and yeah, maybe he's having a good time laughing with me, as a friend.

But as we look at each other, all I can imagine is him moving off of that bench seat, kneeling on the floor of this carriage, and crawling under my skirts. Prince Charming could be a demi-god, and it's still going to be Nate's tongue I'm thinking about when I finally get a chance to relieve myself.

The carriage moves up again, then stops. Nate breaks his gaze, staring out the window.

"Getting closer," I say.

"Yeah," he responds.

He sounds a little breathless, but it's probably my imagination.

I'm sure I've said enough things for the show to embarrass me with; I'm not going to add getting shot down by a producer to the list.

# FOUR

## Nate

Yeah, okay, I am definitely way too into Becca. I expected that I was going to fall a little in love with all the girls I interviewed, but I did six more interviews after Becca—including all the Black girls, but not, the head producer, Levi, assured me, because I'm Black—and while several of them seemed like awesome people and all of them were gorgeous, none of them had the effect on me that Becca had.

*Has*, apparently.

I stare off at one of the lamp posts lining the road outside the castle, trying not to imagine what it would be like to offer to relieve her of her sexual frustration, to lift up her skirts and kiss my way up her thighs and rock her entire world right here in the carriage.

Okay, I am completely failing at not imagining that. But at least I have the self-control not to *offer* and get a horrified rejection and probably lose my job.

Not that I couldn't probably lose my job over some of the things I've said, if Becca took offense to them. I'm not sure what possessed me to ask so many penis-related questions, besides that she was laughing, and I wanted to keep her laughing. She honestly didn't seem uncomfortable with it.

I hope I'm not going to find out later that she was. I would hate myself if I did anything to hurt her.

Which is why I had better get myself under control and this conversation back where it's supposed to be. I can ask about her dating life. I'm being *paid* to ask.

But I need to cut back on the questions I'm only asking because I wish I could take her out and kiss her until she's weak in the knees, then break my first-date-hookups rule and take her home and make love to her all night long.

*Oh my god, Nate. Stop. Get this conversation back on track.*

"So, what do you hope will happen when you meet Prince Charming?" I ask. "This guy could be the one, right?"

"Do you think so?" She frowns, her tone doubtful. "Is this really how it's going to happen for me? On a reality show?"

"When you think about meeting someone and falling in love, how do you imagine it happening?"

There. That's better. That sounds like the kind of question I'm being paid to ask.

"I don't know," she says. "I don't really let myself think about it."

"Really?" I ask. "Never?" Becca is obviously reticent to talk about her late husband. Every time I ask her about him, she dodges. Probably she's still heartbroken. I wonder if she doesn't want to admit that she's already had the great love of her life and doesn't know if she can fall in love again.

"I try to shut my brain down every time it goes in that direction," Becca says.

Huh. "So you don't want to fall in love."

"It's more that I don't want to get my hopes up, I think. As much as I hate to admit it, I'm a romantic. But I don't want to let myself get attached to romantic ideas."

I smile at her. "What about with your late husband? What's the most romantic thing he ever did for you?"

Becca hesitates. "One time, after I had Rosie, he took me out to buy a new dress and then to this nice restaurant. I'd mentioned the week before that I would like to try that place, and he took

41

care of everything—the babysitter, the reservations. It might not sound like much, but as a new mom of two, it was . . . really nice."

It's a sweet story, even though it's obviously hard for her to tell it. "Okay," I say. "So there's a romantic story. And now you're in a carriage, in a ball gown, about to meet Prince Charming. You're allowed have romantic thoughts, right?

She gives me a grudging smile. "I guess so."

"So if you didn't imagine meeting someone on a reality show, then where? How would you want it to go?"

"Okay, fine. If, for the duration of the show, I'm being fanciful, I guess I'd always thought I'd meet someone in a normal way."

"Like on Tinder."

She narrows her eyes, but she's grinning. "Not on Tinder! I don't know, maybe at a coffee shop. Like, I'm sitting there drinking my coffee, enjoying the day, and there's a cute guy at one of the other tables. Our eyes meet, then he comes over and asks if he can join me. We start talking, and he asks if I want half his muffin, and—"

"Are you serious? This cheap-ass dude can't buy you your own muffin?"

"What? I think that would be sweet!"

"Is the shop out of muffins?" I ask. "Because it would be much more polite for him to go get you a muffin. I guess if there's some great muffin shortage and the second half of his muffin represents a huge sacrifice—"

"*Fine*," she says. "Ruin my fantasy. Now I kind of hate Muffin Guy. I do deserve my own muffin."

"Right? Trying to give you half a used muffin. If I pulled that, my mom would be like, 'What's the matter with you, Nate? Get the girl her own muffin!' "

She laughs, shaking her head. "I think I'd like your mom."

"I think you would." I grin. "She'd give you all the Dominican recipes her grandmother has passed down and she doesn't have the patience to make."

"Um, yes please. That sounds amazing. As is the gallantry

when it comes to a woman's muffin needs." Her lips tease up. "You really are old-fashioned. I bet you hold open doors and everything."

"It's not old-fashioned to be polite," I tell her. "I am all for women's rights, but they aren't an excuse for men to be rude. So yeah, I hold open doors. Though I'm not one of those assholes who won't *let* a woman open her own door, because that's also rude."

"It is," she agrees. "But please tell me you don't put up with the girls who just sit there in the car and make you walk all the way around it to open the door and let them out."

"I don't know that I've ever had a woman wait for me to open her car door," I say. "I'll open her door when we're getting in the car."

"Sure. But the women who'll sit there like they can't just open it themselves? Watch out."

"I don't know that it would bother me all that much."

"It should," Becca insists. "It's a red flag. With 'I am super high-maintenance' written on it. In bold."

I'm sure whatever producer listens to her audio is going to salivate over this and do everything they can to get one of the other girls to wait for Prince Charming to open the carriage door so they can play this right over the top of it.

"I think it would only bother me if the woman was pretending to be helpless," I say. "I hate it when girls do that—pretend not to know stuff or to need help doing things when really they don't. Some women do that for attention, but it's not attractive."

"Yeah, totally. And men who only feel good about themselves when they're proving they're stronger or smarter are trouble."

"Have you dated a lot of guys like that?"

"The question," she says, "is whether *Prince Charming* is like that."

I didn't miss her dodge, but I let her have it. I don't want to press her about things she's uncomfortable saying. I hope she'll tell me eventually, though, more for myself than for the job.

The carriage rolls up another slot. Becca was in the second

half of the line, but we're getting closer to the front. Maybe another five or six carriages to go.

I don't want to get there, I realize. Because once I do, she's going to meet Prince Charming, and then everything she has to say to me will be about him.

"Do you believe in soul mates?" I ask her. "Or love at first sight?"

"Not love at first sight," she says.

"So you don't think you could fall in love with Prince Charming tonight?"

"Probably not." She shrugs. "As for soul mates? I don't believe in fate, but I like to think there's a best person for everyone. What about you?"

"I don't believe in fate, either," I say. "And I think there's probably more than one person in the world with whom you could have, say, a ninety-nine percent match. And if you find one of those people, you're lucky. And you can make them your soul mate by choosing them forever, if they choose you back."

She smiles. "You're probably right. I still like to think, though, that there's someone for everyone who is your *best* match. One hundred percent. Not that that means it's always easy or guaranteed—I don't think life is supposed to be that way. You still have to keep choosing the person for it to work."

"Do you think your husband was your best match?"

Becca looks stricken, and I immediately regret the question. There's pain in her eyes, and I didn't mean to hurt her. I was right to be cautious; I shouldn't push her.

Like I just did.

"Sorry," I say.

"It's okay." Her face is a mask, betraying nothing. "What about you? What are you looking for in a partner?"

I'm not honestly sure, except that I know I haven't found it. "Someone who fits in my life, I guess. And someone I fit with. Something comfortable and simple."

"I like that," Becca says. "That's the real fantasy, isn't it? Not some big fancy affair, but an everyday sense of being happy and supported and loved. Able to just be yourself."

I imagine that kind of love is hard to find on a show like this, but I don't say so. "Yeah. My friend Jason—who climbs shit—has been in a relationship for the last couple of years, and I've always been envious of them. They're so natural together. They *fit*, and it's easy, and they're happy. I want to find something like that."

"But you haven't."

"No," I say. "I never have." I've had some girlfriends, but my longest relationship was six months. Every time, after the initial rush of attraction and chemistry wore off, the relationship would become a chore for one or both of us. She'd want too much of my time and get clingy when I had to travel for work. Or I'd be really into the relationship, but she'd slowly have less and less time for me until she told me it wasn't working. We're never on the same page at the same time.

"Do you usually date Black girls?" Becca asks. "Or white girls?"

I'm surprised she asked. "Both," I say. "And I once went on a date with Su-Lin, from *Starving with the Stars*. She's Chinese."

"But that didn't work out?"

"No. Neither of us was all that into it. She's a little too . . . random for me. But she's engaged to her business partner now, and they're happy. What about you?" I know her late husband was white. I saw the pictures of him on her living room wall. He was a buff guy with red hair in a military haircut.

"Um, one of my Tinder dates was Latino," she says. "The rest were white."

I want to ask if she'd ever consider dating a Black guy, but that's too far, even given how familiar we've been with each other in this conversation.

Plus, I don't want to hear her say no, or listen to the excuses about how she would be open to it, but actually she's not.

"I don't know how to talk about this stuff," Becca says a little suddenly. "The race thing, I mean. I'm afraid I'll say something

45

wrong and offend you."

That's more forthright than most white people are. Most have been raised to be colorblind, which means they try to shut down any conversation about racial issues as soon as they can.

"It's okay," I say. "I mean, you haven't said anything that offends me yet."

"If I do, will you tell me? I don't want to do that, but I definitely want to know if I do."

That's a big question. She's asking for more than she knows, because calling white people on their racism usually ends badly for the Black guy. But she's sincere, I think, even if she wouldn't ultimately like the results.

"Sure." I'm not sure if it's a lie or not. That'll depend on what happens, I guess.

I'm about to change the subject, when Becca adds, "This show is really white, yeah?"

That's an understatement. *Chasing Prince Charming* makes nods toward diversity, but the final set of contestants are always white, as is Prince Charming himself. The show has been getting bad press for it lately, though it doesn't seem to have changed much. Didn't stop one of my climbing friends from suggesting it might be easier for me to get a job here because I'm Black.

I stared at him until he shut up and walked away. I didn't know where to begin to tell him that no, being Black doesn't make it easier for me to get hired. It definitely doesn't make it easier for me to succeed in this industry. I wasn't ready to get into an argument about my reality with someone who sees the whole thing as academic. I don't want to have that argument now, either.

"It sure is," I say.

"Does that bother you?"

It seems like she actually wants to know, but the answer is complicated. I mean, of course it bothers me. But also, it's a job, and it's not like Jason's show wasn't white as hell. I was the only Black guy there, too. "I don't know. I guess I'm going to find out."

"I imagine most of the people in production are white, yeah?" she says. "And you mentioned before that there will be twenty blond girls, and there are only thirty contestants, right?"

"Yeah. There are three Black girls in the cast. The producers will make sure at least one of them makes it past night one, so they can pretend they're making an effort."

Becca nods, like that's not unexpected. I'm glad this conversation isn't turning sour, but I'm also glad when she takes it down a different road. "So that's really a thing, huh? The producers picking who stays?"

I don't know how much of this I'm supposed to say to her. I would never tell a contestant that the producers picked them, and I wouldn't say anything about this publicly. But I don't feel the need to lie to her about the generalities—it's a pretty open secret. "Yeah. Prince Charming will choose a few of the girls initially, and then the producers will choose another bunch—the ones they think will cause drama, a few to make the show look good, and anyone whose stories they think will appeal to the audience."

Becca gives me a look, and I smile. She knows which of those groups she's in if she turns out to be a producer pick.

"So clearly it's the producers I need to bribe with my mashed potatoes if I want to stay on the show."

I grin. "I certainly wouldn't turn those down. But I don't get to make those decisions, either. That's up to the senior producers."

"Tell me the truth. Am I going to be the oldest woman here?"

"Yeah." I learned from the dossier on Becca that she's thirty-one. "Prince Charming is twenty-nine, though, so you're pretty close to his age. Much closer than the twenty-two-year-olds."

She winces. "There are a lot of those, I'm guessing?"

"Yep. I think the youngest is twenty-one."

"I'm going to be the cougar of the group."

"You're definitely going to get *called* a cougar," I say.

Becca groans and sinks back on her bench. "How old are you?"

I'm not sure why that's relevant, but maybe she's just looking for solidarity. "Twenty-eight," I say. "Too old to date twenty-one-year-olds, that's for sure."

The carriage rolls again, and the staff member who is leading all the horses forward walks by and waves at me. I lean out the window a little. We're closer to the castle than I thought. Two more carriages in front of us.

I've been in this carriage this whole time, when I was probably supposed to check on Becca and move on to some of the other girls. But no one has come looking for me, so hopefully I haven't been missed.

Besides, my job for the night is to run interviews and get to know the women. I'm getting to know Becca, so I'm not exactly slacking.

Becca wets her lips, her gaze darting out the window. "I'm starting to get nervous again. What if I become the bitch of the season?"

"Do you think you're capable of that?"

She pretends to be offended. "Do you think I'm not?"

"I don't know," I say. "Go ahead. Be a bitch to me."

She purses her lips, eyes narrowed for a moment, then squeezes them shut. "I can't. I can't do it. What am I doing here? What was I thinking?"

"Hey," I say softly. "You were looking for love, and you wanted to give this a chance, right? You were thinking it would be an adventure."

"Maybe I'm not the adventurous type," she says.

"I think you are. I think you're brave and you're going to rock this."

I mean it, even if I hope she doesn't *totally* rock it, because I want her to be available when the show is over.

Even if it means I have to hear her let me down gently.

"Was I crazy to sign up for this?" she asks. "Would you ever do a show like this?"

I laugh before I really think about it. "They would never let me be Prince Charming."

Becca looks worried, like she's already offended me. I'm not offended, though. I was just stating a fact.

"But you're okay," I say. "You're going to do great." The horse handler comes back and gives me a thumbs up. "And you're next, so prepare yourself."

She starts hyperventilating, and I reach over and take her hand. A chill runs over me, but I tell myself I'm just being supportive. I'm just helping her through this. I don't mean anything by it.

I can't mean anything by it, or I surely would.

"I can't do this," she says. "I can't."

"You can. And you will. Take a deep breath for me, Becca."

She does take a deep breath and relaxes her shoulders. She's clearly trying to get a hold of herself, but it takes her a minute, and then the carriage rolls forward a final time. I can see Prince Charming—Preston Carmichael is his name. He's got a square jaw and a sharp haircut and is wearing a royal-looking jacket with epaulets over a fancy dress shirt. His pants are creased and his boots have little golden buckles on them.

He looks like a pansy, honestly, but also every bit the part of the prince.

"Prince Charming is waiting," I say in a low voice. She leans back on her seat like she's trying to become one with it. "If you don't get out in the next ten seconds, he's going to come open your door for you, and then you'll be one of those girls."

She gapes. "I can't be one of those girls."

"Better get out there, then."

I'm leaning forward to hold her hand, and when she looks right into my eyes, she takes my breath away.

She's gorgeous and wonderful, and I'm more into her than I have been with anyone in a long, long time.

And I'm convincing her to run into the arms of another man.

"I'll see you inside, right?" she says. "You'll be in there?"

"Yes. I'll meet you there. I'll interview you. You can tell me how everything went."

And just like that, I'm the friend she talks to about another man.

Shit.

This sucks.

I'm unprepared for how much this sucks.

Preston is standing out there looking at the carriage in confusion. He takes a step toward the door.

"He's coming to open your door, Becks," I tell her. "Now or never."

"Ahhh! I'm going!" Then she flings open the door and rushes out, nearly tripping over her skirts on the way. She bustles up to Preston, and I can't see the look on her face because she's turned away from me, but all the cameras are trained on them, so I'll get to see the footage later.

I do see the look on Preston's face. He seems enchanted, taking her hand and kissing it.

There it is. She's got Prince Charming, the guy she'll be obsessing about for the rest of the show.

And I'm the chump who's going to hang on every word.

# FIVE

## Becca

If my less-than-graceful exit from the carriage is any indication, I'm not going to be on this show very long. I'm bound to get a concussion from tripping in a ball gown, and I can't imagine even a tragic back story will save me then.

Also, why are the driveway stones wet? It hasn't rained in forever. Do the producers purposely spray them down? I'll need to ask Nate.

More importantly, I need to stop thinking of excuses to talk to Nate again and focus on the man I'm walking toward—Prince Charming. I've got to admit, the guy is really good-looking. Not a demi-god, but he's got the clean-cut handsomeness of an actor in some Golden Age of Hollywood film. A film about European royalty, judging by the costume. He's got dark hair styled neatly back and a nice, even smile.

A smile that doesn't have nearly the same effect on me as Nate's.

"My lady," he says when I reach him. He bows and kisses the back of my hand lightly. "I'm Preston."

I can't blame him for the stilted greeting. They always make the princes do this, which means he's already kissed about twenty other hands by now.

My hand is still feeling the tingles from when Nate was

holding it in the carriage; my whole body is tingling from all that talk, risque and otherwise. I *really* need to rein this in. I mean, yeah, five months is a long time, but I've gone way longer between getting laid and not had this level of reaction to a guy. Is it his inherent unattainability? Is it the way he—

*Stop. Focus.*

I force a smile back at Preston and withdraw my hand quickly. I'm going to need it for my greeting, after all. I try to ignore the cameramen and producers and the mic pack taped against my back under my dress.

"It's nice to meet you, Preston," I say, signing as I talk. His eyebrows rise, but I keep going with my prepared speech. "I'm Becca. I have two incredible daughters, and one of them is deaf, so my family speaks sign language." I silently thank Nate for the ideas on how to phrase this. "I'd love to teach you some when we get a chance to talk later."

"I'd love that," Preston says, and he actually sounds sincere. "I look forward to getting to chat with you, Becca." He kisses my hand again, and I make a little curtsy like the producers encouraged me to do when we went over my intro. Then I turn and walk down the (also wet) lantern-lined pathway toward the mansion.

There. Short and sweet. I've met the prince. I managed to make it past step one, and other than the initial tumble in the carriage—*from* the carriage, *from*—I think it went well.

The thick carved-oak door of the mansion is partially ajar, and I push it open and walk in. There's a cameraman inside filming my entrance and reaction to the house. The entryway is large, with dark, shiny tiles and arches that have a similar carved wood to the door. But it's the main gathering room right off the hall that makes my eyes widen, for a few reasons.

First, because it's a gorgeous room, furnished with plush couches and glass-top tables and tufted ottomans. The room wouldn't look out of place in Caesar's Palace in Vegas, what with all the creamy marble and etched columns and delicate golden mosaic patterns in the floor.

I recognize this room from past seasons of *Chasing Prince Charming*, but it's far more impressive in person.

Second, because this room is filled with beautiful women in big ball gowns, and the moment I step inside, they all turn and look at me like they are one creepy, multi-headed entity. The ambient noise dips to virtually nothing for about two seconds. Then they turn back to whatever they were doing before, having either sussed out the latest threat or determined that I'm not Preston. A few keep sneaking looks this way, and one super-model type with long strawberry-blond hair gives me a wide, overeager smile that I feel the instinct not to trust.

It's like I'm the new girl walking into the lunchroom at the Hunger Games Academy. My palms are getting sweaty, and I resist the urge to wipe them on my dress. I look around for Nate. There are lots of crew members around—cameramen, producers, sound people, assistants—but he's not one of them.

He said he'd meet me inside, but probably he didn't mean right away. He's hard at work at a busy job that requires much more of him than to babysit me. I'm a grown woman. I can handle difficult situations and new challenges, all on my own.

It's one of the many things my therapist has had me tell myself over the last three years. I've gotten to where I believe it most of the time. I'm not sure this is one of those times, but "fake it 'til you make it" isn't a terrible strategy. I start forward, hoping to avoid setting my dress on fire from any of the millions of candles clustered on every conceivable surface.

That's never happened on this show, but there's always a first time.

The strawberry-blond girl walks briskly over to me, her movements in her glittering pale-green gown so fluid that it's clear she's not new to fancy evening wear. She's got a champagne flute in her hand. "Hi there," she says with a southern drawl, still smiling too wide. "I'm Madison. I'm from the southern part of Arkansas. You can probably tell from my accent, right?"

She launches on before I can answer that I don't think I could pinpoint Arkansas on a map, let alone the local accent. "I was Miss Arkansas just last year, actually."

Wow, going right into the brag. Okay. "Hi," I say. "I'm Becca. From about an hour away from here."

She watches me expectantly, like she's waiting for me to follow it up with, what? Pageant credentials? I'm tempted to say, "I was Miss Sunset View Apartments. I beat out Mrs. Hubbert next door, but only because she had hip replacement surgery." But I'm not sure my humor would translate well with this crowd, and Thea begged me not to tell stupid jokes.

I think Nate would have laughed, though.

Would Preston?

"Oh," she says when a beat of silence passes. "So, how was meeting Preston? He really is just as charming as the title, don't you think?"

"Sure," I say, though I'm not sure how much charm I can read off a polite greeting. "It went well. We didn't get a chance to say too much, but I figure I'll talk to him more later."

"You can't just assume that, you know," another voice says, and we turn to see a short, perky brunette in sleek, shimmery lavender, also with a champagne flute in hand. "Have you seen this show before? You have to make every minute with Preston count, because you may not get very much time with him." She looks utterly convinced of this—petrified even, her blue eyes comically wide.

Madison's smile turns slightly condescending. "Well, yes. But you also don't want to come off as desperate." She gives a pointed look across the room, where there's a girl wearing a long, braided Rapunzel wig, most of which she's now carrying in her arms like a giant hairball. "Her name's Carline. She made some joke about wanting to make it easy for him to enter her tower."

*Still better than the apple*, I think.

The brunette looks at Rapunzel (er, Carline) and then back at us. "Like, the Dalliance Tower?"

Ah, yes. The Dalliance Tower. Near the end of the show, the three remaining women will each get a chance to have an overnight date with the prince without cameras. With a big bed and lots of wine, I imagine.

Madison gives her a flat look and opens her mouth to say something, but suddenly the swell of chatter dies again, and I find myself looking back at the entryway along with everyone else.

Shit. I've become part of the multi-headed beast. How did that happen so quickly?

We all regard the next girl to arrive. She's another blond (yes, there are about twenty of us) who looks like Kate Upton. She's wearing a two-piece blue and gold gown with a bare midriff. She also doesn't seem nearly as taken aback by the stares, smiling calmly as she strides into the room.

"Hell, no," Madison mutters, then takes a long swig of champagne.

"Who's that?" Brunette asks, eyes still wide. Maybe they're always that way.

"Just some girl from the pageant circuit," Madison says. "Miss Vermont. Which is barely even a state." She waves a dismissive hand. Then her expression turns falsely bright when Miss Vermont looks over at us from across the room. "Addison, hi!"

"Madison!" the other girl says with equally fake brightness. They give each other a very stiff hug, which the nearby cameramen are soaking up. Clearly they already knew about this feud in the making.

"I'm Daisy, by the way," the brunette says.

I smile. She, at least, seems nice enough. "Becca."

"Are you a pageant girl, too?" She bites her lower lip.

I shake my head. "No. I'm a mom to two girls, and I'm going to school for—"

"Oh my god, you're a mom?" she gushes. "That's my biggest dream, to be a mom. When I'm way older, like you."

I can practically feel the camera start to zoom in on my reaction. Which is mostly surprise that it took so long to be called out as the old one. Though I don't love that she knew this just by my looks. "Makes sense," I say evenly.

"I mean, I'm only twenty-one. Way too young to be a mom."

I shrug. "I had my first daughter when I was twenty-one."

She gapes. Then another girl enters, and once again, we all look over. It's like some weird compulsion.

"I'm going to get a drink," I say once the silent beat of room-wide judgment has passed. "Nice to meet you, Daisy."

She's no longer paying attention to me, having turned to squeal in appreciation of some other girl's massive, lace-covered hoop skirt.

I find myself scanning for Nate around the edges of the room, where most of the crew seem to be hovering—staying out of the way of the clumps of girls forming and re-forming amidst quiet chatter and nervous, already intoxicated giggles.

I still don't see him, but a producer appears out of thin air, a tablet in her hand and headset mic over her ear. "The bar's set up right over there," she says with a genial smile, and I remember Nate telling me how eager the producers would be to get us to drink.

I'll have to pace myself. I don't want to doze off during the tiara ceremony.

Another girl arrives while I find the apparently never-ending flutes of champagne. They are set up on large granite and oak bar in the dining room, and beyond that is an enormous, state-of-the art kitchen that I find more exciting than any Vegas-inspired ballroom. We'll be making our own food while we're here, and I'm thrilled to check out all the amenities. I grin at the thought of making some muffins and giving Nate half of one.

I finally spot Nate in the doorway of a room across the hall from the massive kitchen. My heart picks up, even though he's facing back into the room. Through the open double doors, I can see a posh burgundy chair in front of a decorative screen. There's a crew member in there adjusting a light stand. An interview room, I assume.

Then Nate turns and walks into the hallway, and just as

I start to wave to get his attention, a gorgeous redhead in a fluffy gown with a very low-cut neckline comes out of the room behind him. She grins and says something and he laughs just as warmly as he did with me. My hand drops down, my gut tying itself into a knot. I take a swig of champagne, feeling the bubbles fizz down my throat.

Nate's a friendly guy. A genuinely nice guy who's good at making people feel comfortable.

A guy who is good *at his job*. I need to remember that's all this is to him.

The redhead walks into the main room and Nate spots me. He gives me a smile, which I return weakly, trying not to remember the fantasies I've had about him or the way it felt when he held my hand. The fizzy bubbles are making my stomach turn, and his smile drops. I think he might be about to head my way when there's a massive swell of excited cheers.

I turn around, expecting that Preston has stepped into the room, but it's actually the host of the show, Swiss Barrington. "My ladies," he says in his British accent, bowing deeply. As far as I know, the British accent is real, though I imagine the name is not. But I don't know, maybe his parents are sadists. He's dressed in this light blue brocaded jacket with long tails and a ruffled collar, with short silk pants and white tights (are they called hose?) and slipper-like black shoes. The specifics of the outfit—the colors and cut of the coat—differ from season to season, but he always ends up looking like the prince's flamboyant butler. "Gather around, ladies, gather around."

I look back at Nate, who makes an encouraging gesture for me to join the group of women bunching around Swiss.

Right. Because this is what I'm here for.

I take another drink and join the throng in the semi-circle. The room may be big, but with all thirty of us pressed close together like this—many jostling for a better position—it feels like I'm trapped in a stifling cloud of perfumes and ruffles.

"Welcome to the castle," Swiss says with the dimpled smile

he's known for, and the girls cheer some more. Swiss is no Preston (or Nate, for sure) but he's a good-looking guy, probably in his late forties. I remember hearing that just last year he married a lady who used to be on *The Real Housewives*. Reality TV is a small world, I guess. After all, Nate used to work with Jason Winslow and went on a date with Su-Lin, both of whom were on *Starving with the Stars*.

I wonder if Nate has met the rest of that cast? Is he friends with all of them? Would he ever introduce me to celebrity chef Fez Richards?

I blink. *Not unless Fez happens to show up on set here*, I tell myself. *Because it's not like you'll be seeing Nate after this is all over.* I force myself to focus on Swiss and not drain the rest of my glass in one gulp.

"It's always exciting to start a new season," Swiss says, "and to help a new prince—and future princess—on their journey to find love. You've all had a chance to meet Preston, but I know you're eager for more time. So don't let me delay you any further . . ." He gives us a sly smile and gestures back toward the entryway. "Prince Preston Carmichael."

Preston steps into the room, and I feel like I'm at a boy band rock concert in the sixteen hundreds. Granted, there are no sobbing histrionics (those will come later, I'm sure) and most of the women are able to contain themselves from actually jumping up and down and screaming, but the energy is palpable. I've got to admit, I'm starting to feel it too, the excitement of this whole thing.

"Hi again," Preston says, grinning at all of us. He really does have a very nice smile. "I'm just so . . . wow. It's hard to speak with so many gorgeous women all staring at me."

Giggles from the crowd.

"But I'll try my best." He runs a hand through his hair, somehow managing to do so without messing up the style. "I know that each one of you have given up so much to come here and meet me, and I am so grateful. I think this is going to be an incredible experience, and I hope—" He draws in his lips, then nods decisively. "Not just hope. I truly believe my future wife is in this room."

My heart pounds, thinking of Nate's question in the carriage: *This guy could be the one, right?*

The thought brings me more panic than the happy, melting feelings I'm sensing from the women around me.

Is there even a "one" for me? I thought I'd found it before, but I was so wrong. I want to find love—real, unselfish love that builds up instead of tears down. I want to be open to that. I'm a different person now, but it doesn't mean I couldn't be wrong again. It doesn't mean I won't put my trust in the wrong person.

I *can't* be wrong again, not like that.

"Now, Preston," Swiss says, stepping out in front of us. He's holding a glittering tiara that some producer must have given him while Preston was talking. "You'll get your chance to speak with all these lovely women again, but first I want to set out this beauty." He holds up the tiara. "This is the At First Sight Tiara. Preston, when you are ready, you'll give this to the woman that you feel has captivated you most this evening." Swiss carries the tiara over to a glass side table on which sits a puffy red pillow. He rests the tiara on top, where it will sit there throughout the evening, sparkling with the reflected light of the million candles, taunting us with possibility.

Swiss then departs back to wherever he holes up until the next dramatic pronouncement, and barely two seconds go by before Preston is seized by one of the girls. The girl, I am rather delighted to see, is Madison.

So much for not wanting to come off as desperate. She shoots a triumphant look at the other pageant queen, Addison, who was inches away from getting to him first.

I'm cool waiting my turn. I'm not in any rush.

The next hour or so drags on. I try to get to know the other girls, though half the time they're just gossiping about each other and the other half they're saying things like "I can tell

Preston has a really strong connection to his family" or "I can tell Preston is looking for a strong woman, but one who has a softer side." One girl goes on and on about her PhD in Russian literature, possibly because she thinks we'll all bow out under the sheer intimidation of a woman who has written a dissertation on *Anna Karenina*.

I try not to look around for Nate during all of this; I try not to be hurt that he hasn't come to talk to me yet, as I see producers moving among the girls and pulling them out one-by-one for interviews. I try not to track all the commentary I want to share with him or imagine what he might say in return.

There are trays of finger foods set out for us, but the women are drinking way more than they're eating. Carline is showing off some kind of twerking move, her Rapunzel wig half off her head and her face flushed.

"You thinking of joining in that?" a voice says from behind me. This woman is one of the few I haven't talked to yet. Like all the women here, she's beautiful, but she's got a tougher vibe to her. Her black dress is more slinky than poofy, her makeup's a little smokier, and her blond hair is cropped in a pixie cut that manages to look both cute and edgy.

I raise my eyebrow. "Twerking? No. I don't know if you've heard, but I'm way too old for that."

The girl grins. "I think we all are. I'm Jo." She reaches out to shake my hand.

"Becca. It's nice to—Oh, um." I grimace and make a small gesture to her right boob, which shifted when she reached out and is now on the verge of baring itself to the world. I step between her and the camera pointed our way.

"Oh my god," she says, her cheeks turning bright red. She adjusts her top. "This dress has been having side boob issues all fucking night. This happened when I was talking to Preston, too! Of course I didn't know about it until *after*." She rolls her eyes. "I'm totally going to be known as the slutty one."

"Well, I nearly fell on my face getting out of the carriage,"

I say. "So if you're Slutty and I'm Klutzy, who are the other dwarves?"

Jo laughs, a loud bark that startles a cluster of girls lounging on a couch nearby. "I'm thinking we've got Bitchy"—she points at Addison, who is telling a hushed story about how Madison once slept with a pageant show host—"and Ditzy"—this to Daisy, who is squinting at the goat-cheese crostini in her hand like she can't figure it out.

"Drinky," I say, tilting my head toward stripper Rapunzel.

"Evil." Jo's looking over at Madison, who is holding court near the marble fireplace, smiling in that too-sweet way.

I point at PhD girl. "And Doc!" The girls nearby look over at us again and I flush.

Jo laughs, even as I groan. "Oh my god," I say, glancing over at the camera focused right in on us. Feeling that mic pack at my back all over again. "I guess I am going to be known as one of the bitches."

I can almost hear Rob's voice, dripping with sarcasm: *Another great example you've set for the girls, Becca.* My lungs squeeze inward, even though I know I didn't say anything that bad.

But I feel myself relax a little as Nate's smile teases the edge of my thoughts. *Go ahead. Be a bitch to me.*

And then, later: *You're brave, and you're going to rock this.*

Rob never once called me brave. I sure wasn't brave enough to leave him.

"Yeah," Jo says with a sigh, thankfully pulling me away from those thoughts. "Probably by having this conversation, we've become Catty and Judgy." She pauses. "I call Judgy!"

I laugh. "Damn it. Okay. Catty it is."

"So, have you gotten to talk to Preston yet?" Jo takes a few steps over to grab a mini cupcake from a tray of otherwise untouched desserts. I decide she's got the right idea and take one of them myself.

"Not yet," I say around a bite of red velvet.

"You'll want to get on that," she says with a sly smile, making it clear she means the innuendo.

Heat pools low in me, remembering who I really wanted to get on in that carriage. Whose hands I wanted to feel on my skin, whose tongue I wanted on my—

"Are you implying that I'm not here for Preston?" a girl nearby shouts, flinging her arms out and barely missing breaking her champagne glass against a marble column. Attention swivels toward her; cameramen inch closer. "Because I am definitely here for Preston!"

"I'm saying that *I'm* here for Preston," the girl talking to her says firmly, and I notice she's the gorgeous redhead I saw have the interview with Nate. Does he get to pick who he interviews tonight? Did he really request to be in the carriage with me or was he just saying that to make me feel better?

"Oh my god," Jo says loudly in their direction. "We're *all* here for Preston."

The girls don't seem to notice, still sniping with each other.

I turn back to Jo. "Actually, I said in my interview that I'm just here to make friends."

She laughs. "In this crowd? Good luck with . . ." She trails off and raises an eyebrow at a couple of the women on the couch nearby, leaning close to each other.

"Preston needs to know she said that," one of them whispers, though she's a bit too intoxicated to have volume awareness.

Shit. Are we in fourth grade? Are they seriously going to tell Preston that I'm not here for him based on a stupid joke?

Although, when you get right down to it, I'm not really here for *him*. I barely know the guy yet. I'm here for me, and to find out if I can be ready for—

"Go!" Jo says under her breath, giving me a small shove. "Get your time with Preston. I'll stall them."

Right. Time to talk to Preston, to get to know the guy I'm here to date.

Hopefully I'll like him so much I won't wish I was dating Nate instead.

# SIX

## *Becca*

I find myself jogging across the main room for about five
seconds before I realize that jogging across a crowded room
in a ball gown is a great way to get the attention of both fellow
contestants and cameramen. Also, I don't have any idea where
Preston is.

I slow down into what I hope is a casual, stately walk, though
judging by the cameras following me, no one's buying it.

Maybe the other girls snitching on me wouldn't be a bad
thing. Because if Preston can tell right away that it was a joke—
*and a damn good one*, I mentally tell Thea—then that's a positive
sign. If he can't and sends me home, well . . .

Then I go home the first night. Without having proven to
myself that I can be truly open to falling in love. Still left to
wonder if I'm better off sticking with Tinder hookups until I
gracefully age into getting my thrills from the fellow residents
in a nursing home.

I grimace; that's a sobering thought. Probably I should talk
to Preston.

Even in a mansion this size, there are only so many rooms
for us to gather in, and a quick peek around reveals that he's
probably outside. I head out, past a huge pool lit in soothing

blues. It's currently empty of people, though I'm guessing we'll all be encouraged to get in tomorrow for the multitude of bikini shots the show seems to enjoy. Lights are strung up across the yard and lanterns line the pathway. It's much quieter out here, which means that in addition to hearing my own heels click on the stone, I can also hear the cameraman following me.

That is going to take some getting used to.

I also hear a girl's voice just around the corner. A guy's voice follows shortly, and the girl giggles.

Bingo.

Generally I'm not one to bust up some couple's private time—just chatting or otherwise—but Jo's right. Not about the *getting on that*, per se, but I do need to talk to him. I can't date someone if I never get to know him.

Maybe, crazy and improbable though this is, Preston is actually perfect for me. Maybe he's everything Rob wasn't. Maybe he'll be kind and warm and funny and call me brave and make my body ache and want to jump him in a carriage and . . .

I clear my throat and hurry around the corner. And yep, there's Preston on a cushioned outdoor couch, cuddled up with a Black girl dripping in red sequins. I talked to her earlier— Yasmine, I think her name is. She's an Instagram influencer, and I could practically see her framing selfie shots in her mind the entire time we spoke. There's another cameraman filming them.

Preston looks up when I walk into sight and sits straighter, but Yasmine either doesn't notice or chooses to ignore the oncoming threat to her conversation. She has her hand on his upper thigh—emphasis on the "upper."

" . . . I just don't think people understand how difficult it is to really build that level of following," she's saying. "Not to mention the sheer amount of emotional energy it takes to create unique hashtags."

"Definitely," he says, sounding a little overwhelmed. Or maybe underwhelmed, it's hard to tell. "Hashtags are . . . tough."

"Um," I say. "Sorry to interrupt, but can I get a chance to

talk with you?"

Yasmine's head swivels to me. I expect a bitchy glare, but instead she just shrugs. "Okay. I'll talk to you later, Preston." She squeezes his leg, then saunters off around the bend.

"Hey . . ." he says, then winces. "Sorry, remind me of your name again? Feel free to sign it, too."

I appreciate that he remembers something about me, and with thirty women here, I don't blame him for the name thing. "Becca," I say with a smile.

"Right." He smiles back, though there's a tired quality to it, which I also can't blame him for. I'm exhausted myself, and I haven't had to be as constantly social as he has. "You were going to teach me some sign, if I remember correctly." He gestures for me to sit down, and I find myself wondering if Nate would have stood first—that seems like the more old-fashioned, gentlemanly thing to do.

What would his mom have taught him to do in the situation of greeting a continuously rotating door of women he's dating all at once? The thought of hearing his response to that makes me have to bite back a laugh.

"Do you have any requests?" I ask, sitting down next to Preston.

He considers for a moment. "How about 'Becca, that dress is gorgeous and you make it even more so.' "

Now a laugh does escape me. "Smooth."

He chuckles too. "Cheesy, you mean?"

"Maybe." But my cheeks flush as I remember how it felt to hear Nate say I looked amazing. Did he really think that? Probably compared to glitter-covered Becca, at least. "Thank you, though. I do always enjoy a compliment, cheesy or otherwise."

I teach him the signs and he gamely repeats them. I'm sure the show will eat this up.

My mother-in-law, Paula, will appreciate the compliment on the dress. She spent two full days going with me to every fancy dress store we could find to pick out all the different gowns required for the show, and she insisted on paying for every one. She and my father-in-law, Kurt, don't have a ton of money, but they've gone out of their way to support me and the girls as much as possible, helping me save as much insurance money from Rob's death as I can for the girls' college funds and my schooling, as well as seed money for my restaurant.

My own parents have always been mostly uninterested in my life, and much more absorbed in their own. Kurt and Paula are the parents I'd always wanted and the only people who've ever really loved and believed in me—outside of my girls, of course.

It wasn't just fear of being on my own that kept me with Rob; it was also fear of losing the only real family I've ever had.

"So you have kids, right?" Preston asks. "And one is deaf?"

"Yeah, two daughters," I say. "My oldest, Thea, is deaf, and also the most good-hearted and funny and incredibly stubborn kid you'll ever meet. Rosie is my youngest, and is like this beaming, happy light—except when she's not, because, well, she's five."

He laughs, which I take as an encouraging sign that the kids thing doesn't freak him out too much.

"What about your family?" I ask. "No kids, I assume, because otherwise the show would have made a huge deal out of 'single father Prince Preston.' "

"No kids. I'm really close to my family, though. We all try to get together as often as we can. I've got three siblings—two sisters and a brother. They're all married and have kids, so they're just waiting for me to join them. I'm the baby of the family."

"Ah, so you're the little prince. Makes sense." I gesture at his outfit.

He leans in conspiratorially. "You may not know this, but these aren't actually my real clothes."

Okay, so he is kind of charming. That definitely seems like a plus. Even if he doesn't have the same effect on me as Nate did while sitting much farther away in the carriage. But I've spent more time with Nate. Just because I don't feel that same spark (um, *flame*) doesn't mean I won't.

Right?

"Well, you definitely have more personality than Prince Charming," I say. "Then again, most of the Disney princes are seriously lacking on that, so I'm not sure it's a high bar." The moment those words come out of my mouth, I inwardly cringe. I was going for flirty, but that was outright insulting. Flirtation doesn't come naturally to me—for all that Rob would accuse me of cheating, he also made it pretty clear that no one would ever be into me for my conversational skills.

"Hey," Preston says, and I'm pretty sure he only looks mock-wounded. "I've seen some of these movies with my nieces, and not all of the princes lack personality. What about that Hans guy?"

I raise my eyebrow. "You know he turned out to be evil, right?"

Preston grimaces. "Huh. Okay, maybe I didn't watch the entire thing. But he had personality."

"He sang about sandwiches," I concede. "Do you do that?"

"No. Does that make you want to leave?" Before I can answer, he continues on. "I mean, I promise I'm no Eric. That guy was dumb as a rock. Couldn't tell the difference between two girls even though they had different hair colors, just because one said 'AAAAAAAA' in a similar manner." Rather than singing, that last part sounds like pitchy yelling, and I laugh.

"You know that's going in all the promos now."

"God, I hope so," he says with a grin.

There's a nice, funny banter here. It's no muffin-related back and forth, but how many conversations are? Also, I note that he's scooted closer at some point so I'm sort of tucked into his side without my having moved at all—though I'm not exactly sure when that happened. His arm is slung behind me around the back of the chair. Maybe this *could* be a thing. I'm not exactly longing for the conversation to stretch on and on, but I'm not dying to end it, either.

I hear the clicking sound of heels against the stone path, and I figure I've got about three more seconds before being interrupted. "By the way," I say quickly. "Some of the girls are going to try to defame me because I said I was here to make friends. Which is absolutely true. Friends who are all trying to date the same guy are the *best*."

Preston lets out a laugh, just as Addison rounds the corner, her bare midriff somehow gleaming in the lantern light. Did she oil herself at some point? Another cameraman trails behind her.

"There you are!" she says with a huge, pageant-ready smile.

I stand up. "Well, that's my cue. It was nice talking with you."

"Yeah, you too," he says, but Addison has already squeezed herself and her wide skirt between us, so I can't see him when he says this. She plops herself down right where I was sitting— well, even closer to him, actually—and I walk away, doubts pressing in.

Was that actually good enough of a conversation to be kept around after tonight? Should I have gone in for a kiss? It didn't feel like a natural move right there, but I'm guessing lots of other girls made it work just fine.

Maybe I really am terrible at this. Maybe Rob had a point about—

No. I can't let any of this bring me back there.

I walk past the pool again and through the parlor entrance—

And Nate plows right into me.

Um. I mean, not like *that*, just like—

"Hey, Becks," he says, stepping back quickly, his eyes wide. "Sorry."

"Oh, it's totally okay, I was just . . ." I gesture vaguely to the backyard. He was only up against me for, like, half a second, and my body is still flushed all over. My chest flutters, too, at him calling me Becks—just like he did in the carriage. No one's ever called me that before, and it feels personal and cute.

Does he have nicknames for the other girls, too?

"Right, yeah," he says, his gaze flicking over my shoulder. The cameraman following me walks past us. "So you got some time with Preston?"

"Yep." I find myself shifting awkwardly.

"Great," he says after a beat. "So, um. Mind if I interview you?"

"Okay." It's all real, now. I'm on this show and he's doing his job and I can't even pretend for a minute—like I could in the carriage or when we were talking at my house with the camera off—that we're a possibility. That he's someone I could have an actual relationship with. Someone I could finally *want* that with.

Nate tilts his head toward the interview room, and we walk there together. "So how did it go with Preston?" he asks.

My heart thumps unevenly. "Shouldn't we save that for the interview?" I mean it to come out teasingly, but I don't think it does. His dark eyes cut over to me and then back ahead.

"Sure," he says.

I search for something else to say that will take away the awkwardness, but all I can think of is how hyper-aware I am of exactly how close his body is to mine.

There's no way he could ever put his arm around me and draw up against me without me reacting.

We get to the interview room, and I follow him inside. There's a cameraman—camerawoman, actually, the first one I've seen here—already set up. She smiles at me, and I force a smile back.

I take a seat on the interview chair, which is covered in red velvet with a very straight back, probably to discourage slouching. Nate takes a seat across from me. There are candles all over the room, but there are also filming lights—they aren't incredibly bright, but I feel like I'm under interrogation. I'm already sweating before Nate asks the first question.

"So, Becca,"—no nickname now, sadly—"How was your time with Preston?" His tone is also so much more formal, especially compared to the way he was in the carriage.

My throat is feeling dry, and I clear it. "Good," I say. "It was—" I remember belatedly to restate the question. "My time with Preston was really nice. Um, I got to know him some more," (well, at all) "and we talked about his family and my daughters" (for, like, four seconds) "and, uh, Disney princes."

I'm tempted to ramble on, but there's not a lot more to say that we talked about and also I remember Nate telling me that he's not going to cut me off. *When you're done, you can stop talking.*

There's a beat of silence and Nate nods. "Great." He is lying. That was potentially the least great answer in the history of *Chasing Prince Charming*. I need to step it up. They want to hear about how taken I was with this guy. I don't want to out-right lie, but I'm not doing Nate any favors by being such a crappy interviewee.

I can at least try to make his job easier.

"So, did you feel a spark when you met him?" Nate asks.

Shit.

"Well, he was definitely handsome." I force another smile. "And, um. He lived up to Prince Charming's name." I have not actually answered the question, and that was also a very cringey statement, but it's the kind of thing I hear on the show, so that's something.

Another beat. I can't read Nate's expression at all. My throat is even drier, my lips parched. It's like I'm being interviewed in the freaking Sahara. "Do you believe in love in first sight now?" His tone has a teasing note to it, but it sounds off.

Saying yes would be a money answer for him and probably make his day, but I can't, because I don't. I find myself thinking about when I first saw Nate.

"I believe you can be attracted to someone, obviously," I say slowly. "But more than that, I believe you can feel drawn to a person. I believe that, almost immediately, you can tell that you'll feel a real connection."

Now my heart's pounding so hard I hope he can't visibly see it thumping against the top of my dress.

"And you felt that when you first saw Preston?" he asks.

No, I did not. A smile twitches at my lips. "I mean, if I met him at a coffee shop, and he offered to buy me a muffin, I wouldn't turn it—"

"No, no, no," Nate cuts me off, his lips tugging up too. "You don't offer to buy the girl a muffin. That just puts her in a position of feeling like she has to say no. You just buy a muffin and then you offer it to her."

Just like that, my heart feels a million times lighter. "Oh my god, Nate, do you do this a lot?"

He's openly grinning now, and it hits me all over again how incredible that smile is. "No. But if I did do it, I would do so *respectfully*. It's not like she has to accept the muffin."

The camerawomen is looking back and forth between us like we're crazy.

"But," I say, "won't she feel like she has to, if you've already bought the muffin? What if she's not hungry? What if she's gluten intolerant?"

"Then I guess I just got myself a muffin." Nate shrugs. "It's a win either way."

I laugh, and Nate's grinning and there's this moment where it feels like the carriage all over again, like it's just the two of us, and I can't stop looking at his lips and imagining how they would feel—

Nate suddenly seems to notice the camerawoman's presence, and he sits back, his grin slipping.

Right. We're supposed to be talking about Preston.

He dives back into the questions ("What would it mean to you to get the At First Sight Tiara tonight?" "Was there anything you didn't get a chance to say to Preston that you wish you had?" "How would it feel to leave here tonight?") and I do my best to answer them without lying.

I have to be reminded three separate times to restate the question. I'm talking around things and saying "um" way too much and sounding distant even to myself.

I suck at this. Why did I ever think I could be on a dating show when I can't even date?

Finally—dear god, finally—Nate calls it on the interview, and we head out. I expect him to ditch me the minute we leave, but he walks with me to the main room. There's a tension between us again, even worse than when we first walked into that interview room.

We watch the girls milling around the room, many still talking and drinking. Others are slumped on the couches, the exhaustion setting in. Cameras are everywhere, capturing it all.

"I'm glad you had a great conversation with Preston," Nate says after a moment. "And talking about Disney princes? Rosie would love that." He smiles over at me. "Maybe you two really are made for each other."

I'm not sure where one would get that idea from us talking about something my five-year-old would love, but a boulder settles in my gut, because I get what he's doing. He's making it clear he's not interested in me, lest I become confused by all that sexually charged talk in the carriage and our moment in the interview about the muffins.

I look away, anywhere but at him, and my gaze lands on the empty red pillow. "Doesn't look like he agrees, because the tiara's gone, and it's not on *my* head."

Before Nate can say anything, Madison swoops into the room as if summoned by my words, the tiara glittering on her strawberry-blond hair. Several girls swarm around her and congratulate her too brightly, while others roll their eyes or make side comments to each other. Madison is practically bursting with the effort of trying to look shy and "oh my gosh I didn't expect this" humble.

I didn't care much about it before, but now I really wish I had gotten that stupid tiara. Maybe then Nate wouldn't feel like he had to spell out his lack of interest, and I could maintain *some* dignity.

"So how's your goal of making friends going?" he asks quickly.

I'm grateful for the conversation change. "Well, there's Jo." I gesture over to where Jo is standing on the outskirts as one of the eye-rollers. "She's pretty awesome. Even if she apparently does bring out the bitchy side of me. Another reason why I am definitely not wanting my girls to see this."

"Do you think you'll let them watch the show?"

I shrug. "I mean, I'm sure they'll see it all someday—it's going to be out there, you know? But when they're so young . . . Some of it, for sure. They'd both freak out if they didn't get to see all the gowns and fancy stuff." I smile at the thought of their excitement—even Thea's, though she'd try to play it cool. "But definitely not all."

Nate nods. "I guess not the tower episode."

"Yeah," I say with a shaky laugh. "Though no one sees what happens in the Dalliance Tower, right?"

"We shoot the tower and something suggestive and then leave." He shifts a little uncomfortably. Maybe because we're talking about sex again.

"You're assuming I'll still be around to the top three," I say.

He glances over at me. "What do you think your chances are?"

I look out at the mass of women—thirty of them, to be exact. "I guess, technically, it's three in thirty."

"You know," he says with a wry smile, "that there's a simpler fraction for that, right?"

I cringe. "One in ten. That's what I meant."

"Uh-huh." He sounds more amused than judgmental, but I feel my cheeks burning.

*I* should be Ditzy. Here I am in business school, and I can't even do basic math. Rob used to mock me for wanting to go to college. *It would be a waste of money, Becca. I mean, you barely graduated high school.*

Which was true. But I didn't actually try to do well in school. I think what I wanted was to do poorly enough that my parents would pay attention to me. It didn't work.

"So yeah," I say, trying for amused rather than embarrassed. "One in ten."

He studies me for a moment. "Do you really think everyone has an equal chance?" There's a small narrowing of his eyes around a too-neutral expression on his face. He's talking about race, I think, but doesn't want to say it outright.

I look back at the shifting, glittering clumps of gorgeous

women. There are exactly three Black girls. There's one girl who looks like she could be Latina. All the rest appear to be very white—and overwhelmingly blond.

I chew on my lower lip. The lack of diversity is seriously messed up, but all I can think is that if I was "Princess Charming" and Nate was one of three Black guys in a sea of white, I'd still feel this attracted to him, this *drawn* to him. I can't imagine not picking him, over and over again.

"I guess it depends on who Preston really connects with," I say carefully.

He looks away. "Sure."

I feel the disappointment radiating from him. I'm not sure if I've offended him or just let him down, but both feel pretty shitty. Especially because I know what he meant, and I know he's right. I haven't seen every season of this show, but I've never heard of a Black contestant making the top three. Which is terrible, both statistically and in general, so there's a real problem here, and probably I just minimized it.

"You're right," I say. "They don't all have an equal chance, and that sucks."

He gives me a side-eye glance. "So what do you think your real chances are? Not of making it to the tower, but tonight."

I consider this, but it doesn't take long. "Really good," I admit. "I mean, I have a great backstory. Deaf daughter, dead husband. The producers will probably pick me tonight even if Preston doesn't."

I get the feeling he wants to agree with me, but can't quite say it outright, maybe because someone might hear. "It's not just backstory, though," he says. "If a girl isn't good on camera, it doesn't matter what her backstory is."

Great. "Ha, well, I guess that lowers my chances."

"I told you you're good on camera." He sounds irritated. "Are you really concerned about this?"

I fidget with the poofs of silk just below the bodice of my dress. I want to say no, or maybe even snap back that it's none of his business, just to get out of answering the question.

But more than that, I want to tell him the truth. "It's stressful not knowing how I'll be perceived. Not just being in this room full of girls who are judging me—and yeah, I'm doing that to them, too, I know, but—" I shake my head. "It's worse, because it's not just them. It's all of America."

"Do you care what everyone else thinks?"

That's a seriously loaded question, way more than he knows. Because I *shouldn't*. I've spent years trying to repair the damage Rob did to my self-esteem. I've made so much progress.

But this whole process feels like it's knocked my legs out from under me. Like I'm right back to where I was—feeling awkward and dumb and incompetent. Knowing I can't hide that, no matter how hard I try.

"I shouldn't care," I say quietly. "But I do."

I expect to feel more disappointment from him, that maybe he's fully realizing how wrong he was about me being brave and rocking this. But his expression is softer than before. His lips part like he's going to say something and then he closes them. There's another beat, and then, "Can I get you a drink?" he asks, with the hint of a smile. "As a producer, I'm supposed to have tried to ply you with drinks long before now."

My heartbeat picks up again at those warm dark eyes, even if they're so much more guarded than before I stepped into this mansion. "Are you offering and thus making me feel like I have to say no? Or are you just going to get me a drink?"

His dark eyes glint, his smile widening. "Good point. There is a correct option here. I'll be right back."

He goes to the bar and brings back a drink, which I eagerly accept, because god, do I need that. Then he says he needs to get back to his interviews and heads off, and I'm left to mingle with the girls again and vie for Prince Charming when really, I'm interested in someone else.

A guy who doesn't feel the same way and would be off-limits even if he did.

# SEVEN

## Nate

I spend the next hour interviewing Addison, who bitches the entire time about Madison and how she "stole" the At First Sight Tiara before anyone else really had a chance, and dishes about their previous rivalries as pageant girls. It's important stuff, because I'm guessing the two of them are going to be the focus of the first episode's drama.

But my mind is back with Becca. She seemed hesitant and uncomfortable and also somewhat taken with Preston. And why shouldn't she be? He's Prince Charming. Everything we do here is focused on making these women fall in love with him.

There are other things I don't want to read into her hesitance, things I'm more afraid might be there. Like regret over the things she said to me in the carriage. Like she's making sure that I know she didn't mean anything by it. And of course she didn't. She was bored and nervous and looking for someone to pass the time with—nothing more.

It's not a rejection. It shouldn't feel like one. But it stings, anyway, much as I try to ignore it.

I finish my interview with Addison and step out, meaning to ask who's up for interviews next. Instead, Levi, the lead producer, pulls me by the arm into the kitchen. When the girls are living here, this will be stocked with food so they can fix their own meals, but for tonight, it's being used as a break room and staging room for the producers and the crew. Microphones and mic packs are lined up on the counter, and there's a bunch of recording equipment stacked along the counters next to the sink.

I'm half expecting to be chewed out for flirting with a contestant. They've probably reviewed the carriage audio by now, and yeah, some of that got out of hand. But I get that I shouldn't have done that, and I'm committed to maintaining a respectful distance. I'm new at this, and it's a weird night. It's going on one AM by now, what with all the introductions and conversations and interviews, and we're all tired. And yes, I've obviously developed feelings for Becca that I shouldn't have, and after tonight I'm going to have to take some deep breaths and remind myself that she's dating a guy who dresses up like a *prince* and that I don't have a shot in hell and would get fired if I did.

I'd hoped to be able to hide it from my boss until I got a hold of myself.

"Hey," I say, leaning against the counter. "I hope it didn't look like I was—"

"Hey, man," Levi says, "I just wanted to tell you what a fucking great job you're doing out there."

I blink at him. I've been interviewing the contestants like I'm supposed to and trying not to cling to Becca all night like I'm jealous, which I am.

What have I done that's all that special?

"Thanks," I say, because even though I'm confused, I'm not an idiot.

"Seriously, dude." He talks like a surfer and dresses the part in a plain red t-shirt and a pair of cargo shorts. I think this is supposed to make him relatable, but really, it just makes me feel annoyed every time I talk to him. "I had my doubts when we hired you, and I don't mind saying I argued against it. I just didn't get a good vibe from you, and I don't know why."

Now I want to punch him. I force myself to smile, as if I, too, find it a complete mystery why this white guy with his mostly white crew of producers on his mostly white television show could possibly have gotten *bad vibes* from me.

"But, man," he says, clapping me on the shoulder, "you proved me wrong. I was worried about that Becca chick, too. She seemed a little closed off in her initial interview, but she sure opens up to you. I heard some of the audio you got in the carriage. Great stuff! The thing about Tinder—that's going to get people's attention, for sure. The hot mom who's even hotter in bed—people are going to eat this up."

I open my mouth, but nothing comes out. Becca was worried her story would be all about pity for her past, and this is . . . not that.

But not in a good way.

"Thanks," I say weakly.

"Dude, you've got her wrapped around your finger," Levi continues. "Keep that up. We're going to need a connection like that to get the goods from her when the real drama starts."

"Sure," I say, and Levi slaps me on the arm one more time and then breezes out through the kitchen. I brace myself against the counter, feeling sick.

This is my job. This is what I do—I coax stories out of people. I did that with Jason, but Jason was *willing*. And yeah, these girls signed up for this, but they're here for the promise of finding love and maybe having a little adventure. Not being manipulated by douches like Levi.

I am one of those douches now, and if I don't get my priorities straight, this job—and my chance to break into television—are going to be gone. Opportunities like this don't come along every day, and I'd be an idiot to waste it.

Becca wants to date Preston. It's not my fault that the show manipulates people—they'll be doing that whether I'm here or not.

For right now, my boss thinks I'm doing a good job, and that should be enough, no matter what it costs.

I know that's true, but I still don't feel entirely convinced.

The night goes on, and the women get increasingly drunker and louder. Madison parades around imperiously with perfect pageant posture, making sure everyone knows she has the At First Sight Tiara, as if anyone could miss it. Levi has us cut off the alcohol forty minutes before the tiara ceremony starts, because he doesn't want anyone having trouble standing straight. When we line them up on the terrace where we're filming the ceremony—with an ornate iron table covered in nineteen more identical tiaras—Madison is the first to get in place, preening for the camera.

I wonder what she's going to look like on camera, because in person, she looks ridiculous.

I herd the other girls onto the terrace, and find Becca with her head resting on the back of a settee. She looks up at me sleepily. Could be that it's past four AM, and we're all feeling a little droopy, but—

"You weren't kidding about being a sleepy drunk, were you?" I ask.

She yawns. "Can we go home yet?"

"Becks, you are home. Come on. Just the tiara ceremony to go, and then you can get some sleep."

She looks up at me with this world-weary expression, and I laugh. I take her hand to pull her up, and she leans forward a bit, resting against me for a half second before she gets her feet under her.

My whole body warms up—not in a sexual rush like it did when she ran into me earlier, but in this pleasant way that makes me long to take her in my arms and hold her. I want to tell her it's okay to go to sleep, to let her lie down on the settee and put a blanket over her the way people do in romantic comedies.

I take a deep breath and a big step back, once I'm sure Becca's going to stand okay on her own. "Come on," I say. "Time for the big moment."

I realize I've told her she can go to sleep after this like I know what's going to happen, and the truth is, I don't. Preston is in a meeting right now with Levi and the senior producers, making decisions about who stays and who goes. I expect Becca to stay, but I don't know if she will.

I'm torn between hoping she does, so that I can see her more, and hoping she doesn't, so that after all this is over, I can ask her out and see if she feels differently about me when she's not dating Prince Charming.

If someone amazing doesn't snap her up before the show's over and sweep her off her feet for her happily ever after. A woman like Becca isn't going to stay unattached for long, not if she's decided she's ready to give relationships a shot.

I lead her out onto the terrace, while a couple of the other producers usher in the rest of the stragglers. She isn't the only one who looks like she's ready to fall asleep, but when they get a look at the tiara table and the pedestal next to it where Preston will stand, the women all grow more alert. One of the producers, Olivia, is helping them to stand the correct distances from one another so they look good on camera, fussing with their hair, making sure the lighting is right. Becca gives me a look of panic and moves to her place in the second row. Cameras are set up around the edges of the room, and as soon as Olivia is done with the girls, Levi instructs them all to wait while the cameras record.

They stand there for a good twenty minutes, cameras catching every fidget, every uncomfortable twitch, all of which will be used when they need reaction shots.

"Nate, Levi wants you with Preston," Olivia says to me, and I head back down the hall to a shelving unit where all thirty of the women's pictures are set up in frames. Preston stands before the shelves, his hands behind his back, perusing the images and pretending to consider them for the camera, manned by Dustin.

"All right," Dustin tells Preston. "We got it."

Preston immediately deflates, looking even more tired than the girls did. "Okay. Who is in this first batch?"

Levi hands him a list. "These are your first five. Memorize them, then go hand the tiaras out. Come back and we'll give

80

you a new list, okay? If you forget some of them, just come back early. Nate here will walk you up and back." Levi gestures to me, and I wave to Preston in greeting. I'm not assigned to interview him, so I've barely spoken to him. Apparently my newfound favor with Levi means I get the job of walking the guy up and down a hall, but at four AM, Preston is probably capable of forgetting his *own* name, so maybe it's necessary.

"Great," Preston says. He goes over the list, then hands it back to Levi. They don't want him referring to it on camera or—more importantly—in front of the girls.

As I walk Preston up the hall, he takes a deep breath. "If I mess up in interviews, no one sees it but you guys," he says. "I really don't want to fumble in front of the women. One of them could be my future wife."

"You'll be fine," I say. "They're all so nervous, it would probably make them feel better."

Preston chuckles. It's good to know, I guess, that he really is here to find love. It's not as if he needs to pretend for *me*. Though maybe he worries that the producers will be upset with him if he admits he's doing this for notoriety or Instagram followers.

They can't kick him out for it at this point, and he's too worn out to be calculating, so I think he's probably being honest.

Preston steps up to the pedestal, and all the girls are suddenly paying attention. There's not a sleepy face among them as they look at Preston with varying levels of adoration and terror. I wonder if it's the spirit of competition or the weight of expectation or just the atmosphere that makes them capable of feeling so much desperation after just one night.

Whatever it is, it's definitely not only for show.

"Thank you so much for being here," Preston says, his voice full of sincerity.

From the second row, Becca catches my eye and makes a nervous face. I smile at her, giving her a thumbs up, and she nods and turns her attention to Preston.

*Where it belongs*, I tell myself. At best, I'm the supportive friend.

In the real world, I would never put myself in a position to be in the friend zone with a woman like her, and yet, here I am.

"I am so thankful," Preston continues, "that you all took time out of your lives to come here to meet me, and I have cherished our time together." I have to give this to the guy, he sounds like he means it. "But, for some of us, our time will be cut short." He looks dramatically over to the tiaras.

Someone instructed him how to do this. They'll layer that shot with some pre-prepared footage panning over the tiaras.

Thirty women and twenty tiaras, including the one already on Madison's head. A third of these girls are going home tonight, and I can tell they all feel the pressure. Preston steps forward and picks up the first tiara, looking down at it.

"That's good, Preston," Olivia says. "Hold it there."

Preston holds it there for a ridiculously long time, turning the tiara over in his hands, looking as if he's trying to make a decision, when really he's probably counting down the seconds until they let him get on with it.

"Daisy," he says. A perky-looking brunette in the front row grins and rushes over to him. "Daisy, would you wear this tiara?"

"Yes, thank you!" She practically bounces with excitement as he fits it on her head. It catches in her hair and one of the producers comes over to help him with it—that part will be cut out—and then they get a shot of Preston and Daisy hugging before she heads back to the crowd of jealous women.

Becca gives me another nervous look. Some of these women's faces are so pinched that I think they might need to pee.

Preston considers the next tiara for an equally long time—this footage is important, because the tiara ceremony will be the center of whatever narrative they create, the moment everything builds to.

"Jo," Preston says, and Becca's friend with the short hair steps out of line, smiling in a controlled way, like she's trying not to look too eager.

It takes more than twenty minutes to finish the first batch of names. As we head down the hall, Preston looks over at me, his veneer of camera-ready calm disintegrating. "Did I do okay?"

"You did great." This is what I'm here for, I realize. Not to make sure he doesn't get lost, but to ensure he doesn't get too stressed. "How do you feel?"

"Good, I think. I picked a couple of the girls in that batch."

I nod. "The producers want you to keep some of the others around, right?"

"Right," Preston says. "Which I understand. They say some of them are perfect for me, so I need to give them a chance. Like that girl who speaks sign language. She did seem cool, I guess."

Ah. So Becca is a producer pick. I figured she would be—and I don't think this is going to be a secret from the team, so I probably would have found out sooner or later.

But it's good to know that he's not into her. It means she'll probably be around for a few weeks, and then she'll go home.

And be available.

I know Becca really wants this, so I shouldn't be too excited about that, but I am.

Levi gives Preston his next round of names, and we make two more trips up and back before Becca's on his list. We're in the final round of girls, and the fifteen remaining without tiaras can do the math. They're all staring at the remaining tiaras like they're winning lottery tickets, which I guess they basically are.

Preston looks up at the women.

"Go, Preston," Olivia says.

"Becca," he calls.

Her face lights up, and then, like Jo, she seems to tamp down her reaction, like she's afraid of seeming too eager. I've gotten that vibe from her before, so I don't think it's just for the camera. Becca almost seems afraid of hope, afraid of happiness. Which I guess makes sense when you had a fairytale life before and then it was ripped away from you.

I can't imagine being married to someone and then losing them. She's brave as hell for giving this a shot again, and not just because she's doing it on TV.

She makes her way over to Preston and stands before him, looking up into his eyes.

"Becca," he says. "Will you do me the honor of wearing this tiara?"

"Yes," she says, and her face glows as he places it on her. He's getting the hang of that now, so it's going more smoothly each time. He wraps his arms around her waist, and they hug, and jealousy burns in me. I try not to let it show as she catches my eyes over his shoulder and grins.

I give her another thumbs up.

She made it past night one. That's a big deal. There are ten girls standing behind her who won't.

Preston announces the rest of the names, and when the last girl—Addison, who looked like she was going to murder someone if she wasn't chosen—is crowned, ten women all look like they've lost members of their family. The cameras focus in on each of them as they say their (sometimes tearful) goodbyes to Preston, which gives me a chance to catch Becca's eye again.

Her smile at me is so radiant, I don't know how not to smile back. "Good job," I mouth, and she mouths back, "Thank you."

I clearly need to learn these words in sign language, so we can communicate in situations like this. It's my job to make her feel comfortable, and as Levi said, I'm damn good at it.

I just need to figure out how to do it without letting anyone see how, bit by bit, it's breaking my heart.

# EIGHT

## Becca

I'm sitting out by the pool with nineteen other women, all of us in show-mandated bikinis and listening to a girl named Lottie (short for Charlotte, I assume) go on and on about her date yesterday with Preston, in which they learned ballroom dancing and had "the most romantic, fairytale dinner ever."

I'm more interested in what food was served than how far she got with Preston, but I am alone in this.

So, after hearing her chatter on about Preston's graceful dancing (and eating and breathing) for what seems like a hundred years, I am beyond grateful when the town crier shows up on the patio, wearing his tri-corner feathered hat and gold coat with matching silk knee breeches. He dramatically unrolls his scroll.

"Hear ye! Hear ye!" he calls out, and even Lottie goes quiet. "Prince Preston requests the presence of the following eight ladies to accompany him on an outing today." He pauses dramatically, and there are nervous giggles.

*Please let it be me*, I think. I've barely been here two days and I'm already desperate to get out of this house.

He reads off the names, and girls shriek as theirs are called. Mine, thankfully, is one of them—though I stick to a relieved sigh.

"Today," the town-crier continues (in my head, I have named

him Bartholomew), "you will be participating with Preston in *the sport of kings*." Bartholomew emphasizes this last part, the clue to our activity. Then he rolls up his scroll and walks back into the mansion to wherever they keep him. I wonder if he and Swiss hang out in their downtime.

"What do you think that means?" Daisy asks, her perpetually wide eyes still wide.

"I hope it's fox hunting," Madison says. We all look at her, and she shrugs, smiling smugly. "I won the Arkansas Long-Range Rifle Sweetheart Championship three years in a row."

Of course she did. But I'm not particularly worried we're going fox hunting. Animal protection groups aside, the last thing this show wants is the liability of sending a bunch of us out into the woods with fully loaded weaponry.

After our reactions are recorded by the ever-present cameras, a producer named Darlene steps out and tells us to get into our "athletic wear" (also on the mandated clothing list) and be ready to go in a half hour.

Thank god. I'm grateful to be leaving the house, but I'm *really* happy to be getting out of this bikini. I know I've got a decent body, but unlike the rest of the girls here, I'm a mom with stretch marks and a flabby bit of skin puckering around my c-section scar, which no amount of crunches will ever take away. The sarong I'm wearing covers most of this, but I still feel too exposed. I never cared about the Tinder guys seeing it, but now all I can think about is how Rob used to "joke" about whether the military would cover plastic surgery to fix it. *It's essential for soldier morale*, he'd say with a laugh, then tell me I was being too sensitive if I didn't laugh with him.

Would Nate find that part of me so unattractive?

I grimace as I dart into the house. I *should* be asking myself what Preston would think. If I'm going to be body-conscious, I might as well be worrying about the guy who might actually be interested in seeing my body.

I haven't seen Nate much since the tiara ceremony. The twenty

86

of us who got tiaras were hustled up the stairs and allowed to pick our shared bedrooms. There was some drama surrounding that, as some of the rooms are bigger and nicer than others, but Jo and I claimed the one that only slept two, which was worth way more to me than any mountain view.

Yesterday we all slept in—thank god, because we were up past five AM—and we'd barely dragged ourselves out of bed when Bartholomew showed up for the first time and whisked Lottie off on her day-long one-on-one date. I'm pretty sure Lottie is one of the girls Nate's assigned to, so he was sent off with the production team covering the date, leaving me to be sporadically interviewed throughout the day by a woman named Olivia.

I should be grateful, given how awkward the last interview was, but I'm not. I miss that encouraging smile of his that makes my whole body feel floaty. I find myself looking around for him anyway, even though I know he's not here.

I'm practically stalking the poor guy, and I need to stop.

There's virtually nothing to do around the house, without TV or internet or even a spread of magazines. The only dubious "entertainment" we are allowed is a nice leather-bound journal they have given each of us in which we are told we can "record our private thoughts about our journey." They get numerous shots of us doing so, though all I'm doing is writing down recipe ideas and doodling sketches of restaurant layouts.

So by the time we're geared up in our yoga pants and sports bras (though I opt for a t-shirt over the top) and packed into a limo to head to some undisclosed sporting adventure, we're all a bit giddy.

After a half-hour drive, the limo pulls up to a sports complex with a large outdoor field. There are goalposts on either side, but no net in between them. We all squint at it as we get out.

There's a production crew already in place, and I see Nate among them. My pulse starts racing again, especially as he smiles and gives a little wave. God, this gorgeous man is going to give me hypertension. I wave back and catch a girl named Londyn—the redhead I saw him interviewing the first night—next to me doing the same thing. I look away, hoping he didn't see me cringe.

He could have been waving to me or her or both of us. It's his job to be friendly, and that's obviously all it is.

Swiss shows up then in his full regalia and tells us we will be divided into two teams of four, and that each team will need to select a captain.

"But first," he says, with that cheesy smile and a dramatic swoop of the arm toward the complex, "your prince is arriving with everything you need for today's competition. Prince Preston, your ladies await!"

I hear one of producers say into their headset, "Send out Preston," and then Preston emerges from behind the building, striding toward us. He's wearing a billowy white shirt tucked into tight leather pants which are themselves tucked into boots, and he looks like the dashing rogue on the cover of some romance novel—especially given that he's leading two horses. Behind him are several guys wearing helmets and bright blue shirts with white pants and boots. All of them are leading horses and carrying long mallets.

Polo mallets.

We all gape. Londyn jumps up and down and claps her hands together. "We get to ride!" she squeals, maybe missing the big mallets we're going to be expected to swing around from horseback.

"Oh, shit," Jo says from the other side of me. I couldn't agree more.

Preston eventually arrives (it's not a short walk across the field) and greets us all to no shortage of giggles.

"I've always loved horseback riding," Preston says, "and I love a good competitive sport, but I've never gotten the chance to do both at once. So I was really excited to meet with some friends from the Los Angeles Polo Association"—he gestures to the guys behind him—"and set up this fun date for all of us."

I want to look back at Nate and arch an eyebrow at the thought of Prince Charming actually sitting down and ironing out the nitty-gritty of a polo competition date, but I refrain, trying to focus on Preston.

"I know many of you haven't played before or maybe haven't ever ridden a horse," Preston continues, and Jo and I look at each other in commiseration, "but these guys are pros and will show us all what to do. So let's play some polo!"

We all cheer. Even me, because hell, I'm on camera, and isn't this what I wanted? Something different than my normal life? Something adventurous?

Check and check.

We're assigned horses and given basic riding lessons. It's not actually as scary as I had thought, though my horse seems to have a delayed start response. Madison and Londyn are both good at riding, but the rest of us are a pathetic lot, which ends up being really funny—they're getting lots of footage of us shrieking at every jostle of the horse or (in my case) trying desperately to get my horse to actually move.

After that, we're told the rules of polo, the only part of which I remember is "get the ball between the other team's goalposts." My team consists of Jo, Londyn, and Daisy. On the other team are Madison, Addison, Yasmine, and a tall blond law student named Sheree.

Addison immediately claims the captain position on her team, which turns into a clenched-teeth debate with Madison over who is more qualified to lead their team to victory. Meanwhile, my team all looks at each other.

"Not it," Jo says. I open my mouth to say the same, but Daisy jumps in.

"I think Becca should be the captain," she says brightly. "She's the oldest. By far."

Oh my god.

"I don't know," I start, "Londyn can actually ride and—"

"Becca, don't let your age define you," Daisy says very seriously, taking my hand in hers. "You can do anything we can."

"I'm not—*You're* the one letting my age define—" I shake my head and pull my hand back. "Never mind. I'll be captain."

We get our mallets and head over to our horses. I can't help but look over at Nate. He's smiling, and then he signs, "Good luck."

My breath catches. Did he really learn some sign for me? I mean, it's just a small thing, a little phrase, but he didn't have to do that.

"Thanks," I sign back, my heart doing acrobatics in my chest.

We mount up and start playing.

Well, we mount up and start riding at various speeds and in directions we aren't entirely meaning to and only occasionally getting anywhere near the ball. It's actually kind of a blast. We're laughing and cheering for anyone who manages to even come close to the ball, no matter whose team they're on (the exception being Madison and Addison, who might be on the same team but are clearly only competing with each other). Preston's in the game, too, supposedly switching from team to team every so often, but considering teams are essentially useless at this point, it doesn't really matter. He's pretty bad at the game himself and isn't taking it seriously, laughing right along with us. At one point Yasmine manages to get the ball between the posts, but it's the wrong goal and it's because her horse accidentally kicked it in.

It doesn't matter; we all scream and air high-five like she won the world cup.

It's crazy, but this does feel like a fun adventure. A break from the responsible Becca I've had to be ever since I got married— the Becca who was just a wife and a mom.

Now I'm Becca, mom and student, but it's nice, for once, to just be Becca and nothing else.

I know I must not look fantastic, sweaty and red-faced under my helmet, and I'm not impressing anyone with my athleticism, but when I reflexively look over to grin at Nate and see him grinning back at me, I feel downright beautiful.

90

When we get back to the castle, we're told that we have an hour and a half to get ready for the second part of our date, which is a private party in the gardens for Preston and the eight of us. All the girls are excited to get some more one-on-one time with him, but I'm still smiling from the fun of today—and yeah, the way Nate looked at me.

I had a short interview with him right there on the field, and that went much better than the last one. It was easy to talk about how hilarious this all was and who I thought actually won ("Everyone who got to sit back and laugh at us"), and whether I thought anyone made a "love connection" with Preston over polo ("We did talk a lot about his big mallet, if that counts.")

I can't deny it—I wish I could be more to Nate than a girl he's paid to interview, or even a friend. I wish I could have something real with him, everything I came on this show to find and maybe more.

God knows I wish I could feel his body against mine, his hands hot on my skin, his breath ragged in my ear—

But I can't. To any of it.

At least these moments with him are better than nothing.

I put the finishing touches on my makeup. Jo already got herself ready for the garden party—it didn't take nearly so long, with her short hair—and headed downstairs. I study myself, making weird faces in the mirror to check out my makeup, like I'm trying to see how it looks with every expression. I think I've done okay with the eyeshadow and blush. I suck at doing anything fancy with my hair, so it's blow-dried straight and put in a low ponytail. My lipstick game is fierce tonight—a bright coral that matches one of the colors of my dress.

I think even Thea would approve. Rosie, of course, would want to add glitter.

I miss them like crazy. I've never been away from them for longer than one night, and I'm dying to tell them about the gowns and the tiaras and riding horses and arriving in a carriage.

Okay, maybe not *all* about the carriage.

I look at the clock on the dresser. Crap. I need to get down there, and I don't even have my dress on. It's lying on my bed, behind the white ruffly fabric that drapes down from the canopy, which makes me feel like I'm sleeping inside a very luxurious mosquito net. The bed is ridiculous—complete with pale pink silk bedding and matching, lacy-edged pillows—but I have to admit, it adds to the whole insane experience.

I take off my fluffy bathrobe and pull on the dress. It's one of my favorites. Less poofy than the first one, but still gorgeous. It's got a halter top that dips low in the front and especially low in the back. Sexy, but not so much I'd be embarrassed for my kids to see me in it. Really, I think it looks elegant—silk fabric in a gorgeous floral pattern, fitting slim at the top and waist, with a floor-length skirt.

My mother-in-law got tears in her eyes and said I looked like I should be on the red carpet. She might have been overstating that, but the confidence boost isn't bad to have right now.

I hook the halter part around my neck and zip up the back. Or I try to, at least—the zipper catches. Hard.

I tug it as gently as possible, but nothing.

Shit. This dress may have a low back, but I don't want it to be *that* low. I'm not exactly looking to snag the tiara based on my half-exposed ass crack.

Now I try zipping it back down, but it won't go that way, either. Trying to shimmy it off my hips does nothing more than strain the fabric.

Oh god. I'm stuck in a very expensive dress, and I'm not sure I can wiggle out of it, especially without breaking the zipper completely.

I feel myself sweating against the silk. It shouldn't be a big deal, but that searing fear of judgment is back in all its irrational glory. I can't go down there with my ass flapping in the wind; I can't be the girl who is just trying to draw attention to herself, or who is so incompetent she can't get dressed. I can't have the cameras on me during something as stupid as this.

*What did you think was going to happen, Becca?* I can almost hear Rob ask.

I breathe deep, trying to calm myself. If I can find someone up here to help . . . One of the other girls, maybe, or one of the female producers. Or hell, a sound crew person, female or male. Given how tight many of these girls' dresses are, they're used to getting up close and personal to attach a mic pack.

I don't hear anything from the hallway. Everyone must be downstairs already.

What am I going to do? What am I—?

There's a knock at the door and I jump.

"Hey Becks? Are you ready yet?" It's Nate, and I am both beyond relieved to hear his voice and also suddenly flushed for a very different reason.

Could I let *him* help me with my wardrobe malfunction? Would it seem like some obvious ploy, some desperate attempt to—

He knocks again. "Becks?"

What else am I going to do?

"I'm here, just a sec," I say, my voice sounding panicky. I close my eyes.

*You could ask him to get someone else*, the rational part of my brain whispers. But maybe I want to see if he really is so uninterested.

Or maybe I just want to pretend for a few seconds that his hands on me could mean anything.

*Shit*, I think, *this is a bad idea.*

But then I open the door.

# NINE

## Nate

Becca pulls open the door between us and looks up at me nervously. She's wearing a floral-print dress with a neckline that dips right between her breasts and oh god, Nate, get your eyes back to her face.

"Hey," I say, though it comes out a little hoarse. "Can I get an interview with you before everyone meets downst—"

Becca grabs me by the arm and pulls me into the room. She closes the door and presses her back against it. "I need your help."

Um. There are a lot of things I would like to help her with alone in her bedroom, but I'm positive that's not what she means. "What can I do for you?"

Becca winces. "My zipper is stuck. Can you fix it?"

Oh, god. She wants me to—"Should I go grab one of the wardrobe people?"

"I don't want to make a big deal out of it. Can you just fix it?" She looks at me like she's desperate, and I sigh.

Yeah, okay, Becca is hot and amazing and I want to take this as a come-on, but she's an incredible woman in a vulnerable position who is looking to me for help, and there is no way in hell I'm going to take advantage of that.

"Sure," I say, and she spins around and puts her hands against the door. All my blood rushes downward. Her dress is mostly backless, so the zipper hugs the curve of her ass. It's most of the way up, but stuck a few inches from the top, and I can see the elastic edge of her lavender underwear. But it's the smooth skin of her back that leaves me breathless—she's not wearing a bra, though the halter is fastened around her neck, and I want to run my fingers over her skin, to undo the halter and slip the dress off and kiss her neck beneath her ear and whisper all the things I've been thinking and feeling since we met.

*Get a grip*, I tell myself, and while I think I'm going to be getting a very firm grip on myself later, I don't want to make her uncomfortable now.

Which I'm clearly doing by hesitating. Becca looks at me over her shoulder, and I nearly come undone.

I kneel down, inspecting the zipper and definitely not the soft skin at the small of her back. I'm definitely not thinking about how little effort it would take to rock forward and kiss her there, to cup her ass in my hands—

*Oh my god. Zipper.*

It is stuck, and I pull it gently up and down, but it doesn't budge. In fact, it looks like there's a tiny bit of something stuck in the slider, and I try to pick it out with my nail, but it isn't long enough.

"Do you have any, um . . . tweezers?" I ask. "I think there's something stuck in it."

"Sure." Her voice is a little wobbly.

Shit. I am being creepy. I'm making her uncomfortable.

"Or I could go get wardrobe," I offer, because she obviously needs an out here, having miscalculated how awkward I could make this.

"No, I've got it!" she says quickly, then crosses the room to her vanity and bends over her makeup case. She's right next to her bed, which, in show tradition, is covered in a frilly pink comforter and a breezy white canopy. It's the bed every six-year-old girl probably dreams of, and while I certainly never have, I'm

95

dreaming right now of stepping up behind Becca and pulling her against me and then bending her over that bed and—

"Here they are!" Becca says, pulling out tweezers and holding them up triumphantly.

I must be staring at her like an idiot, but Becca doesn't seem to notice. She strides over, hands me the tweezers, and spins around, pulling her hair over her shoulder to give me a full view of her bare back again, even though her hair isn't nearly long enough to reach the zipper.

Her underwear has slipped just slightly, so I can see the ghost of the dip between her ass cheeks. My jeans are mostly containing my raging hard-on—I don't dare wear anything but tight jeans around Becca, not with the effect she has on me. The effect she's always had on me, though it's getting stronger, and having her here so close, with no cameras and no mic packs yet, where I could pull her close and tell her everything and no one would hear—

This is too much temptation, and I need to get this over with as quickly as possible, before I do something to get myself fired and alienate Becca forever. If I want to have a shot in hell of her saying yes when I ask her out after the show, I need to not be that guy who skeeved on her when she asked for help.

I focus on the zipper, using the tweezers to tug out a bit of sheer fabric from the pull. It's a yellow-green color, not even close to the color of Becca's dress. I tuck it in the palm of my hand as I zip Becca's dress the rest of the way up and breathe a sigh of relief.

No, not relief. Frustration. Deep, tangled frustration.

I want this woman so fucking much, but I want to do this right.

There are a *lot* of things I want to do to her right.

"All done," I say, hoping she doesn't notice how breathless I am. I take a step back and she turns and smiles at me. I try to smile back. "Here's the offender." I hand her the bit of green fabric and back up toward the door.

"Thank you so much," she says. I should be relieved that she doesn't seem to have noticed what a wreck I am, but instead, the floor falls out beneath me.

She doesn't notice anything because she doesn't think anything of it, I realize. She's asked me to zip her up like I'm a sexless being to her. Like I'm just a friend and that's all I'll ever be.

That's what she's going to say when this is all over, isn't it? Gee, Nate, that's so sweet of you, but I really only think of you as a friend.

*Shit.*

I put my hand on the doorknob, but Becca takes a step toward me again. She's in my personal space, but not so much so that this would be uncomfortable if I did only think of her as a friend, which I already know I can never do.

"I really appreciate your help," she says in a conspiratorial voice that I feel all the way down in my dick. "It's bad enough, all the embarrassing things they make us do, without parading around in front of the cameras trying to find someone to fix a zipper."

"Yeah, no problem." I know I'm supposed to ask if I can interview her now, but damn it, I need a minute. And I should go and find a corner to breathe and calm down and convince myself that I did the right thing here, not touching her, not begging her to look at me as a man and not as a friend.

But Becca is here, so close, and smiling at me like she's grateful I'm here, too, and the pull she has over me is too powerful. I'm desperate to stay here in her presence just a little longer.

"So what do you think of the accommodations?" I ask, indicating toward the bed. *Oh god, Nate, yes, let's talk about the bed.* "Does it make you feel like a princess?"

Becca giggles. "It makes me feel like I'm five. Rosie would love it. So would Thea, actually, though she would pretend not to."

"That's what you should bring them as a souvenir," I somehow manage to say. Part of me feels like I'm floating outside my body, watching myself have a perfectly normal, friendly

97

conversation as if this is a perfectly normal, friendly thing to do and not a moment when I'm going to desperately wish that I'd taken a chance.

Touching her would be so wrong. I've never wanted something so wrong this badly in my life.

"Can you get me one of these after the show?" Becca asks. "Do they use the same ones every time, or is there, like, a clearance sale I can hit?"

She grins at me, and I smile back. She's got such a great smile, and I'm always taken by it, even if she's smiling about another man.

"Am I your bed broker now?" I'm trying to keep up the friendly banter, but I'm not sure I'm succeeding. "Is there any dirty job you won't have me do?"

Oh. Shit. Becca's eyes flash and her face flushes, and I know mine is too. The heat between us is unbearable, and this is my cue. I have to get the hell out of here before I do something I regret.

"I'm going to go see if they're ready for you," I say, and I flee out the door about as gracefully as Becca exited the carriage.

*Smooth, Nate*, I tell myself. *Way to not make it seem like you're hitting on her.*

But my whole body is aching, and that's not the part I regret.

# TEN

## Becca

Oh my god.

My knees are so weak as I head down the stairs that I'm wondering if maybe I should sit down on the steps for a moment and collect myself. But I already know there will be no collecting myself after that, not for a long while.

Nothing happened, not really. He politely removed the weird piece of fabric that was stuck in my zipper—a piece of fabric that I'm holding in my hand right now—and we joked a bit and he left.

Except.

He hesitated when he was behind me, and when I looked back there was something like hunger in his eyes, and it burned right through to my core. I could feel the whisper of his breath on my skin while he worked at the zipper, and heard the strain in his voice.

I worried I was making him uncomfortable—he asked me twice if I wanted to get wardrobe to help, after all. But that tension in the air, that heat. It didn't feel awkward in some cringey way, like he was thinking of me as this pathetic girl he couldn't wait to escape—even if he did sort of run off at the end there.

He wants me; I could feel it.

And oh, how I want him. More than I've ever wanted anyone. More than I ever imagined I could want anyone (and I have a pretty healthy sexual imagination.)

But that's the problem. Because it's not just sexual for me, no matter how much I want to retreat back to my room and lock the door and relieve the deep, desperate ache. And while I hoped—my throat dry, my heart pounding, my nerves sparking like live wires—that he might cross that line and relieve me right then and there, I know it wouldn't be enough.

I want more and I'm terrified that he doesn't.

I want more and I'm terrified that he does.

Am I even capable of that? I mean, that's what I'm here for, right? Being open to the possibility of a relationship?

But there's relationships and there's *relationships*, and the intensity of the effect he has on me, the connection I feel with him . . .

*There's more than one kind of loss*, I said to him in the carriage. Even if it wouldn't be the same way that it was with Rob. He's nothing like Rob, I can tell. Nate's kind and good and warm and—

"There you are!" a voice says, and I jolt out of my thoughts. It's Olivia, one of the producers, and she impatiently waves me over and hooks up my mic pack. "The party's in full swing." She's got a huge smile on her face, and I can immediately hear why she might be so thrilled.

"I would never call you mentally unstable," Addison is saying from the garden just outside the kitchen door. "I said you were a psycho!"

Holy hell, what am I walking into?

I step out into a fairy land of twinkling string lights and sculptured hedges and a bubbling fountain lit in gold.

As I expected, Addison's shrieking at Madison, who is red-faced and returning a very un-pageantlike scowl.

"Don't you wave your finger in my face," Madison growls at her, even though Addison is several feet away. Madison shimmies forward—the only way she can walk in that skin-tight silver mermaid dress—until she's practically putting her face on Addison's finger, daring her.

To Addison's credit, she doesn't step back. "I will always have my finger in your face!" she says, waving away and nearly poking Madison's eye out with a newly manicured French tip.

The other girls on our group date—minus Yasmine, who is probably off getting one-on-one time with the also-absent Preston—are hanging out at the fringes. Cameras are, of course, focused on the fight, but there are plenty pointed at each of us, getting our reactions.

I'm not sure I'm even capable of a normal reaction to a bitch fight, given that my whole body is still reeling from its earlier reactions to Nate. Who, I notice, is not here.

Is he interviewing someone? Working in one of the production rooms?

Londyn's next to me, wringing her hands. "I hope they stop this."

Jo's on the other side of her, sipping at her wine. "I hope they don't."

"But Preston's going to be so upset!" Londyn looks over at me, and the horror at the thought of Preston's distress vanishes almost instantly. "Oh, Becca, I love your dress," she says.

"Thanks," I say automatically. "Your dress is gorgeous, too." But I'm barely looking at it, barely hearing her, because my mind is still back in that room, remembering Nate kneeling behind me. Picturing him pressing his lips to the skin of my back, running his fingers up my legs under my dress, hiking up my skirt—

"Thank you!" she says back, doing a little twirl, and I see her skirt is covered in peacock feathers. "It's synthetic peacock, of course, but I think it looks real. I just love peacocks."

"Yeah," I say absently, and I'm still back there in that room, Nate up against my ass, bending me over that princess bed— "Cocks are great."

Jo chokes on her wine, and my face burns. Oh my god, did I just say that? *While I am miked?*

I want to die right here on this lovely garden path, but instead I scramble to play it off, giving a sly look to Jo like I meant to say that.

Londyn gapes at me, like she's not sure whether to take offense, but Addison and Madison, who had stepped apart like boxers going to their corners, are now heading back into the ring.

"You were obviously the one who did it," Addison says archly, folding her arms above her exposed midriff. How many of those two-piece dresses does she have? "I heard you were lurking in my room. And I heard you've done this kind of thing before."

"Were you *gossiping* about me?" Madison asks in a tone that indicates she believes this is the most evil thing that one can do outside of not being here "for the right reasons."

"I wasn't *gossiping*. I was literally saying what someone said to me!"

Oh god, Nate's going to hear that audio about cocks—this is going to be my tagline until the end of time, isn't it?—and he's going to know I said that right after he helped with my little wardrobe malfunction.

I'm sure I've made my interest obvious to *him*, but I don't want him thinking I'm trying to be obvious to the whole show. Could this cost him his job? I mean, we didn't actually do anything, but if they suspected—

No, I'm just being paranoid. What's more likely is that he'll hear it and think it's hilarious. He'll get that big grin on his face, which lights me up all over. And maybe knowing how crazy turned on I was—still am—will excite him even more.

"What's that?" Londyn asks, and this time I really try to focus on what's happening around me, lest I blurt out something even worse than my love for cocks. She's looking at my hand, her nose wrinkled. "Is it a bug?"

I look down and see the little piece of green fabric pinched between my fingers. "No, it was stuck in my zipper. That's why I was late, the zipper was caught." I wonder if I'm talking too fast.

"Huh," Jo says, her brow furrowing as she looks at it.

Does she suspect something? Like I planted this myself to get Nate to—

"Why would I do something like that?" Madison says, getting up in Addison's face again. "I'm not threatened by you. Preston is a man of discerning taste."

"He is," Addison says primly, though she looks about one second from going into full fighting stance. "Which is why you tried to ruin my dress. But joke's on you, because cutting the strap only made it sexier." She wiggles her shoulders, and yeah, she does only have one strap holding up that skimpy top. Fortunately it's tight enough around her chest, I don't think she needs even that.

Damn, her boobs are fabulous. Clearly she hasn't breastfed two kids.

Also, did Madison really sabotage her dress? Is that what this is about?

I make the connection just before Londyn blurts out, "Someone broke Becca's zipper, too!"

All eyes turn to me, along with several of the cameras, and my palms start to sweat. "I don't—I mean, it wasn't broken, it was just—"

"This was caught in it!" Londyn says, grabbing my wrist and holding up my hand.

Addison squints and then stomps over to us, snatching the wisp of fabric from me. Then her jaw drops. "It's green organza."

Several girls gasp, and all heads turn to the right side of the garden where Daisy stands, now surreptitiously trying to scoot behind a large, phallic-shaped hedge. I didn't really register her presence before, but she's wearing a slim green dress, with a puff of this very fabric circling the bottom.

Daisy looks flustered. "Why would I do that to Becca's dress? That would be disrespectful, especially because she's so much *older*—"

"Oh my god, Daisy," I can't help but say, putting myself right where I didn't want to be, in the fray. "I'm not eighty, I'm *thirty-one*."

"I know," she says very seriously, and I groan.

"Preston needs to know you did this," Madison says, turning her arch look toward Daisy, who shrinks under it. "Because I have been accused of something I would never do by a girl who called me a skank—"

"I didn't call you a skank," Addison says. "I called you a *snake*."

"Well that's not—" Madison starts, then cuts off as Preston walks into the garden with Yasmine at his side.

"What's going on here?" he asks cautiously. "I've been hearing some . . . tension."

"There's something you need to know, Preston." Madison steps forward with an expression of perfect sorrow for his plight. "Someone isn't here for the right reasons and has been sabotaging other girls' formal wear. If we could chat privately, I'll be happy to—"

"It wasn't me, Preston," Daisy squeals. "Even if my dress was involved."

"I think Daisy might have been framed," Addison says, squinting like she's Sherlock Holmes piecing it all together. "She's my roommate, and if Madison really was lurking around my room—"

"Ladies," Preston says, holding up his hands and looking like he wants to just vanish into the hedge rather than deal with any of this, which I can respect. "Obviously, I need to sort this out. If someone is really sabotaging dresses . . ." He shakes his head. "Honesty is everything to me and is something I need in my future wife."

There's a murmur of agreement from all the women, even as they glare at each other.

I, on the other hand, do and say nothing. Guilt trickles its way down my spine.

I am clearly not the pinnacle of honesty, supposedly dating Prince Charming when I have feelings for another guy.

Telling everyone in my life a big ball of lies about my marriage, never letting anyone know the truth.

Preston sighs. "I need some clarity on this. I'll want to get every side of the story. Madison, would you like to join me first?"

She nods, trying to hide her glee. "Of course." They head down the garden path.

Jo rolls her eyes. "Great party," she says, and chugs the rest of her wine, grabbing another glass at the same time. She's got the right idea there. It's going to be a long night.

can't believe those bitches," Jo says for the third time in twenty minutes. She's sprawled out on her bed, the wispy curtain hanging down around her.

"I know, right?" I murmur. I'm in my own bed, my journal open and my pen poised to write, as it has been since we got back to our room, changed into pajamas, and climbed into bed. Normally Jo falls asleep instantly after these long days, and I'm not far behind—especially if I've had a few drinks.

But tonight we're both having trouble settling in, though for very different reasons.

"I got no time with him," Jo says. "*None*. And it's not like we got a chance to talk on the date today. I was on a horse, for shit's sake. It's those bitches' fault, making all that stupid drama."

"It sucks," I agree, not bothering to point out how much she seemed to enjoy watching the drama. I didn't get any more time with Preston than Jo did, despite my having been slightly more involved in the whole wardrobe sabotage disaster. But Londyn somehow co-opted my side of the story as her own, and I didn't mind at all. It would have been nice, I suppose, to get to know Preston a bit more, but conspiracy theories about my stuck zipper aren't exactly the topic I would choose.

Mainly because there's no way I wouldn't be thinking about Nate the whole damn time.

"We're both going home, you know," Jo says, as if she's hoping to rile me up to match her anger.

I chew on my lip. "Maybe Preston would rather send the drama girls home." It occurs to me that I don't know Preston well enough to know whether he would be inclined to do that or not. Even if he would be, the producers will want to keep the drama rolling as long as possible. Probably the girl with the dead husband isn't quite as compelling to them anymore—especially because I've avoided their increasingly frequent questions on the subject.

Especially with Nate. Because I hate having to lie to him most of all.

But if I get sent home now, will I ever see Nate again? Yeah, he may have wanted to jump me, though I was pretty much putting my ass directly in his face, which probably isn't a great way to see if a guy wants *more* than sex. But if that's all it is for him, then he might not bother contacting me afterward. After all, I'm sure he's not hurting for women wanting to get with him—not even on this show, judging by how many of the girls (cough, *Londyn*) I catch checking him out.

But maybe he does feel that same connection with me that I do with him. Can I really leave before I know for sure?

"Maybe," Jo says. "Preston does seem like he'd prefer a classier woman than all those drama queens."

It's interesting listening to Jo now. She's starting to sound more and more like them—still in her own Jo way, of course—but talking unironically about "the journey" and the kind of woman Preston clearly prefers and how it all feels like a fairy tale. Like the show itself is seeping in through her skin, the constant barrage of leading questions and the sheer boredom of hours pent up in a mansion with nothing to talk about but our shared prince.

Am I doing this, too? Are we all slowly but surely becoming

Stepford Princesses?

I toy with the pen in my hand. I'm writing a journal entry that is really a letter to Thea and Rosie. I'll read it to them when I get home, talking about all the dresses and the fancy dates. I miss them so badly my heart hurts, and I can't wait to curl up with them on the couch and spin this fairytale world for them—all the PG parts of it, at least.

But I stare at the next page and I want to spin a fairytale world for myself. Something I couldn't really bring myself to believe in before and am still not sure I can.

I'm wanting it more and more.

"Do you really think you can see yourself with Preston?" I ask.

"Yeah." There's a note of wistfulness in her voice. "I have to admit, nice guys aren't usually my thing. But Preston . . ." She trails off. "I can really see a future with him."

There it is. *I can see a future with him.* Tick a box off the *Chasing Prince Charming* Bingo card.

But the thought doesn't amuse me as much as it otherwise might. Because I'm picturing myself saying that about Nate.

Can I see a future with him?

"How about you?" Jo peels back the lacy curtain and peeks her head out. "Have they gotten you to admit that you're falling for him yet?"

My heart skips a beat until I realize she's talking about Preston. "Ha. No. I'm, um . . . I'm not sure I'm there yet." I regret the words the minute I say them. We're not miked when we're in our bedrooms at night, and I don't think Jo's the type to go running off to tell Preston (or any of the other girls) that I'm not as into him as I should be.

But I don't know; if she's really falling for him and wants less competition . . .

Ugh. I hate thinking that way. She's my friend. This freaking show is making me paranoid about everything.

"Huh," she says. "Well, probably you just need to spend more time with him. Those stupid bitches cost us *both* our time.

It would really suck if Preston ends up with one of them and not someone he could really spend his life with, you know? He seems so sincere about all this."

Guilt creeps in again. He does seem sincere. Probably I should be feeling worse about still being here when I know full well my attentions are elsewhere. But despite the conceit of the show, it's hard to feel terrible about exploring my own options. After all, Preston's currently dating *nineteen* other girls, and he's gone a hell of a lot further with some of them than I have with Nate.

"Does your producer tell you that you and Preston seem made for each other?" I ask as casually as possible.

"Darlene?"

"Yeah." It's not like the producers don't switch off interviews and handling of contestants (*oh my god, don't think of Nate handling the contestants*), but Darlene is generally assigned to Jo like Nate is to me. "Nate's said stuff like that, but probably they all do, right?"

"I mean, they want to give us hope," Jo says. "Darlene's said similar stuff. They're all full of shit. Though obviously Preston and I *are* made for each other." She gives a little laugh that has more than a trace of the old Jo irony, and that makes me laugh too.

"Obviously." I pause. "I just wonder if Nate really thinks that. Like, if he actually thinks Preston and I would be a good match."

"Why do you care what your producer thinks?"

I try not to cringe. "I don't know. I just feel like he's gotten to know me pretty well, and he probably knows Preston pretty well, too. I think his opinion has some weight to it."

Jo eyes me for a moment, like maybe she suspects something, and I fight to keep from squirming. What if she doesn't buy it? Nate wouldn't really lose his job just because word got around that one of the contestants had a big, fat crush on him, would he?

"That makes sense," she says with a shrug, and I think maybe she doesn't suspect anything, after all.

A few minutes later, I hear her snoring away, and I stare at the journal in front of me. I think of how it feels to talk to Nate, to laugh with him. How much I wish I could tell him everything about me, and how I'm afraid to. How I wish I could feel his lips against mine, his hands in my hair, his sweaty body pressed against me. How it would feel to lie in his arms afterward. Maybe even wake up like that.

I start writing. I'm not a total idiot, despite what Rob always said—I don't use Nate's name or any specifics. The producer who gave us these journals assured us they were for our private thoughts and wouldn't be used by the show, but I'm not about to bet Nate's job on that. I call him "P" and just talk feelings. Fantasies. Hopes I'm afraid to have. Fears I'm not sure I can ever overcome, but want to.

It may all be a fairy tale, but if I'm going to let myself indulge those, this seems like the time to do it.

# ELEVEN

## NATE

The next week, Preston is down to twelve girls, and Becca is still among them. I'm at once glad that I can see her and crushed that the producers are keeping her around. I understand why—they haven't gotten her to open up about her husband yet, and Levi is starting to pressure me to deliver "the goods." I have no intention of abusing my friendship with Becca to get her to say things on the air that she doesn't want to say, but even if I did, I don't think it would do any good. Since the moment I met her, every time I ask about her husband, Becca puts on a fake smile and talks about what a wonderful father he was to the girls.

I don't know what she's covering—a broken heart? Complicated grief that she doesn't want on TV? But whatever it is, Becca's not giving it up, and I'm sure as hell not going to try to trick her into it. If I disappoint my boss, so be it.

With only twelve women left, though, we're headed out of the castle and on the road. After the tiara ceremony, Preston tells the women that we're headed to Bern, Switzerland, and the girls all cheer.

I think he could have announced they were going to Cleveland and they would have been excited, cooped up as they've been without phones or internet or any kind of entertainment besides complaining about each other. That's been great for the show—Addison and Madison especially have been providing some great drama, sure as they both are that the other isn't here for the right reasons. Londyn had a spectacular meltdown on her one-on-one date with Preston, wherein she hinted at some daddy issues that Levi is bent on getting her to expound upon.

Thankfully, Becca isn't avoiding me after my own meltdown in her bedroom, and the girls get packed and board the plane for Switzerland without coming to blows, so all seems to be going well.

Until we arrive in Switzerland, and Levi pulls me aside. "Hey, they lost some of our team's luggage. Can you head over to baggage claim and find out where it is and how long the wait will be?"

"Sure thing." I take our very long printout of baggage claim tickets and head over.

Preston is already there when I arrive, leaning against a support column next to the customer service window. For all that we're in a foreign country, there are a lot of signs in English.

"Hey," Preston says to me. "Do you know what happened to my luggage?"

I wave the papers at him. "Going to find out right now. I'll let you know."

I haven't spent a lot of time with Preston—he has his own producers who have developed relationships with him, and I'm not on that team. He seems like a decent enough guy, if a little bland, and he definitely plays the prince the way he's supposed to. Still, I don't like being around the guy, and I think no small part of that is because he's dating the woman I wish was interested in me.

Preston scrutinizes me, like he's not sure that I'm qualified to handle a customer service counter. "This is ridiculous," he mutters. I'm not sure what he means by that. I just told him I was going to find out what happened to his luggage. Literally anyone could ask this question—including him.

But I'm also not going to pick a fight with Prince Charming just because I'm jealous, so I try to smile reassuringly. "Let me talk to these people and get back to you."

Preston doesn't respond, but he leans back against the post, pulls a magazine out of his pocket, and starts reading it.

I'm not sure where he got that—the entertainment rules are a lot more lax for him than they are for the girls, but they do try to keep him away from any gossip about the show that might be circulating, for the "purity of the experience."

Still, I've been given a job, and it wasn't to take away Preston's copy of *People*.

I go up to the counter, where I am greeted by a woman in German who immediately switches to English when I ask about our luggage. I give her the list of baggage claim numbers, and she sets about plugging the numbers into the computer.

"I'm sorry, sir," she says when she finishes. "It looks like one of the baggage carts containing your group's luggage was loaded onto the wrong plane and the bags are now in New York. They'll come in on the next flight. We'll bring the luggage to your hotel when it arrives, but it may not be until morning."

"Thanks," I say. I don't know yet if my own bags are among those that were lost, but I can survive until morning without the contents of them. The show has travel insurance to cover us if there are any delays, and Levi hadn't seemed panicked about essential equipment being lost. A lot of the cameras and such are rented on location, anyway.

When I turn around, though, I find Preston standing directly behind me. "That's unacceptable," he says to the baggage clerk. "Whose mistake was this? We don't have to put up with this kind of service."

The woman was perfectly friendly with me, but she gives him an icy stare. "I'm sorry, sir," she says in a clipped tone. "We will have your luggage to you as soon as—"

"That's not good enough," Preston says, and then he gives

me a look, like he expects me to back him up.

I'm not going to chew this woman out. She was on a different continent when the mistake was made. "It'll be fine," I tell Preston. "Anything you need before your bags arrive, we'll make sure you get." Some of the women might be told to make do—though I imagine we'll at least be supplying them with toothbrushes. We aren't filming until tomorrow afternoon, and that's just a one-on-one. So, even if there are further delays, only one girl will have to replace her date wear before filming, and she can probably borrow from the other girls. Assuming it's not Daisy, who seems to have alienated most of the girls in the house.

If the team can manage it, they are going to manipulate it so that it's Daisy.

Preston, on the other hand, is the star. If he needs something, we'll find it for him.

"That's it?" Preston leans over the counter, getting in this woman's space. "Do you know who we are?"

Shit. Right now, what he needs is to chill out. "Hey, Preston," I say. "Let's go find your team, okay? I'm sure they'll help us figure out what to do."

Preston gives me a look like I'm stupid, which gets my hackles up. I know Preston is stressed—it's not like I think dating a dozen girls at once is an easy thing. And traveling doesn't bring out the best in anyone—god knows I'm ready to close myself in my hotel room with the TV on and be done.

But seriously, the guy is supposed to be Prince Charming and he can't even be polite to the service people at the airport.

Preston gives one more glare to the baggage clerk, then turns to me in a huff. "Fine. I bet Levi will figure out who's responsible and tear them a new one." He storms off toward the rental car area, where the production team is ushering the girls into vans to be taken to the airport. Preston isn't supposed to be over there right now—we were all on the same plane, but he flew first class with Levi while the girls and the rest of the production team were back in coach. Since we don't have cameras rolling, he's supposed to stay away from the girls, so we don't have to reconstruct any important misunderstandings later for the camera.

But Preston clearly doesn't care about anyone but himself and his precious missing luggage. I sigh and follow after him. I'll find Levi and explain the situation. If Levi decides to call up the airline and "tear them a new one" because of a common travel mistake, that's his right. Levi isn't the one being presented to twelve unsuspecting women as the catch of the century, so I'm a lot less concerned with his juvenile behavior.

One of the reasons I was excited about this job was the travel. I've done plenty of that with Jason and our crew, and it's always a highlight. The night we arrive in Bern, I head out in the old town with some of the other producers, and over the next few days, I get to sightsee a bit more while following Addison and later Yasmine—the lone remaining Black contestant—to interview them about how their dates are going.

Addison's goes well enough that it's clear he's going to keep her this week, but Yasmine drones on about how exactly she would use each and every sight they see as a background to show off her cleavage on Instagram if only she had her phone, and Preston decides that he "isn't feeling it," and sends her home that very night.

I guess I can't blame him for that one.

We arrive at the tiara ceremony with several of the girls distraught about not having gotten "enough time with Preston," despite their group date at a music festival.

I get it. I would be stressed if I was expected to get engaged in a couple of weeks to someone I've barely talked to. About half of the remaining girls haven't had one-on-one dates, and I'm guessing several of them will go home without them.

Not Becca, though. Levi wants to keep her on until she talks about her husband, and he's added a list of prepared questions to my interviews designed to prime her to talk to Preston about Rob on her one-on-one, which we're planning for next week. Levi gave me creative control of the date so long as I could get most of it for free in exchange for exposure on the show, and I've been making phone calls like mad to get everything lined up.

I think Becca is going to love it. If she goes home after the date, at least she'll have some great memories to look back on. She's always talked about the show more as a vehicle to get out of her own head than as a life plan, so I think she'll be okay regardless of what happens, but I still want to give her the best experience I can before she goes.

The tiara ceremony is set up in the gardens of the hotel, with a "ball" taking place around the pool. The women are all in gowns tonight instead of swimsuits, but tensions are running high enough that I think someone might end up in the pool before the night is over. Daisy, in particular, is very concerned about her lack of quality time with Preston and begged the producers to get her some hand-crafted Swiss chocolates to share with him tonight as a bonding exercise. "I swear," she says to her handler of the evening, "you can tell a lot about a man by the chocolates he chooses."

I miss the full explanation about what chocolate preferences say about a man's sexual proclivities because Becca arrives, and I head over to see how she's doing.

"Hey," I say, resisting the urge to give her a hug or wrap an arm around her waist. I have to resist this urge a lot.

She gives me a nervous smile—she's worried about going home tonight, I'm sure. It won't happen, but I can't tell her that.

Damn, it'll be nice to be done with filming. I'm not much for secrets, but as a producer, I have to keep a lot of them. "You look beautiful," I tell her, which is a compliment I'm allowed to give her and also completely true. She's wearing a sea-foam green gown tonight that's sleeveless but not quite as backless as the one with the stuck zipper.

Thank god for that. There's only so much temptation I can handle.

"Thank you," she says.

"Nervous?"

She nods. "Is it obvious?"

It's always obvious to me what Becca is feeling, but I don't think it's going to be as obvious to everyone else. She's cautious and guarded. Levi considers those traits to be liabilities, but I think they're strengths, especially in this situation. "Probably only to me," I tell her, then wince. That was overly familiar. I need to watch it.

"Oh my god," Daisy says loudly from over by the pool where she's talking to her handler. "Is Preston on his way? I don't have enough time to set up my chocolates!" She grabs a bottle of wine that apparently pairs well with chocolate and heads over to the little gas fire pit in the corner of the pool area. "I'm the only one who hasn't kissed him!" she says. "He has to kiss me if I have chocolate in my mouth. He just has to."

My hands go cold, even though the night isn't particularly chilly. I wasn't aware that *all* of the remaining eleven girls had kissed him. It's not like I spy the entire time Becca is talking to Preston—I try to avoid it, actually—but if she'd kissed him, I'd have thought—

"She's not the only one who hasn't kissed him," Becca says beside me. "I haven't."

I hate myself for the wave of relief that crashes over me. I have no right to be relieved, but I am all the same.

She will, though. Next week, Becca has a one-on-one that I'm carefully crafting to be as perfect as possible. Levi will make sure she gets sucked in before Preston breaks her heart, and I'm helping him do it.

"Maybe you'll get your chance tonight," I say. I'm supposed to be pushing her in that direction, and much as I don't want to, I also don't want to seem jealous.

Becca looks dubious about that, and I selfishly hope it's

because she's not ready.

"Preston is here!" Madison shrieks from over by the hotel doors, and all the girls turn, including Becca. Daisy comes flying over from the fire pit, fluffing her hair as she goes. The girls all move in Preston's direction, but Levi waves me over to where he's reviewing some footage with Dustin.

"Hey," he whispers to me when I get over there. "While the girls are all distracted with Preston, you go over and push those chocolates closer to the fire. I want them all melted when he opens the box, understand? Try not to catch the box on fire, but I want those chocolates ruined."

"Seriously?" I say.

Levi gives me a look that says I better not mess this up, and moves over to direct the camera guys who are going to capture Preston's toast to kick off the poolside ball.

I survey the fire pit. Daisy's chocolates are set a safe distance away on the marble bench, but it wouldn't take much to move them close enough to melt them quickly without risking the box going up in flames.

*Am I actually doing this?* I ask myself as I cross the courtyard. Am I really employed to destroy artisan foods and drive already frantic women into full psychotic breakdowns?

I look back toward the group and see Levi's eyes on me, though all the women—including Becca, damn it—are fully engaged listening to Preston's toast.

Shit. Yes, that is exactly my job description. Here I go.

I slide the chocolates along the bench, moving the wine as well so that they will all be in the same configuration. I position the box close enough that it's uncomfortable for me to put my fingers on it—that ought to be enough heat to melt the chocolates quickly, as I'm not sure how long it will be before Daisy gets Preston over here for their romantic moment.

I get back to the group just as Preston is finishing his toast, and all the women giggle and drink. Becca looks over at me and raises her eyebrows, and I give her a sign that, according to

YouTube, roughly translates to "You got this."

She grins. She seems to like it when I sign to her, so if nothing else, I hope I'm bringing her a little bit of comfort.

Most of the women still have their glasses to their lips when Madison announces that she wants to steal Preston away, and Daisy looks like she's going to shit a brick as Madison leads him off. I think Daisy is going to discover what happened to her chocolates and rescue them before they melt, but one of the producers—probably tipped off by Levi—pulls her into an interview before she can check on them.

Sheree interrupts Madison, and she and Madison get into a snit, and half an hour has passed before Daisy escapes from her interview. She interrupts Sheree and manages to bring Preston over to her carefully prepared area.

By now, I'm sure those chocolates are toast. Becca waves to me, and I'm about to make my way over there, mostly to hide from the damage I've wrought, but Levi catches my eye and indicates for me to keep an eye on Daisy and Preston.

So it is that I'm standing not fifteen feet away when Daisy lets out a banshee yell they probably hear all over Europe. "My chocolates!" she screams. "Who moved them? Oh my god, they're chocolate soup!"

Preston looks startled by the screaming, but tries to save the situation by asking if anyone has graham crackers for s'mores. Daisy bursts into tears and storms off to cry in the hallway that leads to the sauna.

Londyn goes to comfort Daisy and is met with immediate shrieks that Daisy *knows* Londyn is the one who did this to her. Preston meanders away from the chocolate looking like he wants to disappear, while Londyn shouts that it was *not* her, and she's sure it was Addison because she saw Addison poking around the chocolates while Daisy was in an interview. Madison charges over and says that she, too, is sure that it was Addison, because Addison is generally lacking in moral character in just about every way.

Levi nods to me approvingly.

This is my life. Getting credit for being a complete douche and ruining a woman's evening while she tries to date a guy who is at least a partial douche.

I feel like I've made some very bad life choices.

# TWELVE

## Becca

As soon as Daisy starts shrieking about her melted chocolates, I slip around the pool to a quieter area and sit down on a marble bench beside a statue of a woman with a high-ruffed collar and her hair braided in a circle around her head like a wreath. She appears to be looking at me judgmentally, like she thinks I'm showing too much neck. Or perhaps like she thinks I have abandoned my children to travel across the world on a dating show where most of my time is spent listening to grown women bitch at each other.

I'm starting to think I deserve judgment for the latter.

I've leaned over to check out the plaque and see who this austere woman is—the author of *Heidi*, apparently—when I hear footsteps coming up behind me. I turn to see Preston approaching, followed by two cameramen and a producer.

"Hey, Becca," Preston says. "Sorry about all that craziness. I think you made a good call, slipping away for a bit. Mind if I join you?"

I smile at him. "Go right ahead. I don't think Johanna Spyri here will mind." I glance back at the statue. "Or at least be any more unhappy than she already is."

Preston laughs, but he sounds tired. Possibly from the

non-stop drain of the show, though I don't think tonight's chocolate escapade is helping. I do like that he doesn't seem to particularly enjoy the drama. Maybe Jo's right, maybe he does want a classier woman. And since I've been fantasizing about all sorts of very non-classy things I'd like to do to a certain producer and I also essentially tried to take advantage of a stuck zipper to seduce said producer, I doubt I fit that description.

But I'm still here, despite Jo's premonition (she, however, is not, which I felt terrible about and not just because now I've got to room with Londyn.) Maybe Preston is more interested in me than I thought. I haven't had a one-on-one date with him, but after the music festival group date, I did get to talk to him some more. We talked about my kids and my dreams of opening a restaurant, though it all felt more surface than it did when talking about those same things with Nate. From the very beginning, I wanted Nate to know more than the surface Becca. I think he does, more than most people do.

What would he think of me if he knew all the things I've been keeping from him, all the things I keep from everyone?

Then again, I've gotten the feeling the last several days that Nate doesn't think of me much beyond what's necessary for the job. He's been friendly and warm during interviews, but I don't get the sense that he's seeking me out, looking for extra time with me, and every day my heart aches more from it.

I didn't imagine that look of hunger in his eyes; I know I didn't. I've played it over in my head a thousand times.

But intense sexual attraction doesn't necessarily mean he wants anything more. It's possible—likely, even, given how insanely gorgeous these other women are—that he feels the same level of attraction for some of them, which makes my chest feel like it's caving in. Besides, he's doing his job here, and I'm sure he doesn't want to risk that for anything, let alone a one-time romp with a contestant.

Or maybe he *does* want more and that's why he's avoiding me?

I'm so confused, and no amount of journal fantasizing about

"P" is helping me know what to do. If I only had the courage to *ask* him—

"You seem quieter than usual tonight," Preston says.

Shit. Right. I'm supposed to be talking with the prince.

"Am I?" I ask.

"It's not a bad thing," he says quickly. "I actually like that you seem to take things in, to think them through. You're not inclined to wade into the conflict."

"Well, if you listen to Daisy, it's due to the wisdom of my advanced age." I wince. Probably I shouldn't be saying bad things about other girls right on the heels of him complimenting me on being above all that.

But he chuckles. "Yeah, well, if thirty's an advanced age, I'm not far from achieving the wisdom of the elders myself."

I smile. He really does seem like a nice guy, and—harem of women he's dating aside—I'm starting to feel guilty about leading him on. Especially if he is interested in something more with me.

I should try to make myself more open to this. I can't put all my hopes and feelings into a guy who is unavailable.

"I do get the sense, though," Preston says slowly, "that you're holding back. And I'm pretty sure I know why."

My stomach drops. "I, uh. I don't—"

"It's hard for you to talk about your late husband, isn't it?"

Oh god. My husband.

"Yeah, it is." This is potentially the most honest statement I can make on the matter.

Preston's lips turn down. "That makes sense. Losing him must have been traumatic, both for you and your daughters."

I swallow. "It was a—a very difficult time for us." I fidget with the fabric of my skirt, and Preston notices. He reaches over and folds my hand into his.

His hand is warm and there's a comfort to the touch, but it's not Nate's. I don't have the longing to entwine my fingers with his; I don't feel that comfort traveling through my whole body. I don't feel the *heat* of it.

"I can imagine," he says. "And I don't want to press, but—"

"It's okay." I knew I'd have to talk about it with him at some point. Half the producers have been intimating that "sharing my pain" with Preston would go a long way to bringing us closer.

Except it won't, because I can't share that. Not all of it, anyway.

"You can ask me anything you want," I say.

He smiles gently, then pauses, like he's gathering his thoughts. Meanwhile, I see the producer motioning, and another producer hurries over. I see him say something into his headset mic, though he covers it with his hand.

I can guess, though. *She's talking now. All hands on deck.*

Well, all hands that aren't dealing with the shit-show by the fire pit, though that does seem to have quieted down.

*Game face, Becca,* I tell myself. *Another round of the story you'll tell again and again for the rest of your life.*

"He died serving overseas, right?" Preston asks. "Three years ago."

"Right. The military was a huge part of his life. He loved being in the army, serving his country. It was really important to him."

Preston nods. "I imagine you and the girls were really important to him, as well."

"Absolutely." Partially true. "He was a wonderful father. They adored him." My voice breaks on the last part. No matter how many times I've told this story, it's still hard to remember the day I had to tell the girls. The wails Thea made, like a wounded animal. The way Rosie, only two, didn't really understand and was terrified by the grief and hid under her bed.

Tears burn at the corners of my eyes.

Preston squeezes my hand. "God, that must have been horrible for them. And for you as well. It sounds like he was an incredible man."

My gut is folding in on itself, more so than it usually does when talking about this. There are so many cameras, and Preston is so earnestly wanting to learn more about me because

123

he's looking to find a wife, for god's sake, and now I'm lying to the whole world—

But I don't have a choice, do I?

"He was," I say. "An incredible guy. Everyone just loved him." Almost everyone. "He was one of those people who made everyone feel at ease and special. He could hold the attention of a whole room, and each person felt like he was paying attention to them."

Preston lets out a breath, and I wonder if I pushed it too far. That's probably not what someone interested in dating me would want to hear.

I want to look for Nate, to find out if he's watching this, but I won't let myself.

"How long were you with him?" Preston asks.

"We met in high school," I say. "Our junior year. He was my first real boyfriend. He proposed on our graduation day, and we got married a year and half later."

Preston's eyebrows raise. He might have done the math on Thea's age, but hearing the age we got married always manages to take people by surprise. "Wow. It sounds like you two had a really special, deep love."

For some reason, my mind goes back to the carriage ride with Nate. To talking about whether we believed in soul mates.

*Do you think your husband was your best match?*

*No*, I suddenly want to scream. *No. We didn't, he's not, please would someone listen to everything I'm not saying?*

My heart is pounding, and sweat beads on my brow. I wish I could take my hand from Preston's, but that seems like it would cause more things to have to explain, and I just want this conversation over with as soon as possible. I need to hold it together.

I didn't respond to Preston's comment about our "special, deep love," but I think he—and the viewing audience—will read my silence as grief.

He wets his lips. "Do you think you're open to falling in love again?"

My throat closes up. Am I? Will I ever be? "It's always scary, wondering if something like that is possible. Again." I wonder if anyone will notice the tiny, accidental hitch between those two words.

Will Nate notice?

Preston considers this. "I would think it might be less scary. If it can happen once, it can happen again."

"Right," I say with what I hope does not look like the world's most forced smile. There's a panic blossoming in my chest, that if I don't say what they want—what he wants, what the producers want, what America wants, what my family wants—then I'll never be free. I straighten. "The reason I'm here, though, is that scary as it is, I believe I can find love. I believe there's someone out there for me, someone I can share the rest of my life with."

Preston leans closer, and I have another panicked second where I think he might kiss me, but instead he smiles. "I'm really glad to hear that, Becca," he says. "I hope that—"

"Oh my god, who put the melted chocolate there?" a girl shrieks from back by the pool. "You! You wanted me to sit in it!"

"Don't blame me. It's *your* ass that apparently can't get enough carbs," another one snipes back.

Preston closes his eyes, looking pained, then opens them again. "I, uh. I should probably go find out what . . ." He tilts his head back to where the commotion is starting all over again. "But thanks for being so open, Becca. I'm so glad to have the opportunity to get to know you."

"You, too," I say. Awkwardly, because he doesn't actually know me and I don't actually know him.

He takes his hand away from mine, and I don't feel the loss of it the way I did with Nate. The tears are burning behind my eyes, and I feel queasy. I look back at the statue, who's still silently judging me.

*I know,* I think to her. *I'm messed up. Go ahead, write a fucking book about it.*

My hands are trembling, but I try to hide that, smoothing out my skirt and standing up, heading slowly back to the pool area. My whole body feels like a rubber band pulled tighter and tighter, but I can't let it snap, not in front of the cameras, not in front of anyone. I hold it together. That's what I've always done.

The camera follows me around the bend, and yeah, the drama is definitely fired up again, accusations flying and Preston trying to rein it all in, and I'm just so, so tired and the weight of everything is a boulder, slowly crushing me.

I can't be here. I can't do this. But what am I going to—

I notice then that there are no cameras on me anymore. Not a single one. They've all focused on Chocolategate. I do see Nate, finally, and my stomach flips all over again, but he's watching the chaos with a grimace on his face I think he's trying his best to hide.

I want him to see me. I don't want him to see me.

I back up until I'm out of sight around the corner. Then I undo the side zipper of my dress and reach underneath to my mic pack and turn it off. I can't breathe. I hurry toward a side door of the hotel and step into the lobby. It's a fancy hotel, with a grand piano in the foyer and a professional pianist playing classical music. Everything shiny and gilded, with lots of mirrors in ornate frames—god, there are so many mirrors, I can see reflections of myself everywhere, like I'm in some horrible funhouse and I can't escape. The room is spinning.

One of the receptionists asks if I'm okay, and I manage to give her a wave, but I keep moving, though I don't know where I'm going. Just away. I head up the thickly carpeted staircase to the second floor, but there's nowhere to hide here and I don't think I can hold myself together long enough to make it back to my room.

I burst through a door to the outside, to the giant wraparound stone balcony that surveys the whole of the hotel property. I'm disoriented as to which side of the hotel I'm on, but the pool's not here. No one's here. I'm alone.

I let myself sink down to the decorative tile and sob.

I don't know what's different now, why I can't keep it together anymore. I just know I'm exhausted. Tired from the stress of the show, from the jet lag and the long days of boredom, from missing my daughters, from wondering if the man I have feelings for could truly want me back.

But it's more than that. I'm exhausted from carrying my past around with me like a locked briefcase chained to my wrist.

*I hate you, Rob,* I think, my knees pulled up to my chest, crying into chiffon. *I hate you for what you did to me. I hate you for what you took from me. I hate what you're still taking from—*

"Becca?"

I startle and look back. It's Nate, standing in the doorway between the balcony and the upper level of the lobby, his eyes wide. He closes the door behind him and crouches next to me. "Are you okay? What's wrong?"

The stark concern in his voice guts me, as does being so close to him. I want him to wrap his arms around me and hold me while I cry.

"I don't know if I can do this anymore," I manage, the words catching in my sobs. "I can't—I can't . . ."

He reaches toward me, and there's this breathless moment where I think he might brush back the hair that's fallen from my bun, that he might tuck it behind my ear, his fingers light on my skin. But then he drops his hand and uses it to brace himself on the tile while he sits, and maybe I imagined it, maybe I imagined everything, after all.

"Hey," he says quietly. "Do you want to talk about it?"

I do. I want him to know, even as I'm terrified of what he'll think of me after.

But. "I can't, Nate, I can't, if I talk about it, everyone will know and I—"

"There aren't any cameras here, and I'm not miked." He wets his lips, his eyes darting down to the mic pack at my back. "Is yours . . . ?"

"I turned it off," I say, sniffling. I must look like a disaster. Good thing we were all told to bring waterproof mascara. The show wants us all to cry, but they don't want us looking like raccoons when we do.

"Do you want me to make sure?" he asks. It's probably a good idea to have him check, though if I failed to turn the stupid thing off, they already have a lot of great audio of me being an emotional wreck. I reach behind me and undo the zipper enough to untape the thing and hand it to him. Then I zip myself back up, though I've clearly lost any trace of dignity long before now.

He eyes the pack. "Okay, yeah, it's off." He sets it down and sits back. "You don't have to talk about it. But if you want to, there's no one here but you and me. No one even knows you're here—I just noticed you weren't down with the others and came looking for you."

I wipe tears away from my cheeks, but more spill out. "You promise you won't tell anyone?"

"I promise, Becks." His eyes are locked on mine, and his voice is so sincere, so kind, that it breaks me apart.

"I lied to you," I say, the words choking me. "I lie to everyone, and I—" I shake my head. "My marriage was awful, Nate. I was miserable the whole time. He was terrible to me, he—" I cut off in a fresh burst of tears.

"He hurt you?" Nate asks, his tone almost too even, like he's trying not to react.

"Not physically," I say. "He never hit me."

"But he hurt you." Not a question this time.

I nod. "He wanted me to feel small and stupid and weak. He told me all the time how dumb I was, how I wouldn't survive ten minutes without him. How everything I had was because of him, and I'd never be anything without him. How I could never get through college. How I was a terrible mother and the girls deserved better."

"Are you serious?" he asks. But I can tell it's not that he's doubting the truth of what I'm saying.

"I wasn't lying about how much he loved them," I say. "They were his little princesses. He was never cruel to them, and the

128

things he would say to me he wouldn't ever say in front of Thea and definitely never sign in front of her. Which was good. I never wanted her to see that, you know?" I close my eyes, letting out a breath. "But he would criticize everything I did. Making me give him lists of everything I fed them, of how much screen time they had, who I let them interact with. I had to tell him everyone I saw, everywhere I went. I had to show him receipts, to account for every cent I spent, or he would accuse me of wasting our money. I didn't even have direct access to our accounts. I had to beg my husband for every fucking dollar, and even though I knew this wasn't the way a marriage was supposed to be, I believed everything he told me about myself. I believed that the girls deserved better and that I could never be good enough."

"Oh god, Becks," Nate says. "I can't even—" He looks up at the night sky and presses his lips together. Then he looks back at me. "I saw you with your kids. I saw how they are with you, how much they love you and you love them. You're an incredible mom. And I don't doubt for a second that you always were, no matter what that asshole said."

I let out a laugh that surprises even me. "No one ever called him an asshole. Not charming, lovable, military hero Rob." I close my eyes against another round of tears.

"I feel like calling him a lot worse," Nate says.

"You and me both."

I look into those dark eyes reflecting the moonlight, and I can feel the bare inches of space between his hand and mine as we sit there side by side. I wish I could cross that distance and know that he would want it the same way I do.

But despite that longing and despite knowing I have more I need to unpack from that briefcase, things I'm ashamed for him to know . . . it already feels a little lighter. *I* feel lighter.

Part of it is just the getting to be open about this, outside of a weekly therapy session.

But the bigger part, I think, is letting myself be truly open with *him*.

# THIRTEEN

## NATE

I sit beside Becca on the hotel balcony, glad there aren't any cameras here right now. I still don't dare hold her hand or put my arm around her—much as I want to—because I understand what a big deal it is that she's opening up to me. This is stuff she doesn't tell anyone, and I can't risk making her feel like she can't trust me, like I'd take advantage of her.

This is too important. *She's* too important.

I'm not sure what to say, though, because at this moment, all I can think is that I hate the asshole who treated her like that. It's probably a horrible thing to think about a dead man, but I'm glad he's gone. I'm glad he's not around to tell her she's unworthy anymore.

"Was it better when he was deployed?" I ask. I assume it would be harder for him to watch her every move when he was gone for months at a time.

"Yeah, it was a lot better," Becca says. "I was always so relieved when he left. I think I was a better mom when he was gone, because I didn't have him constantly telling me how awful I was. But then he would get back and it would all crash down on me again. He'd even accuse me of cheating on him when he was gone. I never did, but it didn't matter."

I can't imagine living under that kind of weight. She still does, like she has to protect him. "Why keep the secret? I mean, I guess because it's nobody's business?" I can see not wanting to deal with the public's opinion about something that obviously still hurts her.

I know it's not my place, but I wish I could take that pain away.

She sighs. "I don't want the girls to hear it. I want them to be able to keep their image of him intact. He's their hero. The father they love, who loved them."

"Makes sense when they're so young," I say carefully. "But I wonder if when they're older they should know the truth."

"I don't know what it would accomplish."

"It might help them to know their mother," I say.

"Maybe," Becca says, but I think she's just being polite. "There's more, though. I don't want my in-laws to know. They're my family now, but if they knew the truth—I don't know if they would believe me, much less support me. I can't lose them."

I close my eyes briefly. "That must be so lonely, feeling like you have to lie even to the people you love."

Becca nods and hunches over, like she's bowing under the weight of that burden. It pisses me off, because she didn't do anything wrong. She's not the one who should carry the shame.

But I know there's nothing I can say that will change it.

"No one else knows," I say. "Not anyone?"

"Just my therapist. I've been in therapy since right after Rob died. My in-laws think it's grief counseling, but it's not. I'm still working my way through everything that happened when we were married."

"You don't have to answer this." I've as much as asked it on camera, though, and I regret now putting her in that position. "But how did you feel when he died?"

Becca sniffles. She's not fully crying anymore, but the tear tracks still shine on her cheeks, and her eyes are rimmed red. "I am the worst person in the world."

"It seems like it would be natural to feel relieved."

"I would never have wanted this to happen to anyone," she says. "Not even him. I would never have wanted my girls to lose their father. I would never have chosen this."

That makes her a better person than I am.

"Ideally," she continues, "I would have left him, and my girls could have kept their father, and my in-laws could have kept their son. But I could never see how I would do it. I had no education, no real work history, and no control over our finances." She huddles in even further. "But yeah. When it happened, I felt relieved. I was just so glad not to be trapped with him anymore."

Her body trembles, and I have to wrap my arms around my knees to keep from putting one around her. I probably could—she'd see it as a friendly gesture. But I'm not going to take advantage of her in this situation. I can't.

"I know I seem stupid for going on TV when I have so many secrets," she says. "I always mock people who do that, you know? But I thought it would be easy to lie about, because I've been lying about it for so long."

I take a deep breath. "Yeah, but this process really gets inside your head." I know I'm a dick for blaming the process. It's my job to get inside her head. I've asked about Rob so many times, because it's my job to ask, and because I wanted to know. I did this to her, when I could have said no.

"I see why you signed up for the show, though," I say. "You've been limiting yourself to hookups because you're scared. After this, what's one date, even one you didn't find on Tinder?" Becca smiles, and even if it's a tremulous one, it's wonderful to see. "You needed to throw down this gauntlet for yourself, and you did it. When you get back, you'll be able to do anything."

"I might not even need Tinder."

"You might go out with somebody twice."

"Let's not get crazy, now," she says, but she's joking. I press my lips together, not allowing myself to tell her I'd like to take her out a lot more than twice.

She's thinking about her future, and it doesn't seem to have

Preston in it. That's enough to make my heart do an improbable dance in my chest.

Becca sighs. "I really had made progress in therapy. But now I'm getting insecure again. And I'm doing even more lying than I do at home."

"You don't really lie. You mostly leave gaps and let other people fill them in. And really, when I interview you, I don't expect you to be totally honest. You probably shouldn't be."

She doesn't look happy about that, and I get it. It's hard to keep up a charade day in and day out, sometimes intoxicated and on very little sleep.

I think back to what she said when I first found her here. "Are you thinking you want to leave the show?" I ask. I'm not going to push her into that, but god, do I want her to. I'd miss her every day, but at least I wouldn't have to watch her with Preston anymore. And maybe I wouldn't even wait for the show to be over. Maybe I'd get her number before she left, and she could call me as soon as she got her phone back. Maybe we'd talk every day until I got back, and then—

"I don't want to," Becca says, and I feel like I've been slapped. "I want to prove I can do this."

I nod. That's not a terrible reason, I suppose. "Yeah, you don't strike me as a quitter."

"What do you think?" she asks. "Do you think I should leave?"

I look up at the sky. Only a few stars are visible above the hotel lights.

*She should quit*, I think. She should quit and we'd talk every night, and then when the job is over I'd take her out, and I'd treat her like a princess, only without dating a dozen other girls at the same time. Maybe she'd fall in love with me and we'd live happily ever after.

It's a crazy fantasy. A long shot, to be sure. But I want it more than I've ever wanted anything, so much that I almost take the chance.

But I don't want to be the reason she quits and later regrets it.

And if she stays, I want her to feel like she can trust me. That's more important than my stupid fantasies.

"I think you're smart," I tell her. "And strong. You'll know if it's time for you to leave, because you're a total badass."

Becca stares at me like she can't believe I've said this, but it's true. "I don't feel like a badass," she says.

"Yeah, well. You definitely are."

She smiles to herself, and I feel like maybe I'm helping. Whatever happens, I'm glad for that.

Another question rises in my throat, and I hate myself for how much it's motivated by self-interest. I can't help it, though. I have to know. "Do you see a future with you and Preston?"

Becca doesn't answer immediately, which seems like a good thing. Any of the other girls would have told me immediately that they do. It's practically all they talk about.

"I don't know," Becca admits. "We talked before about how relationships take time, and I still think that's true. I feel like I need more time with him to know if I could have a future with him, and I'm not getting that."

I nod. It's a variant of the thing all the girls say—they need their time with Preston. But it's true. Becca and I have had more time than she's had with Preston a hundred times over.

Which might mean something, if she saw me as more than a friend.

"But you know him, and you know me," she says slowly. "Do you think we're a good fit?"

Oh, shit. I walked into that one. What the hell am I supposed to say? No, he's an idiot? Pick me instead?

"I'm considering," I say, mostly to stall for time. Honestly, from what I've seen of Preston, he's mostly shallow and a little bit of a prick. He's nice to the girls, and charming and affable enough while the camera is on. But I remember the way he was with the clerk at the airport. *Do you know who we are?* He's obviously got serious entitlement issues and a bit of a chip on his shoulder.

He's not good enough for her, I'm sure of that. Honestly, I'm not good enough either, but that doesn't mean I wouldn't try to be, every day, for as long as she'd let me.

I'm not sure when my fantasies stopped being about taking her out and seeing if there was something there. I'm not sure when I became certain that there would be—at least on my side.

But here we are.

"I think your instincts are good," I say finally. "I think you need more time with him before you'll know. But you're smart—you're going to be able to figure out if he's the one for you. Don't compromise, though. The show will try to make you get swept up in the thrill of it all, so you have to stick to what you know you need. Make sure you get that time, and don't jump into anything until you're certain."

Becca nods like that makes sense, but I get the feeling it isn't what she wanted to hear.

I don't just want her to leave for me. I want her to *want* to. Maybe that will never happen, but if it does, it isn't a decision she should rush. That isn't her style. She thinks so deeply, is so deliberate and considerate. I love that about her, and I wouldn't want to change it, even if it's inconvenient for me at the moment.

"You're not going to be more specific," she says.

I smile. "No. It's your decision. I know you'll make a good one."

She leans back against the balcony railing. "I don't have a great history of that. I think that's why I'm so afraid of relationships."

"You're scared you'll end up in another bad one?"

"I lost so much of myself," she says. "It's taken me years to find myself again. What if there are signs, and I don't see them in time? I've spent years trying to get to this place where I'm happy with who I am, and I don't want to lose that again."

"I have a hard time believing you would. You're so beautiful and amazing. You're too wonderful to get lost for long."

Becca lights up and I smile.

135

"You're pretty awesome yourself," she says.

"I spent my evening positioning a very expensive and delicious-looking box of chocolates close enough to a fire that it would melt and cause an innocent girl a catastrophic breakdown. I'm not feeling so great about myself tonight."

"That was *you*?"

"It wasn't my *idea*," I say. "But yeah. I had the misfortune of being the one who had to do it."

Becca shakes her head. "They really are messing with us."

"We are," I say, forcing myself to take some ownership for it. I didn't think of the chocolate thing, but I also didn't refuse. "Sometimes I wonder what I'm doing on this show."

"Is this not what you want to be doing?"

I take a deep breath. I shouldn't admit that, but the cameras still haven't found us. I'm guessing things at the pool are still pretty dramatic, or they would have noticed Becca was missing. "I want to produce," I say. "I've wanted to move beyond YouTube and do something bigger. I tried for years to convince Jason to try to make a move to TV, but he's comfortable where he is. It took me a long time to start thinking in terms of 'my career' instead of 'our career.' I started applying places, and I was surprised when I got offered this job. It's a big step up from YouTube. This show isn't what I want to do ultimately, but sticking it out for a couple of seasons could open a lot of doors."

"That makes sense. What kind of TV would you ultimately want to do?"

"Reality TV, for sure," I say. "But some shows are more affirming than others, I guess. I'd like to tell stories about triumph, rather than about people tearing each other down."

"I get that. I wanted an adventure. But I guess sometimes adventures suck in the middle."

I laugh. "Um, yes. Trust me, the middle of a big climb always sucks. We get out there, and at first we're all pumped, but then things get difficult and we're all miserable. It's worth it for the triumph at the end, but the middle is awful."

"I guess that's where I'm at right now." She elbows me. "And since you're assigned to me, you get to deal with it."

"Eh," I say. "Talking to you never feels like work. Not like the three hours I had to interview Londyn about her daddy issues." She laughs, so I keep going. "And I'm going to have to get out of interviewing Daisy. I have too much guilt over melting her chocolate. I don't think I could handle that."

"I wonder what happened to the chocolate," Becca says. "If it was really good, we could make it into fondue."

"That's what you would do, isn't it? 'Oops, the chocolate melted. Let's have fondue.'"

"Totally," she says. "I'd look sexy licking it off my fingers."

Oh god, she would. I fight the urge to adjust my pants. "If the chocolate ends up in the green room, I'll sneak you some."

Becca closes her eyes, her voice almost orgasmic. "*Chocolate.* Why haven't you brought me any before, Nate?"

I clearly should have. "I didn't know you had a thing for chocolate." It comes out more suggestive than I meant, and she laughs in surprise.

"Oh my god, you just said that!" she says, slapping me on the arm. "I can't believe you said that."

My face is heating up. I didn't mean it like *that*, but if she wants to take it that way—"Shut up," I say.

"No way, you can't get out of this one."

"It was right there!" I pretend to look at my watch, even though I don't wear one. "And look at that! It's time for the tiara ceremony."

Becca groans, and I help her to her feet. I don't want her to forget about the chocolate comment. I don't want her to move on and go to that ceremony. I already know they're keeping her—they want to get her to spill more about her marriage, and they're hoping my carefully crafted date will do it. I hate myself for being part of trying to get things out of her that are none of their goddamn business.

I wish we could just stay here on this balcony forever, lost in our own little world, away from the cameras. I wish I was brave enough not to play off my suggestive comment, to tell her I want her and I need her and I—

Oh, *shit*.

I can't even think those words, much less say them.

So instead, I usher Becca downstairs again.

At least with the cameras around, I know I won't do anything stupid that will ruin any chance of her ever wanting me back.

# FOURTEEN

## *Nate*

The next week of dates is taking place in Füssen, Germany. Daisy is having her one on one at the Neuschwanstein Castle, having been kept on by the producers in the hopes that she'll continue having catastrophic meltdowns and keeping the other women on edge. There are only six women left, and Preston has been steadfast about keeping Madison, Addison, and Londyn, and decided to bring Sheree along as well when the producers magnanimously suggested that he choose one more. Becca is the other producer pick and the only other one-on-one this week. I feel a little bad I didn't squeeze in a visit to a castle for her, but the rest of what I planned is hopefully better.

Mostly I just want Becca to have an experience she'll never forget. She and Preston start their date with cooking lessons from Jonas Braun, a famous German chef. They'll be joined for lunch by—this is the part of the date I'm proudest of—Becca's kids, who've flown in with her in-laws a week ahead of family visits just for this. The show booked Becca's in-laws with some time at the hotel spa while the kids are on the show with their mom, and since the kids know me, I volunteer to sit with them while we wait for Becca and Preston to finish their cooking lessons at the nearby restaurant we've rented out for the afternoon.

I meet Thea and Rosie in the hotel lobby, where they're sitting with Thea's interpreter, Noah. Thea is slumped over on a plush couch, wearing denim overalls and a t-shirt striped with the same orange-red color as her hair. Rosie, meanwhile, is in a sparkly purple princess dress, running in circles around the coffee table. I smile. In some ways, they couldn't look more different, but they both have so much of Becca in their faces, in the brightness of their smiles (though, admittedly, I've seen that smile more from Rosie than Thea.)

Their grandmother, a woman with a round face, a smattering of freckles like Thea, and chin-length brown hair, gives me a weary look and shakes my hand. Since I don't see him here, I'm guessing their grandfather is upstairs in their room getting a jet-lagged nap.

"So you're Nate," she says. "The girls have told me a lot about you."

I freeze for a second. The kids don't know how big a crush I have on Becca, so obviously that's not what they've been talking about. It was probably a huge novelty to be interviewed, and I hope I made them comfortable enough that they're looking forward to being on camera again.

"I'm Paula," she says, and I try to give her a warm smile.

"It's good to meet you," I tell her. "Becca speaks highly of you."

"How is she doing? This whole experience must be so stressful for her."

Over on the couch, I notice Thea sit up straighter as she watches what the interpreter is signing. She's worried about her mom's well-being, too.

"It is stressful," I say carefully. "But Becca's doing great. She knows what she wants and she's tough."

Paula looks relieved. "Of course she is. But you all better take good care of my daughter. *And* my grandbabies."

"I'll do my best," I say.

Paula seems satisfied with that and, after giving the girls a hug, follows the concierge off to the spa.

I wonder how that conversation would have gone if it was

Preston meeting her instead. She would have had a lot more questions for him, I'm sure, but she'll save all that for the family visit next week in France. Officially, Paula and the girls are scheduled to stay in Europe on the show's dime until that happens, because it's cheaper and easier on everyone than flying them back to LA only to have them turn around and fly to France a few days later.

It won't happen. Preston is narrowing the field to four women for next week, which means that Levi won't be able to continue choosing women for Preston to keep. Becca will be gone at the upcoming tiara ceremony, whether or not she's "given up the goods," as Levi puts it. Which is best for everyone—Becca doesn't seem like she's going to be heartbroken about it, though the romance of the date I've planned may change that. I hate myself for setting her up for that, and I wonder if she's going to hate me for it, too.

If Becca is willing to give me a chance after the show, what is Paula going to think of me then? Would she be as friendly if I was trying to date her daughter?

Rosie stops running around the coffee table and throws herself at my knees. "Nate!" she shouts. "Where's my mom?"

"Your mom is having a cooking lesson with a German chef," I tell her.

Thea raps on the table the same way she did when she wanted her mom's attention, and then she starts furiously signing.

"Does my mom like Prince Charming?" the interpreter says.

Damn. Thea doesn't mess around. It's not really my place to tell Becca's ten-year-old about the complexities of the situation, but I try to be as honest as I can.

"I don't know," I say. "I think maybe she hasn't decided."

"Because he's not a real prince," Rosie says, like this makes all the sense in the world. Then she returns to running around the coffee table and squealing.

I ignore the disgruntled look from the concierge as he returns from escorting Paula to the spa. It's my job to keep the kids happy, not to keep them quiet.

Thea's brow furrows. "Does the prince like her? He has to, right? Because she's awesome. Is he stupid?"

"Yes, I think he likes her." Which isn't exactly a lie, even if he's not as taken with her as he is with Madison and Addison and Londyn, which does not speak well for his taste. I sit on the other end of the couch. "How could he not?"

"Okay, but is he nice?" Thea asks. "Mom needs someone nice."

"She does," I tell her. "I think he's nice to her."

Thea's eyes narrow. "But not to *everyone*?"

The interpreter does a pretty good job adding intonation, but I don't need it. Thea's tightly coiled energy is emphasis enough.

She also doesn't miss a thing. This makes being tactful very difficult. I decide to switch tactics.

"You're very smart," I say.

Thea rolls her eyes before I can go on. "Mom shouldn't be with someone who is only pretend nice."

"I agree. I think you should meet Prince Charming and form your own opinion."

"But what if he's pretend nice to me?"

I'm glad the cameras aren't getting this, but if Levi knew what he was missing, he would die.

"Probably I could tell, though," she answers herself. "People are pretend nice to me a lot."

"I bet you could tell. Nothing gets by you."

"Or me!" Rosie adds. Her blond hair is pulled up in pigtails, and they bounce with every movement. Which means they're bouncing a lot.

I wish I'd brought a coloring book or something. Are five-year-olds too old for coloring books?

"Hey, Rosie," I say. "What's your favorite thing about Germany?"

"The pigeons!" Rosie shouts, as if we don't have pigeons in California.

"My mom is smart like me," Thea says, clearly wanting to get back to important matters. "But she doesn't go on many dates. I think she's scared. I don't want Prince Charming to hurt her."

That's perceptive. I wonder if Becca's aware of how much Thea has gleaned about her feelings on dating. "What do you think she's afraid of?" I ask.

"Someone being mean to her and making her cry."

I blink. That's a pretty definite response, and I wonder if it's based in something Thea's seen. "Why do you think she's afraid of that?"

Thea hesitates, eyeing Rosie. Then she pulls a little notepad out of her pocket and starts writing furiously, her red curls hanging over her face.

Yeah, she definitely knows something. I scoot closer to her and wait for her to turn the notepad so I can see.

*Because my dad used to make her cry,* Thea has written.

Shit. I'm guessing Becca isn't aware that Thea knows this, or she wouldn't be so dead set on maintaining her kids' image of their father. I clearly can't say that I've heard about that. I'm also not going to lie to Thea and say I'm sure it didn't happen.

But I've got to say something.

I take the pen she's holding out to me. *I'm sorry that happened,* I write. The interpreter doesn't seem to care that we've cut him out of the loop. He leans back in his seat and checks his phone.

*I love my dad and I miss him,* Thea writes. *But Mom doesn't cry as much now.*

It breaks my heart that Thea notices this. I'm sure it would break Becca's, too, but it feels like something she needs to know. She carries a heavy burden, hiding the truth from her daughters, and I'm guessing Rosie—who has climbed on the coffee table while I wasn't paying attention and is now pretending to be rowing a boat—doesn't have a clue.

*I don't want Mom to cry anymore,* Thea writes. *That's why she needs someone who is nice to all of us.*

*I agree,* I add, and Thea quickly snatches the notepad back.

*But don't tell Mom I said that.*

Crap. I am definitely going to need to tell her mom she said this, but I'd rather do it with Thea's permission. *Don't you think she'd want to know?*

*She doesn't want me to know,* Thea writes. *She would always try to hide it when she cried, but I saw anyway.*

*Maybe she would be relieved that she doesn't have to hide anymore,* I write.

Thea thinks about that for a moment. Rosie is singing a sea shanty about pigeons, and the concierge comes back with a sheet of paper with an ocean scene on it and a box with four crayons. Rosie beams at him and immediately begins coloring from atop her boat.

Not too old for coloring. Noted.

Thea taps my arm with the notepad, shoving it at me again. *Maybe,* she's written. *But I don't want it to be on TV.*

I know Becca doesn't either. But, for once, I think I can do something about that.

*What if you had a minute alone with her? Would you tell her then?* I'd rather this came from Thea than from me. I don't want Becca to think I put these ideas in Thea's head.

*I don't know,* she writes. *She might feel bad and I don't want that.*

Becca is going to feel terrible about this. I can guarantee it. But that doesn't mean she shouldn't know. *Sometimes people feel bad and good at the same time,* I write. *I think it would be like that. I think your mom would never want you to feel like you can't love your dad, but I don't think she likes hiding things from you, either.*

Thea twists her lips, first one way and then the other, then writes again. *She might feel bad that she thought I didn't know. She hates it when people assume I don't understand things, but then she did that too.*

Wow. That's perceptive. I guess I also assumed that Thea was more clueless than she is. Though, to be fair, I don't think I would have expected any ten-year-old to be this aware of other people's feelings.

*I think she probably hoped you didn't know because she doesn't want YOU to feel bad. Sometimes everyone needs to stop worrying about making other people feel bad and just tell the truth.*

Thea gives me a sharp glance. *Do YOU know the truth?*

Damn. I really do not want Thea's awareness turning on me, but I feel it focusing. *I know some things,* I write. *It's my job to ask questions.*

She raises an eyebrow, and I think the Eye of Thea is now firmly fixed exactly where I don't want it to be.

She doesn't keep me in suspense.

*Does my mom like YOU?* she writes.

I want to stop this conversation right here, but we're waiting for Olivia to come out and tell us they're ready to take the girls to the restaurant.

*Everyone likes me,* I write.

Thea rolls her eyes so hard I can only see the whites. *I mean like LOOOOOOOOOVE.*

I roll my own eyes. *I knew what you meant. Your mom and I are friends.*

She gives me the most skeptical look I have ever seen.

*What?* I write. *You don't think I can have friends?*

Thea grabs the notepad and writes so furiously she rips the page a bit under the pen tip. *You don't think my mom is pretty???*

*Of course your mom is pretty,* I respond. That is an objective fact.

*So do YOU want to ask her on a date?*

Gah. This is getting out of control. But at least there's an easy answer for that one.

*I can't. She has a boyfriend.*

Thea shakes her head firmly. *The prince is not her boyfriend. He's dating other people. And if he can date other people so can she.*

I sigh. Therein lies my problem—or one of them. I'm still pretty sure I've been friend-zoned, but I can't completely give up on the notion that Becca might reconsider me after the show is over.

If she won't, that's going to hurt like hell.

*You're right,* I tell her. *But unfortunately, if she dated someone else, she would get kicked off the show.*

Thea huffs. *That's not fair. You should ask her on a date anyway.*

*Maybe,* I write. God knows I've spent enough time imagining doing it. *But I would get fired.*

*SO????* Thea writes so it takes an entire page. We are burning through this notebook. *She's worth it. You can get another job but not better mashed potatoes.*

She has a point there. *She might say no,* I say.

Thea throws up her hands and grabs the notebook. *You just have to be brave.*

Oh my god. I am getting dating advice from a kid, and it's better than any of the advice or behavior on this train wreck of a show.

*I'll think about it,* I write. *Why do you want me to go out with your mom, anyway?*

*Because then I'll know she's dating someone nice,* Thea writes.

Warmth spreads in my chest. "Thank you," I sign at her.

*You're not pretend nice,* Thea writes. *Most people won't talk to me this long.*

*Most people are stupid,* I write, which may not be the most responsible thing to say, but if people don't give Thea a chance to express herself, it's true. She's a remarkable kid. I expected that, given that she's Becca's daughter, but she's far smarter and more perceptive than I knew a kid her age could be.

*Do you want me to get you a chance to talk to your mom alone?*

Thea presses her lips together. Rosie is still sitting on her coffee table boat, now making up a song about jellyfish *and* pigeons.

*What if it makes her too sad for her date?* Thea asks.

*If you don't want her dating Prince Charming,* I return, *why do you care?*

*What about her date with YOU?* Thea responds.

I laugh. *I think she'd be recovered by then.* I hesitate before I

146

add, *I think your mom is used to pretending to be fine for other people.*

Thea sighs. *OKAY FINE.*

This is going to be hard for Becca, but if I can get her a moment away from the cameras, I think she needs to hear it. *I'm going to tell the camera people you're scared, and that's why you need a few minutes alone. I know it's not true, but they'll believe me because they are dumb.*

Thea nods wearily. *Yes, they seem dumb. One asked if I needed a cup with a lid.*

At least I'm not that clueless when it comes to kids. I write, *I'm sorry people judge you. You're not a baby.*

*I think that person should never have kids,* Thea adds.

If they did, maybe they would know better. *I'm going to go check to see how much longer, okay?*

*Okay,* Thea writes, but then she adds, *Is my mom kissing Prince Charming right now? Because EWWWWW.*

That visual isn't one I particularly want, either. I hope that's not happening. I know Becca was telling the truth about not having kissed Preston yet, because production has a chart about exactly how far each of the women has gone with Preston so we all know who we should be making insecure about how little they've done, and who we should be asking if they feel guilty about how much. Levi is annoyed that no one has cornered Preston and gone all the way yet, which apparently happens at least once on most seasons before Dalliance Week.

None of this I am going to say to Thea. *They're with the chef, so I don't think they're kissing.*

Thea waggles her eyebrows at me. *Do YOU want to kiss my mom?*

*I'm going to go check if they're ready now!* I write, and I shove the notepad in my pocket. Thea doesn't object to me taking it, which is good, because there's no way I'm leaving it around for production to find.

# FIFTEEN

## *Becca*

If my life these last few weeks didn't already feel surreal, it sure does now. I'm on a date in a gorgeous city in southern Germany, and I'm cooking with famous chef Jonas Braun. Preston, too, obviously, but *Jonas Braun*. He doesn't have quite the media presence in America as, say, Guy Fieri or Rachel Ray. But in Europe, he's huge, and being a fan of hearty German and Slavic dishes, he's kind of a dream chef of mine. I might have fangirled a bit when we arrived at this charming little restaurant—reserved just for us, apparently—and he stepped out from the kitchen.

Okay, I definitely fangirled. But I stopped short of having him sign any body parts, so at least there's that.

Of course, I found myself looking back to see Nate, wanting to share my excitement, but he's not here today. I reminded myself that it's Preston I should be excitedly beaming at. And though I don't think he has much enthusiasm for cooking or famous chefs, he seemed pretty happy about it.

Despite the adrenaline of cooking with a world-famous chef, I'm a bit exhausted today—Londyn hogged the bathroom for over an hour last night while I was waiting to brush my teeth. I finally knocked to see if she was okay, and it turned out she was not.

"Becca," she wailed. "I haven't pooped in over a week. It's all the stress and maybe the cheese trays? My stomach hurts, and I don't know what to do. Help me!"

I offered to see if the producers could bring her laxatives, and she broke down into grateful tears. But then, between sniffs and effusive thanks, she said, "But don't ask Nate—I mean, don't ask a guy."

Luckily for her, despite my close relationship with Nate, I had no intention of approaching him with a desperate need for laxatives for "a friend."

When I was down on the floor where the production staff were staying, begging the medical team for laxatives, I did see Nate swiping a key card on one of the doors.

Knowing which room Nate is staying in may have kept me up late into the night, locked away in the bathroom taking care of my own, non-digestion-related needs.

Even as Jonas Braun—*Jonas Braun*—is demonstrating his preferred technique for caramelizing shallots, my mind is back to that night on the balcony. How I told Nate everything, all the pain and shame and secrets I've kept locked away from everyone. How much I wanted him to know, wanted him to see.

Because I felt that he already did see me, in ways no one else ever has.

"Okay, Becca," Preston says close to my ear, and I startle, my knife slipping dangerously toward my finger as I chop the spinach. Shit. I know better than to daydream while using a knife. "I might need your help here. I have no idea what *julienne* means and I'm afraid Mr. Braun will give me that judgy look again if I ask."

I laugh, glancing back at Jonas, who is eyeing a beefsteak tomato critically. "I got you," I say, and take the zucchini Preston's holding out.

Then I flush, realizing how suggestive that sounded, grabbing onto his zucchini. By the glint in his eyes, he didn't miss it. At least I didn't say anything about great cocks this time.

"Um, julienne," I say, "just means cut it into short, thin strips. Like this." I cut a few from the zucchini and Preston makes a playful wince. I force myself to smile at him. I'm on a date. On TV. I'm supposed to be flirting.

I wish I was flirting with Nate instead.

Preston starts julienning, and Jonas walks over to us. "Nice cuts," he says in his thick German accent, nodding in approval at the small pile I already made. It may now appear that Preston was the one who did them, but I feel a bloom of pride anyway. Even though it's only cutting a freaking zucchini, something Thea can do just as well.

But then Jonas winks at me and slaps Preston on the back. "Watch out for a woman who knows how to use a knife like that."

Preston and I both laugh. "Always sound advice," he agrees.

We work more on the meal, sautéing the spinach in olive oil with the shallots, seasoning and shaping the potato dumplings, making the chilled tomato sauce that will be the perfect compliment. Preston is suitably teased by Jonas for his lack of ability to shape dumplings, and plays along gamely. Jonas seems legitimately impressed with my technique, enough so that I get up the courage to suggest a possible seasoning substitution—always a risky move with chefs, but it goes over well. Jonas asks me about my kids while we cook, and shows me how to make a child-friendly, spinach-free option. Preston informs me he needs to practice so he can make them for his nieces and nephews sometime.

"I bet your kids don't turn their noses up at vegetables, though," Preston says with a grin. "With you being a gourmet chef and all."

I snort. "My kids turn their noses up at my cooking all the time. Thea has grown to appreciate vegetables, but Rosie acts like anything green will kill her."

"My son is twenty-two," Jonas says, shaking his head. "And he still does." He gives a long-suffering sigh and I laugh, even as my heart aches from missing them, as it so often does.

Jonas holds up a gorgeously plated circle of spinach and

potato dumplings, drizzled in the tomato sauce. We both clap. "I can tell which dumplings are yours," I tell Preston, gesturing to the most misshapen of the lumps.

He laughs. "They have character!"

"That they do." I grin.

"Do you wish your kids were here to see it?" Preston asks.

The pang in my heart grows stronger. "I do. I've taken to sleeping with a picture of them under my pillow. Isn't that pathetic?"

"I think it's sweet," Preston says. "But not as good as the real thing."

I open my mouth to agree, and then the kitchen door opens behind me. Before I even turn, my whole body floods with joy, because I know.

"Mommy!" I hear in that next second, and oh my god, there are my babies, both of them. Rosie is running toward me in one of her princess dresses, her arms outstretched, and Thea right behind, a huge smile lighting up her face. They're right there, hugging me, and I feel tears tracking down my cheeks as I hug them both back, all three of us together. "Oh, I missed you so much," I say, and then pull back to repeat it again while signing. "Every single day."

"Me too," Thea signs, while an interpreter translates. Then Thea's lips twist up wryly. "Maybe not every day. Grandma did let us have extra dessert."

I laugh with a little sob. "I bet," I sign back.

Then I pull them into a hug again, and looking past them, I see Nate standing by the door, grinning at me. My heart swells even more.

I want to sign "Thank you" to him, but the cameras are all pointed directly at me, and I don't want to make anyone suspicious. I'm supposed to be giving credit for this date to Preston, after all, though I doubt he did any of the actual planning.

"Are you the prince?" Rosie asks, wiggling out of my arms and looking up at Preston. "But not a real prince."

Preston laughs. "No, not a real prince. My name is Preston. And you're Rosie, right? And you . . . are Thea."

It was only the slightest pause there, and maybe no one else would catch it, but I recognize it well. It's that little mental hiccup most people have when they first meet Thea, where it occurs to them that they're talking to Thea but she can't hear them. This tiny pause is usually followed by an uncomfortable shift, or, in Preston's case, a squint of the eyes, like he's trying to figure out how this works.

I don't blame people for this instinctive reaction, but it still makes me wince inwardly every time, because I know Thea notices it, too. That immediately she's categorized as someone who needs to be treated differently.

I don't remember seeing that reaction from Nate.

Thea smiles back at him, though it's a little stiff. "Yes, I am," she signs. "It's nice to meet you." Very polite. Which is good, even if she seems stilted.

"You too," Preston says. "Should we all sit down and eat? We have some great food your mom made." I notice that he says this mostly to Rosie.

"Preston helped too," I add.

He chuckles. "Don't worry, girls, you won't have to eat any of the ones I cooked. In fact, we made some of these dumplings without spinach, just for you two."

Ha, that's right. I should have caught on then.

Rosie cheers. "Spinach looks like long boogers!" she announces proudly.

Thea raises her eyebrow at Preston. "I love spinach."

I raise my eyebrow back as the interpreter translates, because I happen to know she only tolerates spinach.

Sadly, we have to say goodbye to Jonas, but while I've been greeting my children, the production team has swept in and taken the food out to the dining area, so that when we leave the kitchen, we're presented with a table that's all set for us, with our plates and glasses of wine and an old porcelain soup tureen filled with daisies.

"This is incredible," I breathe, taking in the table, the surroundings. We have this quaint, charming little restaurant all to ourselves. With its mis-matched, well-loved tables and chairs and the character in every decorative piece—items that might be found in the house of a German grandma—it feels so much like my dreams for my own restaurant. Though not the stuffed deer head above the fireplace.

"I knew you'd love it," Preston says, pulling out my chair. "And you haven't even tried our dumplings yet."

He pulls out the chair next to him for Rosie, who climbs up eagerly, looking wide-eyed at the beautiful table setting. Thea plops herself into a seat, picking out the most green-dotted dumpling and plopping it onto her plate like she's proving a point.

We all begin to eat. The dumplings are perfection, and I have to hold in an orgasmic groan at the first bite. Rosie barely touches her non-spinach dumplings, bouncing in her seat and brimming with questions for Preston. Does he live in a castle? Does he have a horse? If he had a horse, what would its name be? Would its name be Freckles? Would it be a boy or a girl?

Preston manages to answer very seriously, but looks a little relieved when I tell her she needs to eat a few bites, mainly so the rest of us can eat without being peppered with questions. I can't wait to tell her all about getting to ride a horse for that polo date, but for right now, I want more dumplings.

Thea is eating her spinach dumplings—*at* Preston, I think—and staying oddly quiet. She's clearly not enthused about all of this, which I both understand and don't. On the one hand, I imagined she'd be a little judgmental of someone I'm dating. On the other, she wanted me to start dating again.

That must be a lot of conflicting feelings for a ten-year-old to process.

Thea takes a long drink of her apple juice, then finally starts talking. "What do you like about my mom?" she signs directly at Preston, who seems more comfortable watching the interpreter as he translates.

"Oh, okay," Preston says. "I think your mom is beautiful inside and out."

It's a very nice answer, if a bit general. Though I only have myself to blame for that, given how little of myself I've actually shown him. He smiles winningly at Thea after this answer, but I don't think she's swayed.

"What do you like about your mom?" Preston asks her.

Thea pauses. "Her mashed potatoes," she says, staring him down without cracking a smile.

I laugh, and Preston chuckles too, but it seems forced. I don't get the sense he's incredibly comfortable around kids, but I do think he's trying. Thea's not exactly making it easy on him.

Rosie cuts back in with more questions, this time about whether he's seen *My Little Pony* and if he thinks Twilight Sparkle is the best or Applejack, and on and on for awhile until we're pretty much done eating. I realize belatedly that we're eating spinach, and oh god, am I going to have spinach in my teeth on camera?

At least I have Thea with me today. If I do, she'll tell me in a heartbeat.

"Hey, guys," Nate says, and his voice sends a thrill through me. He crouches down between my seat and Thea's and lowers his voice. "Thea told me earlier that she's scared of being on camera, so we wanted to make sure she had some time alone with you to help her get comfortable before the second part of the date."

I look at Thea in surprise. She is avoiding my eyes and shifting nervously in her seat. Is that why she's been acting off since she got here? She didn't have a problem being on camera before.

Clearly *something* is going on. "Of course," I say, reaching over to squeeze Thea's hand. She squeezes tightly back and a prickle of fear stabs at me. Is she okay? Did something happen while I was gone?

"Thea, are you afraid of the camera?" Rosie demands, signing for herself, and Thea glares at her.

"Hey, Rosie," Nate says, standing back up. "Why don't you come with me while Preston gets interviewed and your mom and Thea talk. There's a cool fountain across the street you might like to see."

Rosie cheers and jumps from her seat, grabbing Nate's hand and tugging on it. "Let's go!"

He grins, and the sight of how easily she takes to him warms me all over.

"Why don't you and Thea take a walk," he suggests. "Production will follow to make sure you're all right, but they've agreed not to record."

Production never agrees not to record, so Nate must really have worked his magic on this one. We head outside, leaving the interpreter behind for the moment, and I lift up the back of my shirt just enough to turn off my mic. Thea and I pass a cute little bakery that could be pulled straight out of some storybook.

"You're not wearing a gown today," Thea signs, looking over my silk halter top and slim dark jeans.

"Probably a good thing, considering I was cooking."

"He was in prince clothes," she points out. Preston had another of those formal jackets with the gold buttons and braiding, though he took that off for the actual cooking.

"He's the prince. He always gets stuck wearing those."

"You look really pretty." She pauses, sucking in her lips. "Did he tell you that?"

I blink at her. "He did."

At the end of the block, we reach a small park. Olivia has followed us, but she's waiting down the block, and there are no cameras or microphones in sight. There's a colorful playground being used by a couple of kids, their parents chatting on a bench nearby. Thea and I find our way to an unoccupied bench that's across the way from the others and blocked from Olivia's view by the slide.

We sit together and Thea scuffs her feet on the ground

beneath the bench.

"Thea, what's wrong?" I ask.

She holds up her hands for moment before signing. "I know Daddy was mean to you sometimes."

My heart stops.

"What?" I ask.

She frowns. "I know he said things that made you cry. I know he would be mad at you and you would be sad a lot when he was there."

I don't think I can breathe; my hands are trembling as I sign. "You saw that?"

She nods and tugs at one of her curls.

I want to tell her that she misunderstood. I want to tell her that it was just because people cry sometimes even in good relationships, that her dad was never *mean*, just stressed out and upset sometimes.

But she'll know I'm lying, and I can't do that to her. Not anymore.

"He was mean to me sometimes," I admit, "and I was sad a lot. I didn't want you to think of your dad as mean, though. He loved you and Rosie so much."

She nods again. "I know he did. I love Daddy. But I don't want you to date someone who is mean to you again."

Tears are burning in my eyes. Relief that she can separate her love for Rob from what she saw in the way he treated me. But sadness that she carried this with her, locked away like I did. "Is that why you're telling me now?" I ask. "Because I'm dating again?"

"Yes. I didn't think you wanted me to know and I didn't want to make you sad."

The tears spill over and I hug her close, then release her to say, "I don't want you to be sad, either. But I'm so sorry I made you feel like you couldn't talk to me about it. And I'm sorry I treated you like you see and understand less than other kids. I should have known better." The guilt is a vise, squeezing me tight.

She shrugs. "I was really young."

It was three years ago, and she wasn't *that* young, but I appreciate the out she's trying to give me. And I do get the sense that that aspect doesn't actually bother her very much.

She's just sad for me. She wants the best for me.

What did I ever do to deserve such an incredible daughter? Let alone *two* such incredible daughters—these bright, shining lights in my life. I wish I could make everything perfect for them.

*It might help them to know their mother*, I can hear Nate say.

Maybe he's right. Maybe they don't need perfect; maybe they just need to know me.

Not that I think they should know all the details, not this young. And I do think Rosie is too young for even this much. But one day, if they want to know—

"Do you think Preston is pretend nice or real nice?" Thea asks.

I pause, considering. "I think he's real nice," I finally say. "But I don't know him very well yet. What do you think? You're always good at reading people."

She gets a mischievous smile. "I think Nate's real nice."

I raise my eyebrows, pretty sure I know where she's headed with this. "I think so too." I pause. "Did you spend more time with Nate today?"

"He stayed with me and Rosie while you were cooking. I asked him if he wanted to kiss you."

I choke on my own spit, and she grins at me.

Oh my god.

Probably I shouldn't encourage her on this, but I have to ask. "What did he say?"

"He wouldn't tell me. But he didn't say no!" She gives me a very pointed look, and I feel a little flushed.

"He can't kiss me," I say, trying very hard not to show the regret in those words—though it's Thea, so probably she can see it anyway. "He can't date me. He's a producer. I'm dating Preston."

Sort of.

Thea wrinkles her nose. "I told Nate if the prince can date other people, so can you. It's a double standard."

She's not wrong there. But—"Did he say he wants to date me?"

She squirms. "He said he'd think about it."

*What?* What does that mean? He'd think about whether he *wants* to date me? Or whether it's possible?

Probably he was just saying that to get Thea to stop pressuring him—something she's very good at. She's the freaking Spanish Inquisition when she sets her mind to it.

I desperately want to ask her to describe the way he said that, his body language, all the things—but she is my daughter, not a girlfriend I'm having drinks with, and I can't use her as some go-between in my love life because I'm too chicken to ask Nate these questions myself.

Even if Thea would clearly enjoy it if I did.

"Well," I say, "I'm glad you're friends with him. He is really nice."

I expect that look from her that says she knows why I'm changing the topic, but instead she looks down at her feet again, scuffing them some more.

"I told Nate about Daddy being mean to you," she says. "Is that okay? I asked if he already knew and he said yes."

I gape, then close my mouth. "Yes, that's okay. I'm glad you could talk about it with him. I'm even more glad you could talk to me."

"He told me I should tell you," she says. "I was afraid to make you sad, but he said you would want to know."

The tears are back in my eyes again. I'm a little terrified that there might have been cameras around while he had this conversation, or other producers who might have overheard. But Nate went to the trouble to make sure we could talk privately, and he probably wouldn't have been so careful if the secret was already out. "He was right. Thank you." I hug her tight again and she clings back, and we sit without talking for a few more moments, just feeling the breeze ruffling through our hair. I sign

"I love you" and she does too, our hands side by side.

Nate made sure we had time to talk about this, away from everyone else, rather than encouraging her to wait until I got home.

Nate knew what I needed, what she needed. He *knows* me.

I feel lightheaded again, but not in the panicky way of before. More like a floaty feeling all over.

I don't want Nate to get in trouble for giving us this time, so I pull reluctantly away from Thea. "We can talk more about this when I get home," I say. "But right now, I think we need to get back to the show before Rosie glitter-bombs someone."

Thea giggles and nods, and we head back to the others. Nate is across the street helping a chattering Rosie balance on the edge of the fountain as she walks around the rim, and I'm kind of amazed she hasn't jumped away from him and into the water. He looks over at us as we approach, his brows drawn together in concern.

I smile at him and sign, "Thank you."

His whole posture seems to relax, and he grins and signs it back—which is how deaf people say "You're welcome."

He's been doing his research.

And more and more, I feel like it may have nothing to do with his job.

# SIXTEEN

## Becca

I have about two minutes of Rosie excitedly babbling at me about a pigeon that landed "in the fountain, Mommy!" before Nate walks over with a cameraman right behind and somewhat apologetically tells me they need an interview.

I don't mind. I'm not going to pass up on any time I can talk to Nate, even if it's in an official capacity.

He has me switch my mic pack back on and stand in the street in front of the restaurant so they can get a scenic shot of me and the charming facade of the building.

"Was it a surprise seeing the girls?" he asks with a grin that tells me he already knows the answer.

I laugh. "The biggest surprise. The best surprise ever. I missed them so much, and I—I needed this." I hope Nate can feel me thanking him specifically for this. And for giving me that time alone with Thea—which I still haven't fully processed.

Nate's smile is so wide, his warm eyes so soft. "That's great, Becca." He pauses for a moment. "And how was it introducing your kids to Preston?"

My mouth turns dry. I know the show wants to hear how incredible it was to have my kids spend time with the man I'm falling for, and that's true, if not about Preston. I can't say that,

160

obviously, though I wish I could—off camera. Alone with Nate and in his arms.

I could lie, give Nate some answers that'll make his bosses happy and thus be great for his career, but if he is starting to feel the way for me that I do for him—could he really be?—I don't want to hurt him.

So I go for truths I can say. "I've always been curious to see how my girls would handle meeting a guy I was dating, since they've never done that before. I could tell Thea was a little reticent. She's protective of me. But I thought Preston did well with them and Rosie was excited to meet a TV prince."

"Fantastic," he says. He opens his mouth like he's going to start another question, but then closes it, squinting off to the side. "Sounds good," he says, and I recognize that he's just gotten a message in his headset from another producer. He looks back at me. "Part two of the date coming right up, Becks."

Him calling me Becks makes my knees weak, every freaking time.

"Well, part one will be hard to top," I say.

He winks at me. "Just you wait."

The wink, too. Now my knees are jelly.

Luckily he turns away before he sees the wobble in my step. When we walk back into the restaurant, I can see that my kids are being filmed interacting with Preston, and I think he really is trying his hardest to connect with them. He does that magic trick where he pretends to pull a quarter from behind Thea's ear. "See, I told you I have princely magic!"

I cringe, because I already know that's going to go over like a ton of bricks. And yeah, she's already giving him a *for the love of god, I am ten years old* stare-down. The interpreter definitely doesn't need to translate *that*.

Even Rosie looks less than impressed. "Money doesn't come from ears," she informs him. Then her eyes light up. "You should say a swear word!"

Nate and I look at each other and try valiantly to keep from laughing. Preston, however, gapes a bit, and I figure I should step in and save him.

"I'm guessing you didn't bring your swear jar with you," I say to Rosie, and she wrinkles her nose, realizing the fatal flaw in her money-making scheme. "So you might have to wait until the next time I step on one of your Legos."

Thea snickers and Rosie looks like she's about to start whining, but then a few of the cameras turn to the door, and Bartholomew the town-crier strides in, wearing his full jaunty regalia—feathered hat, gold breeches, and all.

"Hear ye, hear ye," he proclaims, unrolling the scroll. "The ladies Thea and Rosie are summoned for a special task—to help a fairy godmother as she provides the Lady Becca with a gown befitting a true princess."

Rosie squeals, jumping up and down. Even Thea looks eager. I'm pretty excited myself. A fairy godmother?

I remember telling Nate about the most romantic thing Rob had ever done for me, one of the few days of our marriage in which I actually felt loved. The beautiful dress he'd picked out just for me, the surprise dinner at a restaurant I'd wanted to go to, but never thought he'd be willing to spend the money on.

I meet eyes with Nate. He raises his eyebrows a bit, like, *I told you.*

I bite my lip, wanting nothing more than to keep staring into those eyes.

"I think you'll all really like this fairy godmother," Preston says. "I picked her out special for your mom."

I very much doubt he picked anything out—I'm pretty sure it's always the producers. But I don't blame him for claiming it; the princes always do, and I think the show tells them to.

"You don't pick a fairy godmother," Rosie points out. "She comes by magic."

"Prince magic?" Preston says, trying once again to salvage things.

Rosie seems to consider this. Until about two seconds later

when she forgets and dances around. "I want to see the fairy godmother!" she says excitedly, tugging on my hand.

"Me too!" I say, picking her up and balancing her on my hip—something that's becoming less easy as she gets bigger, but I'm not willing to give up yet. She giggles.

"Then I will bid you farewell for now, ladies," Preston says. He takes my free hand and kisses the back of it like he did the first night.

Thea gives a very pointed look to someone behind me, and I don't have to guess who it is. I give Preston a small smile and extricate my hand to grab Thea's. "Yes, um . . . farewell. To you, um, lord. Or Your Highness? Right. Your Highness."

Wow, I suck at this. Especially when my brain is fully engaged imagining what it would be like for Nate to press his lips to the back of my hand. Or other places.

Thankfully, Bartholomew leads us out to a waiting carriage.

Both girls gasp. And I have to force myself not to look back at Nate, remembering the time we spent in a carriage. My cheeks are burning—and a few other parts of me too.

This carriage is only big enough for me, the girls, a lone cameraman, and the interpreter, so Nate doesn't ride with us. Which helps as I try to smother all the inappropriate thoughts while interacting with my daughters.

We ride through the streets of downtown Füssen, cars zipping past us, and I have to clutch Rosie tight to keep her from leaping out the window at every exciting sight (and pigeon). It's not too long, though, before the carriage rolls to a stop in front of a high-end boutique—no old-world cobblestones or medieval-looking signs here. There's a slender, middle-aged woman standing on the steps in front. She's severe-looking, with cheekbones so sharp they could classify as deadly weapons, and she's wearing a crisp, dark business suit. She's the type of woman that I feel immediately intimidated by, who looks like she could run a Fortune 500 company in her sleep.

Except she's also wearing big, pink fairy wings.

Rosie shrieks happily, and Thea gapes. They both practically haul me out of the carriage and down the steps.

"Well, hello, my fairy apprentices," the woman says somberly, with a strong German accent. "And princess-to-be. I am Katrin, your fairy godmother. Welcome to my shop." She has a look on her face like she's about to work my kids to the bone in the fairy sweat shop.

Rosie doesn't seem to mind, clearly enchanted by the whole concept. Thea squeezes my hand so tightly my fingers hurt.

"But first," the woman continues, "you must become fairies yourselves." She snaps her fingers and two shop associates scurry out from the store bearing smaller versions of her own wings and also little sparkly wands. The girls put their arms through the wing straps and take their wands. Rosie looks so overcome with joy that for once in her life, she's speechless. "And now the magic begins," the woman says loudly, and suddenly she grins, her whole face instantly transformed into humor and happiness. The shop associates toss up handfuls of colorful confetti—not glitter, thank god—and both girls squeal in joy. Even Thea, who then looks embarrassed about it.

We're ushered inside, where cameramen are waiting to film us entering the shop. Glittering dresses are spaced on mannequins throughout the brightly-lit space. Jewelry shimmers in cases. My eyes widen. Thea's eyes widen. Rosie dances and waves her wand around and runs from dress to dress.

"Don't touch anything!" I say, afraid she's going to knock over some multi-thousand-dollar gown, but Rosie points her wand at each one in turn and says, "I make you! And I make you! And I make you!"

Katrin laughs, unconcerned about the potential destructive power of my five-year-old. "These are all beautiful gowns, yes? But . . ." She leans in close to Thea, lowering her voice like she's telling a secret, which is so nice—she's treating Thea like she would any other child, even though it's clear she's deaf. The interpreter walks next to her, signing everything. "I have a very special gown for your mother. Would you like to see it?"

Thea nods eagerly.

Katrin snaps her fingers again, and her shop associates emerge from the back, holding the most beautiful dress I have ever seen. It's got a full skirt and a tight, sleeveless bodice. The fabric is done to look like stained glass windows, the kind you might see in some gorgeous medieval cathedral, each pane outlined in black, glittering beads.

It's so beautiful it steals my breath. Is this really the gown I'm going to wear? There's no way they'll let me keep something like this, but to even wear it . . .

In front of Nate. Who probably didn't choose the actual dress? But who is very likely behind the planning of this date, considering how perfectly every detail has been arranged.

I focus on Katrin and my girls and the most beautiful gown in the world. Which, I am told, I will not be allowed to wear until I have had my makeup and hair done. With fairy apprentice assistance, of course. The girls are thrilled, and I am, too. Even if I have many times been the recipient of my girls doing my makeup and hair, and it's not exactly the most flattering look.

Katrin introduces us to "the makeup fairy" and "the hair fairy"—professionals who can probably improve whatever disaster my kids want to create on my face (excepting glitter, of course, which takes actual magic to remove.)

I'm taken back to a makeshift salon, and the beautifying begins. The girls are given things they can do, and they are in heaven. Thea carefully applies my eyeshadow under the makeup fairy's instruction, then pretends to fly around the room with Rosie when they get bored watching my hair get curled into loose waves that fall over my shoulder.

I look up to see that Nate has arrived, probably to interview me before the next portion of the date. He looks me over appreciatively before the girls beg him to join in their flying. For a few minutes he does, laughing along with them. My heart turns to jelly like my knees did earlier.

I need to talk to him. I have to. It's so hard to talk without being caught on camera, even in the halls at the hotel—

But I still know where his room is. If I snuck out tonight, could I knock on his door and see him? My whole body heats up, thinking of being with Nate in his hotel room. Telling him I have feelings for him. Asking if he feels the same.

It would be a huge risk. With my own heart, certainly—the thought of him rejecting me, of the pity on his face while he tries to do it gently . . . it terrifies me. But more importantly, I'd be risking Nate's job. Would he let me into his room? Would he be angry with me for seeking him out?

"Now time for the princess to wear her gown," Katrin announces and the girls cheer. One of the shop assistants guides me back into a lavish fitting room and helps me remove my clothes in a way that doesn't mess up my makeup or my newly-styled hair. Then she helps me into that beaded, shimmering gown and zips me up.

I stare at myself in the mirror, stunned.

I'm me, but a different version of me—a beautiful woman who is wearing this incredible gown like she was made for it. A woman who is confident and assured and glamorous.

I have never in my life felt like a princess—not as a kid, not at prom, sure as hell not at my wedding, when I already knew Rob would never see me that way.

But I feel it now.

My heart is hammering with that thought as I walk back out into the main room of the shop, where all the cameras are waiting with the producers and sound guys and Katrin and my girls. I wonder if this is how Cinderella felt walking into that ball, seeing all eyes turn to her.

"Mommy, you're so pretty!" Rosie gasps, and Thea's jaw drops. Katrin clasps her hands together with a broad smile.

I let my gaze flick quickly over to Nate. Is it all in my mind, or does he look awestruck? His lips are parted, and then they close again. His Adam's apple bobs up and down with a swallow.

"What a lovely princess, don't you think, girls?" Katrin asks.

Thea nods, her eyes still wide, but then signs back. "Do you get to keep the dress?"

Katrin chuckles. "Sadly, the magic will wear off at midnight and this dress will become rags."

Ha. That's a better answer than, "Sorry, honey, the show's not paying thousands of dollars for your mom to keep a designer dress to wear while she vacuums the living room."

I expect Rosie to pout at this answer, but she is in some elevated state of princess euphoria and starts belting "Let It Go" like it's the only way to express her depth of feeling. Thea rolls her eyes, but she smiles at me. "You look beautiful," she says. "And you don't need any glitter."

God, I want to look over at Nate again; does he still look so admiring? Did I read too much into it?

But I can't keep doing that. I can't be so obvious, for his sake as well as mine.

Before Rosie can transition into another princess song—I think she's gearing up for "Part of Your World"—Katrin gets a signal from one of the producers and announces that the princess needs to leave to meet Prince Charming, which means she needs to say goodbye to her little fairy apprentices.

Another producer—the guy the contestants call "Mustache Dan" for self-explanatory reasons—steps in to inform us that after I leave, a car is waiting to take the girls back to their grandparents at the hotel. My heart sinks. This day has been so incredible, but I'm not ready to let my girls go yet. I know I need to, though. I was lucky to get this much time with them. We hug and I mess up my lipstick kissing them on their cheeks, but I don't care.

Then we say goodbye to Katrin, and I'm ushered out of the boutique, where Preston is standing in front of the carriage. It's evening now, and the gold buttons and epaulets on his jacket gleam in the light spilling out from the store windows.

His smile broadens as he looks me up and down. "You look incredible. Stunning, in fact."

"Thank you," I respond. "The fairy godmother and her apprentices worked their magic."

"I don't think they needed much of that," he says and takes my hand, leading me up into the carriage.

My hand feels heavy in his, not right. But I force a smile anyway, because I'm on a date with Preston, and I need to try to be present and appreciative.

How much longer can I keep doing this?

My whole body feels heavy as we sit in the carriage, and it's not just because the beads on this gown have the combined weight of an elephant. Preston sits next to me on the padded bench and there's a cameraman opposite us. We talk as the carriage starts moving—Preston tells me how great it was to meet the girls, how adorable they are and how much they clearly love me.

"I get the feeling, though," he says, "that Thea's a bit . . . hesitant about you dating again."

I fight a cringe, because I know very well that she's not. I remember her coy smile, telling me about how she'd asked Nate if he wanted to kiss me. "I think she can be, um . . . protective of me."

"I imagine she misses her dad a lot," he says. "Probably no one else is going to be good enough for her mom. Not even a prince." He nudges me playfully.

"Well, you know kids," I say awkwardly.

The carriage lurches to a stop, and a footman opens our door. Which makes me think of my door-opening etiquette conversation with Nate—but I have to admit, despite my opposition to women waiting around in cars for their doors to be opened for them, it does make getting out of a carriage in a ballgown considerably easier.

We're at a park, and there's a table set out on the grass, ringed by hanging lanterns and the string lights this show is so fond of. Preston leads me out there, and we sit down. There are plates of food already set up for us—some sort of beef loin and rhubarb dish—and a bottle of wine.

It's pretty easy to get Preston to open up about the favorite places he's traveled, the places he'd like to go. He asks about places Rob and I traveled, clearly trying to get me to share more about my marriage, but I'm an expert at side-stepping these bombs, and after mentioning that we moved around a bit with the military, I turn the conversation to asking Preston more about his childhood and family, which he's also eager to talk about.

It's all nice and pleasant but I'm still tense, because I know that Nate, the man I really want to be on a date with, is somewhere behind those cameras. I'm becoming more and more sure that I need to find out his feelings, and less and less sure that I'll have the courage to do it.

After a while, Preston gets a signal from someone over my shoulder and nods, setting down his wine glass. "Well, Becca, there's one more surprise for us today." He stands and holds his hand out. "Care to join me?"

I'm a little terrified a band is going to start playing and I'm going to be forced to waltz in the grass in a dress that is probably worth more than my car and about as heavy, but he leads me to a path that winds around a bend of trees to a large patch of craggy ruins—maybe from part of a castle?—which are gorgeous in the moonlight.

"Wow," I say, taking it all in. "This is—"

And then fireworks explode across the sky, blues and greens and reds, the lights shimmering above us and dancing off the ruins. It's breathtaking, and I can practically feel the cameras zooming in on my look of surprise, but I can't stop staring at the sky. I've always loved fireworks. The Fourth of July used to be my favorite holiday when I was a kid, and my girls share my love of it.

I turn to tell this to Preston, whose eyes dip down to my lips, and then, before I can react, he leans in and kisses me.

I'm pretty sure my whole body stiffens, and I instinctively want to push him away, but oh my god, am I really going to be the girl who refuses to kiss Prince Charming right here on TV? I don't want to embarrass him, not to mention myself. My lips go on autopilot, and it's not like he's a bad kisser, but my body feels like it's closing in on itself, and I want to tear away and run to Nate and let him know that I don't want to be doing this.

I pull back and break the kiss. It wasn't very long, but I don't think it will come across like I found the whole thing repulsive. It wasn't, in and of itself.

But it wasn't Nate.

Preston smiles gently at me, and I force myself to do the same back. He puts his arm around my shoulders and we look back up at the fireworks and I make myself count to ten before I glance to the side, where I can almost feel Nate's presence, like I'm tied to him with an invisible string.

There's this moment where our eyes meet, but there's not even a ghost of a smile on his face. His jaw is hard, his posture stiff and hunched all at once. Then he looks quickly down, staring at the ground.

He doesn't look at all like a producer happy to see that his planned date got the romantic result that he wanted. He looks like he hated every second of that.

I feel terrible and hopeful all at once. Is he really jealous? I mean, I don't want to hurt him, but if he's jealous, then that means—that means—

My heart is pounding so hard I think I can hear it above the fireworks, my mind flashing to that plan again.

Can I really do it?

Preston and I stand there until the fireworks die down. I guess the producers decide they aren't getting any more kissing at the moment, so Mustache Dan calls Preston over for an interview. I see Nate saying something to Olivia, who nods. "Yeah, sure," she says, then waves at me. "We'll get your interview over here, Becca. Just let us get the lighting right."

She and the cameraman discuss places for me to stand, and I see Nate start to walk away. My heart is beating in my throat and

I try not to trip over my beaded skirt as I hurry over to him. I know I can't say anything real here, but I want to say *something*.

After everything he did for me, making me this perfect day, showing how much he knows me . . .

"Nate," I say, and he looks back at me warily. "I just wanted to thank you. Um. For letting me have that time with Thea." I hope he can hear how much I mean that; how it meant everything to me that he knew how much we both needed that. "I think it really helped her . . . get over some of her fear."

His lips twitch up, but it doesn't reach his eyes. "Of course. I'm glad. I just—Olivia will do your interview. I'll see you tomorrow, okay?"

"Yeah," I say, barely a breath, and he hurries off.

"Becca?" Olivia calls, and I head over to her, my mind spinning. They get me positioned.

"So," Olivia says with a teasing smile, "This was a pretty big date, huh? What would you say it meant to you?"

Everything from the day is shuffling through my mind—the incredible cooking lesson, the time with my girls, the dress, the fireworks—and it's all framing itself around that hurt look on Nate's face.

He does feel something. Maybe he feels everything I do.

That thought makes me dizzy. It makes me feel . . . brave.

"It's the kind of date that says 'I love you,' " I say without thinking.

My heart stops, and not because Olivia is practically salivating at the direction she can take the interview.

But because, though I don't know that Nate's feelings are that strong, it hits me that mine are.

I'm in love with him.

Olivia dives in with the questions I knew she was going to ask—what was it like kissing Preston? Do you think he's falling in love with you? Do you think you're falling in love with him? On and on and on. I fall back into my usual answering routine—dodge, sidestep, say noncommittal things. Talk about "the journey" some more.

But the whole time, my mind is one hundred percent elsewhere, shoring up plans, my nerves sparking with fear and giddy anticipation.

I have to do this tonight. I have to know.

I'm terrified, there's no question. Of rejection, of getting caught, and most of all, of the depth of my own feelings. But there's his voice in my head from the balcony that night: *You're a total badass.*

It's time for me to prove him right.

# SEVENTEEN

## *Nate*

I was unprepared for how awful it was going to feel to watch Becca kiss Preston. She had every right to. She's dating him, after all. But I still feel like I've been punched in the gut, and I can't wait to be done filming. Some of the other producers are heading down to the hotel bar, and as good as a drink sounds right now, I just want to be alone. I tell them no thanks and head back to my room, where I shut the door and turn on the television to nothing in particular and then turn it off again after a while because the noise is intolerable.

It was my job to convince Becca to kiss Preston. She didn't say anything on the date about Rob, so I'm guessing Levi isn't going to be happy with me. He'll give up on her and she'll go home.

I hope Becca isn't going to be heartbroken. I know I've participated in bringing her along this far, but I wonder how real her feelings for Preston have become.

That kiss sure as hell *looked* real. And afterward, when she caught me leaving, she looked so *happy*. Practically radiant, in fact. I should be pleased—I put a lot of work into making that date as spectacular as possible. I'm *glad* she had a good time. That's what I *wanted*.

But I wish it was me she'd been kissing, instead of Preston.

I kick off my jeans, lie back on the bed in just my boxers and t-shirt, and debate whether I should call Jason. It's a more reasonable hour in California than it is here, and I'd really like to talk to someone about all this. But Jason isn't the most articulate dude, and he'd probably just tell me this situation sucks and he's sorry, which I already know and don't want to hear right now. I don't think anyone in my family would be particularly helpful, either. I wonder how weird it would be for me to call Jason's girlfriend, Emily, and whine to her. She'd be easier to talk to about it, and Emily is my friend, for sure, but I don't just call up my best friend's girlfriend—ever. Still, any awkwardness that might cause could be worth it just to—

There's a knock on my door, and I close my eyes. I really don't want to deal with anyone else tonight, but if it's work related, I can't ignore it. I drag myself off the bed and answer in my boxers, hoping to convince whoever it is that they woke me up and should go the hell away.

I crack the door open, and it takes me a second to process what I'm seeing.

Becca is standing there, wearing a white zip-up hoodie and some yoga pants, looking at me with a nervous expression.

"Hey—" I say, and I've barely got the word out before she's ducking under my arm and inside the room, then pressing her back to the door, shutting it again.

Oh my god. Becca is in my hotel room, and I'm not wearing pants. I've still got my hand on the door frame, which means I'm leaning way too close and—

I step back toward the bed, staring at her. "Becca, hey," I say, trying not to act as thrown off by this as I am. Is she here to tell me more about her date? More likely, she wants to talk off-camera about her time with Thea.

"Hey, was that really okay, what happened with Thea today?" I ask. She thanked me earlier, so I thought so, but I still blind-sided her with all that. Probably, I should have handled that better, and—

174

"Yeah," Becca says. "That was fine. *Better* than fine, it was a great . . ." She shakes her head, like she's clearing it. "Thank you for doing that, but I'm not here to talk about the kids."

"Okay." That was a much safer topic than her date with Preston, which I definitely don't want to—

"I have feelings for you," Becca blurts out. "Strong feelings. All the strong feelings."

I blink at her, wondering if I did, in fact, fall asleep or am somehow hallucinating this. Did she seriously just say that?

"And I came here to ask if maybe you have feelings for me too," she continues, "and if you do, to ask if you wanted to see where this could go."

She wants to—

"Really?" I say. It comes out hoarse, because I'm still adjusting to the idea that Becca, who was just kissing Prince fucking Charming, is here asking *me* if I want to—

"It's okay if you don't, of course," she says, squirming. "Have feelings for me, I mean. I know you were just doing your job, and I didn't mean—"

"Yes, I have feelings for you," I say, and she looks about as stunned as I probably do right now. "Strong feelings," I add. "All the strong feelings."

Becca smiles tentatively. "Really?"

She sounds so hopeful, and I want to close the distance between us and put my arms around her and tell her that of course I do. She's so wonderful and perfect, how could I not?

Can I do that? Is she saying I can do that?

"Yeah, really." I incline my head toward the bed. "You want to sit down?"

She takes a seat on the edge of my bed. I debate whether I should put on some damn pants before I join her, but it's not like my boxers are super revealing, and I don't want her to read it as a sign of discomfort.

So I sit next to her and hope I don't soon need to put a pillow on my lap to stay decent.

Shit. Maybe I should have put on pants.

Becca is still watching me nervously, but she's radiating that happy glow from the date. It makes me much happier when she's here with me than it did then.

Becca is here. With me. In my hotel room. Which could definitely, absolutely get me fired, but at this moment I really don't care.

"What about Preston?" I ask.

She gets a sly look on her face. "I know you planned that date today."

That wasn't really an answer to the question, but it still makes me happy that she figured it out. "Yeah, I did."

"I knew it. Everything was so perfect, so totally geared toward me and what I love. But the whole time, I kept wishing I was on the date with you."

That takes my breath away. It's everything I wanted and didn't dare hope for.

"I wished that, too." I want to point out that it didn't stop her from kissing him, but I don't want sound like a prick. "I was really jealous."

"I thought you were," she says, biting her lip. "Especially after he kissed me. I'm sorry about that. But seeing how much you hated it—that's what gave me the courage to come here." She knots her fingers in her lap. "I wanted to be on the show to take a chance, to become more open to dating. But I think what it's done is made me open to dating *you*. So if you want to see where this can go, I'll leave the show."

She looks at me hopefully, and I'm struck so speechless it takes me a minute to answer.

She'd leave the show for me.

For *me*.

"You'd really do that?" I ask.

She nods. "If you want me."

"Yeah, I want you." My body is starting to heat up, and I think in a minute that's going to become painfully obvious, but maybe that isn't a bad thing. She's saying she wants this, and god, I want her so much.

Can this happen? Is this really okay? It feels too damn good to be true.

She's looking at me with this intense hunger in her eyes, and I'm guessing I'm doing the same.

But we need to have a plan, don't we? An exit strategy. Becca matters too much to me to do anything rash.

"What will you tell Preston?" I ask.

She shrugs. "What is it that women always say? I don't feel a strong enough connection. I don't think I can continue with this journey. I don't want to take the place of someone who can get there with you."

"You'll have to go home," I say, feeling a pang in my chest. I don't want her to go. I don't want to be away from her. "But it's only a few more weeks, and then I'll be back. And once you get home, you'll have a phone again."

Her smile turns coy. "I will," she says, and I'm pretty sure she's thinking, like I am, about all the things we could do over the phone. Yeah, my body's starting to have all kinds of reactions that are incredibly obvious and Becca's eyes travel down, just for a second, and I know that she notices.

"You really want this." I'm stating the obvious, but it's just so hard for me to believe that after all of that longing, she's really here.

"I do," Becca says. "I've wanted this since I met you. And especially after we talked in the carriage."

Oh god, the carriage. "Me too." I chuckle in a way that is seriously wound up. "You were talking about how long it had been and how sexually frustrated you were and I wanted so bad to offer to help you out with that."

"I wanted you to!" she says with her own wound-up laugh. Then she pauses and her hand slips over, resting on top of mine. It's a simple touch, but it ignites a current that runs through my body, vibrating down to my bones.

Maybe this is too much, but it's true: "I was about *this close* to offering to crawl under your skirts and take care of you right there."

Becca lets out a faint groan and her eyes blink closed. "I might have had a few fantasies about that myself."

Holy shit, we're doing this. We're really doing this. I lean in, running a hand up her leg, and she whimpers softly, looking up into my eyes.

She looks so open, so vulnerable, more so even than when she told me the truth about her marriage. It's incredible to me that she's been feeling the same way I have this whole time, but looking back, it feels so obvious.

"And oh my god, you making me fix your stuck zipper."

Her face is so close, I feel her breath on my cheek when she laughs. "Yeah, I might have done that on purpose, to see if you were attracted to me. I mean, not the getting the zipper stuck part, but, um. Insisting you be the one to help me."

Of course she did. I can see it, now, and I don't mind at all. "When you got the tweezers out of the makeup case. You were bending over like that on purpose, to turn me on."

Becca giggles, and I put a hand on her cheek, pulling her face close to mine, resting our foreheads together. I don't care that she kissed Preston tonight. I don't care, so long as I'm the one she wants. "Good thing I have so much self-control," I say, "or I would have bent you right over your bed."

"I wish you had," she says and reaches up to her hoodie and pulls down the zipper. She's not wearing a shirt underneath, just a black, lacy bra. That's the end of my self-control. I close the space and kiss her and we both moan softly against each other's lips. I cup her face in my hands and kiss her and kiss her, every forbidden thought I've had about everything I want with her racing through my mind, my whole body tense and ready and desperate for this.

The kiss breaks, and we're both panting, and Becca lays her forehead against my chest. "Nate," she whispers.

God, she wants me. *Me.*

I want to give her everything and never look back.

# EIGHTEEN

## *Becca and Nate*

Kissing Nate is better than I thought a kiss could ever be. It breaks apart those last reservations holding back pure hope, pure happiness. It breaks me apart, but not the way Rob did—this is the very opposite. Not tearing me apart to make me less, but letting in the space to make me see that I am so much more.

And god, the things it does to my body.

Nate's tongue brushes along mine, and waves of heat run through me. His hands are so soft and warm, cupping my face, and then they pull away so they can be replaced with his lips, working his way down, tracing fire and need along my jaw, then down my neck. I moan softly, gripping his shoulders—and damn, his shoulders. Lean, tight muscle that feels like delicious sin under my hands. I need to see more, I want to see every muscle on his whole body, want to taste every dip and ridge of him.

I'm about to start pulling his shirt off, but his hands have been busy too, and I'm distracted from any coherent thought by him drawing me closer with his palm on the small of my back, under my sweatshirt. His lips light across the tops of my breasts, and I can feel my nipples hardening, begging for him there. My whole body is begging for him everywhere.

I arch against him. "Nate," I whisper again, like I'm afraid to say it louder, afraid this is all a dream. Afraid to wake up.

He has feelings for me. This incredible man who makes me not only believe in real love but feel it, more powerfully than I ever thought I could.

I want to say those words, want to whisper them in his ear, but the fear that it's too much, too soon, stops me just as it did when I first entered the room.

Strong feelings, I said. So inadequate to describe this.

I shouldn't be doing this. I know it. It's not just that I'll get fired if we're caught, but Becca will be kicked off the show, instead of leaving on her own terms. She's still technically dating Preston—although Thea made the really good point that Preston is dating other women, so it's not entirely fair if Becca is shamed for doing so.

And I've had sex with women I'm not seeing exclusively, but I've never been in this deep with anyone, which ought to terrify me into taking it slow.

But it's that same depth, that same pressure that makes me unable to step back. I need her like I need the air I breathe; I'm in no condition to be sensible. We're kissing desperately, like we're trying to devour each other, and I've never felt so consumed.

So *ready.*

Becca's body arches against mine and she whispers my name again. I'll never tire of hearing her say it. Never in a million years.

I move my hands up to the back of her bra, meaning to undo it, but I can't find the clasp. I'm fumbling like a sixteen-year-old, and Becca reaches her hands up to the front of her bra—okay, there's the clasp—and pulls it open for me and leans back on the bed, giving me full access.

Her breasts are just like I imagined they'd be—gorgeous and perfect, just like the rest of her. I pull one of her nipples into my mouth and Becca whimpers and runs her nails up my back, giving me full-body shivers.

It's funny to think I can read her so well and somehow missed that she was attracted to me.

I would have seen it, I think, if I hadn't been so afraid it wasn't true.

My fingers have found the hem of Nate's shirt and I'm pulling it off. He helps me, and then his bare chest is right there, and it's sexy as hell. The guy's a climber, and I could already tell with his clothes on that he was seriously fit, but wow—that expanse of gorgeous brown skin, the taut muscles. I can't keep my hands from traveling across him, and I don't think he wants me to.

He could be a freaking statue of male perfection, except that he's so warm I can feel the heat radiating from him, and he's no statue, he's Nate and he's real and he's mine. The hungry way Nate looks at me makes me lean back, wanting him to take me in. Wanting him to take me.

He lets out a sigh that might be awe or need or both, and then he's leaning over me and his mouth, hot and wet, is on my nipple, tugging it with his tongue, and sending electricity down, down, until I feel it pulsing between my legs. I'm whimpering, begging wordlessly for more, and he moves off the bed so he's kneeling right there, so close to that pulsing ache.

Insecurity prickles under my skin. Because he's close to other things, too—the stretch marks, the scar. Things I should be proud of, proof my body gave me the two most amazing gifts in the world. But that pride has been buried under Rob's disdain.

I feel my body go stiff. Just a bit, maybe not enough for Nate to tell that—

He pulls back, looking concerned. "Are you okay?"

"Yeah, of course," I say. It won't matter, right? He won't want me less, right?

He frowns. "What's wrong?" he asks gently.

I don't want to tell him, but in the grand tradition of me and him, I also do. "You have to notice everything, don't you?"

He smiles, and I melt for it, like I always do. "It never seemed to bother you before."

It's true. I love that about him. "I'm just self-conscious about my scars."

His brow furrows; clearly he has no idea what I'm talking about. He looks down me and his eyes stop on the loose, puckered skin folding together just above my pants.

He runs a finger over it. "Surgery?" he asks.

"C-section. With Rosie."

His expression is so gentle, and he leans down and presses his lips against the hollow of my hip, which causes my eyelids to flutter. "I would never wish that away."

I can feel tears forming behind my eyes. This is a man who sees my flaws, my imperfections, but sees me as so much more than that. He wants me, as I am.

"You're beautiful, Becks," he says, and I close my eyes as those tears come even closer to the surface.

Y ou make me feel beautiful," Becca says.

It breaks my heart that she doesn't feel that way all the time, and I'm guessing this, too, is because of Rob.

I'm not going to bring him up tonight. I'm going to make sure every thought of him is a million miles away. I kiss her skin just above the hem of her pants and then slip my fingers beneath the waistband. "Mmm," Becca says, and she lies back on the bed again, which I take for an invitation to slide her yoga pants off, revealing the matching lacy underwear beneath.

"You are so sexy," I say. She always has been, but the fact that she wore this for me—she was wearing more practical underwear

182

when I helped her with her zipper, so I'm guessing she brought these for the Dalliance Tower—makes her even more so.

Becca meets my eyes, and there's a different kind of tension between us now, taut like a rope with no slack in it.

I don't look away from her eyes as I hook my thumbs in the stretchy lace of her underwear and pull them down, as I lift her knee up over my shoulder and turn slightly, kissing the soft skin on the inside of her thigh. Her eyes close and her head falls back, her mouth parting, and watching her respond to me like that undoes me completely.

I kiss my way up her thigh slowly, savoring every inch. "Would you really have let me go down on you in the carriage?" I ask against her skin.

"Mmm," she says. "Yes."

"You would have had to be quieter there," I say, reaching the top of her thigh and nibbling it gently.

"I should probably be quiet here," Becca says, then gasps as I run my tongue up her outer lip.

She should—it's not a good idea for us to be heard from the hallway. But—"Not too quiet," I say. "I want to hear you." I lift her other knee over my other shoulder and then run my tongue back down and up the other side.

She groans, and it's exactly as delicious as I imagined.



I don't think Nate needs to worry—I don't think I could keep him from hearing me if I tried.

His tongue traces me up and down, up and down, heat lancing through me with each motion, the low pulse becoming its own heartbeat. The thought that in the carriage we were having the same fantasies at the same time drives me wild, makes the ache deeper. I groan, words caught in my throat.

Except this one: "Nate."

"Becks," he says, and the way he says it makes me shudder.

And then he lowers his mouth to me and begins in earnest. His lips, his tongue, his breath, the faintest brush of his teeth— all of it working together, sending waves and waves of pleasure through me, making my body feel like it's pulling together with need and desire and fire. I'm definitely not being too quiet—I'm moaning and gasping and shifting closer to him, wanting him tighter against me.

His hands are under my ass, massaging as he works me with his mouth, and I'm shaking and arching and whimpering. Saying his name again, pleading and pleading as the heat rises higher and higher.

He's working me faster, harder, and my fingers are in his hair, tangled in those dark, gorgeous curls he keeps tied back, and I hope I'm not pulling too hard, I hope I'm not hurting him, but I can't let go, I can't ever let him go—

I cry out as my whole body comes deliriously apart in blinding ecstasy like I've never felt before, never in my whole life. I'm shuddering and shaking, and he pulls me through it until I fall back on the bed, my muscles so weak they might as well have dissolved.

He's grinning at me. "I wish I'd done that in the carriage."

Oh my god, yes. "Me too. I never even would have met the prince."

Becca says that like it's a good thing, which makes me smile. She spreads her legs and I climb over her, lying on the bed on top of her.

First times are generally not my favorite—I prefer the comfort of knowing a person to the novelty of discovery. Maybe it's all the time I spent wanting this, but there's no awkwardness, just a feeling of belonging, like this is exactly how things are meant to be.

It's a delirious mix, having the pleasure of discovering her body for the first time, and feeling like I know her so well, all at once. She's trembling beneath me, and I want to be the one who makes her feel this way, always. I've tried so hard not to contemplate what that means, but now it's right there, so close to the surface.

Her fingers slip under the waistband of my boxers. I'm so hard that I'm testing the strength of the elastic, and Becca wastes no time gliding her hand inside and gripping me in her fist so tight my vision loses focus.

"Oh, Becks," I say, burying my face in her neck. Her long hair smells like strawberries, and I remember what she looked like in that dress—like a fucking princess, with her shoulders bare and the jewels glittering. I'm scared I'll never be able to be the kind of man she deserves. It's not something I've worried about with anyone else, but Becca deserves everything good in the world and I feel like an asshole thinking I could ever be enough.

What she's doing with her hands is rapidly going to be enough to tip me right over the edge, though, and I gasp against her shoulder, tilting my hips to change the angle, then turning my head to whisper her name in her ear.

"Nate," Becca says, her voice deep and raw. "Would you really have bent me over the bed if I'd asked you to?"

My groan comes out more as a growl. "Roll over."

My body is fire. I turn over so I'm kneeling in front of Nate, feeling myself opening to him, that low pulsing back and stronger than ever, a constant beat of desire. There's movement behind me as he takes off his boxers and then suddenly he's right there between my thighs, not yet inside me but so close, and I let out another moan.

"Do we need a condom?" he asks.

The thought of him pulling away right now is unbearable, and I'm so glad that I can tell him this: "I'm on the pill, and I'm clean." The show made us take tests beforehand, so I know

185

that for sure.

"Me, too," he says, and then he enters me and fills me up and I groan at how incredible that feels. We both pause for this long, delirious moment, feeling the headiness of this, and then, as if we both can't wait a second longer, he thrusts at the same time I shift back, and we're moving against each other and completely together, hard and fast and glorious, lifting me higher and higher—

Oh my god, she feels *so good*. She clenches me tight, and we're moving faster and faster, fucking desperately like we've both been searching for this release since the moment we met, and I think maybe we have.

I love her, I realize. I knew it before, but I didn't want it to be true, not this gorgeous woman who wanted someone else. I've loved her for a while, I think, long before I realized what was happening, and being with her now feels so good and so right. Like something I've been waiting my entire life to find.

I'm suddenly hit by this wave of need to kiss her, to look her in the eyes, to connect. I slip out of her, and she lets out a groan like she doesn't want me to stop.

I don't mean to.

Nate draws back, and the ache pulls a low, pleading sound from me. I look back around, fear prickling under my skin. Wasn't he enjoying that? Does he not want to—

No, the expression on his face is still hungry.

"Come here," he says, his voice quiet but intense.

I do, because I don't want to be away from him. Not now. Not ever. He draws me onto his lap so I'm straddling his waist, my legs out behind him. His eyes are locked on mine, and I want so much to read love in that intensity—desperate, raw, everything kind of love. The kind that I know is in mine, because it's in every part of me.

*I love you*, I can imagine him saying. *I need you.*

Oh, how I love and need him too.

And then he enters me again, pushing into me so deep I see stars. No, not stars. Fireworks. Blues and reds and greens and yellows flashing in my vision, more beautiful than they've ever been before.

My eyes are closed, but I feel him lean against me, the heat of his chest pressed against mine, just an instant before we're kissing again. His lips taste like sex and salt and fire. I wrap my arms around his neck, our mouths crashing harder as he moves under me, thrusting with his hips, rocking me against him with his hands. The fireworks are brighter and bolder and loud in my ears, right alongside the sounds of rising pleasure, and then everything splits apart all over again, even stronger—

Bright. Blinding.

All-consuming bliss.

I never believed that being with someone could feel this true and right. But I should have known.

I should have known, because it's Nate.

# NINETEEN

## *Nate*

ecca trembles against me as I rock back on my hands, unable to stay upright. My muscles are weak with satisfaction, my heart filled to bursting. I still can't believe this is happening.

This is all I want, her and me, for the rest of my life. I can't imagine wanting anything more.

*I love you*, I want to tell her, but nothing kills a new relationship faster than premature declarations. If she's willing to give me a chance, she deserves the space to decide how she feels about me, to try this out and see if she can get there. I'm so damn lucky that she's here with me—she had Prince Charming kissing her tonight, and she wants *me*—that I'm not taking any chances.

Becca rests her head on my shoulder, her legs still locked around my waist. "Oh my god," she says, and I grin.

"Right?" I ask, and we both laugh, like we're lost in this incredible haze of just being together.

"This was definitely a good idea," she says as I run my hand up her back, holding her against me. "I am a badass, after all."

"Did you doubt it?"

"I did! I don't feel like one, except when I'm with you."

"Well, you are," I say. "Anyone can see it."

She looks up at me, and there's this sweetness to her expression, and I wonder if this is the first time I've seen her purely happy, without the nerves and the worries and the pressure.

At that moment, there's a knock on my door.

"Shit," I whisper, and Becca startles, rolling off my lap like we're teenagers who've gotten caught. Only we are fucking *adults* and there are *consequences* to getting caught here like this.

I move to the door and look through the peephole while Becca searches for her clothes. "It's Olivia," I whisper.

Becca looks like she's about to have a heart attack.

Olivia knocks on my door again. "Nate?" she calls.

*Fuck.*

I pick up Becca's panties and toss them to her, then grab my boxers and pull them on. "Hang on!" I yell to Olivia, then whisper to Becca, "Go in the bathroom and turn on the shower."

Becca looks confused. "Turn on the—"

"Trust me," I say, doing one last sweep of the room for articles of clothing that are not mine while I haul on my jeans.

I run a hand through my hair. The elastic band fell out at some point, but it fits with my story. I hear the shower start. I open the door without putting on my shirt. "Olivia," I say. "What do you need? I was just about to jump in the shower."

Olivia's face is flushed, and she seems unsteady. "No, you're not," she says. "You have to come down to the bar. You're missing everything. Levi is so happy, it's ridiculous."

I resist the urge to step into the hallway and shut the door behind me. *That* wouldn't fit with the story. "What's he so happy about?"

"You!" she says. "I mean, everyone, I guess. He gave Darlene a bonus just for breathing. But that date tonight went so well, and with the footage you got the other day, you're killing it, big time."

I want Olivia to shut up and go away, but what she's saying doesn't add up. "What do you mean the date went well? I thought he wanted Becca to talk about her husband, but she didn't, did she?"

Olivia waves a hand and the motion nearly knocks her over. She leans against the door frame. "No, but who cares? You already got her to admit what a douchebag her husband was, so they don't need her to say it in an interview. They'll just layer it over other crap, you know?"

My stomach sinks.

I . . . what? "When did I . . ."

She slaps me on the arm. "I can't believe you didn't tell me you got that! Anyway, Levi is ready to give you a big, fat bonus, so get your ass downstairs to the bar with the rest of us."

I'm not totally processing everything she's saying. My mind is still stuck on this: "I got her to admit . . ."

"That her husband was a dick to her! And wow, he really was. Shit." She stops and studies me. "Were you seriously trying to keep it a secret? Didn't want the rest of us to get jealous of your skills?"

"No," I say, rubbing the back of my neck. I probably have a raging case of sex hair—man, can it get out of control when it's teased—but Olivia doesn't seem to have noticed anything amiss. "I just . . . I didn't think they were able to get that on camera."

She shrugs. "Oh, yeah, Dustin says the actual footage is crap. Something about a balcony railing being in the way? But apparently Wilson got the whole thing with one of those bullet mics and Levi says the audio is gold, so good on you."

*Shit.* That's what happened. The cameras *did* follow us that night on the balcony, but they did it from a far enough distance that they wouldn't spook Becca. I'm surprised neither Dustin nor Wilson said anything to me, but they probably thought I planned the whole thing.

Which means all that stuff Becca told me in confidence, all those things she never wanted her girls or her in-laws or the world to know—

Oh, god.

The shower is on, but the door is cracked. I wonder if she's hearing all this, or if I'm going to have to be the one to tell her.

Olivia is still staring at me like she expects me to go downstairs with her, and maybe that would be a good thing, because it would give Becca an opportunity to sneak back to her room. But that's not happening, no way.

"Sorry, Liv," I say. "But I'm exhausted. I'm going to take that shower and get some sleep."

"Seriously? You're missing out. Levi gives better bonuses when he's wasted, and between this and you getting Londyn to open up about her daddy issues, you're pretty much the golden boy. You're so *good* with these girls, you know? You just smile that pretty smile and know exactly what to say, and they all trust you like you're their fucking priest. I should take lessons."

"Yeah, thanks," I say, but I'm already closing the door. Olivia stumbles back a few steps, and I think she's wasted enough that she's not going to remember the details of this encounter, much less be suspicious about them.

As I close the door, I'm no longer worried about getting caught. Because this is a thousand times worse: I told Becca she was safe, and she wasn't. She trusted me, and I let her talk when I knew it wasn't totally impossible we'd be recorded.

I let her down, and she's going to pay the price for it. I don't know how I'm ever going to make up for that.

I don't think there's any way I can.

# TWENTY

## Becca

I'm standing in a bathroom that is rapidly filling up with steam, but I'm frozen through. Only minutes ago, every part of me was fire, searing and brilliant and flickering up to the sky, and now I'm ice, encased in shock and dread.

They recorded it all. Every word.

And Nate . . . Nate . . .

The hotel door closes with that definitive snick and I'm backing up, feeling the tile on my bare feet, the way my heels bump against the tub. I'm cold and numb, and when I reach into the shower to turn it off, the hot water sprays across my skin like razor blades.

There's a second of deafening silence.

They recorded it all, and they're going to show it.

*You're so good with these girls.*

*They trust you.*

I trusted him, and he—

I can't think the words, they feel so clumped together.

In my other arm, I'm still clutching my clothes tight against my naked body. I didn't bother putting them on. When I first came in here, I thought I wouldn't need to—that Nate would get rid of Olivia and we'd go back to . . .

I'm not sure how I'm moving at all, but I am. I throw open

the bathroom door and I step out—

Nate's there at the doorway and I barrel right into him.

"Becks," he says, his eyes wide.

I make a noise like a wounded animal and shove past him.

He doesn't try to stop me. "Becks, I'm so sorry."

That nickname on his lips, the one I loved so much, the one he whispered in my ear, the one he moaned—it's a stab in my gut now. "They know everything," I manage. "Everyone will know. They'll hear me say—" I choke.

There's no ending to that. It's too awful.

He cringes. "I should have known better. I should never have encouraged you to talk to me when—"

"Really? Is that what happened?" My thoughts are separating from each other and crystallizing into hideous shapes. "Are you sure you didn't know those cameras were there?" My voice doesn't sound like me anymore—it's sharp and cutting.

I'm surprised it's not shaking, because my whole body is.

Nate looks like he's been slapped, and I immediately want to take it back. But—

*You smile that pretty smile and you know exactly what to say.*

He's so very good at his job. I've thought that so many times before.

He told Olivia that he didn't know they'd gotten the footage, but maybe because he already knew the shot was ruined. Or, more likely, he said that because he knew I was in the bathroom, listening. And it didn't seem to occur to Olivia that Nate didn't set the whole thing up himself. Because that's what the producers do. They get the drama.

"I didn't know, Becks. I promise. I never would have said that if I thought they were there." He runs his hands through his curly hair that just minutes ago was tangled in my fingers, that brushed against my cheek when he leaned close. My stomach turns, because I want so desperately to believe him, but I've been so dumb before, over and over.

I've believed when I never should have, because I was so

desperate to think I could be loved. That I could be *seen*. And instead I disappeared even more. Instead, I discovered that love was this shimmering mirage I couldn't reach.

And now I believed again. I thought I was there in that oasis, that it actually existed for me.

*What's wrong with you, Becca? So fucking naive. You wouldn't last a minute in the real world.* Rob was fond of that one.

Nate takes a step toward me, and I flinch back. I'm suddenly aware of how naked I am, how exposed, and I clutch the ball of clothes tighter to my chest.

Nate freezes, then lowers his arm. "I didn't know," he repeats. He squeezes his eyes shut. "But it's still my fault. I should never have assumed we wouldn't be recorded."

"I trusted you!" The words burst out of me, and he recoils. "I trusted you," I repeat, my voice lowered, because what if someone out there hears, and—

Oh my god, why am I still trying to protect his fucking job? The job he might have destroyed me for.

But did he? Can *Nate* really have done this?

Do I know him at all?

"I know," he says. "I know you trusted me, and I'm so sorry."

I don't feel the tears before they're running down my cheeks. "My in-laws are going to hear this. Paula and Kurt are going to hear me tell the world that their son was a terrible person. My girls—they're going to hear about everything Rob said to me." I'm hit with the worst of all, and I whimper. "They're going to hear their mother say she's relieved that their father is dead. They'll know how horrible I am."

"You're not horrible," Nate insists, taking a tiny step forward. "The way you said it, in context, it's completely understa—"

"You think they're going to show that in *context*?"

His mouth closes with a snap. "No. Probably not."

For years and years I hid this to protect myself. To protect the people I love. Years of watching every word I said about the terrible things Rob did to me, because others needed him to

194

be a good person. Because I was terrified that they'd know he was right.

Maybe I should be relieved that I don't need to hide anymore, but I'm not. I feel like my entire world is crashing down.

I sway on my feet.

"Becks." Nate's fingers brush my arm, trying to steady me, and I wrench away, my bare hip banging against the edge of the cheap hotel table.

"Don't touch me," I say. Suddenly I need my clothes on. I wanted more than anything for Nate to see me, all of me, and now I can't bear that he has. I pull up my pants, then shove my arms through my hoodie and have to shove them through again when I discover the sleeves are inside out.

How the hell did this show ever seem like a good idea? What the fuck was I thinking, coming to Nate's room and handing him my heart, which I'd kept locked up for years, long before Rob died. Locked up and cold and alone, but *safe*.

Nate makes a small, helpless noise, and it hurts to hear, because I'm in love with him and I can't just turn that off, even if it was built on lies. "Please," he says. His dark eyes shine with tears. "I didn't do this on purpose. Please believe me."

I want to. I still want to. Can he fake tears like that? Can he fake looking so stricken? Can he fake the way he made me feel when I was in his arms? The way he looked at me like I was the most precious thing in his world?

*So fucking naive, Becca,* Rob whispers in my head.

"I don't know that I can," I say. "How can I ever know for sure? I was manipulated for so long. I was sucked into believing someone loved me and then I was torn apart, piece by piece. Made to feel like I was being crazy, too sensitive, too weak. And he was *so* good at making people trust him. Making them feel like they were special. Until they weren't." I've finally managed to get my hoodie on. I didn't bother with my bra or underwear; I shove those into my pockets. "So how can I ever know that I can trust you? How can I know I'm not being manipulated all

195

over again?"

"If this was all for my job, what would I be getting out of this now?" Frustration punctuates each word. "You were going to leave the show."

"Sex? Maybe you're afraid I'm going to tell Levi about this? It could be anything. What did Rob ever get out of it? Some people just get off on controlling other people." I put my shaking hands up to my face. "I can't do it anymore, I can't . . ."

There's this long moment of quiet, and I know I should leave, I should just go, but I feel tethered to him.

I still want him to convince me, want him to prove it somehow. I still want *him*, more than anything. And I hate myself for it.

"What are you going to do?" he asks quietly.

I narrow my eyes. "I'm not going to tell anyone about this, if that's what you're asking." My heart thumps heavily, slowly, and I look down at the ground. "I know what this means for your career."

I can't take that away from him. Even if I had absolute proof that he'd used me.

"That's not what I meant," he says, and there's a desperate quality to his voice. "Can I contact you?" He bites his lower lip. "If you give me a chance, I'll prove that you can trust me."

My whole being feels racked. It's what I want, but—"People can pretend for a long time," I say, barely above a whisper.

"Are you still leaving the show?" he asks.

I want to. And I don't.

Do I leave with my tail between my legs, wait for them to air my shit all over the world? Do I run and hide?

The thought makes me furious, and the fury feels *good*, cutting through the hurt and fear and loss that are smothering me.

"You were the one who said that I don't strike you as a quitter," I say.

His expression darkens. "So you're just going to go back to dating *him*?"

I want to bark out the bitterest laugh, but there's no humor in any of this, even the bitter kind. I honestly wasn't even thinking about dating Preston when I said that. I'm not sure what that says about me, but whatever it is, it's not good.

None of this is good. No matter what I do.

"I don't know, Nate," I say honestly. "I really don't know."

There's this look of hurt on his face, and I can't bear wondering if it's real.

So I leave, and Nate doesn't try to stop me.

I peek out the door, see that the hallway is empty. I make my way out and down the hall, duck back when I see someone pass by the cross hall, and let out a small sigh of relief when it's only room service.

I don't care at this moment about being caught for myself. So they throw me off the show; they make that choice for me. Better than me slinking off.

But I still want to protect Nate. I think I'll always want to. I think I'll always want to believe, and I hate myself for it.

It's not even him I'm furious at. It's me. I trusted myself, my heart.

*What's wrong with you, Becca?*

I make my way back to my bedroom. Londyn's already in bed, sound asleep. The girl can sleep like the dead, but snores a hell of a lot louder.

I sit on the edge of my bed, feeling like I might shatter.

I have to hold it together. I have to try to make the best of this.

They're going to make me a victim with that footage. They only have the audio, and they'll use the worst pieces. No context. Just me as a weak, sobbing puddle. There's no way I can control what they release, no way to salvage Rob's reputation for my in-laws and the girls.

Thea may know some of it already, but I'd rather she—and Rosie—not find out the details that way.

If they're going to anyway, though, I want them to know me as a survivor. I want them to know me on my terms, as much as I can manage.

Which means I need to give the show what they want. I need to make the story *mine*.

The room is mostly dark, but I can see the outline of the journal on my desk. Pages and pages of dreams of a future with Nate. A future that, for a moment, I let myself believe I could have. But I'm too messed up for that. I'm too broken to know what I can trust and what I can't.

I'm too likely to get destroyed all over again.

Part of me wants to rip up every page, throw it in the trash. But I can't bring myself to do it, so I just curl up in my bed and cry.

# TWENTY-ONE

## Nate

I wake up to pounding on my door and in my head, which aches like a hangover, even though I haven't had anything to drink. I didn't get much sleep—*couldn't* sleep after Becca left, just played that whole clusterfuck over and over again in my mind, trying to figure out what I could have done better.

I could have done the right thing originally, told Becca that it's never safe to assume we're not on camera at an official event, maybe come up with some way to see her privately later. I was selfish; I wanted to know about her past for my own reasons. Because I'm in love with her.

I'm in love with her. And I fucked it all up.

Last night, though, I think there was nothing I could have said. Becca had her mind made up about me from the moment Olivia opened her mouth.

It's my own fault, but that only makes it hurt more.

The pounding resumes on my door. "Hang on!" I shout. I pull on my jeans and answer the door, for a second time, without a shirt on.

It's Darlene—the producer Olivia said got a bonus last night. "Get up," she says. "Becca's going to talk to Preston and you need to be there to interview her after."

"Yeah, okay," I say, and Darlene stalks away. The door closes.

This makes sense, really. Becca won't just leave. She'll need to tell Preston it's not working out, she's not feeling it, whatever she's going to say. I should be glad for that, but all I can think is how hard it's going to be not to see her every day.

How much it's going to hurt if she refuses my calls when she gets home, if she's *done* with me.

Not that I could blame her. It was my job to manipulate her. I'm still culpable in the whole mess. I was trying to protect her. I told her I'd watch her back, and I failed her, because you can't protect someone and work for the enemy at the same time.

Maybe *I* should quit. What does it matter if Levi suspects I'm leaving because of Becca? I'd be gone, and maybe I could convince Becca to see me when we're both back in LA. Maybe my apologies would have more weight if she knew for sure I wasn't still trying to protect my job.

I pull a clean t-shirt out of my suitcase and put it on. I need a shower, but I'll probably get time after the interview. I imagine the rest of the crew is going to slink back to their rooms to nurse their actual hangovers.

I'll do Becca's exit interview and then tell Levi I'm out. Technically I have a contract, but they can't enforce it. It would be better for my resume if I finished the season, but Becca is worth it.

Even if she never gives me another chance, I don't want to face being here without her.

I throw on my shoes and head out to find Darlene and the others. They're setting up a two-seat couch in one of the hotel rooms with portable lights and getting the cameras ready. Neither Becca nor Preston are here yet. I don't see Levi anywhere. I wonder if he's still in bed.

"Here," Darlene says, giving me a headset. "We don't want to crowd them while they talk, but you can listen in so you know what to ask in her interview."

I step out into the hall in time to see Becca approaching with one of the other producers escorting her. She's put together, wearing makeup and a pair of jeans with a shirt that falls off her shoulder. She looks beautiful as ever, but I almost don't recognize her—I've never seen that expression on her face before, somewhere between suspicion and regret.

I stand against the wall as she passes, and she doesn't acknowledge me. I wonder if the others think that's strange—we've always been friendly before. Inside, I hear Darlene coaching Becca about where to sit and which way to face, fitting her with her mic pack.

"Thank you," Becca says over the headset.

I close my eyes.

Is this how it's going to be now? We can't even talk? I wonder if she's going to let me interview her, or if she'll request someone else and then go quietly home and never speak to me again. I wonder if last night meant anything to her, if she felt even a fraction of what I felt while we were making love, the connection and the depth and the sheer happiness.

I wish I knew what to say to make her look at me like that again, like someone she wants. But I know how hurt she is, and really, with her secret inevitably going to be revealed to the world, this isn't about me.

I'm being selfish again.

Footsteps approach, and I open my eyes to see Preston coming up the hallway with Levi at his side. Levi looks a little worse for wear, but he's awake, at least. Darlene comes out and fits Preston with his mic pack, then sends him in and closes the door.

"Becca!" Preston says. "I heard you wanted to talk."

"Yes." Her voice is even, and if I didn't know her so well, I'd never be able to tell she's nervous. "Thank you for taking the time to see me."

"Of course," he says.

Levi stands outside the door, and he motions me closer. "Do you know what this is about?" he asks in a low voice, clearly irritated. It's important to Levi that he's always aware of what's going on, always in control.

I'm pretty sure I do know what this is about, but I shake my head. My involvement isn't going to help Becca's situation or mine.

Levi puts his headset on, listening. The headsets are wireless and have a decent range, so I pace down the hall a ways so Levi can't watch me react. I look out a window that faces into the hotel gardens. A sprinkler is watering the grass so it sparkles in the early morning light.

"I don't know how to talk about this," Becca says, "so I'm just going to come out and say it."

"Go ahead," Preston says.

I hold my breath, waiting for her to tell him that she's leaving, that she doesn't feel a connection with him, that it's not fair to him or the other women for her to stay through the tiara ceremony.

"I lied to you about my husband," she says. "I lie to everyone about him, but I think it's time for me to tell you the truth."

A chill washes over me. Becca sounds so confident, so steady, and maybe a little resigned.

I see what she's doing. She's going to tell the story on her own terms before she goes.

"Okay." Preston sounds uncertain, now, and a little off-kilter, which is unusual for him. He's pretty good at keeping his composure, even when all the women are losing it.

"Rob and I didn't have a good relationship. What I told you about him being a good father was true. He loved his girls with all his heart. But as a husband, he was critical and hurtful. He told me all the time how incapable I was, how unfit to be a mother and a wife. It seemed like I could never do anything right." Her voice trembles, but she quickly steadies it. This is nothing like when she told me, crying and curled into a ball.

She's hidden these things for so long, yet here she is, saying them out loud with confidence, like she's not the least bit afraid. I know that must be an act, but I'm impressed and proud of her all the same.

"Wow," Preston says. "That must have been difficult."

It's the understatement of the century. Becca is the fucking war hero.

"It was," she says. "I didn't want to lie about it, but I've tried so hard to preserve my girls' memories of their father. Rosie hardly remembers him, but she knows him from stories and pictures. Thea remembers him well, and I never wanted her to feel like the father who loved her wasn't real. He was. It just isn't *all* he was."

"That makes sense." Preston hesitates for a second. "What made you decide to tell me now?"

I bite my lip, staring out at the sprinkler pivoting back and forth. She's telling him because she knows now that she has to, because she wants to own the narrative. But she can't tell him that. I wonder how she'll—

"I had a wonderful time yesterday," she says. "And this morning I realized that I need to be honest with you, if I'm really going to give this relationship a chance."

What? *No.* Did she say—

"Because relationships can't grow in secrecy. They depend on the truth."

Those words feel like a dagger aimed right for my heart, and I think maybe that's how she meant them.

"Thank you," Preston says. "For being open to this process and brave enough to tell me this. You're an incredible woman."

I press my fingers to the glass, waiting, praying she's going to tell him that she can't stay.

But no. She just told him she wants to give their relationship a chance.

Damn it. She's not leaving. This was what I was afraid of last night, that she's just going to go back to dating *him* like what happened between us was nothing to her.

Like *I'm* nothing to her.

I can't breathe. I feel like I'm suspended in water, hearing everything thick and slow.

"Thank you," Becca says. "It's not easy to talk about, but I'm going to try. I don't want to lie anymore. I want you to know who I really am."

My hands are shaking, and I barely hear the rest of their pleasantries. Preston doesn't ask any meaningful questions and Becca doesn't offer any more details. She knows they already have those, but now she's given them some better footage, a way to reveal her secret on her terms. I'm still impressed with her for doing this—I know how hard it must have been.

But the other message keeps ringing in my ears.

*Relationships can't grow in secrecy.*

*I don't want to lie anymore.*

*I'm really going to give this relationship a chance.*

No one else will have heard it, but she couldn't be any more clear.

She's done with me. She's choosing him. And I guess I can't blame her. He's Prince Charming, after all, and I'm the asshole who hurt her.

I'm not seeing the garden anymore, or the glass, only the image of Becca's face last night when she first came into my room. *I have feelings for you*, she said, and like an idiot, I filled in the gaps. I hoped she felt the way I do, but if she did, she wouldn't be able to push me aside so easily.

"Nate," Levi says from behind me, and I startle and spin around, probably looking guilty as hell. "Becca wants a minute to compose herself and then you can interview her."

"Of course," I say.

So she's not going to request someone else. She's going to make me go in there and ask her how she feels about what she just did, and what she thinks it means for her relationship to Preston.

I could ask someone else to do it, but Levi is already looking at me like he notices something's off.

More importantly, I *want* to talk to Becca, even if I can't ask what I really want to know: *How could you do this to me?*

"You ready?" Levi asks.

"Yeah. Still waking up, I guess."

Levi smiles at me and claps me on the shoulder, a habit of his that I hate. "Aren't we all," he says, then turns to where Preston is being ushered into another hotel room to be interviewed.

He's still wearing his mic pack, so I hear the beginning of his interview through the headset.

"Wow," he says. "That was, wow. After our date yesterday, I knew she was incredible, but I had no idea she'd been through something like that."

I squeeze my eyes shut. Their date yesterday, the one she said she spent wishing was with *me*.

"I've overlooked Becca," Preston says. "I'm so glad she's still here. I feel like I'm only now starting to get to know her, but on our date yesterday—I knew then that she was someone I could fall in love with. She's just so *different* from the others. I'm going to give her a tiara this week, for sure."

I look up at the ceiling. Of *course* he is. He hasn't chosen her any other week, and now that Levi has his footage, he's not going to insist that Preston keep her. I've been wishing all this time that Becca would go home so that I could have a chance with her, and now I probably won't, either way.

She's going to stay here and date Preston, and he's going to keep her because he's only now waking up to what he's been missing.

"I can't believe I didn't see how wonderful she is," he continues. "She's been right here, right under my nose, all along."

I tear off my headset, resisting the urge to throw it against the wall.

"Nate," Darlene calls from down the hall. "Becca's almost ready for you."

The fuck she is. Becca's made her choice, and what am I supposed to do now? I could still quit, but for what? She's not going to give me a chance, not going to listen to a damn word I have to say. She was a wreck last night, and I understood, but I hoped she'd give me at least one more chance to explain.

But no. She's back on the show, and I'm back to being the producer who gets a front row seat to watch her chase a happily ever after.

Just not with me.

Fuck.

I can't do this. I can't.

But what's the alternative? Quit and go home with nothing? No chance with her, no credit for my resume, *nothing?* Pretend this never happened?

As if I ever could.

"Nate?" Darlene calls again.

"Coming," I respond. Darlene barely acknowledges me as she makes sure the camera is ready.

I should go. I know I should. There's nothing for me here except resume fodder, and it's not going to be worth watching this.

But if I leave now, I'll never see her again.

So I take a deep breath and walk into the hotel room where I'll do my goddamn job and interview Becca like nothing ever happened between us.

If that's the way she wants it, *fine.* She can have what she wants.

I'll stay and let her twist the knife.

# TWENTY-TWO

## Becca

I'm standing in the hotel bathroom, trying to breathe deeply. I washed my hands several minutes ago and turned off the water, but I'm still holding onto the faucet handles to keep my hands from shaking.

Which is ridiculous. Telling Preston about Rob went fine. I told the story on my own terms, recited it word for word the way I planned in the pre-dawn hours. I was able to say it in a calm, composed way, I think. Definitely different than the way I told it on that balcony, my whole heart bleeding out. Wanting someone—no, not just someone, *Nate*—to know the real me.

This was the truth, but it wasn't the real me. Which is better; I've learned my lesson on that.

I stare at myself in the mirror. My blue eyes look empty. There are dark smudges from lack of sleep under them that I was only mostly able to cover with concealer. They aren't nearly as bloodshot as they were a few hours ago, and the puffiness has died down. There are no tears brimming over.

I don't imagine it's going to stay that way. But I'm hell-driven to keep them like this in front of other people. In front of the camera.

In front of Nate.

Who will likely be the one interviewing me as soon as I can extricate myself from the bathroom. If he wasn't listening when I was talking to Preston, he certainly knows by now about my decision to stay. It was a decision I wavered on throughout the night—can I bring myself to stay and have to face all these people who know this huge secret about me? Can I bring myself to slink back home in shame? Can I force myself to deal with the hurt of seeing Nate every day?

Can I leave and never see him again?

I peel my hands off the faucets. They're trembling, but not outright shaking; that's a good sign. I need to get out of here or they're going to send Darlene or Olivia in after me. I told them I just needed to use the restroom and then I'd be ready for the follow-up interview. I'll answer Nate's questions about Preston and me and wonder if Nate really did use and manipulate me. If he felt anything like I did last night. If I was just being stupid and naive.

Will he be genuinely hurt by my choice to stay? Will he act hurt to keep up the charade? Some combination of both?

My mind is clouded by doubt, cluttered with questions I can't sort through—every time I think I've come to a conclusion, another one pops up, and I'm even more confused.

*Of course you are, Becca*, I can hear Rob say snidely. I thought I had mostly exorcised his voice, but it's getting stronger now as the show goes on.

And maybe that was the deciding factor to stay—I can't give Rob the satisfaction. I'm doubtful I'll last the week anyway. Even if Preston was moved by my tragic tale, I've seen him with the other girls. He has more chemistry with every one of them, and from the girls' various bragging about their time with him, I know he's done a lot more than a chaste end-of-date kiss with each one.

So I'm guessing he'll send me home this week or next, and I can leave with my pride intact. I didn't quit. It just didn't work out.

And maybe, if he doesn't send me home . . . maybe there

*could* be something there. I don't feel it, but I've been so wrapped up in Nate, fell so hard for him, that it's not like I've given Preston an actual chance. Clearly, my intuition isn't something I should trust. It never has been.

I blink at myself one last time in the mirror. I look put together enough. I can keep myself from breaking down in front of Nate. I can keep him from seeing the pain that makes it hard to breathe, hard to think, hard to move.

Darlene knocks on the door.

"Becca!" she calls with her trademark sweet, motherly tone, which manages to hide her shark-like ability to sense blood in the water. "You ready for the interview?"

"Yeah." Because I am. I have to be.

"Great. Nate's waiting for you."

Just the mention of his name knifes my heart, but I paste on a tight smile and open the bathroom door. I return to the padded ottoman in front of the decorative folding screen (the show seems to really like those) and, of course, lit candles. Nate's standing next to the cameraman, his posture stiff. He turns and looks at me, stone-faced; expressionless. But those eyes . . .

I see hurt there, what looks like real pain, and my chest squeezes in. Maybe this *is* killing him the way it's killing me.

Maybe he wasn't lying. Or maybe I'm desperate for his feelings to have been real. Maybe I'm just desperate to believe.

I'm swimming in maybes, and I can't let myself drown. I have to build up walls again, create a protective dam so thick not a drop can squeeze through.

"Have a seat," he says coldly.

I sit on the ottoman and try to reflect the stone-faced look right back at him.

"So, Becca," he says. "What made you decide to tell this to Preston today?" There's the tiniest emphasis on the word "today."

Because I had to seize control of a story I never wanted to tell at all. Because the man I thought I had a connection with used my pain to further his fucking career and I just found out about it last night, that's why.

My anger is back, and that's good. I can use that. "I told him today," I say, very carefully and deliberately restating the question, "because I knew I couldn't hide it any longer. On a journey to love, it's important to be honest and straightforward."

Nate's jaw tightens. Probably pissiness at getting called out, at getting caught with his pants down (literally). I force myself to believe it's that.

"Makes sense," he says flatly. "So would you say your feelings for Preston have changed since yesterday?" He clears his throat. "Since your date, I mean."

The cameraman gives him an odd look, and I remember the last time I noticed the camera crew looking at Nate oddly during an interview—when we were joking about muffins. Flirting, the sexual tension thick in the air.

This is so very far from that. Even if I still remember the way my body felt against his; even if I know I'll never forget the way he moved inside me, the way his tongue traced along my most sensitive parts.

I don't doubt that the sexual tension was real for him, too. But wanting to bang someone doesn't necessarily equate to real feelings.

It doesn't equate to love. Another lesson I should have learned a long time ago.

I realize the silence has stretched on too long. I need to answer the question.

"The date yesterday was a pivotal moment for me," I say with a tacked-on smile, though I know the words sound as flat as his are. "I'm really looking forward to seeing where this journey will take us."

It wasn't exactly an answer to the question, but I've said "journey" now twice within two answers, so Levi will probably be happy. If I talk about feeling "like I've finally found my prince," or how "I'm starting to believe in happily-ever-afters," he'd throw Nate an effing parade.

I'm not inclined to go that far.

"What would getting this week's tiara mean to you?" He's asked this question in almost every interview—I'm pretty sure it's a requirement. But he's never said it with this snide little edge to it before.

Which makes my hackles rise further. "I believe that getting this week's tiara would mean that Preston also wants to see where this relationship can go. I believe it would mean that he has real feelings for me." I put a tiny emphasis on the "real" the way he did before with "today."

Nate looks down at his knees, and I notice that his hands are gripping them tightly. "I think that's good for now, Becca," he says, not looking back up.

I'm taken aback. These interviews can stretch on for hours sometimes—though it never felt too long when I was with Nate.

Is he really hurt? And if so, does that mean he didn't betray me? Does that mean he feels—

"Town-crier's about to show up," he says, by way of explanation. "So you should go join the others."

Shame creeps in, for starting to let my guard down. "Right. Sure," I say and head toward to the suite that's been set apart for the show.

My face burns the whole way, because I still want to believe in Nate. I never felt about Rob the way I feel about Nate, not even in the very beginning.

Back then, I did trust Rob. He wasn't always awful to me, and I trusted that he loved me, that he always would. He was so good at making that seem real to me, until he didn't have to anymore. By the time we got married, I already knew that was never true and would never be true, but I went with it anyway because I thought it was all I deserved. My therapist says that I felt like negative attention was better than none. That I felt like being with someone was inherently better than being alone—and I was wrong.

Nate isn't Rob, I know that. Not even close. Not even if he did use me and exploit my pain, he could never be Rob.

But if he didn't use me, if what I felt from him was real . . . does it even matter? Can I ever really trust someone when I can't even trust myself?

I sit down with the other girls, who were summoned here too. There are six of us left, and they're talking about who they think will get the next date, as the cameras shoot us from every angle.

Daisy looks bored, picking at her nail polish—she already had her one-on-one earlier this week. My name's not going to be on the scroll, either, for that same reason. Which leaves the other four—Addison, Madison, Londyn, and Sheree—all saying they're sure it's going to be a group date and pretending to be really excited about that.

I eye Londyn. I know she also has a crush on Nate, and according to Olivia, he got her to open up about things she was holding back. Is he building a relationship with her, too? What would have happened if Londyn had been the one to show up at his room?

*Stop, Becca. Stop stop stop.*

Luckily, Bartholomew enters, scroll in hand. And this time, walking next to him is host Swiss Barrington, who we usually don't see much other than at the tiara ceremonies.

"Ladies," he says, flashing that wide, pearly Swiss Barrington smile. "I hope you're enjoying your time with Preston in Germany."

There are a few half-hearted "woooo"s; Daisy preens.

Then Swiss turns deadly serious, in that instant mood shift he does. "You're about to hear the final date for this week, and it won't be long before the next tiara ceremony. I don't think I have to remind you how very important this next ceremony is. The four women who move on will introduce their families to Preston."

He claims he doesn't need to remind us, but that's clearly all he's here for, because then he indicates for Bartholomew to read the date scroll. Meanwhile, the other women sit on the edge of the couch even more tensely than normal, as if hit hard by Swiss's words. They've been talking nonstop the last few days about the importance of the family visit week.

Bartholomew does his grand announcement of what is, in fact, a group date. But it turns out to be a group date of three: Madison, Sheree, and Londyn.

They cheer and rush off to get ready, and Addison looks like she's going to explode from sheer rage. Instead she channels it into doing a set of furious crunches right there on the lobby floor—which, if that's her strategy, no wonder she lives in crop tops and bikinis.

"It's so frustrating," she says, huffing out short breaths between crunches. "I don't think any of them are here for the right reasons."

I slump back on the couch and wonder if any of us are, really. I'm not sure I know what that means anymore.

# TWENTY-THREE

## *Becca*

Preston gives me a tiara at the next ceremony—which Swiss reminds us yet again was "a very important tiara ceremony"—and sends both Sheree and Daisy home. Sheree is pissed as hell and refuses to "take a moment and bid farewell" to any of us, including Preston.

But the real drama comes from Daisy. We're all stunned when Preston doesn't choose her, given that they had a super romantic date at the Neuschwanstein Castle.

Daisy is the most stunned of all, and in a move which will surely go down in *Chasing Prince Charming* history, has a total meltdown right there on the courtyard steps. Like, full-on toddler-level wailing and weeping and becoming a boneless puddle of chiffon and melodrama. She whines that Preston could only be sending her home because she was framed for sabotaging our dresses (an incident I think Preston has long forgotten) and that he never really gave her a chance and how the producers never let her go to a salon to get a facial treatment and if they had, she might not have this gigantic zit on her chin (which I couldn't see even when she pointed it out). She also wails about how unfair it is that men always go for "the old women," which is aimed directly at me and also not a generalization I've ever heard before. She decides she's going to lie down on the steps and die, and it takes a combination of Preston trying to talk to her, then Swiss, then Preston again, then several producers, then finally a threat that she'll be carried out by security, before she at last gets to her feet and stumbles into the waiting carriage.

At one point during this, Nate and I exchange one of those looks of shock and amusement that we used to send each other on the regular. Then it's as if we both remember that this isn't part of our relationship anymore, and he looks away.

I feel gutted all over again.

The next several days, as the contestants and crew fly to our next location in Normandy, France, and get settled in the hotel to begin the round of family visit dates, I hardly see Nate at all. Since I can't control which producers I interact with—short of specifically requesting not to be interviewed by Nate, which would be too suspicious—it seems obvious that he's avoiding me.

Because he's hurt?

Because it's not worth keeping up the facade anymore?

Because the only reason he was spending time with me was to get my secrets on tape, and now that it's done, there's not really a point?

I shuttle back and forth between these and other possibilities. The knot in my mind becomes even more tangled. But the thing I can't deny is how much I miss him. Not only the touch of his skin against mine or the way he whispered my name when we made love. Not only the all-consuming passion of that night, which I already know I'll never feel again with anyone else, not like that. Those memories are intense, crushing. But it's more than that. I miss seeing him grin at me. I miss us communicating without words at the crowded cocktail parties. I miss the bits of sign he would do just for me. I miss hearing him call me "Becks." I miss laughing together, the way our conversations felt like the most natural thing in the world, no matter what we were talking about.

I miss the man I'm desperately in love with, but he wasn't

just that. He was also my best friend, and I miss that man, too.

I think so often of seeking him out. Telling him that I love him. Begging him to tell me the truth and agreeing that I'll trust him now if he says again that he didn't know about the cameras.

But every time I almost take that step, fear seizes me, clamping down on my heart. Fear that I still can't trust myself or anyone, because that was a part of me broken a long time ago. Fear that I'll open myself up and he'll confess that he never did feel strongly for me, after all. Fear that he did, but he doesn't anymore and I've ruined the only chance I'll ever have at love and lost my best friend in the process.

I can't tell him, so I write all these things in that stupid journal—every conflicting thought and worry. My therapist has always recommended I keep a journal, and I've made several half-hearted attempts in the past. Turns out what I really needed was a shattering heartbreak and complete lack of access to mind-numbing TV and Ben and Jerry's New York Super Fudge Chunk.

It's becoming increasingly difficult to mask the details surrounding "P," but I do my best anyway. Most likely, anyone who reads this will think I've cracked under the dating show pressure and am writing one of those crazy stream-of-consciousness manifestos that will be used as evidence if I snap and sew bottom halves on all of Addison's shirts so I don't have to see her perfectly toned stomach anymore.

It's a good thing it's family visit week. I need this, desperately.

For today's date, I'm going to meet Preston—and my family!—at the nearby Mont Saint-Michel, which is breathtaking even from a distance. It's a castle atop a hill on a tidal island. It's low tide in the channel now, which means the castle is surrounded by sand rather than looking like it's floating in a glittering sea, but there's a majestic look to the sand and marsh, too.

The limo takes me—and the camera guy and Mustache Dan—right up to the walled edge of the town that surrounds the castle. I see Preston in his usual princely outfit, with several cameras already filming.

Preston grins as I emerge from the limo, and I smile back, though I'm far more excited to see my family.

I'm trying, though, to be more open to the idea of dating Preston. That was the point of me coming on the show, right?

He gives me a hug and tells me how excited he is for today, and I can truthfully say the same back. Especially when I hear Rosie squeal, "Mommy, look, it's a real castle!" from behind me, and Rosie and Thea come running toward me like they did back in Germany. I hug them, tears running down my cheeks.

Behind them come Paula and Kurt, at a much slower speed, but grinning all the same. Normally Paula's brown hair is streaked with gray, but she's clearly had it dyed since the show and cut in a cute bob that looks great on her. She's also wearing what I'm pretty sure is a new outfit, since I have never in my life seen her wear a silk blouse. Kurt, however—a stocky guy whose hair has been mostly gray since his late twenties—hasn't done a single thing to his appearance and is wearing socks and sandals with his ever-present cargo shorts.

God, I love these two.

I run to meet them, practically launching myself at Paula.

"Oh, honey," she says after our hug, pulling back and putting her hands on my cheeks. "It is so good to see you."

"You too, Mom." I started calling them Mom and Dad soon after Rob and I got married, though they'd been trying to get me to do so for much longer. I was hesitant, though. Could they really mean it?

But it became easier and easier, and they never once seemed to regret offering me that gift.

Will they regret it once they know what I've said about their real child on TV?

Will they even believe me?

Kurt wraps me in a big hug, too, and then the two of them turn to greet Preston, who's waiting behind us with a nervous smile.

"Mr. Hale," he says and shakes Kurt's hand, then bows a bit

to Paula. "Mrs. Hale. It's such a pleasure to meet you."

I can tell instantly that Paula is taken with him; she flushes and fluffs her hair.

"It's quite an honor to meet Prince Charming," she gushes.

Kurt eyes Preston skeptically. "We hope you've been treating our daughter well."

"He's been great," I say, to spare Preston the interrogation—for the moment, at least. I have no doubt that will come later. Though it doesn't escape me that Kurt may not be the best judge of who will treat me well.

"I want to see the castle!" Rosie shrieks happily, running around us in circles.

Preston laughs. "Well, let's go. Do you know that we're getting a private tour today?"

I don't think Rosie particularly cares how private the tour is, but she cheers anyway.

"Hi, Thea," Preston says with a wave.

Thea smiles and waves back, but it's fake. She keeps looking around at the crew, clearly seeking out Nate. She has a different interpreter today—a young woman who can't be more than nineteen or twenty.

It also doesn't appear that Preston has bothered to learn any sign. I mean, I know the guy's busy dating all these women and is probably even more exhausted than the rest of us, but it wouldn't take much. Just a couple minutes on YouTube.

Nate was busy too, and he figured it out.

I try to push that aside for now. It's another thing to examine to death in my journal later. Right now, I'm going to enjoy my family and a date with a nice guy and the fact that we're all together in France.

Neither my in-laws nor the girls had traveled outside the US before the show. I hadn't either. Rob was never stationed overseas except when he deployed, and with money being so tight and then my restaurant dreams, I never thought I'd get the chance. This show may be slowly driving me insane, but this is definitely a perk.

Before we're able to go past the walls and into the quaint little town surrounding the castle, the producers pull everyone aside for interviews. When Kurt and Paula are being jointly interviewed, and Preston is listening to Rosie go on and on about that horse she's still pretty sure he has, Thea tugs at my hand.

"Where's Nate?" she asks.

I suck in my lips. "He's not with the crew today."

Her brow furrows. "Why not? And why did they have someone else with us before we left the hotel?"

Shit. I can already tell Thea isn't going to let this go. But I'm not going to discuss it with her right here around all the producers and cameras.

"I think they switch who does what job," I say carefully. "But we can talk more later, okay?"

Her green eyes squint at me and then she nods. "Okay."

It's not a bullet I can dodge for long, but at least this gives me time to plan what I'm going to say to her. Because I can't let her keep hoping I'm going to end up with Nate. She's already too attached to the idea.

God knows I was.

We spend the morning touring the castle, which is a functioning abbey where a few dozen monks and nuns live and worship. It's got this austere beauty—lots of muted stone and soaring, arched columns reaching up to the heavens. It's awe-inspiring and humbling all at once.

I'm a little disappointed when it's time to leave. We walk around the town, which is adorable and looks every bit the picturesque French village I'd hoped for, and we sit and eat at a place called Crêperie La Cloche, which has crepes so good I try to remember every taste and texture so I can replicate them at home. The kids, tired from all the stairs at the abbey, perk up at the crepes, and the crew eagerly watches as Kurt and Paula grill Preston.

Preston handles it like a champ. His answers are smooth and

considered and exactly the kind of thing parents would want to hear. Which, for some reason, bothers me. Not that I want them to dislike him, but . . .

Maybe part of me does. Maybe part of me wants to be told this isn't right, because I know I can't trust my own gut on anything.

*So fucking naive, Becca.*

We leave the city and go back to the beach that surrounds the town when the tide's gone out. More interviews, in which I talk about how great it is for my in-laws to get to know Preston, how great he is with them, how great the day is, all so *great*. Rosie plays by the wet sand and at one point manages to catch a toad, which she brandishes with glee. "Look, Mommy! A frog! You should kiss it!"

Everyone laughs, and the producers are no doubt ecstatic about how cute this will be on screen, especially as Paula says, "Well, hopefully she's found her prince already," and Preston gives me a big grin, which I attempt to return, even as I'm realizing I'm going to have to make that stupid kissing frogs joke in an interview, after all. Thanks, Rosie.

It's mid-afternoon when we return to the hotel. The producers are giving us some downtime to rest and get changed before we meet Preston for dinner. Paula gushes about how much she likes Preston, and Kurt grudgingly agrees that he seems like "a decent guy," but I think they're finally starting to notice that things aren't quite right with me.

When they're pulled into yet another interview in the lobby, I take the girls to use the bathroom. Rosie oohs and ahhs at the golden faucets and the decorative tile, but Thea wastes no time.

"Did Nate ask you on a date?"

I sigh. "He can't, remember? I'm on the show, and he works for the show."

"Will you go on a date when you get back home?"

I close my eyes briefly, trying to steady myself with a deep breath. Then I open them again. "I don't think I can date Nate."

"Why not? He likes you. He didn't say he *didn't* want to kiss you," she repeats from our last conversation on the subject, as if that's proof enough. "And I know you like him."

I'm not going to deny that.

Fortunately, Rosie's gone into a stall, so she isn't paying attention. "I'm not sure if he liked me for real," I say, trying to be as careful as possible. "Not, like, in a dating way."

She frowns. "Do you mean he was just pretending to want to date you? Was he just pretend nice?" She clearly hates this idea, and for the record, so do I. More than she could ever know.

"I don't know," I say honestly, then cringe. "I don't think he was being pretend nice with you and Rosie. He really likes you guys."

Thea brushes that aside. Either it's so obvious it doesn't bear examination or there are more important fish to fry here. "I don't think he was pretending to like you. Did he *say* he doesn't?" Her eyes widen. "Did you try to kiss him and he said no?"

I gape. I'm definitely not going into the details of what happened when I tried to kiss him, or how very much he did not say no. "It's not that, but he did something that really hurt me."

"Did he say he was sorry?"

I press my lips together, remembering him pleading with me. I feel like I'm breathing shards of glass every time I think about that night. "He did. But I don't know if I can believe him. I don't know if he means it. So I can't date him." I feel the tears burning my eyes. "I'm sorry, Thea."

She raises her hands like she's going to say something else, but then drops them again, frowning at herself in the mirror. Her cheeks are a bit pink from the sun, even though Paula put sunscreen on her twice.

She turns back to me. "Where's Nate?"

Crap. "I don't know. I just got here, too, remember?"

"I need to talk to him."

"Thea, you don't need to—"

"I need to talk to him." Then she pulls a folded piece of

notebook paper out of her pocket, on which she writes, *Where is Nate??*

"Thea," I say, but she waves me off and marches out of the bathroom. I poke my head after her, because Rosie in still in the stall. Thea points the note at Mustache Dan, who looks startled and indicates down a hallway to where the production crew is stationed. I try to get her attention again, but Thea takes off without a backward glance. Honestly, I'm too emotionally exhausted to give chase.

I wish I had the courage to go with her.

# TWENTY-FOUR

## *Nate*

Avoiding Becca is easier the week of the family visits, because there are so many people to be shuttled around and kept separate, so all the producers are scattered. It should feel like a relief but it doesn't, because I miss her with this constant ache that never goes away. I would have missed her if she went home, of course, but maybe then I could have called her.

Not that she would have wanted to hear from me. She's made it quite clear that I was a mistake she doesn't care to repeat. I wish my brain would get with the program and stop conjuring memories at the oddest times, stop running through our one glorious moment together on constant repeat in my dreams.

If my heart wasn't so tender over it, I might have broken my one-night-stand rule and found someone willing to help me work out the tension, but I don't want anyone but Becca.

Becca, on the other hand, apparently now wants Preston. Good for her, I guess. He made good on his vow to keep her another week. Maybe he'll keep her all the way to the end and they'll get married and live happily ever after.

*It's fine*, I tell myself.

But, of course, it isn't. So, on the day Preston and Becca are spending time with her kids and her in-laws, I'm hiding in the production suite, checking on the flights of Addison's parents and siblings who are due to arrive tonight.

The door to the suite is propped open, and I don't see Thea come in until she's standing right in front of me. She's got a sign in her hand that says *Where is Nate??*, which I'm guessing she flashed at the other producers until someone pointed her in my direction. There's no interpreter in sight.

"Hey, Thea," I sign at her. I still don't know much, but I can say that.

Thea is glaring at me, and I wonder if she's mad that I wasn't assigned to keep the girls company this time. I was, but then I asked Olivia to do it, making an excuse about not being good with kids.

Thea pulls out a notepad with the hotel logo on it and starts scribbling. Then she thrusts it at me.

*What did you do to my mom?!* it says.

Oh, god. So many things. None of which I'm going to discuss with her. I take the paper and pen, motioning for her to sit down in one of the other chairs at the little breakfast table. Thea plops down as I write, *The show found out the truth about your dad, and it was my fault—but I didn't do it on purpose.* I follow this with a row of frowning faces and hand the paper back to her.

Thea looks down at the paper and then up at me. *They know?* she writes.

I nod at her, then add, *Your mom is handling it very well, though. It's going to be okay.*

Thea's brow furrows at the paper, and then she sets the pad on the table, sheltering it with her arm as she writes like she's afraid I'll cheat off her answers.

I sigh and push the laptop away. No one has shown up looking for Thea, so I guess we're doing this, then.

*I asked her if you're pretend nice or real nice, and she says she doesn't know anymore,* Thea has written when she shoves the pad back at me. *Which one is it?*

I'm not going to pretend to be an asshole just so that Becca can feel better about herself. *I didn't pretend,* I write.

*But you told about my dad?* Thea asks.

I shake my head. *No. I told your mom there were no cameras, so she thought she could talk to me about it. It turned out there were cameras, but I didn't know they were there. I shouldn't have told her it was safe when it wasn't, but I didn't do it on purpose.*

My handwriting is even messier than usual, and Thea squints at it, but she seems to understand.

*Did you tell her you loooooove her?* Thea writes.

Shit. I didn't. And I'm not about to now. Instead of writing a response, I give Thea a skeptical look, which she seems to correctly read as a no. I grab the paper from her and add, *I think she likes Preston now.*

Oh my god. I am now passing notes about my sad, disintegrated love life with a ten-year-old. I am back in fourth grade.

*I don't think so,* Thea responds. *She still likes you. She can't like him, too.*

I draw a sharp breath and try not to take that too seriously. Did Becca *tell* Thea she still likes me? Probably not. Probably Thea is just inferring. She might be a really sharp kid, but she can still be wrong.

She was invested in Becca and me. She's seeing what she wants to see.

*A person can like two people,* I write. *But I don't think she likes me anymore.*

Thea frowns and scribbles quickly, though her handwriting still comes out small and neat. *Do YOU like two people?*

Oh my god. *I'm not dating Prince Charming!*

Thea rolls her eyes. *I think she's just doing that for the show.*

*Maybe,* I answer. I'm about ready to go out in the hall and flag someone down who knows what room Becca is in right now. It's a little odd that she didn't chase Thea down, but maybe she's in an interview.

Or maybe she *really* doesn't want to see me.

*Do you think it will be okay that my mom told about my dad?* Thea asks. *I don't think grandma and grandpa will be happy.*

She looks up at me like she actually wants my opinion on this, when I met her grandmother for a total of, like, three minutes.

*How do you think your grandparents will react?* I write.

*I think they will cry,* Thea writes immediately. *They still cry a lot about my dad.*

I bet they do. Asshole or not, he was their son.

*Your mom is strong,* I write. *And so are you. It will be okay.*

Thea squints at me. *You should tell her that. And that you love her.*

Gah. This girl does not give up. Kind of like her mom, when she wants something.

Too bad it turned out she doesn't want me.

*Maybe your mom will be happier with Preston,* I write. *You should give him a chance.*

Thea's face turns into a storm cloud. I take it Preston did not make a good impression. *So you don't want her anymore?*

*I didn't say that,* I respond.

*Because it sounds like you're quitting. The hero isn't supposed to give up.*

This is not that kind of story. Not for me, anyway. *Thea, there is literally a guy in this story named Prince Charming. He is probably the hero.* I hesitate, and then I add, *I just want your mom to be happy.*

Thea throws her hands in the air and draws a giant arrow to what I've just written. *THIS is what the HERO says.*

I have to laugh at that. *You're very smart.*

Thea is undeterred, even by flattery. *So what are you going to do?*

*Nothing!* I respond. *She wants to date Preston!*

Thea makes a frustrated grunting sound, and steals the paper back. We've used up almost the whole pad. *I know what you should do! You should tell the show people they are stupid jerks! And do it really loud in front of my mom, so she knows!*

Um. I reach for the paper to tell her that's not a good idea, but she pulls it farther away and keeps writing. *And break all the cameras so she knows you hate that they filmed her without her knowing!*

Okay. This is getting out of hand. I pull the pad back and flip the page, writing on the cardboard insert at the back. *It is their job to film her. I don't think she would like it if I did that. Maybe you should ask her what she would think of that.*

Thea shakes her head resolutely. *It would be a big love jester.*

I'm pretty sure she means gesture. I really need to put an end to all this. I don't want Thea to be any more disappointed than she already is, and I don't want Becca to think I encouraged her. *She doesn't love me, Thea. I'm sorry.*

Thea stares me down for a minute, and then she sighs. *You could at least tell my mom you're sorry.*

*Believe me. I did.*

*You could say you're sorry AGAIN.*

*Fine*, I write. *I will, okay? I'll say I'm sorry again.*

Thea looks somewhat mollified, if still unhappy. I stand and motion for her to follow me. *Come on. Let's get you back to your family.*

Thea marches out of the room, like she knows exactly where she's going, and I trail after her. When we reach the end of the hallway, we find her grandfather looking for her. I can't remember his name right now, but I raise a hand in greeting and he waves back, signs something at Thea, and then ushers her away.

Which is good. She belongs with her family, and I belong far away from all of them. I head back and verify the flights and send messages to the shuttle drivers, making sure that Addison's people are all going to get picked up on time.

But what Thea said eats at me. She seemed so sure that her mom still liked me, and I guess it's possible. Becca was so worried that maybe I'd set her up or manipulated her, and I know she's got some serious trust issues from Rob. I denied it at the time, but I intended to talk to her about it again later, when she was calmer. I didn't, because I felt so hurt that she decided to stay on the show—but I do still owe her another apology.

227

One I really don't want caught on camera, so I'm not going to approach her about it when they're shooting.

Later that night, I look up Becca's room number—she's sharing with Addison this week, while Madison rooms with Londyn, because Madison and Addison can't be in a room for more than twenty seconds without trying to claw each other's eyes out—and head up to her floor.

I knock softly, and Addison opens the door. She's wearing a sports bra and a pair of booty shorts, and she regards me coolly, like she's not at all surprised to see me. "Hey, could we get some more towels?" she says. "I spilled nail polish on one of them and the rest are all wet from my steam treatment."

I don't ask what a steam treatment is. I also don't remind her I'm not the concierge. "Sure," I say. "I need to talk to Becca for a second. Coordinating for tomorrow."

Tomorrow is Addison's turn to have family day with Preston, so there's nothing for me to coordinate with Becca, but Addison doesn't exert herself to consider anything that doesn't involve her. I see motion behind her, and there's Becca, wearing a t-shirt and the same yoga pants she had on that night she came to my room.

A knot forms in my throat, but I step back, motioning for her to come out into the hall.

For a moment, I think maybe she won't, but she steps out into the hall and shuts the door behind her. Just like that, we're alone. Or as alone as we can be in a hallway where anyone could step out of a room at any moment. Becca looks at me warily.

"Hey," I say quietly, shoving my hands in my pockets. "I just wanted to tell you again that I'm sorry."

"Really?" Becca says, like this surprises her.

That stings, but I shrug it off and keep going. So what if she thinks I'm a terrible person? Doesn't mean I have to act like one. "I shouldn't have let you talk to me about Rob that night on the balcony. I didn't know there were cameras, but I still should have told you it wasn't safe, just in case. I was being selfish, because I care about you, and I wanted to know what was wrong. I know

228

it put you in a terrible position, and I'm sorry."

Becca's expression softens. "Thank you," she says.

I don't know what else to say. I want to beg her to give me another chance, but I don't have any right to, not if she wants to be dating someone else. "How are things going with Preston?" I ask. I immediately regret the question. I want her to tell me it's going terribly, that he could never compare to me, that she regrets deciding to stay.

Something I can't read flickers in her eyes and then she shifts uncomfortably, probably because she doesn't want to talk about this with the guy she once slept with. "I don't know. It's so hard to get to know him in these circumstances, you know?"

"Yeah, I bet."

"What do you think?" Becca asks. "Do you think we could be good together?"

My mouth falls open. I feel like she's stabbed me. "Did you seriously just ask me that?"

Becca looks startled, like she didn't expect me to take offense at being asked if I think she's a good fit with the guy she said she'd leave for me. "I, um," she stammers, "I'm sorry."

I shake my head at her. The ache settles in my gut, and I feel like I'm going to be sick. She didn't even consider that the question might hurt me. She wants me to go back to being her friend again. Maybe not even that—just her producer. Just the person who guides her through this whole weird process, in the hopes that Prince Charming will choose her and they'll live happily ever after.

Screw that. I can't do it.

"Good night, Becca," I say, and I turn and leave her standing in the hall without looking back. I take the elevator down to the concierge and tell them that Addison needs more towels, because it's my job to make sure these girls have what they need.

But I don't have to be the fucking wingman for the woman I love more than anything in this world, even if that's the only thing she wants from me anymore.

# TWENTY-FIVE

## *Becca*

A s if I don't have enough painful thoughts about Nate circling through my head, now I've got last night's conversation outside of my hotel room added to the loop.

After the days of him avoiding me, it was a shock to see him show up at my door. An even greater shock when he apologized, telling me again that he didn't know about the cameras but should have.

Probably this was nudged along by Thea, but he certainly didn't have to say anything just because she wants us together. *Which*, I remember vividly thinking, *means that maybe* he *still wants us together.*

But before I could even process whether this could be true, he asked so quickly about Preston. Like he couldn't wait to change the subject.

My heart deflated so quickly it hurt.

The truth is, I miss him so much that if he wants to go back to being friends, it would be so much better than having nothing at all. So I clung to that like a life raft, shoving myself back into the place we were before, asking him about Preston.

He looked like I slapped him. Hurt and angry, like he just realized he barely knew me at all.

*Did you seriously just ask me that?*

I did, and I wish I could take it back.

I can't stop wondering if I should apologize again, or if I'll just hurt him more no matter what I do. I also can't stop wishing he'd answered the question the way I want him to—

*You shouldn't be with Preston. You should be with me.*

I wish I could talk to someone about all of this. Someone who is not that stupid journal and can tell me what the hell I should do.

It's a special kind of torture that this morning I'm getting some private time with my family before they're taken to the airport, and I can't tell them about any of it. We're all in Paula and Kurt's room together, and for one thing, I'm not about to unload everything on them with my daughters right there. Also, I have learned my lesson about trusting that I'm not being recorded.

Rosie is coloring quietly (for now, at least), and Thea keeps eyeing me like she's trying to read something from my face. I ask her what's wrong and she deflects, at least until Paula is busy packing her suitcase and Kurt has stepped out into the hallway.

"Did Nate talk to you?" she asks.

I hold in a sigh. "He did. He apologized. It was very nice of him."

Thea looks at me expectantly. "So? Are you going to date him?"

I hate having to hurt her too, on top of everything else. "I don't think that's going to work out, Thea. I'm sorry."

She juts out her chin and is about to say something else when Kurt walks back in the room. There's awkward silence from all of us, and I'm trying to think of something fun and light to talk about, when Paula and Kurt exchange a look.

"So I'm thinking, girls," Paula says, both out loud and in sign, "that maybe we can have one of those nice producers take you to get a few of those cinnamon buns they had downstairs?"

"I just saw one of the ladies in the hallway," Kurt adds, "and they said they have a new batch. I think I can smell them from here!"

*Subtle, guys*, I want to say. But I would like some time alone with them.

Thea knows she's being had, but I've never known either of my kids to say no to a cinnamon roll for any reason, and this is no exception. Though she does give me a hard look as Kurt ushers her and a cheering Rosie out the door.

Almost immediately when the door closes, Paula and Kurt sit down on the second double bed across from me. For two very different people, their expressions of concern are weirdly identical.

"Becca, honey," Paula says. "You're not acting like yourself. I know this situation must be difficult. They always say that in the interviews, you know. 'It's so much harder than I thought it would be,' that sort of thing. Is it getting to be too much for you?"

"It's a lot," I admit. "We don't get a lot of sleep"—especially lately—"and there's all the travel, and, you know, a lot of the girls don't get along, and . . ."

What can I really say? I can't talk about Nate. And looking at their concerned expressions only makes me feel more guilty about what I said about Rob.

How could I have done this to them?

I'm picking at my cuticles, and Paula and Kurt exchange another glance.

"Is it that Preston fellow?" Kurt asks gruffly. "I don't like that he's seeing all these other women. You think he could just make up his mind and not have a whole goddamn harem—"

"That's the concept of the show." Paula rolls her eyes, and I can tell they've had this discussion before. "And it's not a harem, it's a journey to find love."

"How many women does it take? Especially when he's got our Becca here. Idiot shouldn't need the rest of them."

"Well, obviously, but he's got to at least *pretend* with the others." Paula gives me an encouraging smile.

I appreciate the sentiment, but it only makes me feel worse.

"Honey," Paula says, the smile dropping. "You can talk to

us about anything, you know? We can tell something's wrong. Not that I think it's obvious to anyone else," she hastens to add. "But we know you."

They don't, though. Not fully. Because I've never let them. Because I could never let them really know Rob.

Will they think I'm just telling horrible lies about their son?

Or maybe they'll believe me, and it's like I'm taking the son they loved away from them all over again.

Either way, my stupid mistake will gut the only people who ever really loved me.

Paula moves to sit next to me on the bed and puts her arm around me. "We love you and we're here for you."

"Maybe you should come home," Kurt says.

That won't help, because the damage is done. "It's about Rob," I say, the words bursting out of me. More words I can't take back. "Because I said things about Rob and they've got them on camera."

There's a long moment, and something about the stillness makes me look up at them. They're watching each other carefully, something I can't identify in their faces.

We're going to have to have this conversation eventually, and it's nothing the show doesn't already know. "Rob wasn't who you thought he was," I say. "Not with me, anyway. He was a good father and I know he was a good son, but he wasn't a good husband." I can't bear to look at them. "He was terrible to me. He was controlling and mean. He would tell me how stupid I was, how useless, that I'd never be able to survive without him, that I was a horrible mom, and my girls and everyone else deserved better, and—" I draw in a shuddering breath, and I force myself to open my eyes, to see the pain I'm putting on them.

They're looking at each other again. There's pain in their expressions, definitely.

But I don't see surprise. Disbelief. Horror. Any of the other things I might have expected.

A pit of dread forms. "What?" I say, my voice cracking.

Kurt swallows, links his thick fingers together. "We, um. We had an inkling that maybe things weren't so good with you two. That maybe, well. Maybe Rob wasn't treating you as kindly as we'd like."

The air is sucked out of me. Tears freeze on my eyelids, quivering on my lashes. "What?" I look over to Paula, who isn't meeting my eyes. "You knew?"

"We overheard a few times," she says. "And we suspected there was more. We'd see how you'd get, how low you'd feel about yourself—"

"You knew." I'm stuck on repeat. "You knew."

Kurt clears his throat. "We knew Rob could be a handful sometimes, that he liked to be in charge of things—"

"*Things*?" My voice is too high-pitched. "Like me?'

Paula flinches.

I yank myself away from her and stand. My legs don't feel like they can support my weight, but I can't sit there anymore. "Did you ever say anything to him? When you overheard, did you ever . . ." I trail off, because I can read the answer on their guilty faces. "You didn't. You didn't say anything to him, and you never said anything to me. Years and years of this, and you knew and you never said *anything.*"

"We didn't want to interfere in your marriage," Paula says weakly. "We wanted to support you the best we could, but it didn't feel like our place to—"

"To *what*?" I spit out, and she flinches again. Rage is cutting through the ice, hot and sharp. "To try to stop your son from destroying me? To let me know that what he was doing to me was wrong? That he was wrong about *me*?" The tears are spilling over again. "You left me alone there! You pretended to love me, and you left me there all alone to be abused by him!" I'm yelling now and possibly the show is recording this, but I don't care anymore.

"We do love you, honey," Kurt says, and Paula nods desperately, her own eyes shining with tears.

"We do," she says. "We always told ourselves that if you ever came to talk to us about it, we would tell you that we knew and do whatever we could to help—"

I let out a bitter, incredulous laugh. "So it was on me, then? If *I* came to *you* to talk about it?" I press my shaking hands to my head. I feel more than ever like I'm losing my mind. "I kept this to myself for years because I was terrified of losing you or hurting you, and it was a secret that *buried* me."

"We didn't want you to have to keep it a secret," Paula says, wringing her hands. "We hoped you'd tell the therapist about it, and that she could help you work through it."

Oh my god, the therapist. To help me with my "grief." They were giving me someone else to unload on, because they didn't want to deal with it. Paying for school, too, being so supportive of me working toward my restaurant, dating again.

It was all because of guilt.

"Becca—" Paula stands and reaches for me, but I step back.

I'm struggling to breathe again. *I was manipulated for so long,* I remember telling Nate. *I was sucked into believing someone loved me and then I was torn apart, piece by piece.* "I have to go, and you have to go." I turn toward the door.

"Becca, honey, if you'd just listen—" Paula says.

"I've already heard enough. Send the girls up to my room before you leave so I can say goodbye."

I open the door. Thankfully, no one's in the hallway. I suddenly wish that Nate was standing there, that I could fall into his arms and sob against his chest.

I don't have Nate. I still don't know if I ever did.

Maybe I never had anyone.

# TWENTY-SIX

## Becca

I expect to be sent home after family visits, but somehow Preston sends Londyn packing instead. So I stumble through the endless days of travel, getting desperate enough to seek out Madison and Addison to hang out with. They are both awful in their own unique ways. Madison, who I'm always a little afraid will poison my food but will then no doubt deliver my eulogy with a pageant-ready smile and a "It's too bad she didn't pass up those carbs, bless her heart." And Addison with her constant need to bitch about Madison and Madison only.

Of the two, I prefer Addison; it's kind of nice to have someone to openly bitch about Madison with. It's not like I care much anymore how the show's going to portray me. I lost that battle weeks ago. Really, when it comes down to it, I know this—I'm awful, too.

And now I've arrived at Dalliance night, which will only add fuel to the fire.

We're in Ireland now, and I'm on my final date with Preston. We walk along the edge of a sheer, awe-inspiring cliff where we can look out at the crashing waves or at the rolling hills that are so emerald green it's like they've been through a saturation filter. Then later, we have dinner at a pub where we eat soda bread and boxty and listen to an Irish band.

Like so many other dates I've been on, it's beyond anything I could have expected to experience in my life. And yet, I feel like I'm sleepwalking. Everything is a blur, and I don't want to be here anymore. Much as I miss my girls, I don't want to be home either, having to pretend at happiness and fun to make up for all the weeks I've been gone. Having to pretend that every part of me doesn't feel like it's broken into pieces and being held together by a layer of determination that is thinning by the minute.

I also can't handle facing Paula and Kurt again, but when I get home, I won't be able to avoid them, because I depend on them for childcare.

Staying here, seeing this through, seems more important than ever. But that's killing me, too. Both seeing Nate—when he's interviewing us at our hotel or standing with the other producers at the tiara ceremony—or not seeing Nate, when he's avoiding me.

He seems to be doing that more now, which I suppose makes sense. There are only three girls left—me, Madison and Addison—and they don't need as many producers on the front lines.

Clearly, they don't feel like they need Nate to pry any more out of me.

The cameras follow Preston and I as we emerge from our limo to stand in front of this gorgeous castle in which Preston and I are going to spend the night. Preston gives my limp hand a squeeze and smiles down at me.

He's such a nice guy and really, he deserves better than what I'm doing to him. I keep hoping I can invest myself in this more, give it a real shot, but especially after that chat with my in-laws, my mind isn't here.

And my heart has never been. It's been Nate's from the beginning, and I can't seem to wrest it back no matter how hard I try.

"Here we go," Preston says, holding up the brass key that was brought to us on a tray with our dessert at the pub.

"Here we go," I say back with a wan smile. My eyes flick toward the production team, as they so often do, but Nate wasn't with us for the rest of the date, and he's not here now. Probably that's a good thing.

Preston tugs me forward and we enter the castle. It's an actual hotel, with a lobby and reception desk in the front room, but there are tapestries hanging from stone walls and big oaken chairs with high, carved backs and a roaring fireplace.

"Your highness," one of the hotel clerks says with a smile on his face as he bows low. "My lady."

From the amusement on the clerk's face, it's pretty clear this isn't the first time he's greeted Preston this way. We've been in Ireland for several days now, and I'm the last Dalliance week date of the three. The clerk's face confirms to me that Preston has spent nights already in this very same castle. Possibly the very same room.

It's skeevy as hell, but it doesn't bother me nearly as much as it should. And hey, it's not like I can be angry at him for sleeping with other people.

The hotel clerk leads us up the winding stairs to the room at the top (in the tower, of course), and Preston brandishes the key again. Darlene asks him to keep holding it up for a few seconds, then says, "Becca, would you mind taking a step to the side, you're blocking the shot." I move. "Okay, we're good," she says. "Preston, insert the key now, but do it slowly."

Very subtle. I only barely manage not to roll my eyes.

Preston gives me a knowing smile, like we're in on the joke together, which I appreciate. Then he opens the door, and we get a look at our Dalliance room, complete with cameramen waiting inside for our reaction. They won't stay, but they're going to get as much footage of this as they can while they're here.

The room itself is gorgeous, with a big canopy bed. No lacy curtains like the bed that—*no, Becca, don't imagine Nate bending you over, wanting that same thing at that exact same time . . .*

This bed isn't so much "princessy" as "queenly." Lots of tasseled pillows in deep golds and maroons. Sconces with candles on the walls. Another fireplace, the fire already crackling away. Rose petals strewn on the bedspread. Wine chilling on the decorative wooden chest at the end of the bed. The room smells a little musty, but is also mixed with a fake garden scent—like someone did a full spray-down of Glade.

That's a little less romantic. But overall, the kind of gorgeous luxury that one could expect when spending a night with a handsome prince. But I'm far less enchanted about the whole thing than I should be.

I blink at that word. Enchanted. I remember writing that in the beginning of my journal, how I felt embarrassed to even say it, like I was giving in to the show pressure to make everything a fairy tale. *I'm enchanted by P,* I said. Everything about Nate drawing me in, everything between us feeling like magic.

Now I think it *was* like magic—something that looks real, but ultimately isn't. And I feel both like the stunned audience watching the magician, trying to figure out how it was done, and also like the woman being sawed in half.

"Becca?" Preston asks, his brow furrowing. "Is everything okay? Is the room not . . ." He looks around, because what bad thing can you say about this room?

"Oh, no, it's—it's gorgeous. I'm just . . . I was just dizzy for a second. But I'm fine." I force a big smile to show how fine I am.

He seems to buy it. "Good. But yeah, I get it. It's been a long day. I'm looking forward to spending the evening in. Here, have a seat and I'll pour us some wine."

The cameras still haven't left, and I don't think they're going to until they have some clear indication that Preston and I are ready to start making some truly non-network-TV-friendly content. Which I am feeling less capable of every second, and I didn't start out feeling all that capable to begin with.

Which is ridiculous. I've been dating on *Tinder,* for god's sake. I had an emotionally abusive nightmare of a marriage for ten years before that. It's not like I need to be madly in love to get it on.

At least not until I was with Nate and never wanted to be with anyone else again.

I sit on the edge of the bed, and Preston uncorks the wine and pours us a couple glasses. He hands me my glass and sits right next to me.

"I'm really looking forward to getting some alone time with you, Becca," he says.

My throat feels dry. "Me too," I manage, before taking a sip of wine. There's a long beat of silence, which I know I need to fill. I can practically feel the producers willing me to say *anything*. "I had a lovely day today."

Oh god. A *lovely day*? Am I going to talk about the *temperate weather* next?

Preston doesn't seem to mind, but really, this probably fits with the Becca he knows. He leans close, reaching past me to set his wine glass on the nightstand, his body shifting toward me. I know what's happening next, and I know what the producers want to happen next, and like everything else in the last several days, I feel like I'm being tugged along without the will to fight it anymore.

I set down my own wine glass and turn back to Preston. Maybe there *can* be a connection, some chemistry. Maybe I'm just not trying hard enough, still holding back.

So when Preston leans in to kiss me, I kiss him back. I try to imagine I feel anything for him like what I feel for Nate. I try to imagine that the very nearness of him makes my body feel alive. I try and try, and our kiss lasts much longer than the previous one, but I'm just going through the motions, like I'm an actress who's done a scene too many times.

Preston pulls back and smiles, and the production team, having gotten the footage they wanted, takes off. Darlene gives us a wink and a none-too-subtle head tilt toward the basket full of condoms they have so graciously provided.

We're alone in the room now. The fire cracks and pops. I take a big drink of wine, and Preston does the same.

He stands. "Do you mind if I take off this prince jacket?" he asks, already unbuttoning the shiny gold buttons. "I've got a shirt on underneath, but god, this thing gets scratchy."

It's nice of him to ask, given that we're in the Dalliance Tower and clothing removal is generally expected. "Sure," I say. I'm wearing a shimmery cocktail dress—overdressed for an Irish pub. I'd like to change into the Snoopy pajama pants and matching tank top I smuggled into the overnight bag they had me pack, but I don't feel like suggesting I want to "get a little more comfortable." Even though Preston would probably see the writing on the wall when I come out of the bathroom looking like I'm attending a sixth-grade sleepover rather than wearing sexy lingerie.

I am definitely not wearing that lingerie tonight. I am probably never going to wear that lingerie again.

So I kick off my heels and stretch out on the bed against the pillow mountain.

"It's nice not to have the cameras in our faces," Preston says, peeling off the jacket and then his boots, so he's wearing a basic white t-shirt and black pants. He sits back on the bed the same way I am. "I could stand to go an hour without talking about my 'journey.'"

I chuckle. The awkward tension dissipates a little. "You know, until Rosie found that damn frog the other day, I had made it this whole time without ever once mentioning in an interview that I had to kiss a bunch of frogs in the quest to find my prince. I think I was the last holdout."

He laughs. "I can't tell you how many women said that directly to me."

"Seriously? I mean, not that I don't believe you, but—"

"Twelve. Twelve women used that line on me, seven of them before the first tiara ceremony. Every single time I had to act like it was the most original thing I'd ever heard."

"I'm starting to see why I've stayed around so long. Lack of fairytale-related pick up lines." I regret the words the minute they leave my mouth, because they sound too flirtatious.

I'm feeling queasy again, or maybe it has never really left and I keep rediscovering it. It's not just because I don't feel that way about Preston—that's a fact now, no denying it—but because it feels like I'm being unfaithful to Nate.

Who I am not dating. Who very well might have used me. Who might never have felt anything for me at all besides sexual attraction.

Or who might have felt that same connection, maybe even love.

"You know, Becca," Preston says, and I blink back to where I am, with the guy I'm actually on a date with. His expression is serious. "I feel like I want to be honest with you." He sucks in his lips and frowns down at the bedspread.

"Okay," I say carefully. Is he going to tell me he's not into this? That he's noticed that when I'm around him, I have the personality of a sack of potatoes? The thought fills me with no small amount of relief.

"I'm really glad I've gotten to know you over these last few weeks," he says, his tone hesitant. "But I think you should know that I didn't feel anything between us at the beginning. It was the producers who kept you around at first." He looks up at me with a cringe.

I'm surprised, but not by that information. I expected I would be a show pick that first night—Tragic Backstory Becca. I'm surprised he's telling me this when he clearly doesn't have to. I'm about to tell him that I already guessed that, no worries, but from his expression, I can see there's a little more to it. That pit of dread forms all over again—it just lives there now, I think.

"How many ceremonies?" I ask.

He pauses. "Until after our first date."

The pit widens. "So, most of them," I say, and he winces.

"Yeah. But I had such a great time on our date, and I realized you were someone really incredible who I'd overlooked." He says this all hurriedly. "And I'm glad they kept you for so long, because I really have enjoyed our time together. I think you're an amazing woman."

"I . . . uh, thank you." I should be responding more, but there's that knife of betrayal again, slicing me all the way through.

Nate knew. He knew the whole time. And yeah, we talked about how confident I was that the producers would keep me that first tiara ceremony, but it never came up again after that. It's not like I expected him to spill all the behind-the-scenes secrets of the show—he's working for them, after all—but that night on the balcony . . .

That night, I opened my heart to him. I told him truths I had never told anyone before. Then I asked him about Preston and me, if he thought we would be a good fit. Sure, I didn't ask him outright if Preston had ever once picked me, but if he really cared about me, wouldn't he feel that I deserved to know that the guy I was "dating" wasn't into me at all? I can see not telling me if he was worried he was going to get caught and lose his job, but that night—

My heart pounds. That night there were cameras. Probably he didn't tell me because he knew they were there. And he knew full well he was getting the footage that would make him the star producer. The golden boy.

My whole body goes cold and then hot, one right after the other.

I'd been believing more and more that I was wrong about all that. But—

"I'm so sorry, Becca," Preston says, putting his hand over mine. "I didn't want to hurt you, but I didn't want there to be this lie between us, you know? You deserve the truth."

I let out a shaky breath. Do I? No one else seems to think so.

"It's okay," I say, forcing the words out past the massive lump in my throat. "I get it, you know? It's hard to feel a connection with so many people at once, and there were so many girls, and I wasn't the most assertive, and . . . I get it. Really."

"Okay, good." He lets out a relieved breath. "I've appreciated you opening up with me about everything, and it felt like you should have the truth in return."

*One would think.* But to him, I say, "I'm grateful that you told me. That you were so honest. That means a lot to me."

More than he could possibly know.

Why can't I be in love with *him*? Why do I always put my trust in the wrong people?

*You're fucking stupid, Becca. You always were.* It's Rob's words, but it's not only his voice—it's mine, too, like they're becoming one again, the way they used to be.

"That's good to hear," he says. There's another long pause, in which I'm playing back that conversation with Nate on the balcony, my body numb. I'm so lost in that, I don't notice Preston leaning over to kiss me again until his lips are inches away, his body shifting like he's about to get on top of mine.

This time I pull away, so quickly I almost fall off the bed. "I don't—sorry, but I don't, um . . ."

He sits back. "Did I make you uncomfortable?"

"No, it's not that. It's just . . . I know we're here in the Dalliance Tower, but I don't want to have sex tonight. I'm not ready for that. I'm just not there."

"Oh. Yeah, okay." There's a flicker of irritation in his face, but it's gone so suddenly I think I might have imagined it. Especially because he so quickly looks so earnest. "That's totally okay with me. So what do you want to do?"

*Cry into my pillow. Go to sleep and turn off my brain for even a few hours.*

"I don't know. Maybe just talk some more?"

"Sure," he says.

And we do. We talk about topics we've already more or less covered—his childhood. My kids. His nieces and nephews. His favorite basketball team. The ex-girlfriend who introduced him to sushi.

Soon it feels like we're both reaching for pretty much anything to say, and it's not just because my mind is still so stuck on this latest hurt.

There is honestly nothing there between Preston and me, and after one particularly painful stretch of silence, I feel like I need to come out and say it. No need for either of us to keep pretending—and he deserves honesty, too, at least as much as I can give him.

"Preston. You know this—" I gesture back and forth between us "—isn't happening, right? Like, it's just not—"

He gives me a half-smile. "Yeah, I know." Then he lifts my hand and gives me a gentle kiss on the back of it that feels like a farewell. "Should we turn in early?"

"That sounds great," I say with a smile back. I didn't want to hurt him, and I'm so glad that it appears I didn't. That despite whatever interest he developed, he sees that we aren't a good fit.

I don't even bother to change out of my cocktail dress. I just get under the covers and we turn the light out and almost instantly, he's fast asleep.

It takes a long time before I join him.

# TWENTY-SEVEN

## *Nate*

The night Becca has her Dalliance Tower date, I am smart enough not to get assigned to be part of the crew, but stupid enough to sit in the production suite on one of the laptops afterward reviewing the footage of her making out with Preston on a bed covered in rose petals before the cameras leave them to their evening alone.

I make myself watch the footage over and over, studying the way she smiles at Preston, the way her fingers curl around the back of his neck. I tell myself over and over again that this is what she wants, that she was never mine, not really. I do it until I'm sure that the jealousy is going to consume me, and then I retreat to my room and crawl into bed in a puddle of self-pity.

As if I'm going to be able to sleep after *that*. I toss and turn, curl up into a tight ball, stretch out on the sheets. I close my eyes and stare into the dark, but all I can see is Becca practically on Preston's lap, making out with him, and then the footage of the door closing. It's been a while. They're probably on round two by now.

*Fuck.*

I reach to the nightstand for my phone, checking out the likes on the latest episode of *Jason Climbs Sh!t*, which I neither produced nor was present for. I torture myself again by watching the last few episodes, watching my friends keep turning out hilarious, awesome climbing vids without me.

It's not like I wanted Jason's show to fall apart. I'll still be involved when I'm in town, I hope, even though Jason's pissed at me for moving on and getting another job. But it still doesn't feel good to see the show keep ticking without me. There's nothing quite like being replaced to make you feel . . . well, completely replaceable.

I turn my phone off and try to sleep some more, but it doesn't work. So it is that at four AM I find myself using the internet to determine what time it is in Los Angeles.

It's eight o'clock in the evening, my phone tells me. A completely reasonable hour to call. I dial Jason, and pray that he'll pick up. Even if I don't tell him about Becca, at least I won't have to be alone with my thoughts.

"Nate!" Jason says. "Dude, I didn't think I'd hear from you until you were back. You're not back yet, are you?"

"No," I say. "I'm in Ireland for Dalliance week."

"Dude! That's awesome!"

It's not, but I understand why he thinks this. Being in Ireland would be pretty cool if I wasn't losing my mind. Plus, he's a fan of the show, so just knowing I'm here filming Dalliance week is a novelty.

"How is it going?" Jason asks.

I don't know how I thought I wouldn't tell him. Jason and I don't usually sit around and dish about our personal lives, but I'm so starved for someone to talk to that what comes out of my mouth is, "I fell in love."

"In Ireland?" He sounds surprised and confused, which is fair. I've never been in love before and he knows it. "Did you fall for some Irish girl?"

"No. I fell in love with a contestant."

"Oh, shit," Jason says. "How's that going?"

"Well, it's Dalliance week, and she's off in the tower."

"Shiiiiiiiiit."

"Yeah," I say. "That pretty much sums it up."

"Does she know you're into her?"

"Unfortunately," I say, and I start from the beginning, filling Jason in about meeting Becca during interviews, the sexually frustrated carriage ride, the fabric in her zipper (which earns a protracted "duuuuuuuuuude" from Jason), her date with Preston, meeting her kids, and then her coming to my hotel room and the subsequent dissolution of all my hopes and dreams.

"She might not have sex with him tonight," I say at the end of all that. "They don't always have sex in the tower, right?"

"That's true," Jason allows. "They don't *always*."

I groan. "Who am I kidding? She's probably banging him right now. She only dates on *Tinder*. It's not like sex is a big deal to her." Obviously, given how easily she could hook up with me and then cast me aside. Of course it meant nothing to her. I was just another way for her to scratch an itch, just another guy who didn't mean anything.

I wonder if Preston is different. He's Prince Charming, after all.

"God, I'm an idiot," I say. "How do you and Emily make it look so easy?"

Jason laughs. "Easy? We almost broke up a couple weeks ago."

*What?* "You can't break up. You guys are so happy together."

"Yeah, we are," he says. "But I let myself get all up in my head about not being good enough for her, and kept trying to keep us from progressing because I thought if we did, eventually I'd lose her. And she decided that since I didn't want to move in together, that meant I wasn't really into the relationship any-more. And then she called me on it, and I didn't react super well—"

"Oh my god. Are you guys okay?" I've always taken for granted that Jason and Emily are going to make it. They're so perfect together, and Jason hasn't so much as looked at another girl since they first met, even though it took Emily several days to get with the program.

If *they* can't make it, everyone is doomed.

"Yeah, we're good now," Jason says. "Though unfortunately we had that meltdown while we were filming the Real Not-Wives show, so a lot of it got caught on camera. And we had to do on-camera couples therapy with Monroe Coco, so there was that."

"You had to do . . . what?"

"Couples therapy with a former Real Housewife. It was ridiculous, but weirdly it worked. So now we're engaged, and—"

"You're engaged? Wow."

"Yep." I can practically hear his grin from all the way across the world. "And we're going to buy a big crappy house and fix it up, because apparently Emily wants eight kids and we need to be able to afford—"

"*What*? Emily wants *eight*—"

"Eight kids. Yeah. It was a surprise to me, too."

I think someone wanting eight kids will always be a surprise, but now that I think about it, I could totally see Emily and Jason as parents to this big family, packing their kids along on all their adventures. "So that's why you're not hassling me about getting involved with a single mom."

"Yeah, pretty much. That, and you're really in love with this girl. I've never heard you talk like this."

I assume he means he's never heard me so unhappy, which is true. "Yeah, but she's done with me. Now I just want this whole thing to be over so I can get back to my normal life." Though I already know it's never going to feel the same again. I hate how desperate I sound when I add, "I can still have my old job back, can't I?"

There's a long beat in which I'm suddenly afraid he's going to reject me, too. But then he says, "Yeah, man. Obviously. But are you sure you're not too cool for us, now that you're producing *Prince Charming*?"

"Hell no," I tell him. "I hate this job. It's not just watching

Becca date some other guy. I'm manipulating women for a living, and it's awful. I'm going to finish out the season for the resume credit, but I'm not doing another one."

"Really?" Jason sounds relieved about this. He didn't want me to do this show, not for ethical reasons, but because he never wants anything to change. "So . . . do you think you'd still be up for trying out some of those ideas you had? Pitching that high adventure show, and all that?" Now he's the one who sounds a little nervous.

I blink. I've been bugging Jason to branch out for years now. He's always shrugged me off, and he's sure as hell never brought it up himself. "Yeah. Would *you*?"

"For sure," he says. "Emily and I have all these plans for the future, and now that I'm not afraid to think about them . . . You were right that we need to try new things, see if we can get our foot in the door somewhere besides YouTube. I was pissed at myself that I only realized it after you'd given up on me and moved on, you know? Not that I can't still do all that shit, but I wanted to do all that shit with you."

This is such a relief to hear that it physically hurts. "Okay. We'll do that, then, when I get back. We can take a look at all the ideas we've tossed around and pick a place to start."

"Sounds good, man," Jason says.

I take a deep breath, staring at the dark ceiling of my hotel room. It hurts to think about a future without Becca in it, even though I don't have any other kind. "Why does she have to be having sex with him tonight and not me?"

"Do you think she is?"

"Maybe not," I say. "Probably."

"Do you think you could forgive that? Like, if she slept with him, but then she doesn't end up with him, do you think you would still want to be with her?"

Would I want to? Hell yes. Would I be able to look past it, knowing she went back to him and had sex with him like I was nothing? "I don't know. Do you think you could have forgiven

250

Emily if she rejected you and went and had sex with some other guy?"

Jason is quiet for a second.

"Oh, ha," I say. "She *did* do that to you." When Jason and Emily first met, our friend Su-Lin tried to talk Emily out of dating Jason by telling her he was a player. Su-Lin was hell-bent on hooking Emily up with her cousin, and Emily went along with it for a while until Su-Lin's cousin turned out to be a cheating asshole.

"That was before we'd slept together, though," Jason says. Thoughtfully, which is not a tone I'm used to hearing from him. "It seems like that could make a difference."

I think it does. It makes the hurt worse, anyway. "I think I could get past it," I say. "If I really believed I was the one she wanted. But if she's sleeping with him and not me, I'm obviously not."

"Yeah, that sucks," Jason says, and I appreciate that he doesn't try to talk me out of it. "Though," he continues, his tone lightening, "if she'd left the show before, you wouldn't be having sex with her right now anyway."

"I don't know. She would have had her phone." I remember the look on Becca's face when I mentioned it, that night in my hotel room. Had she known then that this was just a fling? I thought leaving the show for me meant she wanted a real relationship, but did she actually say that or did I just assume?

"Dude, yeah," Jason says. "I totally wish you were having phone sex right now . . ." He trails off like he realizes how weird this sounds. "Not with me," he clarifies.

"Thanks for that. I'm going to text that quote to Emily right now without context."

"Sweet." He pauses. "You know she's going to grill me for every detail of this conversation."

"I do know. Tell her everything." It'll be nice not to have to tell her myself. I'm suddenly wishing I could go hang out with Jason and watch TV, get a hug from Emily and let her tell me that if Becca doesn't want to be with me, that's her loss.

It's nice to remember that I have a job and friends I love to come home to.

But even that bit of comfort isn't enough to get me even a single wink of sleep.

# TWENTY-EIGHT

## Becca

The next morning, the cameras are back, getting footage of Preston and me in our room, eating breakfast from a tray on the bed. We're both wearing big white bathrobes—handed to us by Mustache Dan as soon as the crew got here. I've got my Snoopy pajamas on underneath (at some point during the night, I decided to finally change, hoping it would help me sleep, though it didn't) and Preston has some flannel pajama pants underneath his. All of which is more comfy-looking than sexy, but for some reason, the bathrobes do make it look like we got it on. Not to mention that neither of us had a chance to tame our bed head before the crew showed up, which will probably be interpreted as sex hair.

I don't love any of this, but I tell myself that it doesn't matter if people think we had sex. It doesn't matter if *Nate* thinks we had sex. He never really cared about me. He kept things from me and he lied to me and he said he'd have my back, but he left me alone here, swimming with the sharks. Everyone does that, and he's no exception.

And I'm no longer numb. I'm pissed.

He's not here with the crew this morning, but I wish he was. Maybe I want him to think Preston and I had sex. That what

Nate and I had didn't mean anything to me. That losing it didn't rip me into irreparable shreds.

Probably I want him to believe this because I want so desperately for it to be true. (Well, not the Preston and I having sex part. I'm more than good with my decision there.)

I'm trying to keep up the amiable breakfast chat with Preston over our traditional Irish breakfast, but I'm stabbing at the bacon rasher like I'm trying to kill the pig all over again. Preston doesn't seem to notice—he's too busy trying not to look disgusted at the black pudding. No judgment from me there; pig's blood congealed into a sausage form isn't for me, either. There are limits to my adventurous palate.

After breakfast, we change into actual clothes—jeans and an off the shoulder, bohemian top for me, and the usual "Harlequin-book-cover rogue" outfit for him—and we're taken in a limo back to the main hotel which has been my prison for the last several days. Mustache Dan directs me immediately to the interview room.

I steel myself to dodge a bunch of questions about the sex I didn't have last night, then walk into the room—

And there's Nate. So gorgeous, his faded t-shirt clinging just the right amount to his toned torso. His curly hair that I once gripped so tight is tied back. His lashes dark and long over deep brown eyes.

My heart squeezes, my body flushing. My hands twitch at my side, like they remember being on him and want nothing more than to be back there. Every goddamn time I see him, it's like this.

He looks at me, his face so impassive I might as well be some woman he's never seen before, then looks back at the cameraman, murmuring something as he points at the decorative screen (where the hell do they find all these things?) that will be behind me. Then he gestures to the seat.

Like I'm nothing.

Like he got what he wanted from me and he finally doesn't

care anymore if I know. Maybe he's no longer worried that I'll tell about us. Maybe he's sure no one will believe me.

I channel that instinctive rush of anger, which feels so much better than despair.

I sit primly on the edge of the seat, trying to make my own face as neutral as his. I may be pissed as hell, but I don't want him to see it.

"Becca, hi," he says calmly, sitting in the folding chair to the side of the camera. "Let's get started."

"Sounds great." I cross my legs, rest my hands on my knee.

"So last night was the Dalliance Tower with Preston."

"It sure was." I manage to sound nicely coy.

His lips twitch up at the sides, but his eyes don't match that amusement. "Don't forget, restate the question with your answer."

As if I haven't been interviewed ten thousand times already and know the damn rules. "I didn't realize that was a question."

That little smile looks frozen on his face. "Was last night your Dalliance Tower date with Preston?"

"Last night was my Dalliance Tower date with Preston." I try to beam, like the very thought of that night of boring conversation and turning in at eleven PM fills me with radiance. After a second, I realize I'm probably giving more of a psychotic "black widow exulting over murdering her mate" vibe and take it down a notch.

Nate eyes me for a second, then looks down at his clipboard. "And how was it to get that special alone time with Preston?"

His words so even. Like asking me about my overnight doesn't faze him any more than if he were asking about my Irish breakfast.

"Getting to spend that time alone with Preston was *amazing*," I say. "A relationship needs time to become something more, and getting that quality time together was exactly what we needed." I'm pretty sure I sound like every one of the other girls, gushing after their date. Which is exactly what I'm going for.

Dreamy. Starry-eyed. In love with a fucking prince.

Not giving Nate the satisfaction of knowing I only ever felt that way about him and maybe only ever will.

"Wonderful. That's great to hear." But his voice sounds tight.

Because it's affecting him to hear this from me?

Probably not. Probably I'm reading too much into every little tiny mannerism. Look where that got me before.

"So you say your relationship has become something more," he says. "What does 'something more' mean to you?"

What does something more mean to me? It means real, true connection. It means friendship and passion and safety and love and trust and belonging, all these ingredients mixed together to create this perfect dish that some people make so effortlessly and others will spend their whole lives trying and failing to create.

And some people think they might finally have it, only to watch it sink like a bad soufflé.

I wet my lips. "'Something more' means that it feels like our relationship took a big step forward last night. Like, really getting to feel that chemistry between us. It was like that future felt so much more real, you know? Something I could *trust*."

"I *bet*," he says with a smile so aggressively polite I feel like I'm being sold extended warranty insurance. "So this chemistry . . . It sounds like you had a lot of *fun* with Preston in the tower."

He wants to go there? Sure thing, Nate.

"Well," I say with a giggly laugh that feels like it should be accompanied by a hair flip, though I can't bring myself to go that far. "I'll keep the details to myself, but spending a night alone in a tower with a hot prince? Oh yeah. We definitely had lots of *fun*."

He blinks too rapidly, and his dark eyes flash. And I know it then, I'm not imagining it. The set of his jaw, the way he's gripping the clipboard—

He's jealous.

My pulse races, guilt creeping in and mingling with stupid, stupid hope, but I'm not going to let myself get carried away with that again. No.

I never doubted that the sexual attraction he felt for me was real. So yeah, maybe he's jealous. Rob used me and didn't actually love me and he sure as hell got jealous.

So if Nate is jealous now, that's good. It's not the heart-stomping he did to me.

"How do you think Preston felt about your night together?" Nate asks. The words sound like they're being pushed through gritted teeth.

I *shouldn't* feel bad about it. But maybe it's because I do that I lean into this even harder.

"Oh, I think Preston felt really good about our night together." My voice is practically a purr. "I would say it was *deeply satisfying* for both of us."

The punch lands. I see it happen, the way he flinches. The way his body curls inward around it.

And it doesn't feel good at all, hurting him back like this. Because that's real hurt, not just wounded pride, and oh god, does that mean—

"Would you—" he starts, then swallows and starts again. "Would you say you're falling in love with—"

He looks up, just for a second, but that's enough for me to see his eyes are wet with tears, reflecting back that despair to me that I've felt every second of every day since I stormed out of his hotel room.

I can't breathe.

"I'll be right back," he says, jumping to his feet and setting the clipboard down so quickly it hits the chair and slides off. He doesn't pick it up. He practically flees from the room.

Oh my god.

Now I'm the one who feels punched in the gut, but he's not the one causing it.

Was he *never* the one causing it?

I want to run after him, but I'm pinned to the chair with uncertainty and fear and guilt.

The cameraman and I stare at each other. He doesn't say

anything, just starts fiddling with some buttons on the camera.

Olivia walks in, all smiles. "Sorry, Becca," she says. "Nate wasn't feeling well, so I'm going to take over."

"Is he—" I try to see around her into the hallway, but of course he's not there. He left because of me. Because I *hurt* him.

Because I had the power to really hurt him, and I used it as a fucking weapon.

Just like Rob did to me, over and over again.

"Oh, he'll be fine," she says with a dismissive hand wave. "Probably something he ate. But let's get started again." She must have been listening to the interview, because she dives right in with, "So we'll get to that question Nate was asking, but first, let's have some serious girl talk." Her eyebrows waggle. "How hot is Preston under that prince getup? It sounds like you got a front-row seat."

"I—um." I can't talk. I can't move. But I have to do one of these things, and I don't think I'm getting out of this room without answering these questions. "He's hot, yeah. Totally hot."

Olivia eagerly continues on with the questioning, pushing hard for sexual sound bites that I am no longer wanting to give, but I manage to sputter out enough to pacify her. She gets back to the "Are you falling in love with Preston?" question, and all I can see is Nate's watery eyes, the hurt there. The betrayal.

I had convinced myself *he* had betrayed *me*. But that look was so raw I felt it in my bones.

"No," I say, before I can consider the ramifications. "I'm not."

Olivia gapes, then recovers. "Because you're *already* in love with Preston," she says hopefully.

Shit. Nate's job. I can't cost him that now, after everything. And if they haven't put two and two together yet, if I deny having feelings for the prince, they're going to start working on that math. But I also don't want him to watch footage of me lying about telling Preston I love him.

Ahhhh, what have I done? Why did I stay on this show?

I stayed here because I couldn't leave Nate, that's why.

Because no matter how betrayed and hurt and angry I was at him, I couldn't let go of the hope that I was wrong.

"When I admit that I love someone," I say slowly, "I want to say it first to *him*, you know?"

Olivia grins. "Okay, I got it. Maybe that'll happen at a certain proposal?"

Good god. "Maybe," I say coyly, like there's a chance in the world I am telling Preston I love him in any situation, let alone at a proposal which isn't going to happen. We both agreed there wasn't anything between us.

After a few more questions, Olivia finally lets me go. I wander around the hotel a bit, but I don't see Nate. I don't know what I'd even say to him right now if I did.

I go back to my room, which I'm thankfully not sharing with anyone this week. I sit on my bed, my mind tracing every emotional note of these last few weeks, and I'm still confused. Do I believe him now?

My gaze lands on my overnight bag, where my journal is. Not that I was planning on doing a lot of writing in the tower, but I've grown increasingly paranoid about leaving it where someone could read it.

I'm not planning on writing now, either, but I get it out and sit back on my bed, flipping through it. Reading from beginning to end. Every word, starting from recipes for the restaurant of my dreams and then moving on to talking about meeting the man of my dreams. How Nate makes me believe in that future, how he makes me want that future with him more than anything. I read myself falling desperately in love with him, well before I could admit those words to myself.

I'm coming up to that night, the most incredibly passionate, amazing night of my life, so quickly turned the worst. I try to prepare myself—

But before I turn the page, my eyes snag on something I'd written and read over and barely thought about, because it read so naturally to me.

*P is the best man I've ever known. Maybe the best person. So good and kind and hilarious and smart and sincere. The kind of man who I know would be the most incredible husband, the most incredible father. I know I don't deserve someone like him, but more than ever before, I want to.*

My eyes flood with tears, and everything—all of it, every twist and knot of emotions that I couldn't untangle—suddenly makes complete and horrible sense.

*I know I don't deserve someone like him.*

I've worked for years trying to build my self-esteem up after my marriage, and I have come so far, but here is the truth.

I didn't feel like I deserved someone like him, so when it got too real, I took the first excuse to push him away. Yeah, I might have had reasons to doubt, given the situation and his job. But I didn't listen to him at all. I let fear brick up those walls around me that he had somehow slipped through before. And every time my gut tried to tell me that he didn't do anything wrong— an instinct I refused to trust, because trusting that would make me vulnerable again—I found something else to cling to, to pile those bricks higher and thicker. My in-laws, which had nothing to do with him. The thing with the producers picking me, which wasn't proof of anything, no matter how much I tried to make it so.

I read down to the next line.

*But he's the first person who makes me feel like I do deserve every-thing. And that maybe, hopefully, that everything includes him.*

I close the book, the tears making it impossible to read. Hope was too scary after a lifetime without it. So I pushed him away and kept pushing. I was petty and cruel in a way I've never been before, not even with Rob, who deserved it.

Nate never did. I know this, like I can finally see through smeared glass to what was actually on the other side.

I was so afraid with Nate, because there was so much to lose. I've been acting like a terrified child, recklessly lashing out as if to prove that I'm not worth loving, while still clinging to the desperate, subconscious hope that he'd still feel that I am.

But I'm not a child. I am a grown woman, and I can't blame my mistakes on my parents, or Rob, or Paula and Kurt. It was me that hurt Nate, not them. I'm done acting this way. I'm done hurting him. The next time I get the chance, I'm going to talk to him like an adult. I'm going to tell him the truth about last night, and try to explain why I said the things I did, even if it's not an excuse. I'm going to try to be vulnerable again, and if he's willing to talk, I'm going to listen to him this time. Be there for him the way he's been there for me.

He might be totally done with me, might not want to hear a single word I have to say, and I wouldn't blame him for that, no matter how much it breaks my heart.

But I need to try.

# TWENTY-NINE

## Nate

I don't have to lie when I claim I don't feel well and hole up in my hotel room. At first I'm not sure what's wrong with me. Yeah, hearing that Becca slept with Preston felt like getting punched in the stomach and leaves me nauseous for hours. But the full body aches that follow feel like I've caught the flu, and I wonder for a minute if I have.

No, I realize finally. It's not viral. It's grief. Until now, some part of me was still holding out hope that she'd forgive me, that she or Preston would decide to end things, and then maybe when we all got back to LA and away from this hell, Becca would give me a chance to show her that I can be worthy of her trust.

The look on her face in that interview was undeniable, though. It's over. She doesn't want me, and maybe she never did. At the very least, she doesn't feel about me the way I feel about her. Despite the pain, I still love her. I don't know how to stop; I can't turn it off like a faucet. That's not how love works, and if she felt even a fraction of what I do, she couldn't turn it off, either.

I never could have carried on with someone else in front of her and then bragged about it. It would have destroyed me to do it.

The way this is destroying me now.

I give myself twenty-four hours to wallow. I crack the door when Olivia stops by to see if I'm feeling better and tell her I feel like death and am probably contagious. Except for a couple of impatient texts from Levi, I'm left alone.

And I've never felt more lonely in my life. Jason texts me a couple of times for updates and I think about calling him, but instead I send him something noncommittal in response and then turn off my phone.

There's nothing anyone can say to make this better. I've been an idiot and let myself get carried away by the show, by the romance of it all. I'm supposed to be engineering people to fall in love, not falling under the spell myself.

Becca clearly isn't the person I thought she was, so I can't be in love with her, not really. I'm just caught up in feelings for someone who isn't real. I'm in love with a person who doesn't exist.

And she saw how badly it hurt me, I know she did. She knows, and there's nothing I can do about it now. All that's left to do is to get through the end of this with what scraps of dignity I have left. When it's time for production to pack up and head to Italy for the proposals, I take a shower and pack my room and tell Levi I'm feeling much better, thanks. It was probably just food poisoning. He gives me a look like he doesn't entirely believe me, and yeah, okay, there were several people who got a long look at my face when Becca gave her recap of the Dalliance Tower. She and I have been so obvious, it's a wonder he didn't start to suspect something before now.

But it doesn't matter, because there's nothing between Becca and me, so there's nothing to be suspicious about. God knows she's willing to forget about it entirely. Neither of us will say anything, and with the exception of Jason and Emily who now know, it'll be like it never happened.

I help with the remainder of the packing, and hang out with a couple of the other producers for long enough to hear that Preston is still saying "There's just something different about

263

Becca," and making noise about choosing her over Addison or Madison because "being with her would mean growing up and having a family, really giving to someone else in a way I never have before," as if Becca and her children are some kind of rite of passage or lifestyle choice instead of people who need to love and be loved. I feel sick all over again.

Of course he's going to choose her. Of course he is. And Becca will say yes and have her happily ever after, and while it's hard for me to imagine the woman I knew being truly happy with the Preston I've met, it's probable I never really knew her to begin with.

Good for her. If that's what she wants, then it's just as well she cut me loose before I got in any deeper.

But no matter how many times I tell myself that, I never feel any better.

At the airport, I'm put in the group that's flying with the women, while Levi and Dan and a couple of the other producers take an earlier flight with Preston. I'm glad, because I have the irrational urge to punch Prince Charming right in his chiseled jaw. At the airport, I say something about being tired and sit apart from the others, who are more than happy to give me space in case I'm still contagious. I put in ear buds and read the news on my phone and try to pretend that Becca (and Addison and Madison, who keep eyeing each other warily and dancing around the inevitable bitch fight) aren't sitting three rows of airport seats away.

Until Becca sits down next to me. "Nate?" she says.

I don't want to do this right now. I don't want to do this ever. But I remember my goal to keep what's left of my dignity and pull out one ear bud, trying to look disinterested.

"Yeah?" I say, glancing over at her.

This is a mistake. Becca looks nervous as hell. She's sitting with her shoulders hunched forward and picking at her cuticles and looking at me like she's racked with guilt.

Fuck, this is not what I need right now. I'm not going to feel bad about walking out of that interview. I'm not.

"I just wanted to tell you," she says in a low voice, "that I didn't sleep with Preston." She looks over her shoulder at the others, like she doesn't want them to hear, which is probably a good call.

I hate how my heart does a cartwheel in my chest. It shouldn't matter if she slept with Preston. It doesn't change that she *told* me she did and broke me all to hell. She and I are not a thing, and we're never going to be. She's made that clear enough.

"Okay," I say, trying to act like this is the least interesting news I've ever heard. "If you say so."

That was snotty, and I know it, and my heart squeezes when she looks like she's been slapped. "I swear I didn't," she says. "I know I made it sound like I did, and it was awful of me to do that to you, and I'm sorry."

"Whatever," I say. "Look, I get it now, okay? This whole process is confusing, and we got caught up in it. That's all it was."

Becca blinks at me, and I can tell this deeply bothers her, but I don't know why. Obviously that's what happened, right? Because the alternative is that she played me like this on purpose from the beginning, and if that's the case, then Becca deserves a fucking Academy Award.

"The reason I said it," she says slowly, "is because Preston told me he hadn't been the one to decide that I should stay, not for weeks. Not until after our one-on-one. And it hurt that I asked what you thought of our relationship, and you didn't say anything. And it seemed to solidify my belief that you had known about the cameras there, and I just—"

"You knew the producers were going to keep you," I say, finally turning off the music on my phone, though I don't take out the other earbud. "I didn't tell you because I thought *you knew* that's why you were making it through the tiara ceremonies. You told me as much."

Becca takes a deep breath, and I hate myself for how good it feels to have her close, even as much as it hurts. "I knew they

265

were going to keep me in the beginning. I didn't know it had gone on all that time."

I'm a little amazed Preston thought it was a good idea to open his big mouth about that. But I didn't ever mean to keep that a secret.

I'm also not sure how it justifies throwing her overnight with Preston in my face.

"And so, finding that out after I'd trusted you to—" she continues, but I glare hard enough at her that her words cut off.

"You never trusted me," I say coldly. Becca looks like she wants to argue, but I don't want to hear it. I can't. "The first time you had doubts about me, you ran with them. That's not trust. It's a lack of doubt."

Becca looks stunned, and when she nods, I realize how much I wanted her to deny it.

"I'm so sorry," she says, barely above a whisper, but I can't hear that right now, either. Because I know it's not going to be followed up with what my traitorous heart still wants—for her to say that she wants to take all that back, start again, actually trust me this time.

"Maybe I should have told you," I say. "But I didn't want to be that guy who was sabotaging your relationship with Preston, trying to get you to leave the show. It was a conflict of interest. I didn't want to cross that line."

Becca doesn't retort that I was fine with crossing dozens of other lines, which is true.

There's a long beat of silence between us, filled with the sounds of the intercom announcing a flight boarding, and the ambient airport noises of chatter and carry-ons being wheeled down the hallway.

Why the hell is she even still here? Why doesn't she just leave me alone to—

"I told my in-laws about what I said on the show about Rob," Becca says suddenly.

I stare at her. "You . . . seriously? During the family visit?"

"Yeah," she says, hugging her arms around herself. She looks so small, and I want to put my arm around her and tell her it's going to be okay.

But even if she didn't sleep with Preston, she's still dating him. Nothing about this conversation is an invitation to get involved again, and even if it was, I'm not going to let her pull me back in just to break my heart all over again.

I still can't keep myself from asking, "How did it go?"

"Not great," Becca says. For a moment I think she's not going to elaborate, and I guess I can imagine the rest. But then she adds, "They already knew."

That catches me by surprise. "What?"

She shrugs. "It turns out they overheard some things over the years and they suspected there was more. So they knew all along about the way Rob treated me, and they never said anything."

"Shit," I say. If I thought the impulse to reach out to hold her was strong before, it's nothing compared to now. "They *knew*?"

She nods miserably but doesn't elaborate.

"Assholes," I say. I expect her to snap at me that they were in a bad situation, they didn't know what to do. That's probably true, but the fact that they didn't even say anything *after* Rob was gone and they wouldn't have been concerned about interfering in their marriage anymore, that they couldn't have once told her that she didn't have to pretend everything was perfect—

It makes my blood boil, thinking about that weight she's carried, how fiercely she felt she had to protect that secret, for her girls, yes, but for her in-laws, too.

"Yeah," Becca whispers. "Pretty much."

She seems so sad and so alone, and I lift my hand, intending at least to rest it on her arm. I don't want her to feel alone, not ever—

This is how I got caught up in this before. Shit, I can't *do* this again. She says one vulnerable thing to me and I'm just going to get swept away again and let her hurt me over and over.

I can't. However much she might act like she wants me, she's still dating *Preston*. "I'm sorry they did that to you," I say, keeping my voice as detached as possible. I clear my throat and put my other ear bud in and turn the phone away from her so she can't see that the music isn't playing.

Becca hesitates, still sitting there and picking at her nails, and I feel like I could crawl out of my skin. All I want is to have back what I thought I had before—this amazing woman who wanted me and who I wanted with all my heart. Turns out none of it was real—god, how do I know this story about her in-laws isn't just a lie concocted to pull me into her web again?

I can't do this. I need her to leave. I pull one of my ear buds out again and turn to her. "Why are you still here?" I snap.

Becca's eyes widen, and she bites her lip. "Sorry," she says, finally, and gets up and hurries away.

I feel her absence, the cold, empty space where she was just a minute ago. Where she'd still be if I hadn't been such a dick about it.

God, she must be hurting. All I want is to be her shoulder to lean on.

Except that isn't *all* I want. It'll never be *all* I want.

And I can't let her reel me in again just to be cut loose. It hurts too much, and it'll hurt even worse when Preston proposes to her and she accepts.

I hold that image in my mind, and that's what keeps me from pulling her aside to talk to her again.

Just one more week, and I can go miserably home, lick my wounds, and try to figure out how to move on with my life.

There is no reality in which I end up with Becca, so I'm better off if I don't let myself imagine there is.

# THIRTY

## *Becca*

It's the final day of filming, and as insane and emotional and devastating as all of this has been, I should be weeping with joy that it will soon be over. Well, at least until the finale I'm contractually obligated to attend.

I'm beyond done, ready to go home and try to scrape myself out of this emotional pit. But even though I know Nate and I are no longer a possibility, it hurts so much to think that, other than maybe at the finale in a couple months, I'll never see him again.

That's the real reason I've stayed. I told myself so many stories about why, but it's all perfectly clear now to me, the excuses stripped away. I stayed for him. I stayed because deep down, I knew that he hadn't betrayed me, that he did have feelings for me. Because no matter how much I pushed him away out of fear, I couldn't leave him.

It's time to let him go, though—to let him move on and find someone who makes him truly happy, who can be everything good and right that he deserves. Someone who would never hurt him like I did.

There's a part of me that regrets that I wasn't brave enough there in the airport to tell him that I'm in love with him. By the end, though, I knew I'd succeeded in pushing him away for good. I couldn't keep the painful truth about my in-laws from bursting out—selfish though it was to tell him, when he clearly wanted me gone. But it felt even more selfish to share the depth of my feelings for him, to put him in the position of having to tell me that he hadn't felt that strongly. Or to tell me that he had, but he knows now that I'm not the one for him.

He was confused, he said, caught up in the show. But he definitely seemed to have figured out that he's better off without me and the mess I am.

Which is probably true, no matter how much I wish otherwise.

The limo pulls to a stop at the official proposal location, and I take a deep breath. Just a few more minutes and this will be over.

All of it.

"You'll go down the steps," Olivia says. "And we'll do one last hair and makeup check, then Swiss will ask if you're ready, and you'll go to meet Preston. Got it?" She eyes me like she's not sure if she's going to have to repeat these directions.

I may be exhausted from yet another full day of travel getting to Sicily, but I can remember how to walk and stand. "Got it."

The limo door is opened for me, and the thought of Nate commenting on that, with his gentle, teasing smile, makes me want to cry. I adjust my gown enough to step out into the bright sunlight of Southern Italy. We're right at the top of an amphitheater full of picturesque ruins and Roman columns. The whole thing is at the edge of this gorgeous cliff overlooking the sea.

It would be an incredible place to be proposed to, but I'm glad that's not going to happen to me.

I hold up the skirts of my dress as I walk down the long path of stone steps into the amphitheater. Inside, the crew is bustling around, sound people and camera people and producers readying themselves for the show's climax. It's very possible I'm the first of the girls here, though I suppose I could be second and either Madison or Addison have already gone and been rejected. I'm guessing they'll save the actual proposal for last.

I wonder which one of them Preston will choose. Since the Dalliance Tower night, when it was clear to both of us that it wasn't going to be me, I've considered just bowing out entirely. But I know how the show would portray that—they'd find every way possible to make it look like Preston is shocked and devastated by this, when he would definitely not be. And I feel like I owe it to him to let him do the rejecting and not have whoever he proposes to question whether she was only picked by default.

Of the two of them, I kind of hope he picks Addison. Maybe without Madison around to constantly bitch about, she could be a reasonably decent person.

I make it to the bottom of the steps, and, as directed, stand there while my hair is fussed over and my forehead is blotted free of the sweat from the heat.

The makeup artist takes a step back and surveys her work, then smiles. "You look gorgeous."

I think she might actually be right. They already did a full round of hair and makeup back at the hotel, and I was shocked at how they were able to cover the dark circles under my eyes and make me look like I haven't been a zombie for the last several weeks.

Instead, in this white, empire-waist dress stitched with swirls of gold embroidery, I look like a bride on her wedding day, going out to stand on the coast with the man of her dreams. Except that, as I saw in the mirror earlier, my blue eyes look as empty as I am inside.

"You really do," a man's voice says, and my heart suddenly pounds, like it just remembered how to beat again.

I turn around and there's Nate, the actual man of my dreams.

"Thank you." I'm surprised I'm able to form words, given that I don't feel like I can breathe. He's so incredibly handsome, his smile gentle, if sad. It's a good thing the makeup artist and hairstylist both left and no one's standing close by us, seeing me look at him like this. Reading the loss on my face.

"You're supposed to put this on now," he says, holding out one of the "glass slippers." This one isn't actually glass, since I'm going to be walking up to the proposal in it, and I imagine real glass shoes aren't the best for hoofing it more than a few feet.

Whoever gets proposed to, though, will get an actual glass slipper, which Preston will kneel down and slide onto their foot, in lieu of a ring. Madison, Addison, and I all had to get fitted for these things, so that Preston can say something cheesy like "The slipper fits!" and it actually will.

My throat closes up seeing Nate holding this shoe out like that, like he's choosing me out of all these beautiful women.

Except that he did, didn't he? And I made him think I chose someone else, when really I chose to hunker down in my fear and self-protection.

I take the shoe from him and slip off my heels, then put this one on. It's not super comfortable, but I don't have very far to go. At the end of the path, up a small rise of stairs, there's a dais framed with an arch formed by the ruins and columns. Beyond that arch is the dark blue of the sea and light blue of the sky. Up on that dais stands Preston, getting his hair and makeup done, too.

Nate follows my gaze, blinks, and then looks back at me. "I'm sorry for the way I acted at the airport," he says quietly. "I was rude, and it was uncalled for."

I let out a little breath. "I think it *was* called for, considering how I—" I stop myself; I doubt he wants to rehash any of that. Especially given that he's not saying he regrets the intent of the words.

"I'm sorry, too," I finish softly. "I really am."

His lips tug up in that sad, sweet smile. "Whatever happens, Becks, I want you to be happy."

Becks. It's kills me that this may be the last time I ever hear him say my name like that.

No, not *may* be. It will be. He's saying goodbye. A kind goodbye, because he's a good man—the best man—but a goodbye all the same.

"I want the same for you," I say, and it's so true. He deserves every happiness in the world.

My eyes are burning, though, knowing it won't be with me.

I have this moment again where I wonder if I should tell him that I love him, that I've known it for weeks now. Not because I think he'll take me back—or even should—but because maybe he would feel better knowing that I wasn't playing him, that he wasn't alone in having feelings and hurting from the loss of possibility. That this was so very real for me, even if ultimately I'm too messed up to be the person he needs.

But I take too long to decide, and he clears his throat. "It looks like Swiss is headed this way," he says.

Swiss is indeed walking toward us, Mustache Dan at his side. Behind them I can see a few canopy tents, shielding the crew from the sun between the proposals (or non-proposals, as the case may be). Weirdly, I see Madison there, mostly obscured by a handful of producers. She's wearing a white dress, too, though a super formal, Renaissance-looking one that has a stiff skirt that stretches so far out to either side, she looks like the upper half of her is perched atop a white, lace-covered wall. She looks upset—furious, more like.

She must have been rejected already. I would have thought they'd send her back to the hotel, but maybe they'll send us back together.

That'll be fun.

I look back at Nate, then down at my feet. One is in a shoe and the other is barefoot. "Am I really supposed to hobble up there with only one shoe? Won't my foot be filthy?"

"Don't worry," he says. "They have people up there to clean it."

Oh my god. The ridiculousness of this show.

Before I can say anything more, Swiss arrives, and Mustache Dan is calling over some sound guys. Nate turns and walks away toward the crew area, his hands in his pockets.

My heart lurches like it's trying to go with him.

273

Swiss ignores me until the cameras and mics are in position. When they start filming again, he looks at me with a fatherly fondness. "So, Becca, are you ready to meet Preston and find out if the slipper fits?"

"I am."

"Best of luck to you, my lady," he says, sweeping his hand toward the ruins. "Your prince awaits."

Then his job is over—how much does this dude get paid for occasionally showing up to ask a question or state something obvious?—and he stands back while I attempt to hobble gracefully up a dirt path.

I fail at this, but I make it to the stone dais without falling over, so that's a win. The ruins all around are gorgeous enough, but they've added pots of colorful flowers, and vines twirl down the two columns of the arch under which Preston is standing. He's wearing a new, even more formal navy-blue princely outfit, and on a pedestal beside him, there is a glass slipper on a velvet cushion. Which will fit Addison, apparently, given what I just saw.

He grins at me—no nerves there, probably because he knows he won't have to deal with another crying mess on this rejection. As Nate said, a couple producers come out when I walk up the steps, and they clean off my bare foot. This part will definitely be cut out of the final product. They back out of the shot, and the cameras zoom in on my feet as I take the last couple of steps toward Preston.

I can't help it—I look back at Nate, who, like most of the crew and producers, is not too far away, watching. I notice Levi standing right next to him and I look quickly away again.

"Becca," Preston says, and he takes both my hands in his. "You look incredible."

I know my role in this. "You, too," I say back with a pasted-on smile.

He pauses for a moment, and then his expression turns serious.

"Our relationship has been quite the journey," he says. "It was a slower build than many of the others, but as I grew to know you better, I became increasingly impressed by the amazing woman you are."

I keep smiling, but I'm wishing he would get on with it. Get into the rejection meat of the compliment sandwich, so I can look properly heartbroken (not hard to reach for these last few weeks) and confirm that the slipper doesn't fit (why do they make the rejected girls go through with that?) then gracefully wish him all the best and get the hell out of here so I can mourn my real loss in private.

"I had such a great time with you on our first one-on-one," he continues. "Honestly, all the time we've spent together has been wonderful, and I can tell you deserve someone truly special to spend the rest of your life with." Still holding my hands, he frowns at the ground.

Fantastic. Here we go.

"I just—" he starts, then looks up at me. "I truly hope that can be me."

Wait. *What?*

"You are the one I want to be with, Becca," he continues. "You are the princess that I want to live happily ever after with."

I'm gaping in shock. Why on god's green earth is he picking *me*? Didn't he agree in the Dalliance Tower that we aren't a thing? Isn't he aware that we have absolutely *nothing* between us?

My gaze flicks back to Nate again, who looks considerably less shocked. But I can't read his expression, not really.

Preston chuckles. "I can tell you're surprised. Honestly, the way I fell so deeply for you surprised me, too. But you were so much more than I ever expected when we first met."

"Preston—" I start, caring far less about the backhanded compliments than getting him to stop before he actually—

He puts a finger over my lips. "Let me finish."

Did he just *shush* me? Now I'm both stunned *and* annoyed.

He picks up the glass slipper, which sparkles in the sunlight, and drops to one knee. "I have a feeling the slipper will fit," he says, all wide, charming smiles.

"Preston, I don't think—"

"Becca Hale, will you marry me?"

I'm frozen for a few seconds, feeling a bead of sweat work its way down between my shoulder blades. Feeling the many, many cameras on me in a way I stopped noticing weeks ago.

He blinks up at me with this expectant expression, but there's only one answer I can give.

"Um," I say. "No."

It may be full daylight out, but I swear I hear the chirping of crickets in the heavy silence that follows.

"What?" Preston asks, confused.

Why is he confused by this?

"I can't, um. I can't marry you. I'm sorry."

He gets back to his feet. "Seriously? Why not?"

There are many reasons why not, but the one that tumbles out is this: "Because I'm in love with someone else." My heart stops again. *Don't look at Nate. Don't look at Nate.*

I guess I decided to let him know, after all.

Preston, though, is now the one gaping. "You never mentioned some other guy. Who is he?"

"He's someone I hurt badly, and I messed everything up, and I—" I swallow, my throat too thick. Shit. I'm in the middle of a proposal here. I try to focus back on Preston. "But regardless of who he is, I can't marry you, and I'm so sorry that—"

"No, I want to know! Who the hell is it?" Preston's face is growing redder by the second.

*Don't look at Nate. Don't look at Nate.*

"It doesn't matter," I say. "What matters is that I can't accept—"

"It matters to me!" He flings his hands outward, and it's a good thing he's got a tight grip on that glass shoe, or it might have clocked the boom mic operator standing several feet to the side. "Dude! I had *twenty-nine* other chicks who wanted to marry me! What's wrong with you?"

Any guilt I might have felt at turning his proposal into a

declaration of my feelings for Nate quickly withers. I narrow my eyes at Preston. "I told you in the Dalliance Tower that this wasn't happening," I say, giving that same back and forth between us gesture I did that night. "You agreed!"

"I thought you meant you still didn't want to have sex! Like, I don't know, you were on your period or something, and didn't want to say it."

Oh. My. God. Are we talking about my *period* on national TV now?

"Look, Preston." I'm trying to hold it together, even though I'm seething. "I'm sorry I wasn't clearer. I thought you understood. But I don't want to marry you." I turn to step away.

"You don't get to walk away from me!" Preston yells, and then he throws the slipper at me. It bounces off my skirt and shatters all over the stone.

I freeze again, surrounded by glittering shards of glass with one of my feet bare. I'm not hurt—thank god for full skirts—but my muscles are tense, my pulse pounding in my ears. The whole amphitheater is echoing with gasps, one of which may or may not be mine.

"What the hell?" I hear Nate yell, and I swivel to look at him. His face is a thundercloud, and he was clearly headed this way, but Levi has a grip on his arm now, tugging him back.

"If you want to keep your job, you'll fucking stay right here," Levi growls, then turns to gesture wildly at someone over by the canopies.

Nate wrenches his arm from Levi's hand and looks like he's going to tell him where he can shove his job—holy shit, is he really going to do that?—when suddenly a woman's voice calls out shrilly, "Preston! Wait!"

We all turn to see Madison in her massive white wall of a wedding dress running this way. She was apparently far enough back that she didn't hear what was happening up here, because she calls out, "Don't propose! Don't marry her, Preston!"

In addition to marksmanship, Madison must also have won

trophies in football, because she is booking it in that dress, ramming through crew like Marie Antoinette turned quarterback, her wide skirts knocking over a camera and its hapless operator, and nearly taking Nate out as well.

She gets to the bottom of the dais, breathing heavily, her strawberry-blond hair falling out of its intricate bun. "Preston, you can't propose to her!" She glares at me so hard I almost take a step back, until I remember that there are shards of glass all around me. "She's not here for you," Madison growls. "She's sleeping with *him*!"

She whirls around and points right at Nate, and my stomach drops to my toes. Nate stares at me, his eyes wide, and I stare right back, neither of us having the faintest clue of what to do. Cameras are pointed every which way—at me and Preston, but also at Madison and Nate.

Levi is still standing next to Nate like he's ready to grab him again. There's this smug expression on Levi's face, and it's all suddenly too clear—he already knew about Nate and me. Maybe someone on the show did get their hands on my journal. Or maybe we weren't nearly as subtle as we'd hoped.

Regardless, he knew and he must have told Madison, and now he's unleashed her like a vengeful, beauty pageant Kraken.

Preston whirls back from gaping at Madison to gaping at me again. "You wouldn't sleep with me, but you slept with a fucking *producer*?"

I'm about to yell at Preston how that *fucking producer* is a hundred times more of a man than he'll ever be, but Levi's own furious proclamation cuts me off.

"Is this true?" he barks at Nate, all smugness gone, replaced by faked indignation. "Because if so, I will fire you so fast your—"

"No need," Nate says. "I quit."

Then he storms up onto the dais, shoving none-too-gently past Preston, and scoops me up in his arms. "I've got you, Becks," he says quietly.

My heart is hammering and my whole body is flushed with

heat as I twine my arms around his neck, holding him tight. Then he carries me past the shards of glass and down the steps, and this feels like the most surreal dream, like maybe I'm deep asleep back at the hotel. Possibly on some sort of drug trip?

"Fine!" Preston yells after us. "Whatever. I don't need you, anyway. It's—It's *her* I need!" He turns back to Madison. "I knew it," he says, clearly trying to recover his princely mask of romantic charmingness that somehow managed to hide his ultimate douchebaggery from every single one of us. "I let myself doubt it, but I knew it was you all along, Madison. It's you I want to spend the rest of my life with."

They're getting farther behind us as Nate carries me through the crowd of crew, which is parting to let us pass, but we're still close enough to hear Madison smugly proclaim, "I knew it too! I love you, Preston."

Yep, if I'm dreaming all of this, I am definitely high.

But Nate feels real, so solid and right as I cling to him, as I feel his strong arms holding me tight. We're near the edge of the amphitheater when he sets me down on my feet—one foot bare and one still in that fake glass slipper.

There are a few cameras following us, though most of them have been summoned by Levi to film the second proposal. Preston is on one knee now and Madison is struggling to get up the stairs to the dais in that horrific dress. But I only see all of this for a heartbeat, before I'm looking into Nate's warm brown eyes and the rest of the world disappears.

He stares back at me with the same intensity I feel in every part of me, and I think that maybe everything else has disappeared for him, too.

"Did you really mean that?" he asks hesitantly, like he's too afraid to hope, and god, so am I, except I can't help it, I can't help but wildly hope. "Are you really—"

"I am," I say, flushing again at cutting him off. "I'm in love with you, Nate. And I know I don't deserve to—"

He cradles my head in his hands and brings his lips to mine, and we're kissing desperately, deeply, recklessly. Everything is him and me and longing and bliss I never thought I'd feel again, not like this.

He pulls back, a stunned smile on his face. "I love you too," he says, pressing his forehead against mine.

I close my eyes, breathe in those words like the first gasp of air I've had in so long.

But I have to know . . . "Are you sure you're not just confused?" I look back up at him, his face right there, warm against mine.

"I was never confused," he says. "Never."

My bliss burns even brighter. I grin at him and he grins back.

"We should get out of here," he says. "Before they come after us."

He's not wrong; it's only a matter of time before they get all the footage they need of Madison and Preston furiously making out under the arch, and Levi decides to storm over here and threaten lawsuits. I doubt we'll make that any worse by running.

"I'm all for that," I say. "But I'm not sure how we'll manage to hijack one of the limos."

"Good point. Do they have Uber here?"

I laugh. "We're going to call an Uber to carry us off into the sunset? Are we going to stand around here and wait for this Uber?"

He gets a mischievous spark in his eye that makes me weak all over. "Nope." He pulls his phone out of his pocket and hands it to me, then scoops me up again so fast, I let out a surprised squeal. "You're calling the Uber, and I'm carrying you off into the sunset to wait for it somewhere else."

I'm not opposed to that. He holds me tight and starts jogging up the stairs out of the amphitheater while I search for the Uber app, bouncing in his arms with every step and giggling like a giddy maniac.

Or maybe a woman who can't believe she's back in the arms of the man she loves.

"Holy god, there are a lot of stairs," he says about halfway up, starting to get winded. "This will be way less romantic if I have to stop and stretch."

"You're a rock climber, man," I say back, still laughing. "You can manage a few stairs. Just don't drop me."

"No way." He grins at me. "I told you, Becks. I've got you."

And he does. Oh, how he does.

# THIRTY-ONE

## *Nate*

Between running down the block and finding our Uber and checking into a motel, it takes thirty minutes before Becca and I can finally sit down together and relax. She's still wearing her gown and limping along without a shoe, and we've left with nothing except my wallet and phone, but it feels so good to be out from under the eye of the cameras—which we lost sometime after we got into the Uber, Levi having thankfully failed to prepare for a slow-speed chase through the streets of Sicily.

Becca collapses onto the bed, groaning.

As near as I can tell, we're on the other side of the city from the hotel where the show is camped, though I know we're going to have to go back there eventually, not in the least because we left our passports behind. But it's nice to have a small reprieve—a place to breathe and regroup and figure out what the hell just happened.

Becca looks up at me and smiles weakly. "We really did that. We ran off together."

I smile back. "I wish we'd done that a long time ago."

Becca rests the heels of her hands against her eyes. "Me too!" She groans again, and I settle onto the bed next to her and reach for her hand.

"Are you okay?" I ask.

"I mean, I'm not injured from having a glass shoe thrown at me, if that's what you're asking."

"That's not what I'm asking. Are you okay?"

She looks up at me, and there's hesitation in her eyes. "I really do love you. So much. I meant that."

"I love you, too." Like I was when we ran away together, I'm surprised at how easily the words come. I'm in love with Becca. It's been true for a long time, and it's still true, after everything.

"I'm so sorry I didn't trust you," Becca says. "That's obviously an issue I have, but it was never about you. I let my fear and my doubts and all my issues get the better of me, and I obviously handled this in the worst way possible. But if you'll give me another chance, I swear I'll work on it. I'll talk about it in therapy, and if you want to take things slow until you can be sure that I won't run again—"

"Is that what you want?" I probably shouldn't have interrupted her, but the idea of taking things slow is agonizing. I'll do it, if it's what she needs, but—

"No," she says. "But I really don't deserve for you to—"

"I don't want that, either. I'm in this, Becks. Completely."

Tears form in her eyes, and I pull her into my arms and kiss her softly, then rest my forehead against hers. "If you need time before you can trust me, you've got it. Take however long you need, but please, give me a chance. I swear, I won't give you any more reasons to doubt."

Becca kisses me again, and we hold each other tightly, like we're both afraid if we let go, the other person is going to slip away again.

"You don't need to prove anything," she says. "If anyone does, it's me. I'm so sorry, Nate." She burrows into me and I nod against her hair. I see it so much more clearly now that I'm not racked with all the pain and bitterness—maybe I wouldn't have done what she did, not in that way, but I don't have the same scars, the same wreckage from the past. She did some hurtful things, but it doesn't mean that she doesn't love me or that she's not the same Becca I fell in love with. It never did.

And really, there's blame to go around.

"I'm sorry, too." I take a deep breath. "It was my job to manipulate you, and while I kept telling myself I was going to protect you from the ways they were trying to exploit you, in the end I couldn't. I became part of it instead, even though I didn't want to. I should have quit a long time ago, but I knew if I did, I'd never see you again."

"I know what you mean," she says. "I wasn't into Preston. I kept trying to convince myself I had all these reasons I needed to stay, but really, the thought of leaving you was unbearable."

Oh my god. We trapped each other there. Looking back, it's obvious what we each should have done, but at the time, neither of us had the foresight to do it.

"It'll be okay, now," I say. Even though I'm still terrified, I'm going to fight like hell to make that true.

"Will it, though? What's going to happen when we go home?"

"I want to be with you."

She lays her head on my shoulder, breathing softly against my neck. "Me too. But the show. What are they going to do?"

Shit, the show. We've escaped them for the moment, but not forever.

"You still have to honor your non-disclosure agreement," I say. "Which means we can't be seen together, at least not after the show starts and people know who you are."

Becca tenses. "Does that mean we won't be able to see each other at all?"

"We'd have to do it in secret. Until the show starts to air, no one will recognize you, so we could go out in public, but we couldn't be open about our relationship online or to our friends." Ha. "Except Jason and Emily. They already know."

"Really?" Becca says.

"I might have called Jason to whine when you were in the

Dalliance Tower."

Becca cringes. "I really didn't sleep with Preston," she says.

"I know," I say softly. "I believe you. But at the time, I was a mess, and I needed someone to talk to."

"I totally get it. He's your best friend, right?" She pauses. "Does he hate me?"

I laugh. "Jason's not a hateful person. He hopes things will work out for us."

"And then he's going to watch the show and it's going to look like I'm into Preston." She groans. "Not to mention your family will see this, and—"

"Hey," I say, rubbing my hand up and down her arm. "It's going to be okay. They're all going to get it, and more importantly, they're going to see how happy I am with you, and they're going to love you. Because you're awesome."

She lets out a shaky breath, and I'm not sure she's convinced, especially of that last part, but damn if I'm not going to do everything I can to help her believe it. "And what do you think they're going to do with that finale? The show, I mean."

"Villainize us, I would guess," I say.

"Villainize *us*. When their Prince Charming threw a shoe."

"They probably won't show that part." Shit. The more I think about it, the more I'm sure the show is going to tear us to pieces. "We'll have to keep everything quiet until we see what they air, so we won't be able to get ahead of it."

Her arms tighten around me. "Do you think when it airs, it'll make you remember how awful I was to you?"

"Well, I was there the first time," I say. "And I didn't exactly handle it with grace."

"A hell of lot more grace than I did. And I'm not even talking about nearly face-planting out of the carriage on night one."

"I think it's safe to say this situation didn't bring out the very best in either of us."

"Welllll . . ." she says with a coy twist to her lips. "I can think of some things that felt like the very best."

My body heats up and I chuckle. "Okay, yeah. I can too."

We look at each other, heat passing between us. "Will I really not be able to see you once the show starts airing?" she asks.

"We can sneak around. If you don't mind me being around a lot, I could camp out at your place at least some of the time."

"I think I'm going to want you around all the time," she says, and I smile. After what we've been through, I pretty much want to attach myself to her, too.

"What do you think the girls will say?"

"Thea came within an inch of starting an official Mom Should Date Nate campaign, so she'll be thrilled. And Rosie will be happy, because Rosie is always happy."

"Except when she's not," I say, and Becca grins.

"Except when she's not. But trust me, this won't be one of those times."

"I'm excited to see them again. And to talk to Thea about something other than whether or not you should be dating Prince Charming. Though I'm going to have to learn a lot more sign language than I've picked up from YouTube."

Becca lights up. "You can practice with us! And you could take a course—online, probably, because I'm guessing you shouldn't do that in person, what with all the sneaking around we're going to be doing."

I take a deep breath. "The sneaking around is going to suck. And the press is probably going to be merciless once the finale airs. Are you sure it's worth it?"

"I'm sure *you're* worth it," she says. "But I don't blame you if you don't think that I am."

"You're worth everything to me," I tell her, and I mean it. "All I want is to be with you, for real, without the cameras and the rules and everything. It's not going to be easy, but there's nothing I want more."

She melts into me, but concern flits across her face. "Do you think our lives will fit together, though? That's what you wanted, right? Someone who fits."

"Becks, anything in my life that doesn't fit with us can go. I want to be with you, and we'll *make* our lives fit. If you want that."

"I do," she says with a sigh. "All I want is to be with you."

I kiss her again, and god, it feels so good. Our future is still uncertain, and when the show airs, I wonder if she'll find all sorts of new reasons to doubt me.

But I'm going to choose her, every day, for as long as she'll let me. "Do you want to stay a couple more days in Italy? We'll have to fly ourselves back, but I can pay for it. We can show up tomorrow and deal with the crap they're going to give us in exchange for our luggage, and then we can take a few days and relax before we have to go back to California and camp out until after the show airs."

"That sounds amazing," She loops her arms around my neck and kisses me again, and there's no better feeling in the world. I lay her back on the bed, and she pulls me down on top of her. Our bodies lock together, and we're kissing and kissing, and I want to devour her. I hope she knows how much it means to me to have her in my arms when I was certain I never would again. Her skirts are spread over the bed, and I draw her body up against mine so I can reach around and unzip the back of her dress.

Becca laughs against my lips. "Thank god it's not stuck this time," she says, and I laugh with her and pull the dress down her body and toss it into a heap on the floor. I'm sure she'll want to hang it up later—she looked so beautiful in it, like an angel—but right now, I don't want to be apart from her even for a moment. She's lying beneath me in a white, strapless bra and cotton panties, much less elaborate than the lacy underwear she wore when she snuck into my room, but no less sexy.

Because it's Becca. She's the most incredible woman in the world and I want her and want her and want her. She lifts my shirt up over my head, and that's enough separation for now. I kiss down her neck and over the tops of her breasts and find the bra catch—in the back this time, where I expect it to be—and prove that I can, in fact, remove that article of clothing without fumbling. I kiss right between her breasts and down, down to her belly button and this time she doesn't tense when I run my tongue over her scars.

Becca whispers my name and grabs me by my arms, hauling me up and on top of her again, and she wraps her legs tight around my waist, pressing us together right there, oh god, right there, *yes*—

We're moving together through my jeans and her underwear and having her body locked around mine like that just about undoes me.

"I love you," I tell her, and she echoes it back, and I can't have all these layers between us, not anymore. I think Becca feels the same, because she's undoing the button on my jeans. I slip my hands down the sides of her underwear and drag them over her thighs and then run my hand back up, sliding my fingers right between her legs.

I think I take her by surprise, because she gasps and arches back, and I'm not teasing her this time. My fingers dip inside her and I groan at how wet she is, how warm and tight. She gives up on my jeans and falls back against the mattress, uttering my name as a moan, and while I've been in love with her for weeks now, I still feel like I'm falling, and wonder if maybe I always will.

Becca's whole body shudders, but I don't think she's gotten there, not yet. She renews focus on my fly and tugs down my pants. My boxers come with them and I have to drag my hand away to help her take them off. I mean to go right back to what I was doing, but Becca has other plans. She twists beneath me and shoves me onto my back, climbing on top of me with her knees on either side of my hips.

I lie back in a daze, watching this goddess as she rides up on me, and then reaches down and pulls me inside her with one fluid movement.

"Becks," I gasp, and she moans as her eyes flicker closed. I keep mine open, watching her move on top of me, lifting my hips to drive into her deeper and deeper.

I still can't believe she's mine, this exquisite, beautiful person I love with all my heart and then some. Becca runs her hands up my chest, and I slip mine up the soft skin of her back, scratching gently with my nails. She responds with the most delicious groan and then we're lost in the rhythm and pleasure and the ever-rising song of *us*. Becca crests and peaks before I do, crying out and then kissing me recklessly as she continues to move on top of me, bringing me to heights I've never reached, not with anyone before, even with her. My voice lacks the control even to form her name, and I moan wordlessly as she brings me through.

After, as I'm holding her tight in my arms with nothing between us, I'm struck with the profound depth of how lucky I am to be here with her. She's my heart and my home and my everything, and all I want is to be with her forever and always.

If we can survive what's coming, I'll have everything I need for the rest of my life.

# THIRTY-TWO

## Becca

## Ten Weeks Later

Nate and I are sitting backstage on a leather couch in front of a mounted flat screen, on which is playing the reunion of my season of *Chasing Prince Charming*. We watch as Swiss Barrington introduces the show and hypes it as the most dramatic finale in *Charming* history.

He says that every season, but at least for Nate and I, it's the truth. We're gripping each other's hands, and I'm tucked up under his arm, exactly where I like to be.

Nate and I survived the last two and a half months mostly by holing up in my apartment with the kids. He snuck out to work with Jason, and I'm glad he won't have to do that anymore now that the finale is airing. He tried to pretend it was no big deal, but it was pretty obvious that being a Black man who's secretly living in a white woman's apartment was terrifying enough without having to skulk through the alley at the back of the complex a couple times a week for Jason to pick him up and take him to a climb.

After this, that will all be done—though it's possible we'll *both* be having to sneak around to avoid aggressive press. Nate swears if it gets bad enough we'll move to a gated community or hire security, but while Nate's a lot better off financially than I am, he's not exactly celebrity-wealthy, so I hope it doesn't come to that.

Swiss stops talking and the footage from the show starts to air. This is a live finale, so we're all here in a studio with an audience of women who will no doubt be convinced over the next forty minutes to hate me to the point of hair pulling and eye gouging. To say I'm not looking forward to stepping on that stage and facing this is an understatement, and I'm so glad to have Nate here beside me.

He didn't have to be. His contract was over after that last day on set. Mine isn't fulfilled until I face Preston again at this finale, where they're airing the pre-recorded proposals and doing live interviews between them. Nate didn't want me to have to take the brunt of this alone.

Really, I wish neither of us were here.

I try to watch as Addison approaches Preston on screen with her one-shoe limp—why do they make us do that?—but I can't focus on the dramatic moment where she discovers the glass slipper doesn't fit.

I grip Nate's hand so tight I'm probably hurting him, and he holds mine back, firm and steady. It won't be long before they reveal my "affair" on screen.

We're probably about to become America's most hated couple, but at least the anticipation will be over. Dreading this day has eaten me alive these last few months.

Thank god for Nate. He's been my rock and my center, and I'm so grateful for him, even if the way we handled our relationship has turned our lives upside down.

Addison leaves sobbing and does a tearful interview about how she can't believe Preston didn't choose her, how their connection was so incredible, and "Why does Madison always win, that bitch!"

She has no idea.

Nate and I have watched every episode of the show, of course, and we decided it was better not to suffer through it alone, so we let Jason and Emily make us the center of their usual viewing parties, which had to switch to my apartment for the sake of privacy. No one in the press seems to have caught wind that Jason of *Climbs Sh!t* fame has been showing up at my house every Tuesday night for the last several weeks. Having them there has helped a lot, though it still didn't make it easy.

There were definitely plenty of hilarious moments—Nate laughed his ass off at my pronouncement that "cocks are great," which was footage he hadn't seen. But it was so painful watching myself date Preston, especially the episode with the terrible make-out footage the night of the Dalliance Tower, which looked a lot more sexy on film than in reality. I was so afraid that Nate would remember how horrible I'd been to him and break up with me, but he held me through every episode, and late at night, after Jason and Emily went home, we talked it all through.

If whatever happens tonight is the price to be with Nate, I'll gladly pay it.

But I still close my eyes as the screen switches back to Swiss, who makes some bland comments about how heartbreaking that was and then invites Preston out so Addison can confront him.

Nate lets out a long breath. "I knew how long it was going to take for them to get to us, but I had no idea how long it was going to *feel*."

"No kidding." I'm glad we're in a room by ourselves, if only so we don't have to pass any more smug production staff who are no doubt looking forward to seeing us get ours for taking the show off script. I desperately want to be back in the apartment with Nate, me cooking and him reading to the girls. He's been practicing his signing skills by reading picture books to Rosie with Thea on the other side of the room refusing to correct him and instead laughing at all of his grammar mistakes. He's a good sport about it, and they've ended up with some pretty great sign-related inside jokes, some of which I still don't completely understand. The girls have been almost as happy to have him around as I have. He's so natural with them. I never would have imagined finding someone who could fit so perfectly into my life.

Which is good, because getting to this point wasn't easy, and I don't know how easy this next chapter is going to be, either.

Addison tearfully leaves the stage after telling Preston several times that no, she *still* doesn't understand why he didn't pick her, and no, *that* explanation doesn't clarify things. Not that Preston is being particularly forthcoming, speaking mostly in the canned answers this show is so fond of. She leaves crying again about Madison always getting everything she wants, and I wonder if Addison remembers that I exist. The show hasn't revealed yet who Preston chose, though from the murmuring in the audience when Swiss cuts to the footage of Madison arriving at the proposal stage, I think everyone assumed it was going to be her.

I can't blame them. Even though the show used the footage where I tried to convince Nate I'd slept with Preston, our relationship still had the least on-camera steam. According to the internet, I have my own contingent of fans, but the general opinion seems to be that I'm too good for Preston.

I doubt that's going to be the case much longer.

Nate squeezes my waist and looks down at me. "You okay?"

"I don't know," I say. "You?"

"Terrified," he says. We both laugh nervously, even though it isn't really funny.

When Preston rejects her, Madison holds it together a lot better than Addison did, but she does give an impassioned speech about how obvious it is that Preston is making a huge mistake not picking someone as gorgeous and accomplished as she is. She storms off, and I take a deep breath. They won't cut it there. They'll show my proposal and refusal, then bring me out, saving the actual engaged couple for the very end.

There are some very shocked reaction shots of the audience as they do just that, without bringing Madison out to talk to Preston first as expected. I wince as I watch myself hobble up

293

to Preston, watch my own shocked and then horrified face as Preston delivers his proposal.

"Tell me how you really felt," Nate says, elbowing me gently.

On screen, I fumble through my refusal, and I expect that the show is going to cut it there, or at least edit out Preston's reaction.

But they don't.

Preston delivers every word of his hissy fit and then throws the shoe, which shatters on the ground with a resounding crash that I think must have been added after the fact.

Nate and I stare at each other. We've spent hours dissecting all the ways they might cut this together, but never did we imagine they'd really air every moment of their star losing his shit at me.

Madison appears, seemingly rushing out of nowhere, though Nate and I have pieced together that Levi must have had her on standby in case I didn't behave the way they wanted me to when Preston offered me the slipper. Madison gives Preston her (second, apparently) impassioned speech, accusing me of sleeping with Nate, though the cameras aren't really focused on us, instead working out a happy ending for their happy couple. On-screen Preston, confronted by one of the other twenty-nine chicks who wanted to marry him, drops immediately to one knee.

The footage ends there, without showing any more of Nate and me. Swiss appears on stage, calling for Madison and Preston to join him.

"No," Nate says. "No way. They're doing *them* first?"

I'm equally stunned. The show *always* ends with the happily ever after. They don't bring out the final couple and *then* drag the Prince through more interviews with women he didn't end up with.

What the hell are they doing?

Madison and Preston both walk onto the stage, but they aren't smiling or holding hands. In fact, they're walking a good six feet apart and looking very uncomfortable.

"Well," Swiss says as he sits them down. "Tell us what has

happened since that day."

"I'm guessing a lot," I say, my eyes wide. Nate silently nods, just as riveted as I am.

"I'm sorry to say, it hasn't all been slippers and roses," Madison says. "We've found we have some irreconcilable differences."

The audience members in the reaction shots look more confused than anything, but they're obviously eating it up, and Madison goes on to say that it "all began with an Instagram post" and elaborates about how Preston, for all she thought she knew him, has turned out to be in favor of gun reform. Which, she says firmly, is *not* what she stands for. "You don't slam the NRA in my house," she says resolutely. "No, sir."

"Oh my god," Nate says, and I echo him.

Swiss asks for Preston's take, and he gives a bland answer about how he's just not sure that Madison is in their relationship "for the right reasons," an answer that makes a whole lot less sense now that they're no longer dating on a show. The two of them begin talking over each other, both clearly intent on coming out of this as the one least at fault.

"They're awful," Nate says.

"They are," I say. "I mean, we knew that, but they *look* awful."

Nate looks over at me. "What are they going to do with *us*?"

I don't know, but as Preston holds up his hands like he can no longer abide to talk with Madison any longer and Madison responds by snatching the roses from the centerpiece on the coffee table in front of him and whipping him across the face with them, it's hard for me to imagine that we're going to come off looking worse than them.

"All right!" Swiss says. "We're not quite done. What about Becca? What about her mystery man?"

"Her *mystery man*?" Nate says.

I appear on the screen again, and Nate steps forward, sweeping me off my feet and carrying me away from the glass. The footage shows Nate and I reuniting and kissing on camera, there for the world to see. This is interspersed with dozens of reaction shots from the audience as some of these women are losing their shit. None of them seem angry. Just shocked and a bit delighted at the drama.

"Oh my god," Nate says again as we run from the cameras, me ordering an Uber on his phone. "Are they making *us* their happy ending?"

I can't quite bring myself to believe that's what's happening. It feels like a trap, like they're trying to make me comfortable before they reveal their actual intentions. But then there's a knock on the door, and it opens.

"Becca," one of the pages says, "Swiss is ready for you."

*Shit.* "Just me?"

"For now."

Nate squeezes my hand. "You can do this."

I hope, for all of our sakes, that he's right.

When I'm ushered onto the stage, I try not to look as off-kilter as I feel, but I doubt I'm succeeding. Preston is still sitting there with Swiss, and I have no idea how they introduced me, because I was backstage with the page at the time.

"Welcome, Becca!" Swiss motions for me to join Preston on the settee among the scattered rose petals from Madison's floral attack. I sit almost as far away from him as she did, and I imagine I look even more uncomfortable.

"Preston," Swiss says. "You were telling me you have some things you'd like to ask Becca."

My palms sweat. I imagine he does have a lot of questions, and from the way the audience is sitting on the edge of their seats, I think they're in agreement.

I take a deep breath, glad that Nate's close by, even if he's not on stage with me yet. Before we left my apartment—in separate cars, with him sneaking out the courtyard exit so as not to be spotted leaving my place—he told me one more time what a badass he thinks I am.

I want to be that person tonight. For him, for my girls, and for me.

"Yes," Preston says. "What I don't understand is how you could do this to me."

My first utterance on the stage is to stutter a bit as I take in that question. Not exactly badass, but definitely deserved. "How I could do this to you?" I ask finally.

"Yes. I was taking this seriously, looking for love, and *you* were carrying on with some producer the entire time."

"Not the *entire* time," I hedge, though that probably isn't making me seem any more sympathetic.

"Really," Preston says. "When exactly did this thing with the producer begin?"

"First of all, his name is Nate," I say, finding my footing. "And yes, Preston, I'm sorry for the way that my actions affected you. I don't regret being with Nate—"

"So you're still together?" Swiss interjects, and I smile.

Talking about being with Nate always makes me smile.

"Yes, we're together," I say. "We're very happy."

There's an uncertain rumble from the audience, but I think I hear a few "awwws" interspersed in there, which give me the courage to keep going. "I don't regret being with Nate, but I do regret that I hurt you."

"You don't regret being with the guy you *cheated* on me with?" Preston says, and I stare at him. Where is the dude who can't speak except in platitudes now?

"I didn't mean to disrespect the process," I say, more loudly than is necessary given that I'm wearing a mic. "But I definitely didn't appreciate the way you reacted when I turned down your proposal."

Preston's mouth falls open, like he can't believe I'm bringing *that* up, even though it should have been obvious. "I just couldn't believe you'd stoop so low."

"As to turn you down?" I ask. "You threw a *shoe* at me."

"You didn't know that then," Preston scoffs. "And who among us hasn't had a shoe thrown at them?"

I do imagine this is something that's happened to Preston

several times in his life. Wonder why. "It was a glass object. You assaulted me, and I could have been hurt."

"But you weren't," Preston insists. "And it wasn't assault! Did you hear what she said?" He seems to be asking this of the audience generally and not of Swiss, who, for all that it's his job to peddle in drama, is looking more than a little uncomfortable himself. "She's delegitimizing real abuse victims everywhere."

My mouth falls open. So do many mouths in the audience.

"I'm *delegitimizing* abuse victims?" I say. I wait for the irony in Preston's statement to sink in, but it doesn't appear to.

"Oh my god!" he says, this time to Swiss. "She's acting like *she's* the victim!"

This earns a chuckle out of the audience, along with a soft hiss and at least one full-on "Boooo." I will probably feel satisfaction about this later, but right now all I can feel is shock that Preston is actually saying these things.

*He's doing you a favor*, Nate would say.

Really, I think he is. It will be very hard for them to paint me as a villain after this.

"Look," I say, trying to get in control of the situation. "I'm sorry that I hurt you, but it's not like you weren't dating a lot of other women at the time."

"I was supposed to be!" Preston shouts. "But you weren't supposed to be dating anyone but me. And did you really *sleep* with him?"

"Yes, I did!" I'm not sure that was the best thing to admit, but damn it, I'm tired of hiding, and I'm not going to do so for the comfort of someone like Preston. "And it was *awesome*."

There's a stunned gasp from the audience and a moment of deafening silence. Then someone far in the back starts to clap, and the rest of the audience joins in with catcalls and applause. I feel my face grow hot, but I let myself grin.

That's right. Being with Nate *is* awesome, and I don't care if everyone knows it.

Preston is sputtering, and before he can figure out what else he wants to shout at me, Swiss cuts him off. "We need to go to commercial break, and after that, we'll have a chat with Becca about what exactly went on with her and Nate the producer."

Then, before I know what's happening, security appears and escorts Preston right off the stage, still sputtering. We've gone to commercial, but the cameras are no doubt still capturing my reaction as the audience claps for this as well.

Holy shit. This is not at all how I expected this to go.

"So, Becca," Swiss says when the break is over. "Tell us when you first started developing feelings for Nate."

"Honestly," I say, "it was when he came to my house to do my first interview." I'm pretty sure that's damning, given that I'm admitting to having feelings for Nate before I even met Preston, but I don't get booed off the stage, so I keep going. I tell them about that night in the carriage (though I leave out the specifics of exactly what we wanted to do to each other), and about the stuck zipper incident. I asked Nate if he wanted me to keep anything that happened between us a secret, and he told me he trusts me and that I'd know what to say.

I hope I'm living up to his belief in me. As I talk about the early days of our relationship, I hope it's all coming out right.

I have regrets from the show but not about us being together, so I don't want to hide. As I'm finishing talking about pouring my heart out to Nate on that balcony, Swiss interrupts me. "I think we all want to know, how did your family react to learning the truth about your marriage?"

I tense, but I try not to let it show for the cameras. The truth is, things with my in-laws are still difficult. I'm working on forgiving them, and I know I will be able to eventually—they're a big part of both my life and my girls', and I don't want to lose that. I also don't want to humiliate them publicly, so I'm hoping not to talk about them at all. Instead, I focus on the girls. "I talked to Thea about it before the show aired," I say, which is true, even though it was when the show was still *filming*. "It turned out she knew more than I thought she did. Rosie still doesn't know—I didn't let the girls watch more than a few pre-screened clips of the show—but I'm going to talk to her about it when she's older. Opening up to Nate about it has helped me to believe I'll be able to tell my girls the truth when they're ready for it, without destroying their memories of their father, which I would never want to do."

The audience applauds, and while it's still hard for me to accept that I deserve accolades for anything concerning my relationship with Rob, I'm still grateful that they seem to understand. I told myself I wouldn't base my own feelings toward this whole situation on the reaction of the audience.

But it still feels good that they're on my side.

"Tell us when things between you and Nate developed further," Swiss says, and I take a deep breath, and then talk about the one-on-one date and wishing I was on it with Nate. And then I confess about sneaking into his hotel room, and the producer coming to the door, and all my doubts and fears about whether or not I could trust him.

"I was a mess," I say, "and I'm not proud of the way I handled everything. Most of all, I regret that I hurt Nate, but in general I wish I'd handled everything better."

"Would you say," Swiss says ominously, "that you were on the show for the right reasons?"

I want to immediately answer no, but I think about it. "Even before I came on the show," I say carefully, "I didn't like the idea of joining a lineup of girls who are all wondering if they're the right one for the prince. I felt like I was there, not to see if I was the one Preston wanted, but to see if he was the one *I* wanted. Not for him, but for me. And in that way, I think I was there for the right reasons. I found the person who is right for me, and it wasn't Preston."

Swiss quirks a smile at the camera. "Well, we've heard from Becca, and we'll have more questions for her. But I think it's time that we bring out Nate and let him tell his side of the story. Becca, should we bring out your man?"

"Please, god, yes," I say, and the audience laughs at how eager I am.

But really, all I want is that man by my side, not just now, but forever and ever.

Everything's better when I'm facing it with Nate.

# THIRTY-THREE

## *Nate*

s I step out onto the stage, all I can see is Becca waiting for me. I watched every word she said, and I couldn't be prouder to call this incredible woman mine. Becca doesn't give herself nearly enough credit. Sure, she's not perfect. She's made some mistakes, and so have I. But watching her stand up to Preston and then tell her story with so much poise and grace (though not nearly enough grace for herself), makes me want to pull her into my arms and kiss the hell out of her.

So when I reach her, that's exactly what I do. I take her hands and lift her up off the couch and put my arms around her and kiss her the way she damn well deserves.

I get cheers from the audience for it, too, which is an added bonus.

We sit together on the couch, Becca so close she's practically in my lap, and Swiss smiles at us. "Nate, we're happy you're here," he tells me, and I bet he is, given that we're apparently saving their happily ever after. Preston has somehow managed to make himself look *even worse* than he did the day of the proposal. It's no wonder the show decided to throw him to the wolves and cast their lots in with us.

I didn't see that coming, but I'm incredibly grateful for it.

It's going to make our lives a whole lot easier if we're not public enemy number one.

"So, Nate," Swiss says. "I have some questions for you, but first, let's take a look at how your relationship progressed throughout the show."

Becca and I look at each other, eyes wide. Take a *look*?

Sure enough, on the giant screen to the side of the stage runs footage of Becca and me together. They generally don't get the producers on camera, so they must have combed like hell to find everything they had. There's a shot of me teasing Thea to get her to smile, and me watching Becca cook with a grin on my face. There's a moment of Becca and I standing in a hallway talking. I remember that day—it was before the incident with the zipper, and we look so happy just to be near each other. They play some more footage of the balcony, of when I told her how wonderful she is. Here on the couch, Becca grips my arm, and when I look down at her, there are tears in her eyes. They, of course, play the footage where Becca talks about the "date that says 'I love you,'" and the audience eats it up, now that they know what it really means.

They end it with the footage of Becca announcing she's in love with somebody else, and us holding each other like we're afraid to let go. Now there are tears in *my* eyes.

I love this woman more than anything in the world, more than I thought it was possible to love someone. These last couple months have been incredible, despite the stress and the hiding out and the sneaking around. Becca and Thea and Rosie feel like my family, and I put my hand on my pocket, feeling the box there.

I'd meant to give it to her after the show, but with things going as they are—

"So Nate," Swiss says. "Tell us how you fell in love with Becca."

That feels too enormous for words, but I'm on camera, so I'm going to try. I tell him my side of meeting her, and the carriage talk, and the stuck zipper. "You've got to understand," I say, "that I wasn't entirely innocent of the way all this went wrong.

Becca takes all the blame on herself, but as a producer, it was literally my job to manipulate her. And I did some manipulative things on this show, things I'm not proud of. I didn't know we were being filmed that night on the balcony, but if I hadn't selfishly wanted to hear what was going on with her, I would have had the good sense not to talk about it there. She was right to be mad at me."

I expect Swiss to turn on me as I'm admitting how the show manipulates women, but somehow he doesn't.

Truth is, Levi did a pretty good job manipulating me, too—after his stunt with keeping Madison as a back-up plan, I'm certain the reason he never mentioned that balcony footage to me wasn't because he thought I already knew, but because he knew I didn't. Even if he hadn't quite clued in yet about how deeply I was falling for Becca, he must have known my loyalty had shifted to her rather than the show. And Levi wasn't about to risk losing out on any more secrets she might confess to me, not until he was willing to let Becca go.

Still, this doesn't absolve me.

"But I wasn't right to go back to dating Preston," Becca says. "I never should have done that to you."

I grip her hand. We've talked a lot about that, and about the moment she asked me again if I thought she'd be good with Preston, and about my hurt that she didn't only reject me, she rejected me for *him*. I've felt bad about how much that still hurts, when I feel like I should just be able to put it aside—especially because now I know she never wanted to be with him. But the wound was real, and as Becca told me late one night, if it was a broken bone, it wouldn't have healed completely yet, so it makes sense that it still hurts.

That helped a lot, and over these last few weeks, the hurt is healing over and leaving nothing but the memory in its place. "We both made some bad decisions," I say. "Either of us could have left the show at any time, and looking back, we should have. But at the time, we were both so scared that it was a one-sided thing, and neither of us wanted to throw our lives away if the other person wasn't totally in it."

"It was hard enough to believe he could really be in love with me," Becca says. "But after thinking he knew the cameras were there that night, and then what Preston told me in the Dalliance Tower—"

"What did he tell you?" Swiss interjects, and Becca winces. She clearly hadn't meant to bring that up.

She fidgets, and I squeeze her hand tighter, even as I'm fighting my own wince. "In the Dalliance suite," she says slowly, "Preston told me that the producers were the ones bringing me along, that he hadn't even chosen to keep me until after our one-on-one."

I look back to Swiss. No way do the producers want that to be public knowledge. I expect him to immediately divert the conversation, but instead—

"So, let me get this straight, Becca," Swiss says. "The man who accuses you of cheating on him hadn't even chosen to keep you around until *after* you and Nate were together?"

"That's absolutely right, Swiss," she says, and the audience makes a sinister murmur that I'm thinking is directed at Preston and not at us.

I want to kiss them, every one.

"So tell us where you're at now," Swiss says, and Becca doesn't hesitate.

"We're living together," she says. We have been pretty much since we got back from Europe. I was surprised Becca was willing to trust me so much so early, but she meant it when she said she was going to work on her issues, and when Becca sets her mind to something, nothing can stop her. "And yes, I definitely regret some of the choices that I made, but ultimately, I can't regret the whole experience, because it led me to Nate."

The audience gives a collective "awww," and I know my cue when I hear it.

"Actually, Swiss, I hope you won't mind," I say, "but I have a question for Becca."

There's a gasp from the audience, and it's like the whole room is holding its breath. Swiss quirks an eyebrow at me but he gives me the floor. I turn to Becca, and she's looking at me like I'm her whole world.

She's mine and I'm hers, and I want to make that a forever thing.

"Becca," I say, already getting choked up. "You're my everything, and as hard as this whole situation was, I am grateful every day to have you in my life. You and Thea and Rosie are my family, and I just want you to know that I'm always going to be here, that you can trust me with your heart, and I'm going to take care of it."

Becca's eyes shine with tears, and she looks like she wants to throw her arms around me, but is hesitating because that wasn't, in fact, a question.

I pull the ring box out of my pocket, and tears slip down her cheeks as she breaks into a grin. We've talked about getting married, but I told her I wanted to get through the show first, to make sure there wasn't anything in the airing that gave her pause about us. She felt the same way, but it was me she was worried would run.

I'm not going anywhere, and I want to make sure that she knows it. "Becks, you're my best match, my one hundred percent," I say, and her grin widens. "I want to be with you forever. Will you marry me?"

"Yes!" Becca says, and then she throws herself at me, tackling me, while the audience cheers. I'm not sure she's even really looked at the ring, which I bought when Jason snuck me out for a work thing, but there will be time for that later. I didn't think I was going to do this on air tonight.

This is better, though, not because I had anything to prove, but because our story, for better or for worse, is tied up in this season of *Chasing Prince Charming*.

I'm ready to put the chase behind us and move on to our happily ever after.

# THIRTY-FOUR

## Becca

We're engaged. *Engaged.* I'm stunned by how well the whole finale went, by the fact that not only did the show *not* villainize us but made us their celebrated love story. What makes me feel like I'm floating, though, is being with Nate and knowing it's official—we're going to get married. We're going to be a family, him and Thea and Rosie and I, for the rest of our lives.

I can't stop smiling. I feel like I never will, and that's totally okay with me. I also think that now that I've had a moment to look at my gorgeous, sparkly ring, I am never taking it off, cooking be damned.

"Did you like the surprise?" Nate asks. We're offstage, tucked away from the crew members, many of whom said things to Nate like "Way to go, man!" Mustache Dan gave him a really awkward high-five.

But right at this moment, while Swiss is out there introducing next season's Prince Charming to a still-captivated audience, we have a tiny reprieve, and Nate's arms are looped around me.

"Um," I say. "Were my feelings not clear, what with shouting 'Yes!' and tackling you?"

"That's usually a good sign you're happy."

I grin up at him. "I can't wait to tell the girls about this. The engagement, I mean. Though I'm sure Thea would appreciate hearing about Madison whipping Preston in the face with a bunch of flowers." Neither of the girls know about Preston proposing to me yet—I trust Thea more with secrets, especially given what she kept to herself about her father, but I've had to remind Rosie before school every day not to tell anyone about Nate living with us. I didn't want to add more she needed to keep from blurting out to the entire kindergarten class.

"Well," he says, twisting his lips to the side. "Thea may already know I was going to propose to you soon. I showed her the ring a couple days ago."

My eyes widen. "Seriously?" Wow, she really is good at keeping secrets. "I bet she was excited."

"She was. She gave me this huge hug. And then said she *told* me I was the hero of this story."

I laugh. "She's a smart girl. I'm guessing Rosie still doesn't know, though."

"God, no. I wasn't about to show that girl a diamond ring and not expect *that* to get back to you." He pulls me tighter. "Maybe when we tell her, she'll toss another mountain of glitter at you in celebration."

"That is what does it for you, isn't it? Me covered in glitter."

"Maybe. And maybe the thought of helping you wash it off in the shower afterwards."

"Mmmm," is all I can manage. Because damn, that definitely does it for me, too.

He tips my chin up and leans in, and once again, I'm kissing the man of my dreams. The man I love so much more than I ever thought I could love anyone but my girls. The man who loves me right back with everything in him.

I still struggle with feeling worthy of a love like this—something I desperately wanted but never thought I could have. I'm still afraid sometimes that all of this will crumble beneath me, but I'm not going to let fear take over. I'm going to trust that he wants this future with me every bit as much as I do, and I'm not going to push him away, not ever again.

His phone buzzes about a hundred times in his pocket and he reluctantly pulls away to check it. We both figured as we walked off that stage that we'd have about ten minutes before getting bombarded with whoever from the press manages to get a hold of our numbers first. But instead of the expected grimace, he smiles.

"So, my parents both say 'Congratulations' and my sister is mad she wasn't here for this and expects us to reenact the whole thing for her in person and my brother says doing that would be super weird—which I agree with, for the record—but he's really happy for us."

I grin. I've only met his family once, at his niece's birthday party, but their immediate welcoming of my girls and I, even after they'd heard the story about our rough patch on the show, was incredible. And his mom has emailed me about a dozen Dominican recipes, a couple of which I'm seriously considering for the restaurant.

Nate chuckles, still looking down at his phone. "Jason says 'Hell yeah.' And then Emily says she's so excited for us and also that this will make her job a hell of a lot easier."

"Oh my god, it seriously will," I say. Emily is a social media and PR consultant and was going to help us get out of the pile of negative press. But I imagine it's going to be a lot easier if the press is actually on our side.

The phone buzzes again. "Jason says that we will still need to pay her back in lifelong free meals at your restaurant. For both of them." Nate shakes his head. "I'm not sure we should agree to that. The dude can *eat*."

"They want free meals forever? They've got it." Jason and Emily have both been incredibly supportive of us, not only in wholeheartedly becoming my friends, but in eagerly joining Nate and me in brainstorming how best to get my restaurant off the ground—when I actually finish business school, that is. Between Emily's social media skills and Jason and Nate's YouTube platform ("It won't be the first time I've climbed a restaurant on air," Jason said with a shrug), getting the attention of the public isn't going to be a problem. And Jason's already planning to pitch a second season of his upcoming show, *Jason Builds Sh!t*, in which he and Nate and their friend Brendan remodel a restaurant.

Nate looks around furtively and then back at me. "You know, I think I saw a coffee shop a couple blocks away. Maybe I can buy my future wife a muffin? Do you think she'll accept?"

I tug my lower lip between my teeth, fighting another smile. "Well, if she doesn't, you end up with a muffin, so I guess you win either way."

He laughs and kisses the top of my head, and as we hear the applause and cheers from the show ending, we sneak out the back of the studio before we're bombarded. We drive to the coffee shop and get a seat in the back, and for now, at least, no one seems to recognize us. We laugh and cuddle and talk about our future and the girls and that insane show.

And yeah, we got here in Nate's Honda Accord, not a carriage. We're eating muffins in a Starbucks in Los Angeles, not caviar in some European castle.

But this is way better than any of that. It's us and our story. And no fairy tale can ever compare.

# ACKNOWLEDGMENTS

Thank you to families, especially our incredibly supportive husbands Glen and Drew, and our amazing kids. Thanks to Michelle of Melissa Williams Design for the fabulous cover. We're also grateful to our proofreaders, Jen Bair, Dantzel Cherry, and Regina Dowling, as well as Lauren Janes and Keri Lockhart for all their help and feedback.

And a very special thanks to you, our readers. We hope you love these characters as much as we do.

Janci Patterson got her start writing contemporary and science fiction young adult novels, and couldn't be happier to now be writing adult romance. She has an MA in creative writing, and lives in Utah with her husband and two adorable kids. When she's not writing she can be found surrounded by dolls, games, and her border collie. She has written collaborative novels with several partners, and is honored to be working on this series with Megan.

Megan Walker lives in Utah with her husband, two kids, and two dogs–all of whom are incredibly supportive of the time she spends writing about romance and crazy Hollywood hijinks. She loves making Barbie dioramas and reading trashy gossip magazines (and, okay, lots of other books and magazines, as well.) She's so excited to be collaborating on this series with Janci. Megan has also written several published fantasy and science-fiction stories under the name Megan Grey.

Find Megan and Janci at www.extraseriesbooks.com

The Extra Series

*The Extra*
*The Girlfriend Stage*
*Everything We Are*
*The Jenna Rollins Real Love Tour*
*Starving with the Stars*
*My Faire Lady*
*You are the Story*
*How Not to Date a Rock Star*
*Beauty and the Bassist*
*Su-Lin's Super-Awesome Casual Dating Plan*
*Ex on the Beach*
*The Real Not-Wives of Red Rock Canyon*
*Chasing Prince Charming*
*Ready to Rumba*
*Save Me (For Later)*

Other Books in The Extra Series

*When We Fell*
*Everything We Might Have Been*

Made in the USA
Coppell, TX
01 April 2022

75871157R00184